THE JOURNEY HOME

P R Adams

THE JOURNEY HOME

Cover Design by Ravven (www.ravven.com)
Formatting by Polgarus Studio (www.polgarusstudio.com)

For updates on new releases and news on other series, visit my website and sign up for my mailing list at:

http://www.p-r-adams.com

The Chain: Shattered
The Journey Home
Rock of Salvation
From the Depths
Ever Shining

⁓

Books in the On The Brink Universe

The Rimes Trilogy
Momentary Stasis
Transition of Order
Awakening to Judgment

The ERF Series
Turning Point
Valley of Death (2017)

To Lynn and Nuku for showing the way.

Chapter One

It was the final day of the Memorial Day weekend, the first day of Elliot Saganash's new life, and he was already late. His stomach growled insistently. As if he needed a reminder of how bad his day had been, the dashboard display cheerfully declared it was 4:29. He should've been in Canada an hour ago, but he was barely halfway through North Dakota. He'd overslept, woke to a queasy stomach from too much greasy food, found a flat tire when he'd finally reached the hotel parking lot, and now…

A bead of sweat trickled down his forehead. Elliot rubbed it away and checked the dashboard display: 75 degrees. It felt closer to 80. Through the front window, I-29 snaked west, awash in summer sunlight, hidden beneath a glistening sea of cars. Unmoving, trapped, shimmering hazily in the afternoon heat.

Trapped.

The air in the Mercedes GLK felt stale, stifling, the doors too close. Elliot shifted anxiously on the leather seat and turned the air conditioner as high as it could go.

The clock shifted to 4:30.

There had been more maintenance crews for the last five miles than functional blacktop. Idle machinery, idle workers, and bare cement. Dull, yellow signs warned everyone to *Give 'em A Brake*. Apathetic crewmen held up signs: *Slow, Stop.*

Mostly, it was *Stop.*

Maintenance crews working on a holiday? Elliot shook his head in disbelief.

The stomach growl came again, louder than the mindless pop drivel coming over the stereo system. Elliot glanced into the back seat; his travel bag rested there. There were protein bars in a side pouch. He pulled the bag up to the passenger seat and unzipped the side pocket. Before he could search the pocket, a maintenance crewman waved the GLK forward. Elliot's stomach growled again, but he couldn't do anything more than grunt back at it. He edged a few feet forward, then stopped and turned back to the pocket.

Nothing. *I know I packed protein bars. I* know *it!*

The traffic was still; the maintenance team once again looked disinterested. Elliot unzipped another side pocket. Also empty.

His stomach growled, demanding now. But it wasn't just hunger anymore. He'd packed the protein bars. He was sure of it. His sanity was on the line.

Elliot blinked away another bead of sweat and unzipped the main flap.

The maintenance crew sensed the flap opening, each of them waving Elliot forward impatiently, insistently.

The protein bar would have to wait. He was holding everyone—every*thing*—up. Schedules were being destroyed; phones were lighting up in the Capitol Building. Elliot growled and edged the GLK forward, pushing his glasses up his nose. A whine escaped his gut, and he shifted in his seat again, sure he was merging with the leather.

The maintenance workers looked away: bored, staring off into the distance. Elliot was onto their game. The second he touched the flap to look into his travel bag, they would snap back to attention and order him forward.

He grabbed for the flap, flinging it up before the maintenance crew had a chance to act.

He stared in disbelief.

A medicine bag—leather aged white and soft to the touch, with a faint medicine wheel barely visible on its front—sat on top of a carefully folded pair of dark blue jeans. It had belonged to Mangas Victorio, the man who more than a century ago had established the home Elliot had spent the last several years in.

How? No one could have—

A horn sounded, and Elliot jumped.

There was a fifteen-foot gap between the GLK and the rust-colored Isuzu in front of it. A maintenance worker was emphatically waving Elliot forward. He waved and pulled up behind the Isuzu.

His eyes shifted back to the medicine bag.

I didn't pack it. I know I didn't. It was in the display area beneath the stairs when I was leaving. I—

Elliot's phone rang, and he nearly jumped out of his seat. It was an unfamiliar tone: *Unknown Caller.* Uncomfortable, unwelcome. He pushed his glasses up, slowly tapping the bridge of his nose once, twice, three times.

The phone kept ringing.

He activated the dashboard hands-free system. "Hello?"

"Elliot?"

Nothing about the voice was familiar. Not the accent, not the tone, not the cadence. Male, deep, almost certainly adult, probably white, Midwestern. "Who's this?"

A pause. "Is this Elliot?"

"Yes." Elliot stared at the dashboard display, wondering how an unknown caller knew his name.

The Isuzu moved forward. The maintenance crew pulled their signs up. Everything suddenly opened up in front of Elliot. He accelerated cautiously.

"Who is this, please?" Elliot demanded.

"I'm Lieutenant Paul Henriksen. I'm with the Major Case Squad of Greater St. Louis."

Major Case Squad? What the heck is that? "How'd you get my number, Lieutenant?"

"Off a phone."

A phone? Who has my phone number? Tammy!

"What phone? Is it Tammy's? Is she okay?"

Plastic crinkled over the connection as if someone were shifting a bag around. A creak—a chair, maybe a door—drowned out the crinkling. "Can I ask you where you are, Elliot?"

"Is Tammy okay?" Elliot struggled to breathe. His decision to leave Harrison Mansion had been much harder than it should have been because of Tammy. Their relationship—once extremely close—had grown strained as she'd grown older and fallen in with her best friend Tessa, but there had been a time where Tammy had been like a little sister to him. She would always be a friend, no matter how stupidly she might behave.

"We're trying to reach Tammy, Elliot. Maybe you can help us. Where are you at the moment?"

Elliot looked around as if he might see a giant, red-tipped pin sticking in the road. He checked the dashboard display. "Um, I-29. North. Just outside of Grand Forks. Why are you trying to reach Tammy? Can you tell me what's going on, please?"

The pause again. "Have you ever been to Missouri? Arlington, Missouri?"

"Sure. Yeah." Elliot's heart had just settled before Henriksen said they were trying to reach Tammy; it accelerated again. "I live there. Lived. I *lived* there. I'm heading back to Winnipeg. That's my home, where I grew up. Winnipeg."

"I'm sorry." The creaking, the crackling, more noise. The sound of paper being torn. "You say you're from Winnipeg? Canada?"

"Yes. Manitoba, Canada."

"Where, exactly?" Henriksen's calm was inhuman, machine-like.

"Cree First Nations reserve. Fisher River 44." Thoughts rushed through Elliot's mind. Police, some sort of Major Case Squad he'd never heard of, looking for Tammy, calling him, getting his number off a phone. "Lieutenant, what's going on? *Please.*"

Another pause, the longest one yet. "Would you happen to know a William Big Bear Saganash?"

"Gran—" Elliot swallowed. He thought of his grandfather, how frail he looked sometimes, his bad heart. "He's my grandfather. Is he okay? Is something wrong?"

A new record for pause length. Elliot pulled the phone from the cradle. It fell to the floor. He glanced at the road ahead, saw it was clear for a distance, then ducked and swatted at the floor mat until he felt the phone's smooth surface. He pulled it to his chest, straightened, and saw the rust-colored Isuzu stopped ahead of him. He pumped the brakes and swerved into the left lane.

The phone was still silent.

"Hello? Are you there?" Elliot winced at the desperate squeal of his voice.

Henriksen cleared his throat gently. "Elliot? If you're driving, maybe you should pull over to the side of the road."

"I'm fine." Elliot knew it was a lie, and he guessed Henriksen probably knew as well. "Is something wrong with my grandfather?"

The dashboard display announced he was now doing 80 miles per hour and would be in Winnipeg in 150 minutes. *So close.*

"Your grandfather's dead, Elliot."

Elliot blinked slowly. Everything around him blurred. Winnipeg was suddenly too far away to drive in a day. Or a lifetime.

"Elliot?" Henriksen's voice was calm, almost concerned.

"Yes?" Thoughts of what could have happened now filled Elliot's mind. It couldn't be trivial or accidental, not with something called Major Case Squad involved.

"Maybe you could tell me your full name?"

"Elliot…Hawk Saganash. I don't usually give my middle name." Hawk had been at his father's insistence. It carried guilt rather than pride, although Elliot would never know whether his mother had actually opposed the name.

"And you lived in Arlington?" Henriksen sounded excited.

Elliot took a deep breath. He'd already cried about saying goodbye to Grandpa William, but he'd never dreamed goodbye had been for eternity. "With my grandfather, yes."

"At the mansion on…"

Elliot closed his eyes against the tears. "Yeah, Harrison Mansion. On 1 Hamilton Lane." *How many mansions are there in that area? One. Just the one.* He held the phone away from his face for a moment and fought to control the tears. A jagged breath, an ineffective swipe of his forearm, and he had the phone back in place. "Wh—what happened?"

"Well, actually, that's what we're trying to figure out." Henriksen released a loud, slow sigh. "We could really use your help."

Elliot shivered. "My help?"

"Sure. Right now, we've got nothing. No witnesses, no useful evidence, no motive." Henriksen's voice trailed off, and the sound of tapping—a pen or pencil bouncing off a notepad—echoed in the background. "When were you last at the mansion?"

"Yesterday morning. Around...eight or nine." Elliot ran through what Henriksen had said. They had nothing. No witnesses, no evidence, no motive. *Motive.* Major Case Squad, not the sheriff's office. "Did someone kill my grandfather?"

The pause returned. Not long this time, but it was there. Henriksen sucked at the air for a moment. "That's what it looks like."

"Where? He's almost never alone. Someone should've seen something. Driss is almost always with him. Praveen, Neda, Daysi, Ms. Nakama, Ms. Fernandez. You checked with them?"

Tapping filled the line again, then it was replaced by the sound of scratching. A pen, writing on a pad of paper.

"Praveen—that's Praveen Thakur?"

"Yes."

Henriksen made a noise that might have been humming or just acknowledgment. "And Neda would be Neda Ebadi?"

"Yes. Driss's name is Zéroual. And Daysi's last name is Pizanga. I don't know Ms. Nakama or Ms. Fernandez's first names. They don't give them out."

"Mm-hmm." Henriksen's voice was clearer now, as if the phone was closer to his mouth. "And Tamment? Tammy?"

"What about her?" Elliot's lips quivered as he talked. He was suddenly aware of how much his arm ached from holding the phone so tight. He set it back in its cradle and stretched his arm out.

"What's her name?"

Elliot's vision went black. "McPhee. Just ask Driss. He's her grandfather; he'll tell you all about her."

Henriksen hummed softly. "I'd rather hear this from you. Actually, I'd rather talk to you in person, if you could come back down here. Or we can send someone to pick you up, if you don't think you can drive."

Elliot glanced at the dashboard display. *So close.* "I can drive." He put his turn signal on and began drifting to the right lane, looking for the next exit. "Where's *here?*"

"We've got space in the Phelps County Sheriff's office on 2nd Street."

Elliot rubbed a trickle of snot from his upper lip. "I know the office." They all knew about the sheriff's office thanks to Tammy and Tessa.

"That's great. The offer stands, though. We don't need you pushing yourself too hard and getting into an accident." Henriksen cleared his throat. "When do you think you may get back down here?"

Elliot rolled his eyes, flabbergasted at Henriksen's insistence. "Tomorrow, probably around noon. I—I have to see how long I can go tonight. I've been on the road since yesterday morning. Can't you talk to the others until I get there? I can't believe *no one* saw anything. Driss spends most of the day with my grandfather. They're very involved in their…studies." *Studying mysticism. How insane would that sound?*

"We're doing all we can already, but we really need your—"

Elliot closed his eyes and tried to control the fury rising over Henriksen's absurd behavior. "Lieutenant Henriksen, I'm on my way, okay? Until I get there, just talk to Driss."

Henriksen's voice raised slightly. "Mr. Zéroual is dead, Elliot. Everyone in the mansion is dead. We really need to talk to you. Please."

As Elliot turned onto the exit ramp, it suddenly hit him.

Where am I? When was I last there? They need me down there. They need to talk to me.

I'm a suspect. And I've got the most valuable item from the mansion, Mangas's medicine bag!

Chapter Two

S ummer had come early to Arlington, Missouri, and it had settled in hard. The days consisted of sweltering, muggy heat, and the nights never quite cooled. Winds blew, but they weren't a relief. Birds sang, but they couldn't appreciate the misery humans felt. The dogwood and redbud bloomed and filled the heavy air with their soothing, subtle aromas, but they were just trees. Only humans actually experienced summer's misery, or at least only humans understood human misery.

Tamment McPhee—Tammy to her friends—was actually fine with the summer. It was her favorite time of the year by default, what with her hating almost everything else. Summer meant freedom from school and structure. It meant tank tops and shorts. It meant she was closing in on another birthday and a life of her own, a life away from Arlington.

She wanted nothing more than to escape the place.

In the late May heat, State Street's clay and dirt became a red cloud of dust swirling up in the wake of Tessa Copeland's speeding Chevy Cavalier coupe. The coupe had faded blue paint—Arrival Blue Metallic was the official name—over about half its body. The rest was a mix of rust, primer, and a faded red that covered the right quarter panel.

Tammy and Tessa—Newburg High's Twin Terrors, or when things were really bad, TnT—danced inside the Cavalier, skidding across their seats, arms pumping, hands gripping imaginary microphones or reaching out windows to touch imaginary fans. Music pounded from the Cavalier's open windows—thumping drums and distorted bass, whistling and soaring synthesizers. Tessa took her hand off the steering wheel long enough to crank up the radio volume, and the whole time the two of them belted out their best off-tune but earnest rendition of their very favorite song of the minute.

They were *best friends forever*, and they wanted to kick the summer off right.

It was Memorial Day weekend, the school year was nearly over, and they were ready. Tammy sipped at an ice-cold soda, savoring its sugary wonderfulness, and then took a deep breath. Their sweet sweat was barely noticeable with the windows down, but it was there, a reminder of the heat. She gave Tessa a big, goofy smile.

They didn't have much in life, but they had each other.

In Arlington, they were as similar yet different a pair as anyone would see. Tammy was a real curiosity in such a small town. She had black hair, deep olive skin, and sharply defined but full, dark lips. Against those, her cobalt blue eyes seemed to smolder. She was the product of a Berber mother from Morocco and an American of Scottish descent. Tessa's father was a Cuban-American soldier who'd been a one-night fling for her mother Emmanuelle, a Euromutt. Tessa's hair hung back from her plain face in loose curls that she'd bleached for the summer. She had pale mocha skin, her mother's traffic-stopping hourglass figure, and a nose that was too broad and long for her small face. With the right makeup, Tammy could be absolutely stunning, and Tessa could be...cute. In favorable lighting.

Tammy wore a loose-fitting, muted coral tank top. Her jean shorts were getting tight around thighs that were finally filling out. Tessa's aqua tank top had spaghetti straps and clung to her breasts like a passionate lover. The top ended just above her pierced belly button. Her jean shorts only came up to the curve of her belly and barely cleared the crease of her thighs and butt.

Tessa knew her assets, and she worked them, hard. Tammy always felt diminished next to her friend, but she never said anything about it. *Best friends forever*.

The Cavalier turned onto a patchwork asphalt parking lot and angled for the center trailer, bald tires bouncing off potholes and cracks, doors and seats loudly squeaking and rattling. It came to a stop with a squeal in front of the dust-covered double-wide that had once been a two-tone beige and brown.

"St. Robert ain't gonna wait all day," Tessa said with a giggle.

"I don't want to keep a saint waiting." Tammy's phone vibrated. She squeezed it out of her pants pocket, checked the identity—*unknown caller*—and took it off vibrate, then she returned it to the pocket with some effort.

Her pants were getting *much* tighter. She really was finally filling out.

They jumped out of the Cavalier and ran up the steps to the trailer, ignoring the lingering smells of marijuana and incense. Tessa's mother was away, probably hooking up with someone for the night. They took turns showering, changed into their best outfits, assured each other they were sexy beyond belief, then ran back out to the car. A minute later, they were on the road to St. Robert and a night of dancing.

Arlington was home, but it had nothing in it. Literally. The IGA grocery store, a small hardware store, and the trailer park where Tessa lived with her mother. The trailer park came as close as anything in Arlington to a social hotspot. Tammy was pretty sure Arlington would have been a ghost town if not for Harrison Mansion and the quarry out by Pillman Cemetery.

The only options for nightlife in the area were Rolla and St. Robert. Rolla was a college town, St. Robert was the civilian support system for Fort Leonard Wood, the nearby Army base. A third of Rolla's population was between eighteen and twenty-four years old, but the social scene still somehow sucked. It was as if the college students were serious about their work or something. St. Robert wasn't much better, but it had two decent clubs.

One day, Tammy wanted to head up to St. Louis, maybe even Chicago!

Tessa turned to smile at Tammy. "You remember Everett from Rachael's party?"

Bad breath, buff body, gangsta poseur. But sorta cute. "Yeah."

"He's gonna be at Area 151." Tessa danced in her seat, her full breasts bouncing beneath a red, semi-sheer, skintight shirt. "Big party tonight, girlfriend."

Sometimes, Tessa's apparent age got her a long way. Like tonight. Other times, it got Tessa into situations that left Tammy skittish. Tessa was dangerous. She was wild and free and fearless.

Tammy thought of herself as adventurous and independent, but she wasn't in Tessa's league. Not by a mile.

Tessa had established her own sort of independent identity, moving through whatever cliques and subcultures interested her at the time; her will demanded acceptance.

Tammy absently rubbed at the *siyâla*—tattoos that would protect her from malicious spirits—she'd drawn on her chin the night before. As if she needed a reminder of how disconnected she was from any sort of identity.

Blending in would be easy enough with her features, if she wanted to. She could pass as Latin American, black, Asian, or anywhere off the Mediterranean, really. But she often found herself dealing with the guilt of abandoning her Berber roots. It wasn't just Jeddo, her grandfather, harping on all the time about their great, disappearing people, either. It just stuck with her. She only knew a smattering of Arabic, even less Berber. Even her French was stronger, and that was a joke.

"Hey, you goin' to sleep over there?" Tessa laughed and turned up the radio, shaking in slow, jerky movements to the music.

"Nah." Tammy dug out her phone and angled it so that Tessa couldn't see the display, then searched for a moment, finally pulling up a picture of her parents. It was from someplace in Germany, where they'd met. *Before me.* They seemed happy. Genuinely happy. Tammy wondered what that felt like.

"Uh-uh, this is Party Night, hear? You schedule Sulk Night for when Tessa's not around, okay?"

Tammy closed the photo app and pushed the phone back into her pocket. "I'm good."

"We gonna get some trance on?"

"Sure." Tammy did enjoy trance, but thinking about her parents was bringing her down.

"Party Night, remember? Fix that shit up."

Tammy gave her best *the World Is Awesome* smile. It seemed to satisfy most people. Everyone just wanted to be sure they weren't caught up in someone else's misery, really.

"That's what I'm talkin' about!" Tessa cranked the radio as high as it would go and danced enthusiastically.

The ride to St. Robert took them through the seemingly endless tracts of gentle, wooded hills that made up a lot of southern Missouri. There were places where their cell phones wouldn't even work.

It was like being hurled back in time.

Area 151 had parking on three sides—front, back, and the east side. Tessa swung the Cavalier in hard and gunned the wheezing engine as she headed for the side lot. She swung into a spot between a couple beat-up trucks, waving and laughing wildly when another driver accelerating toward the same spot honked angrily.

"Law of the Asphalt Jungle, bitch." Tessa grabbed the black clutch she'd brought for the night and checked herself in the rearview mirror, humming in appreciation as she brushed back her blonde curls and inspected the diamond studs in her ears.

Tammy had the exact same studs in her ears, pinched from a shop in Rolla when a counter girl had gone all racist on Tessa. Or maybe before. Tammy couldn't remember for sure. It didn't matter. *Little Miss White Precious* had been watching them from the moment they'd entered the shop, like she thought they were toting AK-47s. A lawsuit for the bad treatment would've netted a lot more than a few hundred dollars worth of diamond studs, so Tammy considered it all even when she plucked them from the counter at the height of the drama. Or maybe just before it started.

"Oh, Tessa is looking dazzling tonight, little sister." Along with the revealing top and studs, Tessa wore a tight, short denim skirt, skinny white belt, and ankle-high, black felt boots. She was going to draw a lot of attention, just like she wanted.

Tammy's focus had already shifted to the club entry. Everything hinged on them knowing the guy at the door. Her fake I.D. was good, not great.

"You ready, girlfriend?"

"Maybe this isn't the best idea, Tessa. I don't see John or Mick at the door."

"Oh, damn. You need a diaper?"

Tammy rolled her eyes dramatically. "Fuck you. This is just stupid."

"No, *you're* stupid, and you're fucking up my fun. Come on!" Tessa pointed at her door with both hands and did another quick dance.

"I don't—"

Tessa was out of the car before Tammy could say anything more.

Tammy hissed. She opened her door, nearly bumping it against the pickup truck parked next to her, then slid out and stomped around to the back of the car. Tessa was smiling impishly, leaning against the trunk lid.

"Tessa, if this doesn't work, we could get busted."

"So?"

"Like go-to-juvie busted! I get one more strike against me, I'm fucked."

"So?" Tessa threw up her arms in exasperation. "Ain't you always goin' on about how shitty your life is and how you wanna escape from big, bad Harrison Mansion?"

Tammy gave up; Tessa had made up her mind. Walking back to the mansion was out of the question. At the very least, she had to make sure Tessa didn't get arrested.

They queued up in the short line. Moments later, a trio of soldiers got in line behind them, young men with lean bodies and short haircuts. They were rowdy, probably already drunk. A few seconds later, several young women got into line behind the soldiers.

Tammy groaned when she recognized them: *the Bitch Brigade*, the popular girls who existed only to make her and Tessa's life miserable. They'd ridden her since the first day of school, when she was just a chubby little seven-year-old girl dealing with her father going off to war and abandoning her at the creepy mansion Jeddo called home. Even after she'd lost all her baby fat and become the bean pole she was now, they'd made her life a living hell. It hadn't mattered to them that she'd spent an entire month in ICU suffering from an undiagnosed condition, slipping in and out of a coma. All that mattered was that when she returned to school, instead of being a fatty, she had become a graceless, clumsy girl with an eating disorder.

She hated them, especially Ashley. Tammy preferred Bitchley.

Tammy tried to get Tessa's attention, but she was preoccupied with a cute young man in line ahead of them. When he was waved through, he twisted back to watch Tessa shake her shoulders and hips. He nearly stumbled over the doorstep.

Tessa giggled. "Gonna be on the floor all night."

The doorman, a bodybuilder with shaved head and a nose that had probably been broken a couple times before, tried to pretend he hadn't noticed Tessa's display, but his thick eyebrows shot up. He waved her forward and pretended to examine her I.D. while staring at her breasts. She winked and shook them some more; he waved her through with a satisfied chuckle.

Tammy tapped the small of Tessa's back; she turned.

"Behind us." Tammy jerked her head back toward the Bitch Brigade.

Tessa turned, face lit up with a smile. "You see that boy checkin' me out? I could handle some of that."

Tammy jerked her head at the line behind her again. "Ashley Parks."

Tessa looked toward the rear of the line. "So?" Her voice was loud, challenging.

Tammy shrank and wished she were invisible. She wished Tessa had an inside voice, a setting other than eleven. "So if she recognizes us—"

Tessa's eyes were still wild when she looked at Tammy. "Fuck that bitch. I'm goin' in, and you are too."

The doorman waved Tammy forward. "Let's go."

Tessa headed for the entry.

Tammy held out her I.D.

"Hey! This isn't an all ages club!" Ashley's snooty, nasal shout filled the air.

Tammy blushed and turned to glare at Ashley.

The bodybuilder gave Tammy a stern look and pushed the I.D. back at her. His pink face reddened as he looked her up and down, his eyes resting on her flat chest and slender hips. "You better be sure that's legal 'fore you show it to me."

Tessa stopped at the entryway, silhouetted by the strobe lights.

Tammy stepped out of the line, shoulders slumped. The music, the dancers, the energy…the doorway: It all called to her, but she didn't want juvie.

Tessa shot back out of the doorway and headed for Ashley. "You stupid little b—"

The bodybuilder shifted slightly to cut Tessa off, taking the opportunity to let his hands drift up to her breasts. "Take it elsewhere, sweetie." He turned to look at the Bitch Brigade. "That includes you, ladies."

Ashley's laughter died, and the men in line around her groaned. She and her friends were dressed for the night, and unlike Tessa and Tammy, they had the money for nice hairdos, makeup, and clothes.

The night's meat market had significantly diminished.

Tessa walked over to Tammy and gave her a hug. Tessa was gloriously soft and warm, and she smelled like candy perfume and sweat. "We still gonna have fun tonight, okay?"

Tammy nodded weakly. "Yeah."

Tessa took Tammy by the hand and escorted her back toward the Cavalier, slowing slightly to glare at Ashley and her friends, who seemed to be content hanging around near the end of the line. The first time Tammy did anything more than let Tessa pull her along was when they passed the Cavalier.

"Hey, where're we going?"

"Not far." Tessa cut across the side parking lot and into the front parking lot. She stopped beneath a flickering lamplight and pointed to a metallic brown Infiniti SUV at the end of the parking spaces, next to the adjoining, adults-only club.

Tammy realized it was Ashley's car. "Shit."

"You gonna let Bitchley push you around the rest o' your life?"

"I'm not gonna be around Arlington after I turn eighteen, Tessa."

Tessa's brow wrinkled. Talking about leaving Arlington was talking about leaving her, and Tammy usually knew better. "You need to worry about the now. You got two more years o' that bitch."

"What do you want me to do, beat her up? Here? In the parking lot? They've probably got cameras everywhere."

"This ain't Fort Knox, girl. Ain't no cameras out here. Their cameras cover their entry, not out here. I've seen what they record."

"Fine. I'm still not doing it. I'm not going to juvie."

"You ain't got to." Tessa squatted down next to the concrete island the light pole was anchored to. A moment later, she stood, a wedge of concrete in her hand. "These things're all fallin' apart. They do all kinds of damage to cars all the time, especially when they're driven by rich little bitches."

"Tear up her car? It's still juvie."

Tessa looked around the small stretch of asphalt abutting the highway entry. The front parking lot was already full. There was no one around. "Bitchley parked out here for those lights. Ain't no cameras. Ain't no one around. No one's gonna see what you do." She stepped forward and dropped the concrete wedge into Tammy's hand.

The wedge was surprisingly heavy. It wasn't big, but it tapered down to a nice edge. There was enough heft to it to crack a windshield or break a headlight.

Tammy turned to search the front of the club. She couldn't see the Bitch Brigade anywhere. She couldn't even see the tail end of the line. "The car alarm. They'll hear it. Someone will."

"Mm-hm. And we'll be over there, movin' down the other side of the building, hidin' in those trees in the dark. No one's gonna see us." She took Tammy's hands and leaned in tight against her back. "C'mon."

Tammy closed her eyes and let Tessa guide her forward. They stopped at the front of the car.

"Window, light…which is it?" Tessa whispered into Tammy's ear. It was seductive, hot. "You just gotta squat down and swing."

Tammy squatted and looked at the car. In the flickering light, it sparkled. Someone had washed and polished it recently. Not Bitchley, obviously, but someone. It was new and perfect and something she would never have while she lived at the mansion, like Elliot's GLK.

"Just think of all the names she called you, baby girl. Fatty. Skinny. *Retard.* Remember how she made you cry and wish you was dead? Remember?"

Every last insult, every effort to humiliate: They had long ago been burned into Tammy's memories. They were scars only she could see. They were marks that had more influence over who she was than the few, precious, loving memories of her childhood with her mother and father.

16

"Bitchley's had everything in her life. Girl ain't never earned a thing, and she gotta show up someone like you for bein' different. Ain't that some shit?"

Tammy closed her eyes, clenched her jaw tight, then swung. She felt the concrete wedge slam into the front passenger door and scrape along the bottom panel. The alarm went off, and she opened her eyes, stunned. There was a dent in the door and paint on the concrete wedge.

She looked around, but Tessa had already sneaked away.

"Shit!"

Tammy dropped the concrete wedge and sneaked around the front of the car. Her heart was pounding, and she felt blood hammering in her ears. She moved slowly across the front of the buildings and into the shadow of the trees lining the western edge of the parking lot, sticking to the shadows where possible. She spotted Tessa leaning against a tree deep in the shadows, her face lit by the blue glow of her phone's display.

After a quick glance around, Tammy joined Tessa, no longer concerned anyone might see them. "Way to back me up."

"You're kidding, right? You all grown up, okay? You can handle escaping on your own. I'm busy gettin' us in."

"Getting us in?" Tammy looked around; they were alone.

"You *do* want to dance, don't you? Or was tonight all about smashing up Bitchley's ride? Hm?"

Tammy tried to appear casual as she looked back at the parking lot. No one was running to check out the alarm. Leaving now would actually be somewhat satisfying.

But she *had* come to dance. "How're you getting us in?"

"Mick's running the club tonight. Big man's back east on family business." Tessa's phone vibrated, and she grinned wickedly. "And now Mick says we in. C'mon."

"Wait. Mick's running the club?"

"That's what I said, right?"

"How long have you known that?"

Tessa made a sour face. "Mm-mm. Don't start. You tryin' to ruin the night?"

"How long?"

Tessa spun on a heel and walked toward the near side of the club.

Tammy followed. Her stomach threatened to flip. "Tessa, how long?"

Tessa didn't say anything until they were in the employee parking lot at the back of the club. When she reached the service door, she spun around and jabbed a finger into Tammy's sternum. "Listen up, you need to get your head on straight, okay? You just goin' around looking to start a fight with everyone, and it's not happenin'."

"Just tell me. Did you know he was running the club tonight? Was that whole thing with Ashley unnecessary?"

Tessa's eyes narrowed, but she didn't say anything more. She tapped away at the keys to her phone. A moment later, it vibrated, and she turned to watch the service door. When it popped open, she shoved her phone into Tammy's hand. "You can stay out here all night. I'm goin' in."

Tammy glanced down at the phone and saw the text exchange between Tessa and Mick. She scrolled up and saw where Tessa had started the whole thing with a text to Mick that she'd been stopped from entering. The very next text, Mick said he was in charge.

Shit.

Tammy caught the door just before it closed. Tessa was already halfway through the bar and following Mick into the manager's office. She wasn't looking back.

Tammy ran after her, head down, embarrassed.

The bar area was half full, dark except for some strip lighting and strobe lights. Mindless jabbering rose over music that was ramping up into a deep, rhythmic drone. People gathered in clumps on the open dance floor, their bodies giving off heat and scents—cologne, perfume, sweat. It was still mostly men and women in separate groups, waiting, watching, hoping. No one paid attention to Tammy as she passed among them, the tingling from passing through the doorway a ghostly, lingering sensation.

She entered the manager's office.

"Close the door, right?" Mick was leaning against the corner of the desk that anchored the office, his attention focused on Tessa, who was smiling and holding his hands.

After an uncertain moment, Tammy closed the door.

She lowered her head, but she still watched Mick. He had a rat's face—narrow, with beady eyes, a long nose, and a jutting chin. His hair was a washed-out brown and wavy. Most of the time, he radiated a strange sort of menace that frightened Tammy but seemed to excite Tessa.

The excitement seemed to be mutual at the moment. Mick playfully pulled at Tessa's top. "I'm takin' a lot of risks for you, girl, so why don't you make it worth my time?"

Tessa pushed his hand away. "You know I will, baby. No need to—"

Tammy turned slightly, uncomfortable in the stuffy room.

Mick stood up suddenly and took Tessa by the wrists. "I'm not fuckin' around, yeah? You caused a big commotion tonight, and I need to let off some steam."

Tammy blinked at the sound in Mick's voice. He was from somewhere in London, but his accent only became noticeable anymore when he was really mad. Tessa's eyes widened; she was finally seeing the danger Tammy had always seen in Mick.

"O-okay, Mick. Sure."

Without meaning to, Tammy gasped.

Tessa shot an apologetic, frightened look at Tammy, then nodded toward her. "She don't need to be here, does she, baby?"

Mick looked Tammy up and down. "Nah. She's just a kid." He sneered. "Get out."

Tammy waited until Tessa smiled—a fake, terrified smile—then stepped back into the club. A slap leaked through the door as it closed, and Tammy imagined she might have heard a whimper.

Back in the club, the music pounded and lights flashed, people danced and every sort of drama imaginable played out, but Tammy's thoughts were stuck on Mick's office. She made her way to the bar and ordered a Coke, taking it into her shaking hands and pressing the cup to her numb lips. The rattle of ice in the glass seemed louder than the thumping bass.

The night of adventure and fun had suddenly lost all of its thrill. She couldn't shake the image of Tessa's frightened eyes.

Minutes ticked by, and Tammy worried she'd made a terrible mistake abandoning Tessa, leaving her when Mick had gone into some sort of murderous rage. Suddenly, the office door opened, and Tessa stumbled out, still adjusting her top and wiping a tear from her face. She shot Tammy a furious look that seemed to carry all the blame in the world in it, then she headed off for the bathroom.

Tammy sipped at the Coke a bit more before digging a vial from a small zip case of hygiene napkins she always kept in her purse. It was a tincture of Seer's Sage, something she'd helped herself to before slipping out of the mansion, something she needed desperately now. She poured the vial's contents into the soda.

She finished the Coke off, wincing at the sting and the bitter taste, then she let the drug slowly work its way through her, bringing a hint of a tingle and the first distortion to her perceptions: colors going a little awry, tastes twisting into lights, and sounds becoming temperatures—bass was heat, treble was cold. She wrapped her arms across her chest and leaned back, enjoying the unreality of the moment.

The taste was a small price to pay for the way the drug reordered the world. Colors, sounds, scents: Everything was leaking from one realm to another. A young man shouted something nearby, and it became…yellow. And heavy.

Tessa pushed through the crowd, strange sounds floating in her wake: whispers, banging. They were scents—store-bought fragrances and alcohol and very human sweat—but they were transforming into a whole new experience. Tessa's face had an unmistakable look to it, though.

Anger. A very red, very loud anger.

"Party's over. I'm leavin'." Tessa leaned in close. "You hear me?"

Tammy blinked slowly, still trying to process the transformations. Tessa almost felt like a lizard with bright, fluorescent scales.

Looked like. She looks…pissed.

"Oh, mm mm. You leave me in there alone, and you come out here and get stoned?" Tessa's scaly face shook side to side, and her pink tongue flicked out. "Damn, girl, ain't that just you?"

An eagle swooped in and landed next to Tessa. Tammy vaguely recognized it as Everett. He was wearing a long-sleeved shirt, the sleeves rolled up to reveal his tattooed arms and the top buttons undone to reveal his pecs. Feathers moved across his chest, then disappeared. He whispered something where Tessa should have had an ear, and she seemed to relax some.

Tessa leaned in again and her tongue flicked over Tammy's nose. It smelled...orange. "I'ma spend a few minutes with Everett, then we gone, you hear? Tammy? You hear?"

Tammy tried to nod, and she apparently succeeded, because Tessa let Everett scoop her up in his talons and carry her into the forest. No, the dance floor. It was a dance floor, and it was full of people swimming in an ocean of light that shifted strangely.

After watching Tessa and Everett twist and slither and merge into a single being that was half reptile-half bird, then separate and begin mating only to separate again and begin a hunter-prey dance, Tammy closed her eyes.

The hallucinations were completely different than what she'd experienced before, and she wasn't sure if that was to be expected or something to worry about. Not nausea or violence or anything like that, just...different. The tincture had been put together by Daysi Pizanga, a *yerberos*, a real, live, withered, old Peruvian shaman who lived in Harrison Mansion with all the other crazy mystics. She was part of Tammy's crazy, extended family. And Daysi had warned a long time ago that the Seer's Sage could cause very different experiences, especially the way she prepared it.

"Your reactions to the drug, that's what we especially worried about."

Tammy was suddenly aware of Daysi's presence, a dark green viper with gold eyes and a strong, earthy sound that seemed to be a natural fit with the rattling, hissing smell she gave off. She hung over Tammy's left shoulder, as if Daysi had just willed a manifestation of herself to be there, either in Area 151 or in Tammy's mind.

Daysi coiled around Tammy's neck. "The doctors never did understand what happened to you, you know. Great care, that is what drove us from that point on with you, child."

"I know." Tammy wondered how she could speak the same language as the snake. She was sure it wasn't Daysi's voice, even if she understood it. "I still think it was a brain-eating amoeba, you know? They stuck enough chemicals in me to kill an elephant, so they probably just got lucky, huh?"

"You were always a special case, Tamment."

"Yay, unique!"

Daysi's head began to bob in time to the throbbing and shaking trees on the dance floor. Tammy reminded herself they were people. She was in Area 151. Dancing. She had come here to dance and have a good time. With Tessa.

"This is some fucked up shit," Tammy said, licking her lips. They felt loud, but they smelled like vanilla that had just dripped from the sun.

Daysi slowly pulled her eyes from the dance floor to look at Tammy. "What you had tonight, it was special, just for you. Special, just like I told you, child. Special for the special one. Rejoice in your youth. Rejoice in the moment. Learn to accept the good with the bad. You hastily embrace misery, but life is not like that, and failure is not inevitable for every challenge you face, even if you convince yourself that is the case. Happiness does not require shame, nor does success require guilt."

"I'm not sure I would understand you even if I wasn't fucked up right now."

"You understand me. Like Elliot, you just refuse to accept what you know."

"Shit. Can't I even have a fucking hallucination without him ruining things?" Tammy stuck her chin out and pursed her lips angrily. "Seriously. Is it asking too much to just do something for *me* for once?"

Daysi lovingly tightened her coils around Tammy's throat. "What is done—everything—is for you. For both of you. We are the past, our time come and gone; you are the future. Where we have failed, it is up to you to succeed."

"Uh uh." Tammy pushed Daysi's head back and loosened the coils from her throat. "I'm done with being treated like a kid, everyone always up in my business and acting like they know what's right for me. You all need to quit smothering me. I'm not like you, and I never will be."

"Being like us, that's not what we ask of you. After all, we did not reach our goals; our ways were wrong. Neda saw this. Praveen tried to tell us this, but the rest of us…" Daysi turned back to watch the dancers, and after a moment, her head was bobbing in time to the music again.

"Wait, what? The rest of you what?"

Daysi turned slightly to consider Tammy with one eye. "When you are old, it is hard. Too much trust in yourself, too much resistance to change, even when it is for the better. And even knowing this, you cannot stop yourself."

Tammy thought of all the times Jeddo had seemed like he was a sampled speech played in a loop over and over again. Always the same message: *You're better than this; you're letting them get to you; you have a destiny;* blah blah blah. He was so stuck in his people's past—*their* people's past, according to him—that he couldn't see the world except through a Berber's eyes. It had cost him his daughter, then it had cost him his tribe. And it was costing him his granddaughter.

"People get tired of the same old message, Daysi."

"What was that, child?" Daysi pulled her head back from watching the dance and tilted closer to Tammy's mouth.

"I was just agreeing with you. Jeddo drove everyone away with his preaching. Usually, a *marabout* has all kinds of influence, at least that's what Jeddo said. But he somehow managed to piss everyone off, even my mother."

"So harsh. Too harsh with your judgment. What do you know of his story?"

"I know enough."

Tammy watched the hypnotizing lights for a moment and quickly found herself detached from time. Everything seemed disconnected and heavy, and she was having a hard time concentrating.

She could feel Daysi nearby, absorbed in the youthful people dancing, then they were back in the mansion's garden, just the two of them. A heartbeat, then Tammy was with Jeddo by the creekside, then they were holding hands and staring into a dark patch of woods that could have been home to a *djinn* for all she knew. Suddenly, she was hugging her father goodbye for the last time at the St. Louis airport, then she was in Germany, holding him tight as they cried over the news her mother was dead, one of dozens lost in a freak sinkhole. The moment shifted, and she was in a cavern, shivering, hiding, listening to approaching footsteps that sent before them a blistering heat that could boil away flesh. The cavern became an orange, desert cave or catacomb or building, and she was engaged in a deadly game of cat-and-mouse. And then she was in the mansion, and she felt something darker and more sinister than anything she had ever known, something that had come to destroy her family.

They weren't dream images. They were vivid memories and undoubtedly real. It was as if time suddenly couldn't even maintain its linear nature.

"Daysi, I think there's something wrong with me. Or maybe it's the tincture?"

Daysi didn't reply, and after a moment, Tammy realized there was no weight on her shoulders.

Daysi was gone, and Tammy suddenly felt so very alone.

Chapter Three

Tammy opened her eyes. The dance club was gone, replaced by a hideous orange shag carpet and a blue down comforter that was long past its expiration date. Everything smelled like stale cigarette smoke and staler cloth, and it was warm, but not as warm as the mansion.

Tessa's trailer!

Tammy sat up, turned around, and became immediately aware of the need to pee. She wanted to shove a power hose into her mouth. It felt like she'd swallowed something long dead and fallen asleep on a compost heap.

She was in the trailer's living room, lying next to a scarred and discolored coffee table that had probably been old before she was born. A small television rested on a newer, uglier TV stand in the corner across from her. To her left, a small, aluminum dining room table and metal folding chairs marked the edge of the kitchen. Emmanuelle swayed in the center of the kitchen and sang along to a Phish tune that was warbling from an ancient portable CD player. She wore a royal blue, fake silk robe that was cinched tight around the waist, but opened wide at the chest, emphasizing the same hourglass figure and deep cleavage Tessa had.

Tammy let out a soft groan, and Emmanuelle turned.

"You finally awake, sweetie?" Emmanuelle's voice was raspy and slow. A cigarette with a long ash tail dangled from her mouth, the ash threatening at any moment to fall into the robe's open top.

Tammy managed a weak wave. "Sorry. When did I get here?"

"Early this morning. You were pretty out of it. Two days partying hard. I'm envious." Emmanuelle was in her late thirties. Her shoulder-length hair was frizzy and henna-dyed a fiery red. Normally, she wore one of two types of outfits: the almost business casual she wore when teaching Philosophy at Columbia College, and the retro, flower power she wore with low-cut jeans when on the prowl. At the moment, she was wearing a bathrobe, open wide enough at the neck to reveal she wasn't wearing anything else. She took a long pull from the cigarette and set it in an ashtray, ignoring the trail of glowing ashes that fell onto the kitchen floor. "What'd you take? Tessa and Everett had to carry you in."

"Something home-brewed." Tammy had to pee, but she felt disoriented and lightheaded. She looked around for the hallway that led to the bathroom and was surprised to find it was still where it had been a moment before. Tammy marveled at the power of whatever it was Daysi had cooked up. "Two days?"

"Yeah."

"Last thing I remember was the club." *Shit! Bitchley's SUV!* "Is anyone else awake?"

"Nah. Just you. They were up later than you. At least Everett was." She pulled her hair back from her face, a face that wasn't plain but wasn't pretty, either. It had impishly gleaming eyes that were a little too close-set and a nose a little too big. "You want some breakfast, sweetie?"

"Sure." Tammy got to her feet with a groan and stumbled toward the bathroom. The floor continuously shifted beneath her feet, as if the trailer were rocking on the ocean.

"I like the Maori tattoo," Emmanuelle shouted through the trailer's paper-thin walls. "You should get it done for real. I know some really good inkers."

"Thanks. It's Berber, *siyâla*. Protection against evil spirits." Tammy glared at her face in the mirror for a moment, wondering what the hell she'd done to herself the night before. Her eyes were red and puffy, and her lips were cracked. She rubbed at the mascara tattoo for a few seconds, smudging it a bit more than it already was, then she gave up and settled on the toilet.

"Berber, yeah. I thought Arabs were against tattoos?"

Tammy squinted and did her best not to sound like she was emptying a gallon of pee all at once. One thing the mansion had over Tessa's place was something at least approximating privacy. "Yeah, a lot of Muslims are against tattoos, not Arabs. And Berbers aren't Arabs."

Emmanuelle was like the ultimate stoner poster model. Tammy did drugs to escape the pain of life; Emmanuelle just did drugs. Nonstop. And it showed.

"Oh, yeah." Emmanuelle began banging around in the kitchen, slamming pots and pans and bowls against the chipped Formica countertop. It wasn't intentional; she just didn't care. "So, the Celtic knot cross I have on the small of my back? The guy who did that, Jimmy? He does really good work. And you can get a discount, you know. Well, sometimes."

"I'm still not sure I'm ready for that sort of commitment, Mi—" Tammy caught herself before she said *Miss Copeland*. It was tough going from Jeddo's strict rules to the home without any rules whatsoever.

"You need to be proud of your heritage. I'm one-thirty-second Cherokee, you know? Back when I was about your age, I went looking for who I was. I traveled all over the Southwest, hung out with some really awesome people, and I finally found me, you know?"

"Sun Hawk," Tammy whispered.

"Sun Hawk. A shaman told me that a coyote whispered that name to him."

Tammy pulled her panties up and rolled her eyes. She felt like a prisoner, forced to listen to the ramblings of an insane warden. "And that's why you got the tattoo on your ankle."

"That's why I got the Sun Hawk tattoo on my ankle. From a guy I met in Albuquerque. Oh, what was his name again?"

"Ricky," Tammy mumbled to herself. She flushed the toilet and washed her hands, then she washed her face.

"God, I can't believe I can't remember his name."

Tammy opened the bathroom door. "Ricky, I think?"

"Oh, right. Ricky. God, he was an awesome fuck."

Tammy settled on the couch and pulled out her phone. It was almost noon, and she was feeling dehydrated, disoriented, hungry, and more than a little worried. There should have been scolding voicemails waiting for her. Jeddo should have sent out an angry search party. She hoped that Emmanuelle would spare her the sloppy details about Tricky Ricky this time. Tessa was open and frank about sex, mostly just complaining how most boys didn't know what the hell they were doing, even after watching all sorts of porn. Emmanuelle had absolutely no filters whatsoever.

Emmanuelle turned, a small butcher knife raised to the ceiling for emphasis. Small slivers of pepper and onion slid down the blade. "So I ended up calling him Tricky Ricky, did I tell you that? Because he had all these trick—"

A sudden pounding at the trailer door cut Emmanuelle off.

"What the fuck?" Emmanuelle set the knife down, took another pull on the cigarette, then almost floated to the door. She popped the door open slightly and peered out, shielding her eyes from the sun. After a second, she closed the robe's top tighter with the hand that had been holding the knife. "Yeah?"

Tammy heard a voice: deep, authoritative, projected. She knew the type of voice instantly: cop.

Fuck. What did I do? Did I attack someone?

She tried to recall what had happened the last two days, to remember anything really stupid she might have done, anything that could have brought the sheriff's deputies out to Arlington.

Bitchley's Infiniti. Oh, shit!

Her heart sank as she remembered that night. She'd made a terrible decision, then she'd used the tincture without testing it first, and that had wiped her out. Now she was stuck in the trailer, and the cops had her.

"Tammy, Deputy Sharper would like a word with you."

Sharper. The name rang a bell. Her heart sank as the day just seemed to spiral out of control.

Emmanuelle stepped back from the door. For the first time Tammy could ever recall, Emmanuelle seemed shaken. She backed into the kitchen, still clutching the top of her robe.

I guess this is it. Tammy tried not to slump too much as she stepped up to the door and leaned her head out. She'd never imagined she'd go to juvie over something as stupid as vandalizing a car. If it had been anyone other than Ashley, Tammy was pretty sure the law firm that took care of all the mansion's legal matters could cut a deal. They'd gotten her out of a few sticky problems over the years. But Ashley came from money, so the only thing that would make her happy was Tammy's head on a platter. The bad blood between them went way back, and Tammy had escalated it to a pretty good ass-kicking that left Ashley with a busted lip and chipped tooth a couple years back.

Suddenly, she remembered Sharper. He'd been the one called to the school to haul Tammy away. Big fiasco, big drama. One-month suspension, three months grounded.

"Tamment McPhee?" Deputy Sharper looked older than she remembered, probably somewhere in his thirties. He was probably as tall as Elliot, and had a good twenty pounds on him, although it wasn't all muscle. He wore aviator sunglasses, standard issue for people who needed to amp up their authority. His hair was brown and short, but not Army short, and he had a silly-looking, bushy mustache, what the kids at school called a porn mustache.

"Yeah." *Like you don't remember me.*

"Would you mind stepping outside, please, Ms. McPhee?" Sharper took a step back and pointed—literally pointed—to a spot at the base of the steps. He seemed agitated, like he was on the verge of going for his cuffs or maybe his gun.

Tammy wished she had her sneakers on. She wished everything wasn't throbbing like her head was a concert hall. She wished Bitchley had never decided to target the chubby new girl for fun all those years ago.

"Ms. McPhee, would you mind telling me where you were between the hours of 6 a.m. and 9 a.m. Sunday morning?"

"Sunday?" Tammy wasn't even sure what day it was suddenly.

"Yesterday," Sharper said through tight-drawn lips.

Yesterday morning? What the hell? "Um, sure. I was here. I mean, I was around. We were driving around." *Hiding from Jeddo and the rest.* "I don't remember. I just woke up a few minutes ago. Why?"

"And you have witnesses who can corroborate this?"

Tammy stared at the sun reflected in Sharper's sunglasses, hating the way he could hide his true intent behind reflective plastic. She could feel the energy coming off of him now, and it wasn't the usual bully thrill she picked up off cops. A chill shot up her spine. "Sure. Emmanuelle—Ms. Copeland—and her daughter."

Sharper screwed up his face, hitching one corner of his mouth up and squeezing his thin lips together. The message was clear: Tessa and Emmanuelle did not qualify as strong witnesses.

"And you live at—" He glanced down at a business card he was holding so tight that it had curled around his thumb. "1 Hamilton Lane?"

"Sure, for the last eight years."

"When were you last at that address?" Sharper seemed to be staring into her, trying to see what was inside her.

She could feel turmoil within him, like he was dancing back and forth from a deep suspicion to…concern? *For me?*

"Ms. McPhee?"

"Um, I left a little after 10 p.m. last night. Two nights ago."

"Which was it: last night, or two nights ago?" Sharper stared at her.

"Two nights ago. I went out with Tessa."

"Tessa Copeland?"

"Yeah." *Okay, so he doesn't have enough to arrest me. So what's this all about?*

Sharper chewed on that for a second, his head bobbing up and down ever so slightly.

Here it comes.

"And where did you go?"

"A few places. The Taco Bell over in Rolla. The convenience store down the street from the Taco Bell." Tammy considered leaving out the trip to St. Robert the night before, but that seemed like a bad idea. "We went over to St. Robert last night." She swallowed, suddenly aware of just how hot the asphalt was, how bright the sun was. She moved back to the bottom step, which was covered in rotting clumps of green indoor-outdoor carpeting. The pain in her feet began to recede immediately.

"From approximately when until when were you at these places?"

Gee, Deputy, I'm too disoriented by a hallucinogen to be exact, but you could check with the Taco Bell and convenience store. Or ask Mick the Rapist at Area 151 for exactly when he illegally let us into the nightclub last night. That'd be just before he started raping Tessa. "Can I ask what this is about?"

Sharper's jaw muscles worked for several seconds as he considered his next move. Tammy was pretty sure the two top options being considered involved one form of police brutality or another.

"I'd like you to accompany me to the station, Ms. McPhee."

"What?" Tammy's heart literally felt like it skipped a beat. "Am I under arrest or something?"

"We'd just like to ask you some questions."

"Yeah, and I'd like to have an attorney present."

Sharper took a deep breath and grabbed his belt with his free hand. The business card shook in the trembling grip of his other hand. "We can arrange that, but it won't be necessary."

"If I don't need an attorney to answer questions, then why do you need to take me down to the station?"

Sharper slipped back into his extended internal conflict.

Tammy's stomach twisted and growled and flipped back and forth between starving and nauseated. Something about Deputy Sharper's behavior was wrong, and it was really starting to scare her. A lot. She was sincerely worried she'd done something in her sleep, maybe something she'd picked up from one of the Elders, some mystical something she hadn't even realized she'd learned.

Could I have seriously hurt Ashley somehow? Even if I did, how could they trace that back to me?

Finally, Sharper stuffed the business card into his breast pocket and looked like he'd reached a decision. "Look, Ms. McPhee, I've been asked to bring you in. You're not under arrest. You're not a person of interest or a suspect. There are just some…things going on, and there are people who want to talk to you. It's very important."

"I want to call Jed—my grandfather."

Sharper let out a defeated sigh and threw his hands up; he wasn't going to stop her. "I'll be by my cruiser."

Tammy pulled her phone out and looked at it. Her hands were shaking. Something was definitely wrong, seriously wrong. She never considered calling Jeddo when she was in trouble. Never. And then there was the strange vibe coming off Sharper.

She punched in the mansion's phone number and set the phone to her ear, then she scraped her front teeth with her thumbnail. She was only vaguely aware of her bad breath and the sweltering heat.

The phone rang, but it sounded far, far away.

When it rang a second time, she began a mental inventory of what she'd even learned from the Elders. Daysi had taught them how to mix a handful of preparations that could get someone stoned in record time. There were other, more dangerous drugs, but Jeddo had refused to allow Tammy to deal with those while she was so young. He'd almost completely refused Ms. Nakama's crazy sex classes, but there had been a few, and they'd been mostly about using someone's lust and desires as weapons against them. Elliot had been miserable in those sessions. He was so uptight about everything, and Ms. Nakama could probably make Emmanuelle blush when she got going. And the way Ms. Nakama looked at Yuki, her snake...*that* was kinkier than any internet videos Tammy had ever watched with Tessa.

The phone kept ringing.

What the fuck?

William Big Bear and Jeddo taught about the spirits: *manitous, baraka.* None of it seemed harmful. They just used different terms and came at things from different ends. It was all sorts of granola, tree-hugger shit, crystals, and other nonsense really. Maybe they knew dangerous things, but they'd never shared any of it with her.

She hung up and dialed again, turning her mind to Praveen and Neda's teachings. Tammy had never really paid much attention to Neda's mumbo jumbo: astrology, numerology, hypnotism, trinkets, wards...it was silly stuff that set Elliot off and caused ridiculous arguments between him and his grandfather, and it was the sort of thing she'd expect in one of those movies about kid wizards or whatever.

Praveen she'd paid attention to, mostly because he tried to make everything down-to-earth. Everything was a story for him: good and evil spirits in an eternal struggle. He was fun. When he wasn't drooling all over Neda.

Tammy remembered Praveen saying that spirituality—what all of the Elders practiced and studied—came down to the same basic things: energy, direction, enlightenment. Jeddo had never agreed with that, but when she thought about it, Praveen's words made sense.

And then there was the time Jeddo had taken her to visit her father's mother Grace in the Ozarks. That was shortly before the mystery illness that nearly killed Tammy—technically had killed her, or at least had stopped her heart, for nearly a minute—so all she could recall of the visit was now just a vague memory. What lingered was more of a sensation than specific memories. She had felt *power* there, and she had felt *danger*. Her father had called his mother and Aunt Bea granny witches. Tammy had the sense her father's family might have known a little more about their own form of mysticism than they let on during the visit.

Deputy Sharper was leaning against the hood of his cruiser, pretending he was half-watching her, half-fucking off. He made a point of checking his watch, and Tammy realized he was actually anxious, not annoyed. It finally hit her: There wasn't going to be an answer.

She *had* done something wrong. Something *terribly* wrong. That was why she couldn't get anybody at the mansion.

Everyone was at the station, waiting for her, probably to say goodbye. That was it. They were all waiting to say goodbye. Forever.

She killed the call and shoved the phone into her pants pocket.

The dread, the feeling of some terrible mistake on her part, felt like she'd swallowed a brick that was now settled at the bottom of her stomach.

I did it. I finally went too far, and I've got some insane drugs in my bloodstream. I'm heading off to juvie, and I can't even remember what I did.

Whatever it was, she knew her life was about to change forever.

Chapter Four

At a little past noon, Elliot pulled into the parking lot of the sheriff's department office. Somehow, southern Missouri had managed to reverse June's approach, at least for the moment. The day felt cool, almost cold, and it had the sort of crisp clarity that only came on those rare, clear winter days. Details popped—the building's squarish bulk, the parking lot's patched blacktop, the bright white of patrol cars, the absolute silence.

Elliot parked the GLK and checked the dashboard display: 12:12; 88 degrees.

The day wasn't cool. He was sweating, yet he was shivering. The day was no clearer than any other. Everything between the hotel and the sheriff's office, everything since hearing the news station refer to the killings as the work of the Memorial Day Killer was a blur.

Memorial Day, all right.

Two deep breaths, then a third, and he exited the vehicle. It was dead quiet, the only scent being that of fresh-mowed grass. Instantly, he missed the sensation of protection the vehicle had provided. In the parking lot, he was exposed, vulnerable.

To what? The killer?

He walked to the front entrance—slow, steady, calm. Dressed in his best pair of Wranglers, an Arrow gray pinstripe shirt, and a pair of brown Hush Puppies, he could be just another student from one of the Rolla campuses.

Maybe he was coming to pay a fine, or to pick up a hungover frat brother, or to identify an assailant.

Or to pick up a kid whose life had gone off the rails, a kid who'd once been as close as a sister. We talked about memories we couldn't share with anyone else. We swore we'd always be there for each other.

What's happened to us, Tammy?

The reflection in the glass entry door snapped Elliot back to reality. It was an illusion, unreal, a brown-tinted image, yet it seemed every bit as real as the world it mirrored.

Elliot pulled the door open, shattering the spell.

A stern-faced, middle-aged deputy gave Elliot directions to Lieutenant Henriksen's office, but only after a protracted, assessing gaze and a once-over with a handheld metal detector. Radio chatter, murmuring, beeping—the silence of the parking lot was now gone. People watched him with lingering stares as he walked the halls.

The stares held the same questions. *Survivor? Person of interest? Suspect?*

It was a long hallway, and the stares and the unfamiliarity of everything made it longer. Elliot turned left and saw the wall plate: Training Room 2.

A fluorescent bulb flickered, as if struggling between the path of darkness and light, life and death. It gave off an unearthly light, bathing everything in an eldritch outline of shadow, where ethereal, half-seen shapes moved for a moment and then were gone. Although disturbing, it felt somehow appropriate.

Grandpa William would see spirits in this. Why not? I've lost everyone I've known. Who's to say they aren't here now?

But despite the appearance, they weren't spirits. Elliot really was alone.

Panic squeezed his stomach until he thought he would puke up the blueberry oatmeal he'd forced down for breakfast. He leaned against the wall next to the door, listening to the voices within the room, waiting for the panic to pass.

"All I'm sayin' is, it makes no sense. You spend all that money on a luxury brand, and for what?" The voice was unfamiliar, deep, with a rhythm and pronunciation that felt Southern, maybe inner-city, black or Hispanic.

"I didn't spend that much. It was pre-owned." Elliot recognized Henriksen's voice, but it was defensive, irritated.

"That doesn't change a thing. And *Acura*? You ever wonder who the hell came up with that? I mean, *Acura*?" The unknown man laughed and clapped his hands.

"What's wrong with Acura?" Henriksen really sounded annoyed.

"They're tryin' to sell you a car built on precision and quality, right? Acura makes you think of accurate, doesn't it?"

"That's the brand's reputation."

"But they misspelled it. A-C-U-R-A? Might as well have used a *K*."

"What? How can you misspell a brand name?"

"Exactly! Talk about a total fuck-up."

Elliot smiled despite the anxiety that was tearing him up. Henriksen had sounded like a stick-in-the-mud on the phone. It was good hearing him knocked around a bit.

A tapping sound came out of the room. It sounded like Henriksen laying down a beat on a pad of paper with a pen or pencil.

"It's a brand name, Lance. They can spell it however they want."

"Sure, sure." The guy who must be Lance laughed again. "I'm just sayin' it defeats the whole point of it."

Elliot edged forward and peered into the room, hand lifted to knock on the doorjamb. He hesitated.

The training room was brightly lit. Cardboard boxes rested on folding tables with scratched faux wood grain tops and legs and frames. Even from the doorway, everything smelled dusty and stale. Matching tables had been turned into desks for two men, one black, the other white, each seated on a wheeled chair that was no better off than the tables. They were both surrounded by manila folders, notepads, and assorted office supplies.

Elliot guessed the white man was Henriksen. Elliot didn't know a lot of black men, but he willed himself not to let his resentment of whites influence his dealings with either man.

The black man looked to be in his mid-forties. He was slender, his face dominated by high, protruding cheekbones and large eyes. A tight-trimmed mustache framed his narrow mouth. Henriksen looked a little younger. He had broad shoulders and a deep chest. Even seated, he looked tall, imposing. His clean-cut face was defined by a strong jaw and chin.

The black man looked up before Elliot could knock. Recognition settled in suddenly. "Elliot Saganash?"

"Hi." He considered the black man for a moment, then looked across the room at Henriksen, with his short, curly blond hair and blue eyes. *Do they both consider me a suspect?* "Lieutenant Henriksen?"

Henriksen stood. He loomed, somehow taller than he really was. "Call me Paul. This is Sergeant Traxler."

The black man gave a quick wave. "Lance." He shot an irritated look at Henriksen. "If we're going by first names."

Henriksen crossed the room in three long strides and extended a hand that completely engulfed Elliot's. "Did you drive all night?"

Elliot nodded. "I got in early this morning. I found a room at the Holiday Inn Express."

A broad smile—practiced, fake—crossed Henriksen's face. He rubbed his jaw, almost as if he were insecure about how broad it was. "Holiday Inn? Nice place. They've put us up at the Super 8."

Traxler snorted and shook his head.

Henriksen didn't miss a beat, apparently determined not to let Traxler get to him. "That's okay. We're going to be spending most of our time here until we get this thing solved." He pointed to the space in front of his desk and hastily plucked a dented folding chair from another table and set it down for Elliot, then Henriksen walked back to his own chair and waited for Elliot to sit before doing the same.

"Have you had any luck finding Tammy?" Elliot hoped the anxiety he was feeling wasn't too obvious.

Henriksen pulled a bottle of Purell from behind a folder and squeezed a shot into his broad palm. As he rubbed the gel into his hands, he seemed to size Elliot up. "She's on her way. A deputy picked her up from her friend's place for us. Ms. McPhee certainly knows how to pick her friends."

Tessa. Great. "Is she okay?"

Henriksen shrugged nonchalantly. "Aside from some underage drinking, yeah."

"She…" Elliot pushed his glasses up, suddenly uncomfortable. *At some point, I'm going to have to quit making excuses for her.*

Traxler pushed his chair over until it was uncomfortably close to Elliot. Traxler settled in, elbows resting on his knees, hands clasped in front of him so that his left pinky—scarred, gnarled as a tree branch, the tip ending abruptly about halfway—hovered just over Elliot's legs. Traxler radiated an unsettling heat and filled the air with a smothering, clove and spice aroma, and beneath that he smelled like cigarette smoke.

"We're not here to judge your friend, Elliot. Kids make bad decisions every day." Traxler opened his hands as if to say there was nothing he could do about it. He saw Elliot looking at the scarred pinky and held it up. "This? Exactly what I'm talkin' about. Twelve years ago, simple drug bust. Kid—smaller than me—jumped me. High on PCP. Tore the tip off and damn near pulverized the rest. Almost lost the whole thing." He flexed the finger, watching its unnatural, diminished movement with noticeable regret.

Henriksen dried his hands with a face tissue, gripped the Purell bottle with the crumpled tissue, and set the bottle back behind the folders. He threw the tissue into a nearby wastebasket with a distracted ease that only came from repetition. "We just need to know if she saw something, or maybe she heard something. Maybe someone was acting oddly at the mansion." He picked up a pen and began tapping a pad of yellow paper. "Any leads at all would help."

Traxler, eyes now squinted, clasped his hands again and stared at Elliot. "She runs with a pretty dangerous crowd."

"Tammy? Dangerous?" Elliot licked his lips. They felt dry and sticky enough that he feared his tongue might get stuck. "Why would you say that?"

"She's got a record. Her friend's got a record." Traxler looked to Henriksen for support.

Henriksen looked away. "It's sealed."

Traxler chortled dismissively. "It's still a record."

"Tessa sold pot. She's not a murderer. And Tammy beat up a girl who'd been bullying her mercilessly. The girl deserved it and more." Elliot fought off another surge of panic. The detectives were doing some sort of good cop, bad cop routine, trying to knock him off-balance. It was as if they already had their case built, even without facts. "Tammy's just a confused kid. She's had a hard life."

Henriksen opened a folder and scanned its contents. "Fights in school. Loitering. Vandalism. Drugs."

"She lost her mother when she was a little kid and her dad not long after that." Elliot hated the way his voice cracked when he was under pressure. "She's had problems dealing with the losses."

Henriksen pointed at whatever it was he was reading, as if Elliot could see it. "She's been suspended twice. She hurt another girl."

"It was retaliation. Ashley's a bull—"

"Drug dealers, assault." Traxler bit his lip and leaned in so close he was almost touching Elliot. "What d'you think? A little blow, some whiskey, maybe she gets a couple of those soldiers at that bar she was at—" He snapped his finger and pointed at Henriksen for help.

"Area 151."

"Area 151." Traxler turned back to Elliot. "She gets a couple of those soldiers to go along for a joy ride? Maybe she offers to give them a little something in return?"

Elliot shook his head. *Not Tammy.*

Traxler leaned in closer, his clasped hands now touching Elliot's knee. "She's a pretty girl. Wild. Dangerous."

Elliot flushed. "She's not like that!" He swallowed. "Tammy's a good kid, like I said. She's just…trying to find her way. She'd never hurt anyone."

Henriksen tapped the contents of the folder. "Ashley Parks doesn't count as 'anyone'? Busted lip, cracked tooth, stitched-up forehead…that sounds painful."

Traxler's left hand gently settled on Elliot's knee. "What about for the money?" The hand lingered for a moment, then Traxler pulled it back, the gnarled pinky catching in the fold of Elliot's jeans.

Elliot pulled his leg back instinctively. "What money?" He looked to Henriksen for help, hating that they were manipulating him despite his best efforts not to let them control the situation. "We had everything we needed at the mansion. She didn't need to steal any money."

Henriksen closed the folder he'd been looking at, running fingers down its cover as if it needed the slight pressure to stay shut, then he opened another. "Were you aware your grandfather was worth several million dollars?"

"Big trust fund." Traxler winced as if he felt terrible for William Big Bear. It wasn't convincing. "I've seen people killed for a lot less. I worked this case where a woman took a knife—"

"What about it, Elliot?" Henriksen set his left arm on the desktop and leaned his chin against the clenched fist. "More than twenty million. That's a nice mansion, but you weren't living like the Hiltons."

Elliot leaned back in his chair. Life at the mansion had always been comfortable, but never excessively so. They'd never gone wanting, but he'd never thought of the sort of money it would take for such a lifestyle. *They never had the place renovated. They never did anything extravagant. The dirt bikes, the mountain bikes, the new clothes, the GLK. That was for Tammy...and me.* His hands began to shake; he clasped them and pulled them in close to his gut. "I never really thought of it. We didn't have money—"

"On the reservation?" Traxler smiled, pretending he understood and sympathized.

"He probably inherited the money when he took over the mansion." Elliot shifted in his chair. The metal felt cold and hard against his back.

Once again, Henriksen closed the folder he'd been looking at, ran his fingers down the front, then opened another folder. "Your grandfather moved to the United States in 1984. Inherited the mansion from Taine Anderson, another immigrant. New Zealand. Maori." Henriksen looked up from the folder, his voice calm, detached. "Was everyone there an immigrant, Elliot?"

"The original owner wasn't." Elliot tried not to sound defiant and failed.

Henriksen glanced at the folder. "Thomas Harrison?" He looked up at Elliot again, eyes widened slightly. "Or did you mean Mangas Victorio?"

"Yes." Elliot shifted in his seat. "Mangas."

Traxler recoiled and tried to appear confused. He was either a bad actor or he was playing a different game than Elliot could figure out. "Mangas? What kind of name is that?"

Henriksen screwed up his lips and pointed to the page he was looking at. "Says here Arapahoe. A celebrity gunslinger around the turn of the century. Bought the mansion from Harrison for a song."

Traxler pulled a set of car keys from his pocket, carefully searched for the perfect one, then began digging in his ear. "Sounds fair to me. After what happened to your people." He pointed the key at Elliot. "Right?"

Henriksen ran through his folder routine again. "You moved to the mansion in 2006? Elliot?"

Elliot nodded absently, his thoughts far away. "After my father died. Grandpa took me in."

"Your mother's dead?" Henriksen looked up from the folder, one eyebrow cocked curiously.

"She died when I was little."

"Damned shame," Traxler said, head shaking as much as the key in his ear allowed. He sneezed suddenly and stood, shoving the keys back into his pocket. He dug out a wrinkled handkerchief and sneezed again, this time catching the worst of it. He walked back to his desk and sneezed again, then again, each time louder and more violent than the last. "Seems like you and Tammy got a lot in common, both losin' your parents so young and all. You got the same anger issues as her?"

"What?" Elliot blinked in disbelief. *Anger issues?*

Henriksen leaned back in his chair, face pinched as if he were holding his breath. He put a handkerchief to his nose for a moment and seemed to relax. Finally, he set the handkerchief down and looked back at Elliot. "You *are* a pretty big guy, Elliot. Bigger than anyone else we found in the mansion. You look like you lift. There were all kinds of weapons lying around the place. Someone might wonder if you ever thought of using those when you got mad."

Traxler snapped his fingers and charged across the room. "Like if they weren't givin' you any of that money. We found paperwork for a Mercedes, but no sign of it. High-end computer, too. And one of those expensive iPhones. Recent purchases."

Why are they doing this? Because of the medicine bag? "They were gifts for my return to Winnipeg."

"Sixty-thousand dollars worth of gifts?" Traxler pinched his nose and rubbed it violently, then he sniffed loudly. "Just out o' the blue? And you didn't start wonderin' if there was more money?"

"No." Elliot fought the urge to cross his arms. It was a defensive posture, exactly the sort of thing he didn't want to do. He tried to relax, barely catching Henriksen giving Traxler a look that seemed to be a signal.

Traxler stepped back to his desk, and Henriksen leaned in closer to Elliot. "So your grandfather was all you had left?"

"Yeah." Elliot sunk in his chair. *And I left him to die.*

Henriksen shook his head. "Why would you leave him?"

"Money?" Traxler called from his desk. He blew his nose, a trumpeting sound in the silence, then made his way back to his seat.

Henriksen shifted his chair back slightly, as if to keep clear of Traxler's germs. "You wouldn't want your grandfather to die over money, would you, Elliot? That doesn't sound like you. Smart kid, really good grades, swim and golf team, no criminal record."

"I was returning to Winnipeg to go to school."

Traxler tapped his chin. "Goin' back to Winnipeg to go to school? Don't they have colleges right here in Rolla? I coulda sworn I saw some mighty fine young women walkin' around town last night. Looked like college girls to me."

Elliot sighed loudly. *They should be focusing on finding the real killer!* "I wanted to be with my people."

"Your people?" Traxler's voice dripped with mockery.

Elliot decided he didn't like Traxler any more than he did Henriksen. He jerked at the sudden sound of a knock. A deputy stood in the doorway, Tammy to his left. She wore a baggy, black T-shirt and a pair of jeans.

"What the—" Elliot tried to make eye contact with Tammy, but she just stared at the ground.

"You ever see this man before, Elliot?" Henriksen pulled a yellow Post-it note off a crisp, black and white photograph and turned the photograph for Elliot to see.

Traxler walked to the door and talked to the uniformed officer for nearly a minute.

Elliot examined the picture closely. It showed a huge man with a shaved head. The man wore a grimy wife-beater that showed off thick, muscular arms and chest, the sort of person Elliot expected to see wandering the free weights area of a prison yard. Tattoos coiled up from the man's hands to his neck and chest. He had a dark goatee and darker eyes. There was nothing but malice and menace in his hard stare. Elliot glanced at the Post-it note and saw the name Glen Stone written on it in crisp, clear block print. "No."

Elliot again tried to make eye contact with Tammy, and she again refused to meet his gaze. Still, he could see that she looked bad, like maybe she'd been roughed up. He reddened, imagining a *brave* deputy knocking her around.

Henriksen cleared his throat. It was just loud enough to regain Elliot's attention. "Have you ever heard of the New Order?"

Elliot looked from Henriksen to the photo that was now face-up on the desk, then looked back at Tammy. "No."

When Traxler dismissed the deputy, Tammy preemptively yanked her arm away from Traxler's extended hand. He turned and followed her into the room, pulling a folding chair over to Henriksen's desk for her. Traxler tapped the photo once with his right forefinger. "They're a skinhead gang out of St. Louis. Nazis."

"Neo-Nazis," Henriksen corrected.

"Whatever." Traxler snorted. "They're involved in all kinds of shit."

Tammy settled in the chair Traxler had set out for her, and Elliot saw her in finer detail. She looked like hell. Her eyes were bloodshot, the lower lids puffy. Her lips looked chapped, and she blinked slowly and seemed disoriented.

"Are you okay?" Elliot turned from Tammy to Henriksen. "Could we get her some water? I think she's dehydrated."

"I'm fine. I just woke up." Tammy stared at Henriksen, and then at Traxler. "What do we have to do with neo-Nazis?"

"In a minute." Henriksen turned the photo toward Tammy. "Have you ever seen this man? Maybe driving around in Rolla? He'd be pretty recognizable. He's about my size."

Traxler let out a short bark that could've been a laugh and tossed a folder on Henriksen's desk. "Minus that lieutenant's gut you're growin'."

Henriksen pretended he hadn't heard Traxler, instead taking the folder and squaring up its contents. Elliot managed to catch a glimpse of one of the protruding sheets before Henriksen stuffed it into the folder and thought it might be more photographs.

Stone's accomplices?

Henriksen squeezed his mouth tight in annoyance as he set the folder deep in the tallest pile and aligned all the folders flush. "This guy Stone, he's about six-three, two-fifty. Very muscular." He glared at Traxler, pulled out the Purell bottle, pumped it twice, and loudly scrubbed his hands. "FBI, DEA, a dozen states—everybody wants him, but they haven't been able to make anything stick. He's careful. But two people saw him parked at the Arlington IGA Sunday morning. He stands out."

Tammy stared at the picture and strained to focus, something she found almost impossible to do at the moment. She did feel dehydrated and had a pounding headache, and the effects from Daysi's tincture were only now fading.

She'd never seen the guy in the picture, but she'd seen his type. Angry, full of hate and violence, always looking to project his failures onto someone or something else. Fort Leonard Wood had a lot of black soldiers and a surprising number of neo-Nazi types. It was like there was an automatic balance in the universe that caused assholes to spontaneously pop up wherever there were innocent people to victimize.

Henriksen plucked face tissues from the box on his desk, then set the Purell bottle back in its place. His chair squeaked as he stood and stretched; the squeak was a cheap, plastic noise, not the deep, honest groan of wood. He gave Traxler a lingering look. "I'm going to grab a bottle of water for her."

"Lieutenant Henriksen?" Elliot's voice was soft in the relative silence.

Henriksen turned, his shoulders back and his body rigid. "Yeah?"

"Who found them…?"

Henriksen and Traxler exchanged a glance that was too quick for Elliot to make sense of, but Henriksen seemed to relax a little. "Someone had apparently called in a grocery order to the IGA in the morning, but no one ever came to pick it up. The grocer sent someone by with the groceries, and they saw ..." Henriksen looked down for a moment, then he slowly walked to the door.

Traxler picked up a folder from Henriksen's desk, then waited until he was gone. Traxler rapped the folder against the crease of his open hand's thumb and forefinger as he looked at Elliot and Tammy. "Either of you know the whereabouts of Luis Juarez?"

"Is he still alive?" Elliot nearly jumped out of his seat. "I thought Lieutenant Henriksen said everyone in the mansion was dead?"

"What?" Tammy felt like someone had poked her with a live wire. Her breath caught. "Elliot, what—" Her voice cracked when she saw the horror in Elliot's eyes. She suddenly realized *his* eyes were red and puffy, too.

"Oh—" Elliot looked at Traxler, mortified. "You didn't tell—she didn't know?"

Traxler didn't react for a moment, but then he blinked and turned away, and Elliot understood.

He'd been set up. They had both been suspects, at least to some extent. Henriksen and Traxler had kept Tammy in the dark, hoping she might let something slip when she came into the room.

"Jeddo ..." Tammy tried to convince herself it was all some sort of elaborate trick, something to get her to admit to banging the shit out of Ashley's car, but she couldn't kid herself, not even for a second. She could sense it in the way the black detective almost slinked away. *They're dead. They thought I was in on it.*

Elliot squatted next to Tammy and wrapped his arms around her. "I am *so* sorry."

"*Everyone?* He killed *everyone?*" Tammy shook and began to bawl loudly. "No! What the *fuck*, Elliot?"

Elliot squeezed her tight against him. "I don't know."

Traxler threw the folder down on Henriksen's desk with a loud slap, clearly uncomfortable. "We don't know if Stone's our killer, or maybe this Juarez is, but we had to eliminate the two of you being involved."

Tammy turned on Traxler. "What the hell is wrong with you? You thought we would kill our family?"

Elliot patted Tammy's back reassuringly. "There's apparently a lot of money involved, Tammy."

Tammy punched Elliot's chest. "So? They were all we had left. We couldn't kill them over *money*." Fat, blubbering tears rolled down her cheeks, and snot bubbled from her nose. Her carefully constructed façade of hard-ass, streetwise, sassy *Little Miss Thing* completely crumbled.

Elliot felt close to losing it himself. He gave Traxler a pleading look. "Could you give us a minute?"

Traxler sniffed loudly, then he walked stiffly out of the room and shut the door behind him.

Elliot stroked Tammy's hair. Anything he said to reassure her would be a lie. "It's all right now"; "We'll get through this together"; "You're strong enough for this". All a lie. They'd lost their family. That wasn't something you got over.

"I …" Tammy choked, her voice a heartbreaking whimper. "Jeddo was so mad at me. I let him down, and then—and then, I sneaked out to go hang out with Tessa."

"You—he didn't …" Elliot couldn't stop her from beating herself up. He'd done the same thing the whole drive back. William Big Bear had given his blessing to leave, had finally accepted that Elliot was doing the right thing, and then…

"Neda tried …" Tammy wiped snot on her forearm and tried to force back the tears.

"Tammy—"

"No! Listen! Neda tried to tell me. She caught me when I was sneaking out, and she was crying. She knew something was going to happen. She *knew*."

Elliot didn't feel like arguing. Neda had fancied herself a seer, and she did have a good way of playing the odds to make it *look* like she could predict things, but her beliefs had been all nonsense. She couldn't have known something was going to happen. It simply wasn't possible.

"Elliot, nothing should have been able to hurt them. The mansion was warded."

"We need to stop with that sort of—" *Silliness? Delusion? Thinking? What can I say that won't upset her? She's scared. She's lost everything, everyone. She can't reach out to others. She won't let herself. And if I tell her she's being silly, she'll cut me off.*

"You need to listen, okay?" Tammy punched him in the chest again. Hard. "For just a minute, *listen*! I took some tinctures from Daysi's room the other day. She *knew* about it, just like Neda knew I stole her bottle of perfume."

"This isn't—"

"Shut *up*! Let me finish! Neda could see the future, Elliot. She *could!* She was waiting for me when I sneaked out. They all knew more than they were ever letting on. Jeddo was dying of cancer. He refused to take any of the things Daysi made for him. He wasn't even trying, okay? Why wouldn't he try to stay alive, even for a little longer? Think about it. Your grandfather argued with you for an entire year, then he suddenly bought you a car and told you to go for it? That never struck you as all 'what the fuck'? Seriously?"

"Try to find calm in the storm." Elliot was stunned at his own calmness, at the quality of his own voice as he tried to console Tammy. The words weren't his; they were Grandpa William's; they were Praveen's. It was both painful and reassuring to find answers in their teachings.

Tammy tried to control her breathing, making snot-gurgling inhales and jagged exhales. She knew she wouldn't get through Elliot's stubborn refusal to accept *anything* other than science and logic while she was crying and screaming, regardless of what was right there in front of him.

"I *am* calm, damn it!" She stood and grabbed a clump of facial tissues from the box on Henriksen's desk. She blew her nose and wiped her eyes and tossed the limp, soggy tissues into the garbage. "Goddamn it! We left them there to die, Elliot."

Tammy's words hit harder than her punches. "I didn't leave them there to die. I was going off to school, with their blessings. You were the one sneaking out to go party." *Shit.* He closed his eyes, ashamed to have even *thought* what he'd just *said*, but he couldn't un-say it.

Tammy shot out of her chair so fast, she knocked it over. "*I* left them? *Me?* You were driving to fucking Manitoba, or wherever it was you were running off to."

Elliot felt anger rise at her challenge, anger born from his own guilt. "You didn't give a damn about them. You didn't give a damn about anyone else but you. I was driving myself crazy wondering if you were dead after Lieutenant Henriksen called. Why the hell didn't you call me, or at least text me?"

"You'd already left. What does it matter? It wasn't like I was ever going to see you again." Tammy's arms were rigid at her side. Her face was stretched and distorted with anger. "You'd already abandoned me, left me alone in that mansion with all…with …" She'd nearly called them fossils. Jeddo's face—weak, strained, concerned for *her*—flashed before her eyes, and the fury drained away as suddenly as it had flared up. She collapsed into a fit of crying again.

Elliot held her. The anger and the guilt were still there, gnawing at him, but it wasn't the time. She'd had no right to lay the blame on him, even if at the same time she was right. She'd been the one who'd abandoned him long before, always turning inward, always finding justification for her anger and bitterness, but they'd both abandoned their home, left the Elders to fend for themselves, left them to deal with a neo-Nazi murderer.

"I'm so sorry, El." Her words were jagged, broken, barely understandable. Nothing was understandable at the moment. "He can't be gone. I'm so alone."

Elliot pulled her closer, but the physical closeness felt less real than the sense she was so far away, her thoughts and emotions stuck on what she'd lost. They had each other now and no one else, but he could feel it: they were alone.

After a long bout of crying, Tammy blew her nose into another tissue, turning it into a dripping mess. She wiped her hand and threw the soiled tissues away. "Why were they asking about Luis?"

"I guess he survived. So that means the attack must've happened Sunday morning, when he was in St. Louis."

"St. Louis?"

"They were looking at—" No. She didn't need to know they were going to get the whole mansion torn apart just to make her happy. "It was some sort of structural work they were going to have done. Some place in St. Louis had the same sort of thing done."

Elliot made his way over to Henriksen's desk and began flipping through the folders stacked there. Stone's accomplices were in that stack.

Elliot had to see them. He *had* to.

Tammy dried her eyes, finally finding a respite from the crying. "What do you think you're doing?"

"There must be some sort of report. I saw a folder. This folder." He opened it and began flipping through the photos. "Something to show who and why—"

He stopped, his eyes bugging out, his stomach ready to flip. The photos weren't of accomplices. They were hi-res photographs—brilliant, sharp, impossibly crisp and detailed—but the images were of death and horror.

He tried to close the folder, to un-see what he'd seen, but instead he flipped to the next photo.

"Elliot?"

The blood. The carnage. The inhumanity.

"Elliot!"

Tammy's nails dug into his flesh like claws. He finally closed the folder and looked at her. He saw the horror in her eyes that reflected his own.

Their family hadn't just been killed, they'd been butchered. Mutilated. It was worse than anything he could have imagined. Glen Stone couldn't be the killer. No human could have done what the photographs showed. No animal could have.

A sinking realization settled into Elliot's brain: Whoever had killed their family was a twisted monster.

Chapter Five

While Henriksen fiddled with a recording device, Traxler seemed to be trying to read Elliot and Tammy. Elliot could sense Tammy seething under the scrutiny; it was exactly the sort of thing she instinctively rebelled against. He tried to take her hand, but she pushed him away. Despite the tight confines of the interrogation room, it felt to Elliot like she'd opened a vast distance between them since taking her seat. The room was stuffy and warm, but Tammy's brush-off seemed to lower the temperature. Even her body odor seemed to intensify with the move. Something strong—but not alcohol—was seeping out of her pores, smothering his Paul Sebastian cologne and the cigarette smell coming off Traxler.

Tammy turned on Henriksen. "Is it really that hard to get that working?"

"Actually, I think I've got it now." Henriksen pushed two microphones forward, one halfway between him and Traxler, the other centered between Tammy and Elliot. "It's Monday, May 25th, 2015. This is Lieutenant Paul Henriksen, Chesterfield Police Department, lead on the Major Case Squad, St. Louis investigation into the Memorial Day Killer." Henriksen pointed at the microphone in front of Tammy and Elliot. "If you would speak your names?"

Tammy glared at Elliot; he leaned closer to the microphone. "I'm Elliot Saganash."

"Tammy McPhee." Just saying her name seemed a strain on her.

Traxler cleared his throat and said, "Detective Lance Traxler, Metropolitan Police Department, City of St. Louis, attached to Major Case Squad, St. Louis."

"Mr. Saganash and Ms. McPhee have agreed to an interview to discuss their last days in Harrison Mansion. Preliminary estimates place the killer or killers on the premises Sunday morning, May 24th, 2015." Henriksen's eyes ran from Tammy to Elliot.

Elliot pushed his glasses up his nose. He wasn't about to get into a war of wills with Tammy. She'd barely agreed to the interview, at first demanding legal representation. Elliot could just imagine the problems that would create. They were innocent. They knew it, and he sensed the police knew it, too.

"Um, I guess I need to go back a little bit." Elliot shifted in the seat, even though he knew he wouldn't find a comfortable position, not on the metal chair. "I was accepted to University of Winnipeg earlier this year, and I told my grandfather—"

Henriksen held up a massive hand. "His name, please?"

"William Big Bear Saganash." When Henriksen nodded, Elliot continued. "Anyway, after I told my grandfather about that, they began—"

"They? Could you provide names?" Henriksen asked.

"Sure. Um, William Big Bear Saganash, Driss Zéroual—Tammy's grandfather—Neda Abadi, Praveen Thakur, Daysi Pizanga and Ms. Nakama. They were our Elders—"

Henriksen's hand came up again. "Elders?"

Elliot looked at Tammy for support, but she was concentrating on something far away. "My grandfather was a traditionalist. They all were. They believed in seeing the world…spiritually."

Traxler's face screwed up. "They were religious? I thought they were all immigrants—India, Japan, Peru…What religion connected them?"

"Not religion. Spirituality. Different forms, but they were always sort of seeking common ground." Elliot could barely keep himself from squirming. It had always been embarrassing, but in light of the murders, it was unbearable. "A lot of their teachings were sort of similar."

"Uh huh." Traxler looked at Henriksen, eyebrow cocked. "So maybe not just an immigrant angle? Maybe they were a threat to his religion?"

"Stone? Stone's religious?" Elliot couldn't conceive of a cold-blooded murderer being religious. Then again, he made a point of actively ignoring religious activity.

Henriksen frowned. "Militantly, you might say, but not traditionally religious, no. The New Order isn't embraced by any mainstream churches, but they certainly proclaim themselves holy warriors."

"Sick fucks—" Traxler flinched and covered his mouth when Henriksen glanced at the microphone, then continued on. "Always gotta find something to justify their actions somehow. It's never their problem; it's someone else's."

Scratching filled the room as Henriksen jotted a note on the pad in front of him. He pointed at the microphone in front of Elliot. "Go ahead, Elliot. You said your elders began something?"

"Oh. After we got past the fighting, they began—"

"Fighting?" Henriksen seemed to focus even more intensely than before.

Tammy came to life, sneering at Elliot. "Elliot wasn't supposed to leave. He'd agreed to stay on at the mansion after he graduated high school, but then he pulled the whole 'I got accepted' thing out and everyone had a shit fit."

Elliot blushed and sank in on himself. "I told Grandpa William I'd have to go to school eventually. I just couldn't stay there any longer, not with so much ahead of me."

Henriksen scratched some more notes, then he pointed at the microphone again.

Elliot straightened and cleared his throat. "So, a couple weeks ago, Grandpa William suddenly changed his mind. He said it was probably the right thing to do. That's when he gave me the Mercedes and MacBook and iPhone you found the receipts to."

Traxler scratched his chin, loud in the small room. "Just like that? No reason?"

Elliot shook his head. He'd always wondered what had changed, but he hadn't wanted to press his luck. "I just assumed he realized it was a fight he couldn't win."

Tammy's eyes narrowed angrily. The pain of death apparently could not outweigh the pain of abandonment. She had always been inclined toward irrationally strong grudges, and Elliot had no doubt her grudge against him was one for the ages. *It's just my fault. Everything. All of it. My fault.*

"So he bought you all those neat toys and said goodbye after raising you for, what, nine years?" Traxler snorted and shook his head. He smiled at Elliot, but it wasn't a pleasant smile. Traxler's dark eyes were scrutinizing Elliot, judging him. "That's a lot of love."

"I know." Elliot's voice cracked.

"And you left the mansion when?" Henriksen's pen was poised over the notepad.

"Saturday morning."

"May 23rd?" Henriksen's pen moved closer to the notepad, but his eyes were focused on Elliot.

"Yeah. The 23rd."

Henriksen scratched a quick note. "Okay, Elliot. I want you to think back. Saturday morning. You're getting ready to leave. What happened? Think hard. What did you see? What did you hear?"

"We'd had a picnic the night before—"

Tammy sighed heavily. "A going away picnic for the hero."

Elliot wiped away a tear. The picnic had been the last time he'd seen Neda, radiant in the burnt orange shorts and sleeveless white-and-burnt-orange-striped top. Her dark brown hair and exquisite eyes, her firm thighs and full, perfectly shaped lips; he couldn't understand how someone like Glen Stone could exist. Who could hurt a beautiful, delicate, and wonderful person like Neda?

"Elliot?" Henriksen put on a fairly believable and encouraging smile. "Saturday morning?"

"I'm sorry." Elliot breathed deep, brought his emotions under control, then pressed on. "I guess I woke around 8 a.m. Showered and dressed ..." He thought back, concentrated. What had he seen that morning?

"And then?" Henriksen jotted a lazy note, waiting for Elliot to continue.

"And then." Elliot closed his eyes. "And then—"

≈

Brilliant sunlight washed everything out, muting colors and merging shapes in the distance so that Elliot found himself wondering if he was even really in his bedroom in Harrison Mansion. Despite his ceiling fan running full speed, Elliot's skin was damp, a sure sign he was still in the miserable Missouri humidity. He hated the heat, but to some extent, the humidity, the sounds of animals returning to life, and the fresh scents of forest rebirth reminded him of the Fisher River reserve.

Home. In Manitoba. Not here.

A dust devil swept south across the lawn below, twisting grass and kicking up loose twigs and leaves in its serpentine path. It threw itself against the tower's north face, blowing debris high, rattling it off the window. He recoiled at the strength of the thing, momentarily wondering if it were some mystical test of the mansion walls.

A mystical test? Now I sound like Grandpa William.

Elliot turned from the window, wincing as the soles of his sneakers squeaked on the bedroom's hardwood floor. All he wanted now was silence and to leave no lasting trace. He looked at the floor and almost saw his reflection in the wood's dark stain. There was a minor scuff, but it was nothing Luis couldn't undo later. No one had taught Elliot more about caring for the creepy mansion than Luis.

Now that I'm leaving, Grandpa will need to find someone else for this room.

Elliot pushed aside the uncomfortable fact that, despite the Elders' best efforts, they hadn't taken in anyone new since Tammy arrived.

He touched the down-stuffed comforter. Its smooth surface was a wild pattern of browns and golds that reminded him of home. He patted the bed, admiring the sturdy cherry wood bedposts that were as thick as his leg and the soft but firm mattress he'd lain on for the last few years.

His signature was here, in the room. It was here simply by him choosing it. The tower. The third floor. He viewed the north lawn and, beyond that, the low stone wall and the road and the woods and the creek.

It was a smaller room than he could have had, colder in the winter, hotter in the summer, but, everything considered, it was a natural fit for him. His father's place in Manitoba had been small and cold, and Elliot could see a river from his window there as well.

So long ago, really. Is the river still there?

He laughed softly at the thought. The river would outlast him. It would outlast his people.

Hoping he might truly be quiet, he gathered the last of his belongings from the cherry wood nightstand, the bed's little brother. He stopped to inspect the bronze-framed photo of his father and mother holding a little bundle Grandpa William proudly swore was Elliot a few days after his birth. He couldn't see himself in the baby's tiny face, but Grandpa William would never lie about such a thing. Next was his high school diploma, now in a frame that had once held a picture of his mother. Finally, he took up the leather pouch that contained the last of his parents' ashes. They had died a handful of years apart, but, despite his atheistic views, Elliot liked to assure himself they had found peace together now.

He pulled the leather necklace from inside his navy blue Nautica shirt until he could wrap his long, elegant fingers around the dun leather strip knotted at its center. A bear crafted from a rainbow of small, glass beads stared up at him from the worn front. Elliot solemnly pressed the strip to his forehead, then reverently lowered it and unstitched the back, revealing a silver cross secured by a strip of leather that ran beneath the crossbar.

Is this the right decision?

It wasn't a prayer to the white man's god. Any value the cross represented was a connection to his mother, or at least to the memories he had of her.

Once again, he chuckled at his own foolishness. His mother's spirit wouldn't answer him. There would be no divine guidance, no assistance from the *manitous*. It was the twenty-first century, and he was an educated man.

No one could answer the question but himself, and at that exact moment, all he knew was that leaving *felt* right.

He closed his eyes and kissed the top of the cross, then he sealed the back of the leather strip again and dropped it inside the front of his shirt. Moving quickly and silently, he gathered up the photo of his parents, the high school diploma, and the leather pouch and stuffed them into the new, black Samsonite travel bag he'd laid on the center of the bed. Uncertainty froze him in place for just a moment, and then he zipped the bag shut with a single, quick tug.

There wasn't time for uncertainty, not anymore. He'd thought the decision through many times already.

He slid a backpack over his shoulder and reached for the travel bag's handle, pausing momentarily to look at the copper hand at the end of an arm much softer and smaller than his father's. The hand lacked the calluses and scars of a laborer.

Or a drunk.

He pulled the bag off his…off *the* bed and carefully walked to the hallway. At the door, he took a final look at the room, shaking his head at a crow that had settled at the northern window ledge to watch him through the glass.

"What are you?" he whispered to the black bird. It cocked his head as if listening and considering the question. "Grandpa William would quiz me if you're ill tidings or not. My days of answering are over. I'm done here."

The crow nodded in reply and took to the air.

Elliot shivered anxiously. A simple bird landing and then flying away had gotten to him. He felt pathetic.

He opened the door onto the hall, nearly bumping into Ms. Nakama. In her black silk kimono, she almost matched Yuki, the long, black snake that followed her everywhere. Elliot bowed slightly, and Ms. Nakama considered him through inscrutable eyes.

"I'm leaving now." He pointed to the travel bag and immediately felt like an idiot. Ms. Nakama and Yuki both glanced at the bag for a moment, then they looked back at him.

Elliot thought Ms. Nakama might be ready to launch into him, to read him the riot act as his school teachers used to say. Given how rarely she spoke to him outside of the uncomfortable training she provided, it would have been surprising. Instead, she coldly bowed back, strands of her graying black hair floating out from the thick bun she'd pinned with simple balsa sticks. Her face was heavily made up, but not so he couldn't see the wrinkles, or the pinched, disapproving frown on her thin, shapeless lips. She walked past slowly, her kimono rustling louder than her footfalls.

Yuki paused to look him over as a young woman might, eyes traveling up and down his body before settling first on his crotch, then on his face. She flicked her—it flicked its—tongue at him before also slowly returning his bow, then slithering past.

He watched them until Ms. Nakama entered the study that occupied the eastern section of the third floor, just south of his room. He waited for Yuki to follow Ms. Nakama inside. Yuki's cold, reptilian eyes watched him from the study's entryway for several seconds longer, then the head turned and it slithered inside to join Ms. Nakama.

It took real effort not to snort at the moment. From his first day there, he'd found everything in Hamilton Mansion strange, freakish even. Mystics from around the world, gathered in a bizarre, castle-like mansion in the middle of nowhere.

Freakish felt appropriate. They were all good people, and they were sincere, but they were…nuts.

Elliot stepped into the hallway, nearly stumbling as the carpet runner in front of his door tangled around the toes of his sneakers. He rolled his eyes as he pulled his feet free, an easy task made harder by the runner's seeming stubborn resolve. He finally had to pin the runner down with the travel bag to pull free.

Everything about the mansion seemed bent on working against him most days. Today seemed worse than normal.

"You're not going to change my mind." His voice was a little louder and more forceful than he'd meant. He shook his head, embarrassed.

Now I've convinced myself this place is alive. I need to get out of here before it's too late.

He walked the hallway slowly, choosing his steps carefully. It didn't matter where he stepped, though. The floor groaned and creaked loudly each time his feet made contact, as if he were a giant, lumbering, uncaring bear instead of a graceful, 180-pound young man taking feather-light steps.

At the head of the stairs, Elliot stopped and glanced at the doors he'd seen for far too long, putting a name to each occupant and a face to the name— Ms. Nakama, Neda, and in the southwestern corner opposite his tower room, Praveen.

As Elliot thought of Praveen, his door opened and his head poked out.

Praveen was shorter than Elliot, without any of the muscle Elliot had developed from his archery, swim team, and outdoor activities, but with his perfectly combed hair and handsome features, he was very handsome. Praveen gave a toothy smile, bright white against the black of his close-trimmed mustache and beard.

"You are leaving now?" Praveen stepped out of his room, but he left the door open behind him. Gentle incense trailed in his wake, filling the corridor. He wore a plain, white silk *dhoti*, bright in the glow framing him. He tugged at the *dhoti's* sleeves distractedly.

Elliot started to take a step, but he stopped. "Yes. It's a long drive."

"It is good weather, though." Praveen tapped his feet for a moment, as if admonishing the runners to behave, then he walked around the stairway banister until he stood next to Elliot. He extended a hand. "It has been a great pleasure to have you with us, Elliot."

Elliot took the hand—dark like his, but with scars and wrinkles that told the story of Praveen's life before coming to the mansion. It had been a harder life than Elliot's. They shook hands.

"Thank you. You always made me feel welcome, Praveen."

"Welcome in your own home? That is indeed an accomplishment. I must truly be a powerful mystic." Praveen laughed and clapped his hands once.

Elliot looked down, ashamed at the subtle reminder that it was him leaving his family, not them pushing him away. "It is possible to have more than one home and family."

"Of course. That's a very wise observation. There's a reason your grandfather holds out so much hope for you." Praveen looked toward the study, then turned to glance at Neda's door. "Did you already say goodbye to Ms. Nakama and Neda?"

"I nearly knocked Ms. Nakama and Yuki over a second ago. They were outside my door. It was like they were just hovering there. And Yuki...kind of hung around."

Praveen's face broke into a puckish smirk, one eyebrow raised conspiratorially. "I told you before, she is a beautiful, young woman. It is a shame you two did not hit it off."

Elliot rubbed the back of his neck. Talking about Yuki always made him uncomfortable.

Praveen clapped his hands again, delighted. "You see Yuki's core form, even when she does not wish you to. It is a gift that you see what is, not what others wish you to see. So few people can shrug off the veils of illusion. Hold fast to this, and it will serve you well."

"Uh …" Illusion. Deception. Manipulation. It was the lifeblood of a mystic.

Praveen laughed again, a lighthearted, uplifting sound. "I can see I've upset you. No more about Yuki, then. What about Neda? You have said goodbye to her?"

Elliot looked away, embarrassed. "We said goodbye yesterday."

Praveen pursed his lips and arched his eyebrows. "Of course. It is none of my business, but …"

"I'd rather not talk about it."

Praveen clutched his hands behind his back and became more serious. "Neda says you have a great journey ahead of you. I wish I could tell you of it, but you have always been closed to me. I hope that means good things for you."

"Thanks." Elliot struggled through an awkward silence, searching for the right words. He still couldn't meet Praveen's gaze. *Guilt? Shame? What's wrong with me?*

Elliot finally looked up. Praveen had stepped closer, his hand resting on the travel bag as if to steady himself, or possibly to somehow use it to keep Elliot in the mansion.

No. He knows I have to go.

"Uh, yesterday, Tammy said…you were leaving too?"

Praveen's brow wrinkled in confusion. "I…Oh! Yes, the journey. Not really my choice. We all take such a journey eventually. It cannot be helped, I'm afraid."

Elliot considered Praveen's words, but the fact he was leaving right after Elliot was so annoying, he couldn't worry about how it wasn't really a choice. "Tammy thinks a lot of you. You know how she is about…well, being abandoned. With me leaving, she's going through this big drama about how she's all alone in this 'big old castle of fossils.'"

"We will meet again. That is the way of things. You should not concern yourself over this."

Elliot looked at his baggage and realized he had no room to speak about anyone else leaving. Praveen had just as much right to some time away as anyone else did. "Okay. Just be safe, okay?"

"I will hope the same for you." Praveen gave Elliot a final pat on the back, but it quickly became a hug.

"Okay." Elliot pulled away, gave a little wave, and then descended the stairs. The whole way down to the landing, he fought the urge to look at Neda's door in case she was waiting there for him. The stairs swayed slightly, forcing him to grab the banister for support. Above him, Praveen laughed.

"The mansion does not wish to see you go, either." The banister vibrated from Praveen's quick, reprimanding strike. "Let him go, old fool. You cannot stop him, and you know it."

Instantly, the swaying stopped, as if the admonishment had been heeded. Elliot hesitated, then he hurried the rest of the way to the bottom floor.

When he looked up, Praveen was nowhere to be seen.

Elliot checked his phone and saw it was already past eight; he was behind schedule. The water not working in his shower, then only the cold when he did get it working, the toilet backing up, his toiletry bag somehow falling under the bed—nothing was going as planned. He opened his travel app and deleted one of his planned stops, adjusting the route to get back on schedule. Then he shoved the phone back into his pocket and headed for the kitchen.

A reflection caught his eye, drawing him into the open room across from the foot of the stairs. It was a semi-circular space, the upper half painted a soft cream, the bottom half covered in pale paneling. Resting on top of the paneling was a shelf of the same pale wood as the paneling. Arrayed above the shelf were photos, portraits, and lithographs, a continuous chain of history going back a century.

Something about the images drew Elliot into the room. He set his travel bag on the ground and drew up the telescoping handle, then turned to look at the walls. He'd seen the framed images a hundred times before, but they seemed different at the moment—clearer, brighter, more intense.

How can an image be more intense?

He smirked and pulled off his glasses. He gave his eyes a frustrated rub and shifted his grip on the travel bag's handle.

The mansion was playing tricks on him. Again. It was always toying with him, trying to get him to consider the teachings of the mystics, their silly beliefs and practices, their nonsensical adherence to ancient—

Now I'm seeing the mansion as a person. It's just a mansion. Stone. Wood. Glass.

He opened his eyes, and the image of Mangas Victorio stared back at him from a photograph.

Mangas had been an Arapahoe shaman who'd made his money touring with various Wild West groups at the end of the 1800s. He'd purchased the mansion from Walter Harrison, the grandson of one of Arlington's founding fathers, shortly after the turn of the century. The history was fairly common knowledge, mundane.

I can't let them get to me. I'm on a schedule.

In the photograph, Mangas was older, wrinkled, almost shrunken, but his eyes were indeed full of an intensity Elliot couldn't recall noticing before. There wasn't a hint of judgment in the eyes, despite the intensity.

Elliot stepped closer. Mangas's eyes followed Elliot until his hands rested on the shelf.

"*Ta'nisi*, Mangas," Elliot whispered, surprised at the reverence in his voice and even more surprised at the authenticity of the feeling. "*Kinana'skomitin.* I thank you for what you've done for me and for others, but mostly for me. I may not believe in your...our people's ways, but I can believe in what you stood for. I only wish ..." Elliot's fingers brushed the medicine bag that rested on the shelf beneath Mangas's picture. Even the bag seemed unnaturally vibrant and intense.

The medicine bag was probably the most valuable item in the mansion, even more than some of the museum piece weapons and shamanistic implements. A collector had supposedly offered high seven figures for the medicine bag not so long ago—an outrageous amount—yet there it sat for all to see. It was Mangas's legacy. No one would dream of endangering it, much less stealing it.

No one ever comes here. It's like the wards Grandpa William says protect this place are …

Elliot snorted and smacked the heel of his hand against his forehead.

It's just a prop from Mangas's touring shows. He was a showman, a charlatan, just like everyone else here. And now I have to ask myself, is this my show, or do I really feel I owe Mangas something for giving us—giving me—a chance?

Or is my leaving too great a slap in the face for me to say anything to him at all?

He turned this place into a home for shamans and sorcerers and witches from around the world, to share knowledge and to bring about peace. What's bad about that? And here I am turning it down. Why? Because I don't believe in the mumbo jumbo? Because I feel a greater debt to my own people? Or because I want to live my own life?

Or none of those.

Elliot touched the photo—no hint of dust was on the glass or frame. "*Ki'htwa'm ka-wa'pamitin*, Mangas—I will see you again."

The mansion was quiet until Elliot reached the kitchen doorway. The door was propped open this morning. He heard the clatter of pans, water running, the scraping of forks on plates, and the soft rhythm of conversation. People were up and eating in the dining room.

Elliot recognized William Big Bear's voice and pulled up short.

Grandpa William.

Elliot took a breath, willed himself to push through the moment, then took a step past the kitchen door, then another, until he reached the doorway that opened onto the dining room. He stepped through.

William Big Bear turned at the sound of the travel bag's wheels and pushed back the wooden chair he sat upon; it rattled slightly across the stone tiled floor. He braced himself on the table with a hand grown thick and rigid from arthritis. His hair, like Ms. Nakama's, was graying. Unlike her, the arthritis was attacking his joints, and as a result, he was slowing down and putting on weight. He wore a simple, blue, long-sleeve shirt and weathered jeans of about the same color. A leather strip like the one Elliot hid beneath his shirt hung over the front of Grandpa William's shirt. The leather strip, too, had a bear crafted from beads hanging from it.

To Grandpa William's left sat Driss, his shaking hands wrapped tight around a half-full coffee cup. He'd been looking sickly for several months, refusing even Daysi's concoctions, but now he looked absolutely terrible. His eyes were bloodshot, his skin yellow, and his lips pale. A necklace of stones hung from his neck. Elliot couldn't recall seeing the necklace before. Along with the blue turban that never seemed to leave Driss's head, he wore a faded black t-shirt with some sort of logo on it and a blue flannel shirt. His jeans were even more faded than William's, almost white. Daysi sat opposite the two men, staring into an empty coffee cup.

Elliot came to a stop and spread his feet uncomfortably. "Morning, Mr. Zéroual—Driss. Grandpa. Ms. Pizanga."

Driss, bottom lip quivering, continued staring into his coffee cup rather than meet Elliot's gaze. Grandpa William just stared at Elliot, stone-faced. Daysi looked up with sad eyes; she was biting her bottom lip hard enough that it was losing its color.

Elliot shifted slightly. "I was going to say goodbye to Tamment before I left. I didn't want to leave it like it was yesterday." His eyes drifted down to the stone tiles, embarrassed.

Clattering from the kitchen—pans banging around loudly—drew Elliot's attention. He waved weakly at Ms. Fernandez. "Morning, Ms. Fernandez."

Even with a face that seemed caught in a perpetual scowl, Ms. Fernandez—that's all she allowed anyone to call her and that was all Elliot knew her by—was an attractive woman most likely approaching middle age and doing so gracefully. Her hair was as dark as Elliot's, and her skin had an olive tone to it that was somewhat reminiscent of Daysi's. She was Filipina, a relatively recent addition to the household. She set a pan in the sink and walked to the dining room table, gathering up the yolk- and crumb-covered plates.

She paused for a moment to glare at Elliot. "Tamment is gone. She sneaked out last night." Ms. Fernandez looked down at Driss, then back at Elliot. It seemed like she was getting angrier. "Again."

Elliot sighed. Tammy was making a mess of her life, and there was nothing he could do about it.

"If something were to happen to her …" Daysi wiped tears from her eyes and seemed to consider reaching across to Driss, but her hands moved no more than an inch.

"She'll be fine. She's probably the most resourceful person I've ever met." Elliot looked at the three of them. It was like they were planning her funeral or something, which didn't make any sense. She'd already survived losing both her parents, pretty intense school bullying, and an illness that had technically killed her, plus she was as mean and stubborn as any mostly functional person he'd ever met. She would probably make some terrible decisions and come out of it fine, just like always.

As if sensing his thoughts, Daysi gave Elliot an almost pleading look. "She just seeks direction."

"I understand." *It's not like everyone hasn't tried to help, though.* Elliot looked Grandpa William in the eye. "Grandpa, I need to get going. I know you don't think this is the right thing for me to do. I know you think I just need to give this more time. I—"

Grandpa William stood, his right hand held out waist high, shaking. He waved away Elliot's words. "You have chosen, son. You are a man. I am not the one to judge. Now I just support you." He hugged Elliot tight. "Your path takes you to the reserve?"

Elliot hugged Grandpa William back and blinked away a tear. *Son. Man.* The words carried great weight. "Eventually, yeah. I think so. I'll be stopping by Winnipeg first, though. I need to get an apartment, finish registering at the university, that sort of thing."

"Your parents would be proud." Grandpa William stepped back and gave Elliot a look up and down. There was a clear sense of pride in Grandpa William's posture.

"And you, Grandpa?" Elliot let his eyes drift away, unwilling to see the disappointment and pain in the old man's eyes. "Would you be proud?"

"I am."

Elliot looked at the old man and saw a smile—genuine but incomplete.

"*You are?*" *After all the arguments and lectures? Why the change of heart?*

Grandpa William gave an ambivalent shrug of his shoulders. "Why shouldn't I be? You have accomplished so much already, and you will accomplish more. This was not the time for you. The time will come. We have seen this."

"I'll swing back down for the holidays, I promise."

Grandpa William's eyes were sad rather than happy as if he didn't believe Elliot's promise. "You will always be part of us, even after you go."

"I mean it, Grandpa. I will come back to visit."

"And I mean it as well, son. You are a part of us, and you always will be, even after we are gone."

Elliot winced and fought back the urge to hug his grandfather again. The Elders were getting up in their years, and there would come a time when they wouldn't be there for him and Tammy.

Driss set his cup down, and covered his eyes with frail, shaking hands.

Suddenly, Elliot understood that the concern wasn't just for Tammy, but for what she was putting Driss through. Elliot wondered what would become of Tammy if Driss passed away before she turned eighteen. Guardianship had already been worked out; Elliot was pretty sure about that, but that didn't mean it would be an easy thing. Tammy still had family on her father's side, poor mountain folk down in the Ozarks, and Elliot could easily see her manipulating them into fighting for custody, even if they couldn't afford it. It wasn't like she ever bothered to consider the implications of her actions.

The drama of the mansion, of Tammy and all the others, was wearing on him, replacing his excitement with more anxiety. He dug his key fob from his pocket and held it up. Like the laptop and phone they'd bought him, it was shiny, new, the vehicle an uncomfortable indulgence given the simple way of life in the mansion. He shoved the guilt and anxiety away.

"I need to get on the road. Could you tell Luis I accidentally scuffed my floor? I'm running so late, I didn't have time to get to it. I swear the mansion ..."

Grandpa William patted Elliot's shoulder. "He's up in St. Louis."

"St. Louis? Are you thinking of moving?" *After all these years?*

William chuckled. "You know we can't move. Luis is inspecting a contractor's work."

"Inspecting?"

"We are looking at what it would take to get central air installed." Grandpa William looked back at Driss. "For Tamment."

They really are trying to keep her here, but even if she stays, she'll leave the second she turns eighteen, just like me. "If any place can handle that kind of work, it's this place. Sometimes, it feels like it's cut right from the earth. Maybe that story they tell about the basement foundation being taken from the Ozarks is true?"

"It is, but that does not guarantee this place will last forever. It is like a chain, and a chain is only as strong as its weakest link. For this place to last as Mangas intended, we must all do our part." Grandpa William gave Elliot a look that was probably meant to convey something, but Elliot had already reached some level of peace with his obligations to Mangas.

"I have to go, Grandpa."

Ms. Fernandez dropped the dishes and her scrubbing pad in the water with a loud splash. "You don't want breakfast?" She angrily toweled off her hands.

"I'll get something on the way. There's a McDonald's in Rolla."

Ms. Fernandez's scowl intensified. "My cooking is better." She threw the towel down and returned to the sink, where she began loudly scrubbing the plates again.

Grandpa William chuckled and squeezed his eyes shut as if he feared an explosion. "Best go now, son. It could only get worse. We will see you again in the by-and-by."

"The holidays, I swear. I'll bore you with stories about school, you'll see. You guys will be anxious to see me go again, you watch."

Tears welled up in the corners of Grandpa William's eyes. "No one would ever want you to go. It is as it is, though. You must leave, and the family must go on."

After managing another awkward wave at Driss and Daysi and a handshake with Grandpa William, Elliot walked out of the dining room door onto the veranda. He let the wind splash his tears across his face until he was sure no one could see him from the mansion, then he dragged the back of his hand across his eyes. He stopped long enough to load his luggage into the back of his silver Mercedes GLK SUV, then he climbed into the driver's seat and started the engine.

Grand Forks today, Winnipeg tomorrow.

He had a long trip ahead of him. There would be plenty of time to cry on the way.

Chapter Six

E lliot's words were too painful, too great a reminder of what Tammy had lost. When she closed her eyes, the faces of the Elders were there, like ghosts. She tried to focus and block out the pain. Sealed off from the outside world, she was aware of her own stench. It wasn't just body odor. Daysi's Seer's Sage tincture was leaking through Tammy's pores, filling the interrogation room with a pungent, earthy smell. Thankfully, no one was saying anything.

Tammy thought back to Daysi's visit at Area 151, the snake coiling and hissing. She'd been dead by then, but the hallucination had felt so real. *Maybe she sent that to me from the grave?*

Henriksen cleared his throat, and when Tammy opened her eyes, he shifted the microphone slightly closer to her. "What about you, Ms. McPhee? Are you up for making a statement about your last memories of the mansion?"

Traxler's face stretched tight, and his eyes flicked toward Henriksen for a moment. Traxler didn't seem comfortable with the whole interview, but he also didn't seem willing to stop it. He looked ready to say something, then instead he crossed his arms over his chest.

"I'm good." Tammy's voice felt and sounded raw. She knew she wasn't fooling anyone, and that was fine. Losing family, losing so many people she loved, no one was expecting her to be strong.

"You were last in Harrison Mansion when?" Henriksen's pen hovered over the notepad.

"Friday night. After the picnic." Tammy glared at Elliot again. She'd run away because of him. Everyone had died because of him.

"That would be May 22nd?" Henriksen hesitated, pen ready to scratch the date.

"Sure." *Like I can remember the exact date.* "Whatever the most recent Friday was."

Elliot leaned toward the microphone. "The 22nd."

Boy Scout. She wanted to punch him.

Traxler leaned forward and settled his elbows on his knees. He gave a smile that, if it wasn't real, sure as hell *looked* real. "Can you recall anything about the day? Before you left? Elliot said there was fighting. Did you see any of that?"

Alarm bells went off in Tammy's head. Traxler seemed to be trying to turn her against Elliot, and that wasn't going to happen. Elliot was a jerk, but he was *her* jerk. He was all she had left. "The last fight they had was over me skipping school Friday. They grounded me for that. Elliot was out shooting his bow with William Big Bear and Jeddo—"

"Your grandfather, Driss." Henriksen didn't look up from his note taking. Being an OCD jerk apparently was effortless for him.

Tammy fought back a snarl. "They were in a clearing in the woods out beyond the west lawn. Elliot wasn't even trying, because, you know, he wasn't through breaking his grandfather's heart."

Elliot flinched, and Tammy smiled inside. She'd landed a good shot.

Henriksen looked up from his notes, first at Tammy, then at Elliot. "What kind of bow?"

"Super Kodiak." Elliot pulled his glasses off and rubbed the bridge of his nose, a sure sign he was stressing out.

"What kind of pull?" Henriksen casually flipped back through old pages on the notepad.

"Sixty pound," Elliot mumbled.

"Hunting bow, right?" Henriksen ran his finger down the center of a page of clear block text notes. It wasn't the usual sloppy cursive handwriting visible on most of the pages.

"We went hunting a few times. It wasn't really something I enjoyed."
Elliot settled his glasses back on his nose.

Tammy had to give Elliot credit for his honesty: no macho posturing in
front of the big, bad cops. She'd gone with Elliot and William Big Bear the
first couple hunts, and she'd even killed her own pheasant. But, same as Elliot,
the killing had left her feeling uncomfortable.

"What color was the bow?" Henriksen shot a curious glance at Elliot.

Tammy could feel Elliot tense up. He didn't seem to like Henriksen.
"Green."

"Okay. Yeah. I missed that earlier." Henriksen shifted his attention back
to Tammy. "Anything else you can remember from the day? Maybe you saw
someone on the property? That's an awfully big chunk of land. And you only
have the one person to take care of it and the mansion? Or did Ms. Fernandez
work outside as well?"

"Just Luis. He's a—" Tammy saw Elliot making a sour face, lips downturned,
eyes straight ahead. *Sure, El. I'll cut him some slack. But he's a major fucking
creepasaurus.* She shrugged, pretending she was at a loss for words. "He works
hard."

"So, you don't recall anyone on or around the property?" Henriksen didn't
hide his disappointment. "Maybe in the last week?"

"Nope." Tammy didn't appreciate the 'gee, golly, kid, you failed to stop
the killer' vibe Henriksen was giving off. "It's not like I wouldn't notice a
scumbag like Stone."

Henriksen sighed and eased back in his chair. "I understand. Can you tell
us about the last night? Before you left the mansion?"

Tammy thrust her chin out defiantly. She wasn't going to let anyone
portray her behavior as the fault for everything that happened. "I went
upstairs after the picnic." She refused to meet Elliot's gaze. There was no need
to go into the fight they'd had on the veranda. Elliot deserved the earful she'd
given him. He was an asshole for leaving her. "I took a nap, and then I
showered."

Traxler seemed completely absorbed in her story. "You'd already arranged
for your friend to pick you up. This Tessa Copeland?"

"Yeah. I just needed to get out of the mansion." Tammy closed her eyes, and the heat of the night came back to her.

⌒∞⌒

Tammy dashed out of her bathroom with a wet facecloth clutched in her right hand. It dripped cold water on the throw rug and on the clothes strewn in clumps across the hardwood floor. She wasn't concerned about that. She stopped at the antique cedar dresser and hastily dabbed at the mascara she'd spilled. The doily was a lost cause, but she hoped to save the wood.

"C'mon, c'mon."

The last of the mascara finally came up, and she let out a relieved sigh. She stared at the spot in the weak light reflected from her vanity mirror. At such a late hour, she had to trust her cell phone display's glow and the faint moonlight that shone through her windows.

A gentle evening breeze fluttered the room's sheer drapes, sucking away the remnants of the day's heat, leaving behind a sweet, pine scent.

It was time.

The floor was an obstacle course of discrete debris heaps: clothes that smelled like grill smoke, school papers ready for the garbage, magazines full of clothes and makeup she couldn't afford. She maneuvered through it all without a sound and tossed the facecloth into the bathroom sink.

One last thing.

She returned to the mirror and examined her face. The mascara was still drying. It gave her a temporary *siyâla*, a tattoo common among Berber women. Her design was a simple line that ran vertically from the base of her lower lip to the bottom of her chin. Eight dots hugged the line, four on each side, evenly distributed from top to bottom. It was a simple, non-intrusive design, something that shouldn't even stand out in a world with so much inked flesh, but it bugged her. It only emphasized her lack of identity. She didn't believe the pattern held *baraka*—the spirit energy Jeddo placed so much faith in—and she certainly didn't believe it would protect her from imaginary *djinn*, the evil spirits Jeddo railed against.

It wasn't djinn *that drove momma away or got you kicked out of your tribe,*

71

old man. You've got no one to blame but yourself.

But it gave her *something*. It made her *unique*.

She dug into the top drawer of the dresser, carefully moving aside her panties and bras until only a small, rectangular box with a rounded top remained. It was pressed into the back corner, so no one would see it without digging through her underwear.

She ran her fingers over the surface, a faux wood finish that made the box look like a pirate's treasure chest. She'd built it in a craft class her first year after moving to Arlington. Miniature hearts and ponies were glued to the narrow sides. It was corny and cutesy, the sort of thing she hated now, and yet it meant the world to her. She set her phone inside the drawer so that it lit the interior, then she popped the box lid.

There wasn't really any need for the light. She knew the box's contents by heart. The top layer held pictures of her family. Her favorite, with both her parents holding her when she was a little three-year-old butterball, was on top. Their smiles could wipe away the pain of her worst days, at least for a while. Below the pictures were the physical artifacts: her father's dog tags and Distinguished Service Cross and her mother's wedding ring. Tammy held each artifact for a moment and flipped through the pictures, warming at the way her parents had held her.

It had been special, magical.

She lifted the tray out to examine the contents of the bottom section: a photo of Elliot from the day he'd beat up a kid who'd called her a fat terrorist after Jeddo came to school wearing his turban, photos of Jeddo from when Tammy was a baby in Europe and he was still a good man, and the focus William Big Bear had given her.

She looked at the pictures of Jeddo with a frown. He had been hard on her mother, that much Tammy could remember, but her mother had never accepted anything but respect for him from Tammy.

I try to respect you still, Jeddo, even with what you've become here.

There was still warmth and happiness to be taken from the pictures. Despite all the troubles, Jeddo had clearly loved his daughter and granddaughter. He was just a hard man.

Elliot's picture was him at his fearless best. He was still a little twig, and his lip was slightly swollen where Eddie Rivera had landed a punch, but the fierceness in Elliot's hazel eyes all but glowed in the dark.

He had been her hero that day and for years after.

He was holding her hand in the photo. He'd always done that for her when she'd been a frightened little girl. She desperately missed it sometimes.

She examined the focus last, holding it out at arm's length. The gold chain was pretty, and the pendant was interesting. She couldn't understand why she'd been given an amber piece of quartz, but it sparkled nicely enough.

She returned the focus to the bottom of the box, then set the photos of Elliot and Jeddo on top. The separator went in next, then the artifacts, then the family photos.

As careful as if it held priceless diamonds, she closed the lid and latch. She stacked her underwear around and on top of the box, then she gave the drawer a quick inspection to be sure the box was hidden.

The drawer closed with a quiet hiss, and she looked at the mirror again.

The more she looked at the faux tattoo, the more the design felt silly, out of place, out of *time*, but she didn't have time to scrub it off. Where she was going, it wouldn't stand out. She checked her phone: nearly 10:00.

A last, quick look: black, sleeveless shirt that didn't cling enough to embarrass her; her tightest jean shorts; a small, black purse; a pair of simple, black heels looped around the clutch's strap. She was wearing her jogging shoes.

They would be climbing shoes tonight.

At the last moment, she remembered to dig a small, near-empty bottle of Cashmere Mist from the back of her bottom drawer. She sprayed a little on each wrist and rubbed her wrists against the back of her neck as she'd seen Neda do. The bottle had been Neda's, lifted when it was nearly empty. Tammy reasoned that unlike her, Neda had enough money to buy the perfume in the first place, so there was no problem taking it. And Tammy never wore it around Neda, so no one would ever know.

Tammy's lips twisted up into a satisfied smirk at the irony of the fortune teller not seeing her own belongings stolen. Elliot was right, it was all smoke and mirrors.

The smirk faded, replaced by an angry frown. *Elliot.*

Phone in hand, she crossed the obstacle course, this time stopping at the rightmost of the room's two windows. She lived on the north side of the second floor. Next to Jeddo's room. One too many sloppy escapes earlier in the year had led to her being moved down from the third floor. It had actually been beneficial to her, making escape easier.

If she didn't screw up. That was always the key.

Yellow light glowed from beneath the front porch roof. Beyond the reach of the light, the breeze shook leaves in the nearby trees. The trees on the opposite side of the low stone wall that separated the mansion from the private lane—everyone other than the Elders called it Harrison Lane—were just swaying shadows against the road's ghostly gray.

Suddenly, the yellow light winked out. Tammy checked her phone: 10:00. Like clockwork.

Jeddo and the Elders were set in their ways, predictable. Even Praveen and Neda had patterns and rhythms they couldn't seem to break. For Jeddo, every night at dusk, the porch light went on, and at 10:00 sharp it went off.

Creaking rumbled through the floor. Jeddo would be slowly climbing the stairs now. The creaking would stop, and a moment later he would knock on her door.

She settled at the end of her bed and waited.

The knock came. "Tamment?"

"Yes?"

"I—" It sounded like he might be struggling to breathe. He was getting weaker and weaker by the day, and he refused to see a doctor. "Kahina was a human, too. Like your mother."

Kahina. Always Kahina. Tammy stuck her bottom lip out angrily. She hated being compared to some legendary Berber warrior queen. "Night, Jeddo."

The floor creaked beneath his meager weight. "Good night, Tamment."

She glared at the window screen sitting on the floor below the window until she heard his door close, then she slid her phone into her pants and slipped the purse strap around her neck. With the utmost patience, she squeezed through the window frame, shivering slightly at the tingling sensation she often felt when passing through entryways.

This time, the tingle felt like saying goodbye.

Getting out the window wasn't easy. Although she was skinny, she had broad shoulders and long limbs, and the mansion never seemed to cooperate when she tried to escape. At any minute, she expected the window to slide down on her or for the frame to squeak. Even as good as she was at fitting through tight places, she'd twice gotten stuck in the window. This time, she managed to slip out without a sound and began the slow, risky process of planting her feet on the porch overhang below her room. She stretched her feet out, trying to feel the firmness of shingles through the sneakers. Stretching…stretching…

Her phone blasted a quick, catchy tone. She had a text. *Wonderful.*

Trusting the overhang would be there, she let go of the sill and dropped. Somehow, her shoes caught on the shingles with little more than a hushed crunch. She twisted and settled to her butt, hurriedly digging the phone out before the text tone could sound again.

The message glowed on the screen: *You gonna make it?*

Tammy thumb-typed back: *Still on schedule.*

She muted the phone and slipped it back into her purse, then she carefully edged down the rooftop on her hands and sneaker tips, each time checking the shoes' grip before placing any weight on them. When she was at the bottom edge of the overhang, she curled up tight, twisted, and lowered herself to the ground.

Gold medal for the Moroccan team—

"Does your grandfather know you're going out?" Neda separated from the shadows of the front porch. She wore a dark, oversized T-shirt that covered her upper arms and thighs. Her voice was soft, not challenging.

Tammy glared into Neda's dark eyes. "No. And I don't care."

Neda looked across the lawn and seemed to shiver, even though the night breeze was warm. "You know, I lost my father when I was a child."

"Praveen told me before." Her lips quivered, and her arms shook with nervous tension.

"I thought—"

"Don't even start. You don't know what it's like to be me."

Neda sighed. The sound was quickly swallowed by the evening breeze. "Your grandfather loves you, Tammy. We all love you."

Tammy snorted derisively and crossed her arms. "Are you going to tell Jeddo?"

"No."

The tension seemed to magically slip from Tammy's body. "Well, good. Because I'm going. I have a right to. I'm *sixteen*. I'm not a kid. I can do what I want, and *that* isn't rotting in this retirement home with a bunch of…whatever you are."

Neda lowered her head and brought a hand up to it, but her dark hair fell forward, hiding her hand and face from sight. Tammy could've sworn she heard a sniffle.

Is she…crying? Seriously?

"Are—are you okay?" Tammy shifted her weight from one foot to the next, suddenly feeling awkward.

Neda looked up, and her eyes glistened wetly in the moonlight. She smiled, but it didn't seem authentic. "Yes. It's just sometimes…knowing the future can be painful." She wiped at her eyes again. "I do mean it when I tell you we love you, Tammy. Some of us being old, or being different, or being …" She waved her hand as if to say *whatever*. "It doesn't change that we're all here, together, a circle, a family. All of us. Even you."

Neda reached out and wrapped her arms tightly around Tammy. Tammy recoiled, but she didn't completely pull away.

"Neda …"

Neda's tears were hot against Tammy's chest. Tammy felt off-balance and confused, as if Neda were sucking away angry and hateful thoughts with just the little contact she was making. It didn't make sense. Neda was too perfect to cry.

Neda released Tammy and stepped back into the shadows, still sniffling, but laughing now. "That smells good on you. You should buy some."

She smells the perfume. Fuck. "I just—"

"I know. I've known for a while. We all have. One day, Tammy, you'll look back and see that this wasn't a prison, and all the people you considered such a strain in your life weren't so bad after all. It's hard to do that when you have so much anger in you, but that anger will pass. One day. Be careful what you let fill the void."

"You're trying to make me feel like I'm a bad person. I'm not!"

"Of course you're not. You've just had a very hard life. Not many people lose their parents so young, and then to be stuck here? We all understand."

"No, you don't. You have no idea what it's like living here. It's like a fucking mausoleum or a hospice." Tammy stomped a foot in protest and immediately felt like a sitcom caricature. That only made her angrier. Neda—everyone—seemed determined to push and push, taking away freedoms until the only option left was…anger. "Look, we're done here, okay? I've got to go."

"I know. You've made your decision. The dance is out there, waiting for you, and you think it's delightful and liberating. I—we—just hope you understand that decisions have consequences."

"Sure, like dragging me out to this nuthouse, making me the target of every loser in school, making me feel like a freak because I'm stuck in some weird cult. Consequences like that? Or only *my* decisions have consequences? I get busted for doing a little pot, and you're all out here cruising on mushrooms. Those sorts of consequences? See any hypocrisy there?" Tammy closed her eyes and tried to pull her anger back in. It was never good when she lost control. She said hurtful things she often regretted.

Neda turned and opened the front door. "When we use the things Daysi prepares for us, it's to *find* something, not to hide from it. That's the difference between being an adult and being a child. You keep saying you're an adult. I hope you will remember what that means." Neda softly closed the door behind her.

Tammy stared for a moment. Neda had been waiting. It hadn't been a coincidence. Like Elliot said, it was a production, theatrics.

Goddammit. Elliot. *Always* Elliot.

She stomped away, doing her best to shake off the sense of crazy coming off the mansion. She loved the residents—well, most of them—but she had

77

to get away from all the *old*. It just saturated everything. The world she was heading into was rejuvenating, revitalizing, exciting. It was freedom from the prison.

As she headed for Harrison Lane, she looked at the sky. It was clear, lit by the moon and stars, but it was still dark. Yellow-green firefly flashes flared and faded all around her as she crossed the lawn.

She passed through the mansion's front gateway, once again registering the slightest buzz, then she stepped onto the shoulder of Harrison Lane and began a half-jog, half-walk. She dug her phone out again and turned on its flashlight app. It wouldn't do to get a foot tangled and face-plant. After several steps, she nearly did exactly that. She slowed and switched to the phone's texting app.

She typed: *Where the hell r u?*

The phone glowed for a moment, and Tammy thought of just tossing it into the woods and returning to the mansion. Tessa was supposed to be waiting for her just down the road, just out of sight. As always, Tammy could feel the fates conspiring against her, trying to stick it to her.

Her phone vibrated.

Tessa had replied: *St. Robert awaits.*

Chapter Seven

Elliot slowly walked the long hallway from the stairwell to the Holiday Inn Express hotel lobby, his and Tammy's home for the past sixteen days while the police and assorted legal entities worked out all the intricacies of life after. That's what he considered it now—life after losing everyone.

He was barely aware of everything that had become commonplace for him in the past sixteen days: the hum of the vacuum cleaner and citrusy-detergent scent of the cleaning staff at work, the distant clatter of dishes and serving trays, the mouthwatering aroma of syrup and waffles from the breakfast bar, the morning sun's iridescent sparkle playing across the lobby floor. His thoughts were too caught up in the trips to the police station, the visits to the mortuary, discussions with Tammy, even more discussions with Nathan Van Buren, the lead attorney who ran the trust that now fell to Elliot's management.

Where discussions with Tammy frequently turned into fights, discussions with Van Buren inevitably led to stress.

Obligations, expectations, temptation.

Elliot stopped and closed his eyes for a heartbeat, sighing quietly. It was enough to clear the fatigue and sorrow for just a moment.

The ring of a phone and the front desk attendant's pleasant drone drew Elliot back to the moment. Someone had opened the breakfast bar's outer door and curtains, turning the bar and lobby into a radiant, stifling oven.

Elliot wiped perspiration from his brow and cheeks, tasted its salt on his lips. It was a typical Missouri summer day. Probably his last.

The manager stepped from her office behind the front desk, a box under her meaty arm. She strained to maneuver it to the counter. As Elliot approached, the strained frown became a sincere, warm smile.

"Is this the last one?" She dabbed at the sweat on her brow with the cuff of her white shirt, leaving a faint line of foundation barely perceptible on the material.

Elliot bowed his head, embarrassed. He wished he could remember the woman's name—Karen? Carla? Corrine? He moved close enough to steal a look at her name tag. *Carla.* He and Tammy—especially Tammy—had put a heavy load on the hotel staff.

"Last one, I promise. Sergeant Traxler called late last night when they found this one. That should be it, this time for real."

Carla's smile broadened. "Still planning to check out today?"

Elliot pushed his glasses up with nervously trembling fingers. "My flight leaves this afternoon. I need to hit the road in a little bit."

"And your...friend?" Carla's smile didn't change, but her voice did, and the warmth disappeared from her face. Tammy was a paying customer, but one the hotel staff probably wouldn't miss once she was gone. A few too many temper tantrums and unsafe levels of histrionics; any reasonable person would have had enough.

"Yeah. They've found a place for her until they can work something out with the state of Arkansas. Her family down there is apparently pretty poor, so there's a lot of back-and-forth over...well, money. I'm really sorry for all the drama. She's going through a tough phase." *And me leaving her in the care of some random foster care facility isn't helping things, but I need to wrap up this piece of my life and move on, and she needs to understand that.*

Carla's smile, quite possibly painted on, didn't budge. "No drama at all. It's been wonderful having you both with us here. Have they had any luck with the case?"

The Memorial Day Killer case was just the sort of sordid thing to put Rolla and its surroundings on the map, especially with the killer still on the loose and the whole immigrant hate crime angle. Two days of Luis's face being plastered all over the news as a potential mass murderer had made the matter national news, especially for the anti-immigrant crowd. When Luis was cleared and Glen Stone was named a person of interest, the cable news network that had been focusing almost exclusively on the story suddenly dropped it. Apparently, the network didn't have as much of an appetite for stories about white, neo-Nazi mass murderers.

Elliot scratched the back of his head. "Nothing new." He took the box from the counter. "If you want to ring my bill up, I should be ready to go in a few more minutes."

The smile reached Carla's eyes, twinkling now, no doubt the result of thinking of Tammy's departure. "We'll have it ready for you. Are you going to need any help getting everything into your vehicle?"

Elliot broke eye contact, embarrassed. "Probably best if I do it. It's all personal belongings. Of the victims."

He shuffled back to his room, barely aware of the box's heft. He couldn't transport everything, but he had the most important personal effects or at least the ones the police would release. It was already costing him a small fortune to carry what he could on the flight.

The box made a solid thump when he dropped it on the desktop. It was simply labeled with a case number and *Personal Effects*. It definitely felt more like Traxler's work. Henriksen would've printed a label out and had some inventory data on it, maybe some sort of secret code.

All neat and orderly, the way Elliot liked it.

Elliot reached for the lid and saw how badly his hand was shaking. He pulled it back to his side. After a moment, he sucked in a big gulp of air and closed his eyes, repeating some of the concentration and relaxation exercises Praveen had taught him.

Praveen. Dead, like the others. I can't believe I thought he might have put the medicine bag in my luggage, even for a second. Some friend I am. Then again, it's not like I stuck up for Luis as much as I should have, either.

As they had in the rare quiet moments of the last two weeks, Elliot's thoughts turned back to Tammy's claim that Neda had seen what was coming. It was a preposterous idea, one he didn't want to think too long and hard about, but there were too many oddities about the whole situation, and they constantly gnawed at him.

Grandpa William's sudden change of heart about the return to Manitoba, his words about the mansion lasting forever if everyone played their part, and more ominously, his comment about the chain only being as strong as its weakest link.

He was talking about me. What a disappointment I've been. I made them all so sad.

Elliot reached for the lid again. His hand was steady now.

Inside was a chaotic array of belongings, although it was packed carefully. The lack of structure and order annoyed Elliot. He wondered if it was a sign the police didn't care or if it was a sign of just how irrelevant the belongings were as evidence.

Ms. Nakama's hairbrush sat on top—polished mother of pearl, clean of any sign of hair, free of dust, just as she had kept it. There was also a silk scarf he couldn't recall seeing before, but it was beautiful, and no doubt it had meant a good deal to her. Praveen's mother's family heirlooms—intricately fashioned bangles and matching earrings and arm cuffs; shining gold, with swirling platinum designs. Neda's necklaces and talismans—a gold chain with a cross potent, a smooth stone with crude carvings freed of details by the ages, and several stones embedded in jewelry that Neda had sworn held power over spirits and demons. He didn't see her favorite talisman among the belongings.

Evidence, probably.

He could make out a couple of Daysi's rocks and a mask. The police weren't about to release her drugs and associated paraphernalia. The DEA had apparently swooped down quickly, working an angle tied to Stone and the New Order.

Had Ms. Pizanga ever sold or manufactured drugs? No, Daysi had exclusively cooked up concoctions for her and the other Elders. It was all for…religious use. And, no, they weren't some weird cult. They were…students, researchers. She also made natural, herbal medicines. No one was sick at the mansion for extended periods. Except for Driss, and that had been his decision.

Do you have any details on William Big Bear's international travels? Grandpa William's international travels were always part of the ongoing research, and the search for more…students, gifted people, like-minded seekers. Mangas, the founder of the—no, they weren't a cult—group had always envisioned the mansion hosting twelve seekers. Elders. The Circle and their "Chain". No, there had never been twelve; in fact, never more than eight. But they kept trying.

What about Grandpa William's travels in-country? What do you know about those? More of the same. Grandpa William never went into detail about any of that.

Did Praveen Thakur ever mention anything about relatives in the drug trade? Praveen only ever talked about his life in India in guarded, embarrassed tones.

The questions had been absurd, but they had also been troubling.

There was so much he didn't know about those who had raised him and been his family. Even when he'd tried to ask—like he had with Praveen and Neda—he had been gently redirected after a bit. Everyone who'd called the mansion home had a history of pain.

Elliot quickly emptied the box and sorted the belongings into piles—Daysi, Neda, Praveen, Ms. Nakama.

Mr. Van Buren had already arranged for Grandpa William's remains to be shipped to Manitoba, Driss's to Morocco, and Ms. Fernandez's to the Philippines. That left only the last four to deal with.

His hands lingered over Neda's pile: a revealing blouse she'd worn too rarely and that always made him stare; a pair of Daisy Duke shorts she'd worn once, enough to leave him with an embarrassing memory after she'd caught him watching her groom Sunshine while wearing them. He wondered if she'd ever known, or suspected the effect she'd had on him. Their final talk made it seem so.

She's gone now. What's it matter?

He moved the belongings to boxes he'd already prepared, labeled and inventoried, each stacked in a specific place within the room—Praveen's boxes just inside the door and to the right, Ms. Nakama's boxes to the right of those, Daysi's boxes to the left of the dresser, and Neda's at the bedside. The most precious items would travel with him, returning to their homelands along with their owners' ashes to be handed off to family. The rest would go into storage until he knew what to do with them. He'd already rented out the storage and filled out a spreadsheet to track what would go where.

Daysi, with no family to claim her and no known disposition request, presented a challenge. Her belongings and ashes would have to stay in storage until something could be figured out.

Ms. Nakama was probably the easiest of the four to deal with. She just wanted her ashes released at a Kumano shrine in Japan.

Praveen had only ever mentioned one relative, the aunt who had taken him in for a few years before he'd moved to the mansion. Neda had only her mother and brother, both still living in Iran.

That was Elliot's itinerary: Bangalore, India; Bandar Abbas, Iran; and Tanegashima, Japan.

Grandpa William said I would do plenty of traveling.

When Elliot returned, he would carry his grandfather's ashes to Manitoba and bring an end to their time in Missouri.

Once the last of the goods was packed, Elliot sealed the boxes and set them into two groups. The ones that would be going on the plane with him and everything else. Then he took off his shirt and pulled on the T-shirt he'd slept in the night before.

He checked the clock on his phone. It was almost time to go.

He'd already sketched out and calculated the best packing arrangement: luggage first, then boxes going on the plane with him, then boxes that would go into storage. It would be a tight fit.

Elliot carried the boxes to the GLK two at a time. Beneath the merciless yellow sun, the parking lot blacktop smelled like a sea of bubbling tar. Heat clung to the dark surface until he passed over it, then it followed in his wake until he came to a stop. The GLK's cramped back captured and amplified the heat and the chemical smell, quickly making Elliot lightheaded. It was miserable, sweaty work, even though it took less than an hour to complete. When he was done, he gave the GLK one last look and confirmed it was locked up tight. There wasn't much of actual value in the boxes, but there was a great deal of sentimental value, and that meant more.

A breeze hit him as he admired his work. It was too hot and muggy to be pleasant, but it was better than the dead air he'd been working in. He fanned his T-shirt to try and cool himself and dry off some of the sweat, but the day was too hot and the air too humid for that to be of any use.

Another check of the time, and he realized he wouldn't be able to shower again before leaving. He hated traveling grimy as he was, and it would only be worse in the storage facility. He shook his head, annoyed that all his planning had ultimately failed him.

"You leaving now?"

Elliot turned at the sound of Tammy's voice. She stood in the morning sun, arms crossed angrily. She wore an indigo T-shirt and white, short shorts. The legs that were revealed were toned and much thicker and shapelier than the little toothpicks Elliot remembered from the previous summer.

She's not a kid anymore. Neither of us are.

"I need to check out first." Elliot headed back toward the lobby entry.

Tammy followed him through the automatic doors. "You hear anything more on Stone?"

"No."

"Mr. Van Buren called. He said they should have everything worked out by tomorrow. My grandmother might be moving into the mansion. I wouldn't have to move down to Arkansas."

Great. You can just keep hanging out with Tessa and ruin your life. Elliot stopped at the lobby desk and pulled out his wallet. He instinctively shielded it from Tammy, then felt hypocritical for doing so. *She's not a thief.* "That means you won't have to stay with the home for long." He handed his credit card to the young man behind the counter—a gangly, pale, redheaded beanpole—and then turned to stare at Tammy while waiting for the receipt.

Tammy rolled her eyes and sighed dramatically. *What is wrong with you, El?* "I don't want to go to the home. I'd rather go up to the Ozarks."

"Down. South."

Tammy tensed, annoyed at Elliot's patronizing attitude. Even after they'd lost everyone they loved, he kept pushing her away. "I meant up in the mountains. Up? High?"

"Mr. Saganash?" The beanpole pushed the receipt across the countertop.

His eyes drifted over to Tammy and lingered long enough that he registered on her ever-growing creep list: a creepling.

Elliot signed the receipt and pushed it and the spare room key back toward the beanpole and caught his lingering stare. Elliot slapped the pen down on the countertop to yank the beanpole back to reality; the beanpole threw him a stupid, almost conspiratorial smile, completely ignoring the receipt.

Tammy bounded forward, doing her best to imitate Tessa, knowing the whole time there wouldn't be Tessa's trademark bounciness. It was enough, though. The beanpole liked what he saw, and he wanted to see more. The beanpole's smile broadened, and he completely missed the way her palm covered the spare room key.

"What time does the pool open? I've got a bikini I've been dying to try out."

The beanpole's face reddened. "It—it's open now."

Tammy did a quick, clumsy pirouette, barely covering the card with her hand. The beanpole wasn't looking at her hands. "Thanks!" She slid the card into her pants pocket and took a couple steps toward the stairwell.

Elliot headed for the stairwell at an angry pace, quickly passing her; she followed. He slammed the door open and jumped to the second step. She took each step carefully.

"You know how this works," he called over his shoulder. "Your father did the whole power of attorney thing, and that left you with Driss. Now that he's dead, it's a whole lot more complicated."

He stopped and looked back at Tammy. Her chin jutted out angrily.

"I don't want to get stuck in a home, El." She cautiously jogged past him, banging open the door onto their floor. There was no pleasure in the soft tingle that came from passing through the doorway. She was too pissed at the sense of powerlessness she felt. And at the abandonment. Definitely the abandonment. She stopped at his door and crossed her arms again, then she leaned against the wall. "You're not that much older than me, and you're going to fly all over the world. Do you think that's fair?"

"Nothing is fair." Elliot groaned inwardly when he realized how old and stuffy he sounded. As he slid the keycard into the door, he caught a whiff of himself and winced. The shower wasn't an option; it was a requirement. He turned to look at Tammy one last time. "No one is going to be around to cover for your mistakes anymore, Tammy. I'm really sorry about that. You were—you *are*—a great friend to me. Everyone in the mansion was like family. But we have to move on. I'm not flying all over the world because I want to."

"Really?" Tammy stepped in close, invading his personal space. She knew how that unsettled him, and she wanted him on edge. "It's 'cause you have to?" She let just enough mockery slip into her voice to prick him.

Elliot shrank back, pushing the door in. "Yes. That's how obligations work. These people deserve to be returned to their homes."

"Homes that didn't even want them." Tammy was almost snarling, and the emotion was raw and real. *They were all rejects, like me!*

"We're not going through this endless cycle of arguments." Elliot opened the door the rest of the way and turned to look back at her. "This is what I have to do before I begin the next part of my life. It just feels right. Why don't you ask yourself what you need to do to begin the next part of your life? You know, the step toward adulthood?"

He started to close the door, but Tammy slapped it with her open palm. "I already know what I need to do, but no one will *let* me. Everyone's too busy telling me how to live my life while abandoning me. You're so quick to get past this. You'd already dumped us so you could go back to your precious Manitoba, so don't act like this is something that hurts you."

"Tammy—"

She pulled her hand off the door. "I know. You've got to go. You've got *obligations*. Whatever. I'll just go pack my stuff up so I can get ready for the state van to carry me away."

Elliot slumped.

"Don't worry about me. You've made your point." Tammy turned, then stopped. "And take a shower, El. You *stink*."

Elliot blinked. He watched until Tammy had crossed the hall and entered her room. Once he saw her door close, he closed his own. *She's so bitter and hurtful. I don't know how to reach her. Who am I kidding? I haven't known how to reach her for years. No one has.*

He crossed to the bed and hastily pulled a fresh T-shirt and underwear from his carry-on luggage. He thumbed through the cash he'd stuffed into a yellow envelope—just enough to feel confident it was all there—then he stripped and ran for the bathroom. He was really up against the time, but Tammy's words had sealed the deal: He needed a shower.

Tammy waited inside her door for a few heartbeats, then she slipped out of her room and darted across the hall. She made sure no one was around to see what she was doing, then she leaned against the wall of Elliot's room. When she heard the water kick on, she slipped the keycard she had borrowed from the front desk into Elliot's door and pushed the door open enough to poke her head in.

The shower was running; Elliot was moving under the water.

Elliot had to shower once she'd said something about his body odor. It wasn't actually that noticeable, but she knew he wouldn't be able to help himself.

He never could.

She ran to his bed, excited to see he'd left the envelope out. She'd expected to have to dig through his carry-on bag. Ever since seeing the bank receipt he'd left out the day before, she'd wanted her fair share of the money.

Don't you tell me nothing's fair. This is money you got from William Big Bear, money from the trust fund. That's money that belongs to both of us.

She had fifty one-dollar bills in her pockets, just about the last of her money. Those bills went onto the bed, next to the envelope. Next, she scooped a bundle of bills from the middle of the envelope.

Hundreds.

She split the bundle in half, setting one half on the edge of the bed, then hurriedly working the ones into the other half. One hundred, one, one hundred, one.

The shower turned off.

Tammy abandoned the idea of working the ones in, instead simply pushing all the bills back into the envelope and closing it back up. The flap scratched loudly; she froze. The shower curtain hooks scraped along the rod.

Tammy walked to the door and opened it with as much patience and control as she could muster. It was silent in the room.

The money! She'd left it on the bed!

Elliot stepped out of the shower, loudly toweling himself off. Tammy ran back to the bed, scooped up the bills, then turned back for the door. She paused to check that the bathroom door was closed. Elliot had left it open a bit. Tendrils of steam crept around the edge, dropping to a fog above the floor in the room's cooler air. She had a moment to escape.

She saw Elliot in the steamed mirror, his form largely obscured, but not all of it. A strange curiosity overcame her. A curiosity she hadn't really had even about Everett. It felt awkward, wrong. *Still...*

Her phone vibrated. Loudly. She nearly passed out.

Elliot froze.

Tammy moved to the door, her bare feet whispering over the carpet. She worked the knob when she heard Elliot move again in the bathroom. Her phone vibrated again, and Elliot went silent once more. She slipped out and closed the door as quietly as she could. A vacuum cleaner kicked on in a nearby room, covering the door's click.

Tammy ran for her door and let herself in, her heart pounding madly. She pulled her phone out, saw the incoming call display: Tessa.

"What?"

"What you mean *what?*" Tessa's voice rose as she spoke. "Are we on?"

Tammy looked at the money in her hand. It was a lot. "Yeah." She strode to her bed and dropped onto the mattress, counting quickly. Seventy-eight bills. *Nearly eight thousand dollars.*

Tessa laughed. Tammy imagined there was a dance going on at the other end of the call. "Don't you go getting all self-conscious and guilty about this. That's yo' money. You said he got it from *your* trust fund, right?"

Tammy closed her eyes. She'd already convinced herself that's where it had come from. "Yeah." *His trust fund, probably, but I have a trust fund, too. Like, seventeen months from now, when I turn eighteen. This isn't really my money, but I can pay him back.*

"Mm-mm," Tessa said impatiently. "You can just stop right there. I can hear it in your voice, plain as day. What you need is somethin' to take your mind off things. You need a good time: dancing and fun."

Tammy's luggage—a pair of simple, bright blue, carry-on Samsonite pieces—was packed and sitting next to her on the bed. "I think I'd like that."

"I'll be there in ten." Tessa disconnected.

Tammy shivered, but it wasn't a pleasant sensation like she had when she passed through doorways. It was something uncomfortable, miserable.

It was the sense she was doing something terribly wrong.

Chapter Eight

By the time Tammy reached the hotel parking lot, it was mid-afternoon, and the lot was mostly empty except for staff vehicles. Waves of heat rolled up from the black surface and through the doorway, which she kept partially opened while she scanned for any sign of police surveillance. Sulfuric diesel exhaust fumes drifted down from the nearby road; she coughed and gagged.

It was quiet except for the occasional car passing outside. Tammy slipped the rest of the way out the door and hurried across the parking lot, her bags swinging and squeaking. Bright sunlight reflected off her dusky skin.

She felt free, no longer trapped inside the hotel, but she also felt exposed.

Is this what an animal feels when it has to cross into the open to get food?

She'd gone hunting with Elliot and William Big Bear once. That had been enough. It had been a lot less macho and exciting than she'd expected. William Big Bear didn't kill for fun or sport, and Elliot wasn't comfortable with killing at all. When they took down a buck, it was with a single arrow deep in the chest, and they'd chased it through the woods for what felt like an eternity. It had been Elliot's first kill, and it had left him shaken, almost unable to get through the prayer of thanks to the *manitous*.

She could only watch the dressing for a few seconds. When the knife went into the soft flesh beneath the sternum and Elliot began the cut down the abdomen, the soft cutting sound—a ripping sound, really—and the hot smell of blood and guts had finished the moment.

Target practice with the rifles, shotguns, and pistols they kept in the workshop had been enough for her from then on. She was actually a pretty good shot. But she'd imagined the sort of fear that animal had felt in the moment before the arrow struck, and she knew that she would never forget the sensation.

Never.

Tammy looked around as she approached the edge of the parking lot. The hotel was on the far western side of Rolla. To the north of the hotel was a band of woods, to the west another little hotel. East a little ways, she could see steel storage sheds. A frontage road was south of the hotel, and beyond that frontage road, the highway.

Tessa would be waiting on the driveway leading up to the storage units. It would be the shortest dash and offered the most cover.

The plan had taken a lot of map searches and a lot of arguing. They both liked to argue, sometimes over the most pointless things. Tammy figured it was a hobby, something they did to make up for not having anything else to do.

Just beyond the east side of the parking lot, she stopped and looked around nervously. It looked clear.

She shook off her nerves and casually walked toward a white Impala. Instead of climbing in, she walked past it and into a narrow band of trees. All the while, she kept telling herself to look casual and comfortable and calm. Half of pulling something off involved not looking like you were pulling something off.

Her bags were quickly getting heavy. She wore the one with tuck-away shoulder straps like a backpack and had the other slung over her right shoulder like a small duffle bag. They weren't just heavy, they were bouncing against each other.

Everything she owned was in the bags. Or, at least, it was everything the police would release to her. What mattered was she had enough to get away for a while.

It occurred to her that her life could fit in the overhead bin of a plane.

There was a freedom implied in that, a freedom she found appealing. Too many possessions meant she would be tied down, and that meant she would have obligations. That was more Elliot's thing.

After a quick glance around to be sure no one was watching her, Tammy casually strolled from the trees toward Tessa's waiting Cavalier. The passenger door greeted Tammy with its familiar squeak. She tossed the duffel bag between the seats; it landed on the backseat with a solid thud. She tried to slide the shoulder straps off the other bag, but they were tight and her arms were tingly.

Tessa stared at the rearview mirror, rubbing a pimple on her forehead. "Y'know, maybe you could go faster? With the cops keepin' an eye out and all that."

"Maybe you could bite my ass?" Tammy smiled sweetly as she heaved the second bag in. It landed with a more substantial thump and slid to rest against the first bag. She slid into the passenger seat and pulled the door closed, immediately taking comfort from the familiar scent of the car's ratty interior. It felt like a sauna, and she was fine with that.

Tessa floored the accelerator. The front tires spun in the gravel and managed a feeble chirp once they touched concrete. Tessa made several turns until she reached the on-ramp to I-44 East. She accelerated as she merged into the light traffic.

Tammy watched the outskirts of Rolla roll past. "Where we going?"

"Arlington ain't no hideout. They know about St. Robert, and they know you hang out in Rolla, so I thought we could maybe, you know, hit the Lou."

Shit. She's right. They found me awfully easy. Tammy turned her phone off. It felt like a big, electronic arrow pointing right to her.

"You know anybody in St. Louis?"

"Friends of friends. We go to St. Lou; we can find some *real* boys. Not those dickless soldier wannabes out in St. Robert."

Tammy caught the meaning behind the words. Tessa was looking for guys that weren't going to treat her like shit. That meant Everett had dumped her, just like all the other boys she'd gone after. *Dickhead.* "Fine, whatever."

It was tough to believe guys would be any nicer in the big city, but Tammy hoped she'd get there and the horrible skin-crawling feeling—like having the eyes of a predator on her—would go away. It wasn't like they had a lot of options. Elliot might not care about her anymore, but as soon as the police figured out she'd slipped away, they'd be looking for her.

The ride was mostly rolling hills, woods, and then more woods. It seemed like they were alone for parts of it. Tessa's stereo was cranked, and they belted out songs along with it.

Tammy felt free, happy.

The farther they went, the less Tammy felt the creepy sensation she was being watched.

Eventually, the wooded areas came to an end, replaced by the outlying industrial parts of the greater St. Louis metropolitan area. Tessa turned the car north onto the I-270 outer belt.

The road was carved into the bedrock in places there. It seemed like it was still heavily wooded, but Tammy caught glimpses of houses here and there through the trees, hints at shaded neighborhoods almost hidden from view. They drove beneath overpasses, sometimes stacked three high, crisscrossing in marvelous patterns. Concrete pillars rose from the ground to hold up roads resting on blue-green steel beams.

Awe, almost fear, and a little shame gripped her as she took in the complex construction. She felt like a backwater hick, and she had to remind herself she'd seen older and more impressive works when she was younger, living in Europe.

Before her life had unraveled.

They drove for another half hour, taking completely unfamiliar roads, highways lined with tall, concrete noise barriers. Finally, Tessa pulled off the highway.

Tammy craned her neck around as they descended the off-ramp. There was a glass building to her right. It wasn't quite a skyscraper, but it was tall, maybe ten stories high. The sun was a dazzling reflection off the glass, a fabulous, white, distorted globe of fire.

Tessa smiled, leaning forward to find a spot on her window that was clean enough to see out of. When she was sure she was clear, she turned. "We goin' shoppin'! You didn't bring hardly nothing, and you need some clothes if we gonna hit the club."

Tammy hadn't thought about the club scene, but Tessa was right. Good enough for St. Robert was one thing, but this was the big leagues, the big city.

"I gotta get a phone, too."

Tessa's face scrunched up like she thought Tammy was crazy. "Why you need a phone?"

Tammy dug her phone out and examined it, imagining she could see through the plastic shell. "I think it's how the cops keep tracking me down. Plus, I'm not even sure who was paying my phone bill before. I want to get a prepaid. And I want to ditch some of this cash, put it on a prepaid card."

"Whatevs. The Galleria got you covered." Tessa's eyes fluttered, her signal that Tammy had gone all complex and ridiculous. Their favorite song of the minute came on, and Tessa cranked up the stereo volume with a delighted squeal.

The matter was history.

As malls went, the Galleria was big. Tammy noticed that Macy's, Nordstrom, and Dillard's were the big anchor stores, not Sears or JCPenney.

It was upscale. They would stick out, just like Tessa wanted to.

Tessa turned off of Brentwood Boulevard and into the mall's parking lot, angling for a parking garage attached to the north side. They drove past rows of luxury cars, with representation from all the major names: Audi, BMW, Cadillac, Infiniti, Jaguar, Lexus, Mercedes-Benz. Tammy felt intimidated just by the gleaming chrome and clear windows. Tessa didn't seem to be bothered. It was as if she just *knew* she fit in.

They parked near the second-floor entrance. Tessa stopped once she'd exited the Cavalier to admire her reflection in the Jaguar next to her door. It was a glossy black lined with narrow, chrome accents. "Oh, baby girl, I wanna fuck me a football star in the back seat o' one o' these."

Tammy smiled. She didn't care about the sex, but the car was pretty.

It was like being a little kid again. They almost skipped as they walked up to the breezeway, then they giggled at the arctic chill. The little strip malls in Rolla didn't keep their stores nearly as cool. Like the anchor stores, the temperature was a clear indication of the mall's high-end demographic.

There were probably more upscale places to shop, but the Galleria was about as far as Tammy's tastes would ever need to go. Sparkling glass and polished chrome, complex aromas—the musk of leather; the rich tang of tobacco; untold layers of perfumes and colognes…she stopped at the center of the mall and slowly spun, breathing in everything.

She could feel eyes on them. Admiring, lustful eyes. Not just on Tessa, on *both* of them. Admiration for the way Tammy filled out her tight pants, her shapely legs.

She spotted a young, stocky man looking at her, his eyes lingering on her thighs. She could almost feel his hands gripping them passionately, squeezing. She shivered at the wave of erotic thought.

She felt invaded, then realized she was invading his energy.

There was a certain pleasure in the surprising discovery that people actually found her attractive, but it still felt wrong and unwelcome. Sort of.

She wrapped her arms around her and returned her attention to her shopping.

Entering the Galleria had been strange. Its energy wasn't like a regular store. It didn't have the mansion's antiquity and sense of permanence. It was almost the exact opposite of driving through Missouri's open, rural areas. There were so many people bustling around, and Tammy was bombarded by their unique signatures and those of the mall.

It was heady and a bit overwhelming. If it didn't drive away her grief, it at least distracted her from it.

But with all the sensations and the crowd, the sense of paranoia returned. She looked around again, watching for security or police. Or for an inked-up skinhead, a white man in a wife-beater.

Someone who can do terrible things to corpses, from what Elliot had hinted.

Tammy shivered, the magic of the Galleria now shattered. It was just another shopping center now that Glen Stone had gotten into her head.

"You okay, baby girl?"

"Yeah. Sure." Tammy noticed Tessa wasn't buying it. Her mouth was twisted up into a doubting smirk.

Tammy made her way over to a directory kiosk. She prioritized her needs: prepaid phone, some clothes, and an outfit for clubbing. She settled on the Best Buy mobile store for her phone, Banana Republic for her clothes, and

Bebe for her club dress. Shoes would be tougher, but she at least noted where the shoe stores were.

Tessa seemed to relax a little more the longer their shopping ran, but Tammy could tell she'd spoiled the plan for the day. She felt bad for maybe a second.

Sorry if my family getting slaughtered put a kink in your plans.

But even Tammy began to relax a little after a couple hours had passed and the mall still wasn't under siege by a bunch of gun-toting neo-Nazis. She had her clothes, her phone, her shoes, and a tight, black, barely there dress with spaghetti straps that was perfect for a night on the town.

They grabbed a late lunch at a Cajun restaurant, then headed back to the garage.

Almost immediately, the sense of a hunter watching her returned.

"Whassup now?" Tessa glared, annoyed. She sucked orange slush from a clear, plastic straw and cup.

"Nothing."

"Mm-mm." Tessa tapped her foot on the parking garage cement impatiently. "You been all wild-eyed and terrified since I picked you up, and you only got worse since we got here."

"It's nothing."

Tessa sucked at the orange slush. "I got enough o' this drink to last me all day."

Tammy sighed, defeated. "It's just a stupid sensation. You know, like...like someone's watching you? You know what I mean?"

"Like when you take a shower and you hope—"

"Tessa. I'm serious."

"Is this about Luis? You think he did what they say and he's after you?"

Tammy threw up her arms in disbelief. "Luis is a creep, but he's not a killer, okay? They were...I don't know what the hell they were doing with trying to say he was involved, but the only crime they could pin on Luis was really bad taste in movies."

Tessa's mouth formed an *O*. "What, did they bust him with some sort of porn?"

"No. Something called 'luchador'? I guess it's really hokey Mexican wrestling? One of the cops said they found boxes of videos, some going way back."

"No shit? So you afraid a bunch o' Mexican wrestlers are after you now?"

Tammy glared at Tessa, caught somewhere between exasperation and fury. "I thought you seriously cared."

"I do. You're the one talking 'bout lucha-whatevers."

"Forget about it, okay? I'm just creeped out right now. Let's get the prepaid card and find someplace to crash. I'm wiped out."

During the rush hour crush, driving downtown was unbelievably slow. Tammy felt anonymous in the press of cars, just another face among thousands.

It was perfect.

After a few minutes, Tammy turned her attention to her new iPhone. It was just like Elliot's, but pretty. She had an account set up on it and a few apps downloaded by the time Tessa pulled onto Washington Avenue. Tammy checked the phone's display: 5:58, Thursday, June 11. The Gateway Arch shone like a diamond in the setting sun. The map application showed they were approaching the Mississippi River.

Tammy pulled the prepaid Visa from her purse and examined it. It felt as fake as her ID, but she had enough on it for a week at a reasonable hotel. Mr. Van Buren would get the details worked out with Grandmother Grace before then.

Fuck foster care, El.

Tessa pulled into a parking garage and Tammy immediately felt her heart drop. The height of the buildings alone told her it was going to be more expensive than what she'd had in mind. "Whoa! Why'd you pick here? Can't we find something cheaper?"

"Uh-uh." Tessa's eyes went wide, and her head bobbed slowly side to side as if she were explaining something to a child. She made a broad circle with an index finger. "See where we at? There are like ten clubs within walkin' distance. Don't you figure if they looking for your phone they'd be looking for my car? We put it in a parking garage and walk, ain't nobody find us."

Tammy blinked, stunned that Tessa was actually operating based off a plan. Neither of them was good at that. It was like a secret handshake to get into Club TnT—do everything on the fly.

Tessa stopped and waited for the ticket machine. Once the barrier arm lifted, she accelerated deeper into the garage, circling upward in the parking structure, ignoring the speed limit. It seemed certain they would crash, but Tessa just laughed. Tammy reflexively braced her arms against the dashboard, only relaxing once they found an empty spot and parked. It was another of Tessa's annoying traits, taking fearlessness to the level of recklessness, then tipping just over into stupid.

Tammy let it go. They were here to have fun, to get away, not fight.

Once they were back on the street, Tammy felt like a tourist again. Surrounded by tall buildings and all manner of traffic, she felt safer, once again draped in anonymity. The city's energy was alive, vibrant. She tingled with the sensation, especially when they passed near doorways.

A vagrant holding a cardboard sign with something unintelligible scrawled on it called out to them. He smelled like urine and body odor. It only made the experience more authentic and legitimate.

They were in a real city.

Tessa led them to the entry of the Embassy Suites. When they entered the lobby, Tammy made a conscious effort not to look around. She already felt like a bobblehead.

The interior was clean and neat, everything orderly and precise. Tammy was sure there was a name for the décor style, but she didn't know it. She considered it utilitarian and nice, the sort of thing that would appeal to Elliot. She scolded herself for even thinking about him. They were done; their friendship was over.

And I already do not *miss you, El.*

She presented her fake ID and the Visa at the front desk. She wondered if she looked as underdressed as she felt. "Do you have a room available, a double?"

The receptionist—bronze skin from a can and black hair from a bottle, but cute despite an overbite—smiled courteously. Her name tag, if it could be believed, declared she was Rebecca. "Do you have a reservation?"

"No. We're looking at staying three days, maybe longer, depending. Is that all right?"

Rebecca tapped at a touch monitor. "We have a double suite on the fourth floor. Will that do?"

Tammy nodded. Rebecca took the card and ID, and Tammy did her best to maintain a calm, almost bored smile.

After some more tapping, Rebecca slid a small envelope with two magnetic key cards across the counter and into Tammy's hand. Rebecca offered a perky smile and said, "Enjoy your stay."

Like the lobby, the room's style was clean, with strong lines and tasteful colors. A common sitting area dominated by a large, flat-screen TV joined the two rooms.

Tessa made a beeline for the door on the left. "Dibs!"

Tammy moved to the door to see Tessa rolling on a giant bed. Tammy checked the other bedroom. A slightly smaller bed occupied that one.

Tammy shrugged off her little pack and the mound of shopping bags she'd been hauling around. She pulled a new, little handbag from one of the shopping bags, tore off the price tag, and started loading it up.

Tessa came to the door, bouncing energetically. "Girlfriend, this is what it's like to be rich. Think you could get used to it?"

Tammy looked around the room. "I guess. It's really nice, isn't it?"

Tessa nodded and smiled giddily. "I could get used to a life like this. Find me a man. Maybe like a doctor or somethin'. I think I'd be a good wife."

"I think you would, too. And a good mama."

"Ah. I ain't ready for that yet. Maybe someday, when some guy can see me for …" Tessa's smile faded as she looked at her reflection in the TV screen. "You know. See past all this."

Tammy walked over and hugged Tessa. "I see past all that, and I think you're perfect."

"Yeah, but that's because deep down inside, you really a lesbian, and you got the hots for me." The dark moment had passed, the same old saucy Tessa had returned. "Let's get dinner, 'kay?"

She didn't wait for Tammy to answer, instead running out and plopping down on the sitting room sofa and pulling out her phone. After a minute, she offered the phone to Tammy. "Here, see what you want, and give me your iPhone."

While Tessa typed a number into Tammy's phone, she examined the tiny map Tessa's phone displayed. Tammy patiently arrowed over pinpoints, reading each one carefully.

"Hey, Emmanuelle." Tessa wandered around the room while talking. "Yeah, I know. It's borrowed. You got any hookups in the Lou? Yeah? Yeah. Hang on." Tessa took a pad of paper from a nearby side table and started writing. "Uh-huh. He's got good stuff? She, whatever. She's got good stuff? Great, I'll—" She cocked her head, listening intently. "I don't know. A couple days. Okay. Okay. *O-KAY!* Love you, too. Bye."

Tessa ended the call and immediately dialed again. While she waited for the answer, she glanced at Tammy's choice of restaurant and nodded.

"This Misha? Hey, I'm Emmanuelle's daughter. I'm in the Lou, lookin' for some fun. Yeah. Down by the Riverfront. Yeah. Hey, what's the hottest club tonight? Uh-huh. Just down the street. Sweet. You wanna—what? Yeah. See you there about—Yeah. Uh, I dunno. Put me down for a quarter of bud, four skittles, and fuck it, how about a hard rock. Hang on." She covered the phone. "You want anything?"

"I brought my own." Tammy thought about the two remaining vials of Seer's Sage she had in her purse. They were powerful, almost frightening. Whatever she took at Area 151 had seriously changed her perceptions.

She stared out the windows that looked onto US Bank Plaza. Long shadows covered the street. Pedestrians moved hurriedly in small clumps, like herds seeking protection from predators. A man stood alone in a doorway, ignoring the flow of foot traffic, staring at the front of the hotel.

Staring at *her.*

"You gonna cover for me?"

Tammy tried to make out details. He was big, maybe as tall as Elliot, probably as big, and he was bald. In the shadows, it was impossible to tell if he had tattoos or not. She could feel...hunger? Pain? Something. Like he was hunting her. The sensation was radiating off of him like heat from the sun. He was too small to be Stone.

"Yo, girlfriend!"

Tammy turned at Tessa's shout. "What?"

"Are you gonna cover for me?" Tessa pointed at the phone.

"Yeah." The money was running out fast, the trip was getting shorter. Tammy turned back to look more closely at the man, but he was gone now, a figment of her imagination.

Tessa concluded the call, disappointment clear on her face. "You bring that stuff you took at 151?"

"Yeah. I'm not gonna do another full vial, though. Did you order a crack rock?"

"We're in the big city now. Gotta step it up."

Yeah. Gotta get away from the hell out there.

Tammy thought back to that night at 151. She'd flown free then, even if it was only for a night. She just wanted something that would make her dream of—

She didn't know what. It didn't really matter. Anything was better than the bloody massacre of everyone she loved. And now she just wanted to get past the horrid creeping anxiety building in her, like there was something out there, coming for her, hunting her, intent on killing her.

She was sure it was Glen Stone, and that he was out there somewhere, waiting for the opportunity to strike.

Waiting to rip her to pieces.

Chapter Nine

They were still 600 miles northwest of Bangalore when a stewardess shot past Elliot's seat in a rush of whispery footsteps. Her dusky features were pinched and strained; her scent rolled up behind her: a mix of stale clothes, perfume, and anxiety.

The anxiety was infectious, floating out and over the nearby passengers.

Elliot's mouth felt dry, grungy. An awful taste lingered, the residue of too many hours stuck on a plane. They were heading into trouble again; he just knew it. He hated turbulence, *hated* it.

Seconds later, a gentle bell sounded, and Elliot prepared himself for the inevitable message that would follow, filling the cabin with its echoes of dread.

Before the stewardess could utter a single word, the plane seemed to plunge, stopping suddenly as if it had slammed into the ground below. Frightened voices echoed inside the cabin. The plunging done, the plane began to shake and rattle.

Elliot's stomach lurched and bitter bile jetted into the back of his throat. People started to scream, and the cabin's tired, re-circulated air took on a new scent, turmeric and cumin replaced by the rank sweat of fear. Raw heat—real or imagined, drawn from him or from an external source—replaced the cool air from the panel over his head. Lights blinked off, then on, then off again.

"Please remain seated …" The stewardess managed a few other words between the worst of the rattling, and she said something about Bangalore, but the rattling took most of what she said.

Elliot fought back a panicked laugh. He'd managed an upgrade to first class in Paris for the last leg of the flight to Bangalore. For some reason, he couldn't find any comfort in the idea he would die seated on luxurious leather with expanded legroom, or that his body parts would be strewn across some forsaken stretch of northwestern India, surrounded by the body parts of the affluent.

No nap now; I doubt I'll sleep the rest of the way. He gripped the armrest as another tremor shook the plane.

The stewardess said something about seat belts, but the banging and clattering and the rising panicked screams drowned the message out. Elliot's mouth was a desert. His lips seemed to be stuck together, the inside of his mouth a single piece. His hands and face were damp and slick.

A popping sound issued from the speaker system, and the stewardess's pointless exercise came to an end. The lights flickered again before settling into darkness, and the plane seemed to drift to the right as if sliding on a sheet of ice. The sliding stopped, and Elliot's hip crashed against his armrest. He gasped in pain, happy that at least he could make a fool of himself with some anonymity: Along with the dark, the seat to his left was empty.

More shuddering shook the plane for several long seconds, and then the lights came back on. The vents began blowing cool air again, and another pop—this one softer—announced the speakers were working again.

Once again, the stewardess said something about seat belts.

Nervous laughter ran through the cabin; Elliot realized he was one of those laughing. He pushed his glasses back into position before clenching his hand into a fist to hide the shaking. He closed his eyes and began a slow count to 100, promising he would only open his eyes if the plane had truly exited the turbulence when he was done. He was nearly done counting when the intercom announced they could move about again.

"Are you okay?"

Elliot's eyes shot open. Something about the voice—it was rich and warm and pleasant—made the interruption acceptable. A young Indian woman with long, dark brown hair, full lips, and big, almost translucent hazel eyes gave him a mesmerizing smile as she leaned in from the aisle. Her teeth were a brilliant white, and large, almost too large. *Like mine. Sort of, but sharper.*

"I—yes, I'm okay."

"Nerves?" She was dressed elegantly, in Western clothes, her blouse and skirt expensive looking, the sort of thing a business executive might wear. She straightened to let an older stewardess slip past, barely even acknowledging the older woman.

Elliot blinked in surprise. Flight attendants were usually sticklers about movement in the cabin. "Yeah, just nerves. I've never liked flying." He stared at her for a moment, seeing in her face some of Neda's beauty. He realized he was likely projecting more similarities than existed, but she was quite pretty.

A middle-aged Indian man walked behind the young woman, giving her a sour look before walking past her.

Was that because she's talking to me, or because she's standing in the aisle? Everyone seems so on edge since we left Paris. Now all this turbulence.

That's probably what it is, the turbulence.

The young woman looked over her shoulder at the middle-aged man for a moment, her face suddenly flat and expressionless, then she turned back to Elliot, once more pleasant. "Would it be all right if I sat here? I don't think they're all that concerned about seating at the moment, and I could certainly use someone to talk to."

Elliot looked at the seat. His thoughts were frozen, his brain a mass of the purest stupid. "Um." *Um? A pretty woman wants to sit next to me, and I say um?* "Sure. If you don't think it'll be any trouble."

The woman settled into the seat and turned so that she was looking at Elliot. She extended a hand, slightly larger than seemed right for her frame. "Simirita Khosla."

Elliot took her hand, surprised at the strength of her grip. "Elliot. Um, Saganash." *Enough with the ums! She's just another frightened person, like me.*

"Was that entertaining enough for you?" She looked straight ahead, watching him out of the corner of her eye. There was a mischievous quality to her voice, as if she were a cat and he the mouse she'd chosen to play with before dinner.

"I'm not really much of a thrill-seeker," Elliot admitted, embarrassed by the weakness in his voice and words. He realized he'd broken eye contact; he struggled to regain it. For a moment, he saw her face—just her face—and felt certain he was looking at Neda. Memories of the last two weeks hit him hard, and he hastily looked away, pulling his glasses off and digging out his handkerchief to clean them. "I'm not much for flying." *Good grief, could I possibly sound any weaker?*

Simirita shifted in her seat, adjusting to it as if it were her new home. "It can be exciting." Her left hand drifted lazily from the armrest until it rested on her flat stomach; she let it slowly drift lower. She turned suddenly to look at Elliot again, her right hand clamping onto his left bicep. "What do you do for fun, Elliot? You do have fun, right?"

Elliot set his glasses back over his nose and gave them a single push. "Sure. I like having fun." He heard the defensiveness in his voice and flinched. "I mean, who doesn't?"

"What do you do?" Simirita's left hand now rested in the crease of her thighs. It was innocent enough, outside of what her words seemed to imply.

"Dirt biking, ATVs, swimming, golf. Archery, I guess." Elliot struggled not to look at Simirita's hand, which made a subtle, stroking motion over her crotch. *Or did it? I can't trust what I see right now, not in my state of mind.*

"An outdoorsman?" Simirita touched his arm, then licked the tips of her fingers. It might have been seductive; it might have been an innocent, absent-minded thing. "I pictured you more as a bookish sort. There were a lot of really sexy guys at Stanford—glasses, smart, but still in great shape. Like you." She stroked herself again, this time quite obviously, driving her skirt down between her legs.

Elliot shifted uncomfortably. He couldn't stop thinking of his fantasies about Neda and the guilt that came with them. "Y-you went to Stanford?"

Simirita leaned in. She had alcohol on her breath, but her eyes weren't those of a drunk; they were lucid, focused. Hungry. Very hungry, ravenous. "Sure. Business school. MBA." She shifted so that her blouse top opened, revealing the soft curve of her breasts and the silky, low-cut bra she wore. "It was hard, you know? Very demanding. But it was worth it. I like it hard, don't you?"

"I—I never could get that whole debits and credits thing." Elliot suddenly felt trapped and helpless. Simirita might as well have been hunkered down in high grass with a rifle, watching a salt lick the way she was hitting all his vulnerabilities. *What's that fish that lures other fish right up to it with a glowing protrusion? It's all instinctive, completely beyond their control; even if they figure it out, they can't resist.*

"My focus was on finance: ROI studies, risk analysis, effective capitalization, maximizing leverage." She leaned closer, her left hand now on his chest, pressing gently. "There's just something so…intoxicating about risk and leverage. You should really try it, especially risk." She giggled—a husky, flirtatious sound.

Her face was so close to his, he could see every element in vivid detail: luxurious eyes that seemed too old for such a youthful face; long, narrow nose above a deep philtrum; full, curved lips. And the teeth, the brilliant white teeth.

Neda. Except for the teeth, the similarities are so strong.

Simirita leaned her head in until her nose and mouth were over Elliot's neck, then she breathed in deep. She relaxed and leaned back in her chair, slowly closing her eyes as if momentarily sated. "Why Bangalore? Confused about your homeland?" She winked slyly. "Saganash. Native American, right? The *other* Indian?"

Elliot forced a quick laugh. Even relaxed as she was, Simirita's vibe was just as much threatening as it was alluring. He stretched and tried to seem nonchalant. "Family obligations, sort of."

"You have family in Bangalore?" Simirita's face creased incredulously.

"Someone close to me. He was like an older brother, really." Elliot bowed his head and swallowed. "I'm returning his ashes to his family."

Simirita sobered suddenly. She sat up in her seat and looked straight ahead, self-consciously adjusting her blouse. "I'm sorry."

"No, no." Elliot blushed, and he shook his head. "You couldn't have known."

Simirita went silent, her eyes closed. After what seemed several seconds, she looked at Elliot again. "Was he infirm? Or weak?"

"Weak?" Elliot struggled to keep the offense out of his voice, but he knew he'd blinked at the way she'd said *weak*, or at least the way he'd heard it, like Praveen had been pathetic.

Simirita placed a hand over his. "I'm sorry. There are times where I wish I'd never heard anything other than English. So many words, so easy to screw up. Sickly? Frail? Some sort of chronic or congenital problem? I think I'm looking for…wasting?"

Elliot managed a low grunt. *Praveen was full of life. And wisdom.* "No. Nothing like that. It was violent. He was murdered."

"Oh…my …" She squeezed his hand, a reminder that he was still alive and in the presence of someone young and healthy.

Elliot thought of pulling his hand away, putting an appropriate amount of distance between them, but he knew at a rational level there was nothing wrong with her intimacy other than what twisted meaning he was projecting onto it. She wasn't Neda. There was a vague resemblance, nothing more. He was letting his guilt run rampant, looking for an excuse to deny himself even a moment of pleasure.

"Tell me about him." Simirita leaned closer, but this time the intimacy seemed more tender and caring, less hungry.

"Praveen?"

"That was his name?"

"Praveen Thakur." Elliot's throat tightened as he said the name. It felt like saying goodbye all over again, and it hurt doubly knowing that they'd parted—

No, they didn't know what was coming. They couldn't have.

Simirita closed her eyes and her voice became a whisper. "Praveen. Praveen. Artful, I think. Or crafty. Maybe it's capable. Something like that. Was he?"

Elliot thought of Praveen's gifts—his ability to stay centered, to find peace during the worst of times, and his ability to draw people out, even the older residents. *He couldn't reach Tammy, not like he reached me. That's definitely an art, and he was definitely capable.* "Yeah, I'd say so."

"And he was a friend?"

Elliot bit his lip, adjusted the glasses on his nose. "They all were."

"They? You lost someone else?" Simirita put her other hand over his. "What happened?"

"My grandfather William, my friend's grandfather Driss, Neda, Praveen, Daysi, Ms. Nakama, Ms. Fernandez. No one knows what happened yet, other than someone broke into our home and killed them."

"So many." She shook her head, astonished. "You were close to all of them?"

"Well, Ms. Fernandez had only been there a short while, and Ms. Nakama wasn't really close to anyone, I don't think. And Daysi…she was closer to my friend Tammy." Elliot realized he was holding Simirita's hand. He relaxed his grip slightly. "Sorry."

Simirita patted his hand gently. "Tell me about them."

Elliot took a long, slow breath. "Okay. Well, there was Neda. She was a…researcher. She did a lot of studying of old belief systems, mythology, history. She tried to teach me about that—history, mythology, what we all had in common rather than what made us different. She had a strong belief in, well, people. The good in people." He smiled ruefully at the irony of the most hopeful among them being murdered by a neo-Nazi. "I had a hard time accepting that."

"Was she pretty?" Simirita's eyes seemed larger somehow. She brushed hair off her face, and once again the resemblance to Neda seemed uncanny.

How could she know to ask that? Did I say something or do something? Am I that obvious in everything? "She was, yes. I guess I had a crush on her, sort of a schoolboy crush on a teacher."

Simirita laughed. It was a pleasant but disturbing sound: happy, deep, but tinged with something almost bestial. She gently arched her back so that her blouse tightened; her body was young, feminine, more slender than Neda's. She caught him watching her and slowly closed her eyes. "That's nothing to be ashamed of. You can't let guilt and shame destroy your life. So much experience will never be known if you don't open yourself up."

"I-I know. It was just …" Elliot adjusted his glasses, uncomfortable again with her closeness and implied intimacy. "Um, Praveen was the youngest. I don't think he was even thirty yet. He didn't like talking about his age or his life here in India. I don't think it was very pleasant. I know he always felt like an outcast. And I think there were fights and trouble with the law."

"Was he a Jainist or Sikh or something?" Simirita's forehead furrowed. "My parents were Catholic converts when they immigrated to the United States. Despite what you might hear about Hindu being a peaceful religion, there are some pretty intolerant groups. It can be hard for others."

"He was sort of a mystic. He said his people's beliefs predated the modern, organized religions."

Simirita frowned. "That wouldn't make it any better. Out in the rural areas, they either worship or kill mystics, depending."

"He was always so calm and level-headed, like he'd already seen the worst he could see in life." Elliot caught Simirita smirking. "What?"

Simirita's smirk widened until it was less playful and more mirthful. "Nothing. It's just that I know exactly what you mean. I had an uncle like that. I think he spent his entire life convinced nothing could shake him, like he was ready for anything."

"Yeah. I was always jealous of that. I try to see things from a rational, logical viewpoint. I guess that's why I was drawn to engineering and math. Even then, Praveen was there to help me when something wasn't rational or couldn't be explained. While my grandfather talked about the spirits of our ancestors and the *manitous*, Praveen talked about balance and focus and seeking harmony with your surroundings to attain inner peace."

"That's wonderful." Simirita looked into Elliot's eyes, her own eyes deep and calm and unreadable. "Is that what you believe?"

"Believe? Like in faith?" Elliot paused to think. "I don't know. My mother's family was Catholic, but they abandoned her when she married my father. My grandfather held the tribe's old beliefs." Elliot winced uncomfortably at the idea of holding onto something so primitive: spirits everywhere—in the wind, the trees, the animals. "I'm not really much about faith and belief. If I were, there would probably be greater appeal in some of the primitive beliefs. The Christians' fire and brimstone, worship me or be an enemy condemned to hell ..."

Simirita's face screwed up.

Elliot recalled that she'd said her parents had fled India due to persecution as Catholics. "Oh, I'm sorry. I didn't mean—"

Simirita forced a weak smile. "No, it's not you. You just made me remember my parents and all the things they structured their lives around. Mass, the sacraments, and all the little rituals." She sighed. "I understand completely where you're coming from. If I have a religion, it's a belief in self."

"Makes sense."

Simirita's brow wrinkled again. "You said someone broke into your home and killed everyone."

Elliot felt his stomach knot in fear. "Except me and my friend, yeah."

"So, did you see the killer? Could he be coming after you?"

"I wasn't there." Elliot choked as the guilt gripped him again. It felt like claws tearing into his guts. "I was headed to Winnipeg. My grandfather and I had been fighting for a while about what I should do with my life. He wanted me there, with him. I wanted to attend university back home and be with my people. He took me in after my father died, so he was really like a father to me. I lived a better life with him than I'd ever known. But when it came time, all I could think about was how I'd lost my parents before really getting to know them, and how I was living away from my people, and how I needed to choose my own path."

"That's normal for a young person: self-absorption, guilt, that sense that everything—good and bad—revolves around you. But you're overlooking the obvious. Something led to you not being there when the murder happened." Simirita lifted his hand, holding it just beneath the curve of her lower lip. "It almost makes you believe in karma, doesn't it? How fortunate you were to have survived something so terrible. You should be thankful, don't you think? It's like someone or something pushed you out before everything fell apart."

"Or, maybe I was supposed to be there to help them, but I was so caught up in what *I* wanted and what *I* needed, I couldn't be bothered." Elliot wanted to shake free of Simirita, but he knew that he couldn't, not after abandoning his grandfather. *Maybe she's right? Maybe he sent me away to save me, but that would mean he knew what was coming, like Tammy said, and that means everything he tried to tell me in life was true, so I failed him even more by not listening. Or maybe he simply didn't have the strength to deal with me anymore. Either way, it's my fault.*

Simirita kissed the hand she held close to her lips. "Elliot, can I ask you a question?"

Once more, Elliot tensed. Simirita's questions were turning out to be little knives, cutting at his resolve and confidence. "Sure."

"What you're doing—carrying the ashes back. Is that for your friends, or is it for you?"

Even suspecting Simirita's question would hurt, Elliot wasn't ready for the raw flash of pain that hit him. *Is it for them, or is it for me? Which is it?*

"I-I don't know."

"I want to believe it's for them," Simirita said, unaffected by his answer. "But even if it's for you, there's a noble element to what you're doing. There's nothing wrong with seeking understanding of yourself."

Elliot considered her words, but he couldn't really derive much solace from them. The idea he was spending thousands of dollars to fly ashes and trinkets across the globe to satisfy his own needs seemed petty. He wasn't sure he liked the person that might describe.

"Look, Elliot, I know Bangalore fairly well. I've been there a few times, and I have friends there. I know enough Hindi that I can be a decent interpreter." She kissed his knuckles again. "Let me help you."

Help me? She hardly knows me. "I don't know. You hardly know me. I mean, I could be dangerous."

She let out a disarming, almost hurtful laugh at that. "You're not dangerous. Look at you." She seemed to sense the insult, because her face suddenly became more serious. "Oh, don't be that way. I meant you the person." She touched his chest again. "In here. Beneath those powerful muscles, you have a good heart."

"Well, what about the killer?" *What about the killer? I've never given that much thought. It's been more than two weeks. Could he be interested in me? In Tammy? We never gave that serious thought. I need to text Tammy when we land, warn her.* "I don't want to take the chance he's coming after me."

Simirita frowned petulantly, half sticking her lower lip out. "If you haven't noticed already, I *am* an adult, and I happen to find you attractive and sweet. I want to be there when you find Praveen's family and return him to them.

And I want to be there before then and after. India can be a dangerous place if you're not careful."

Elliot knew about the upswing in violence in India the last few years, but he felt confident he could handle himself. Had Tammy come with him, he would have been worried. And Simirita? She was a woman, a very attractive woman, and she was aware of her sexuality. "I find you attractive as well, but I'd rather—"

"Let's make a deal, then? Okay?" She opened her eyes wide, challenging. "Give me a day to prove I can take care of us. Just stay in my hotel room with me long enough for me to make some calls and see if I can't get you where you need to go. One day. If it doesn't work out, you've lost a day."

Elliot squirmed anxiously. She was taking away his choices, forcing him down the path she wanted, the same path he wanted at a primal level. He couldn't stop imagining being with her.

"One day." The words were like a croak, feeble and strained. They were an admission of defeat.

"You won't regret this." Simirita's voice was confident, the voice of a conqueror.

Deep in his gut, Elliot worried he had made a terrible mistake, a terrible, deadly mistake.

Chapter Ten

Tammy woke to the sound of screaming and crashing. Something heavy thudded against the ground, and seconds later she heard something tearing, then everything went quiet. She sat up in the bed, momentarily disoriented.

She was in a dark, hot room. It *felt* wrong, unfamiliar. Her baby blue Thundercats night shirt stuck wetly to her chest, and she could smell her own sweat mingled with Daysi's tincture. The tincture had left a fine coating of crud on her teeth and tongue, and there was the faintest bitterness about them. Worse, her breath could peel paint.

She'd eaten late, then she'd gone to bed and mixed the concoction with a Coke. But where was she? *When* was she? She could remember saying goodbye to Jeddo, seeing his ashes in the urn, taking some of her money from Elliot.

She concentrated and leaned forward on her bed, finally catching a sound. Weak, choking gasps of someone being strangled.

Tessa! The hotel! Fuck!

Tammy crawled out of bed and ran her hands over the floor until she found her shorts. She slipped them on as quickly as she could without making any noise, then she sneaked over to the door to her room. It was closed but unlocked.

For a moment, she went back and forth over whether to simply lock the door or go to Tessa's room and check on her.

The sound of breaking glass came from the sitting room outside, followed by more weak choking sounds.

Tammy squeezed the doorknob and twisted it, then she slowly pulled the door inward. It opened quietly, and she immediately saw an overturned table. She poked her head out and spotted clothes—Tessa's top and pants, both torn in half.

Tammy listened, heard another weak gasp coming from deeper in the sitting room. She leaned out a little more and froze.

Stone had Tessa pinned to the sofa, one knee driven into her sternum, both hands wrapped around her throat. They were both naked, and Stone was clearly aroused. Blood trickled down his arms from deep gouges where Tessa had scratched and clawed, but her hands were slipping away from his arms. She looked at Tammy with accusing eyes so full of terror and betrayal that Tammy gasped. Then the hint of life was gone from Tessa's eyes.

Stone turned, his face as bloody as his arms.

"Motha fuckin' bitch tore me up, huh? Izzat what they teach you bitches back in Africa? Yer from Africa, right?" He casually backhanded Tessa's dead face.

Tammy retreated back into her room and tried to slam the door, but Stone somehow got a couple fingertips between the door and jamb. Tammy pushed with everything she had, but Stone was bigger and far stronger. She heard his fingers snap, and Stone let out a pain-filled yelp, but a second later, he shoved the door open and sent her sprawling backward into the dark room. She fell to the floor and banged her head hard. Everything blurred for a moment.

Stone stepped into the room, sucking on his mangled fingers. He was breathing hard, and the violence seemed to have aroused him even more. "Y'all know I like it when ya fight, but I ain't keen on gettin' hurt none."

She tried to get to her feet, but he was on her too quickly, straddling her and driving his knees into her armpits. He thrust his penis at her face and laughed evilly. His eyes glowed in the darkness. "Now, damn, just look at ya, all pretty and shit. I ain't never had me no Arab bitch. Ya suck away the pain from my fingers, and I jus' might let ya live, hmm? Ya like that?"

Images, sensations, desires...Men—shadowy and indistinct, but with a very real sense of…age—chanting around a fire, like William Big Bear. Doing something to Stone. And Stone, he had no intent of leaving her alone. He satisfied his needs—his hunger—with Tessa, but Tammy, the shadow men had promised him Tammy when they were done with her, and Stone had already dreamed up so many horrible things he would do to her, do *with* her.

Who the hell are *they? What does he mean 'when they're done'? What the fuck?*

He probed at Tammy's mouth with his mangled fingers, letting blood drip onto her lips. A twisted smile played across his bloody face. "C'mon, now, open up, little Arab princess. Lemme have muh wish."

Tammy slowly opened her mouth and let him push the fingers in. She nearly gagged at the foul taste, like they'd been buried in viscera and never cleaned.

"That'a girl. Ya just suck away the—owww, bitch!" Stone fell back, clutching his hand in disbelief.

Tammy spat out the fingertips she'd bitten off. She'd nearly gagged on them. She spat again to get the blood and remaining flesh out of her mouth while sitting up enough to rake a hand across Stone's face. "Fuck you!"

One of her nails caught in a furrow left earlier by Tessa's nails; Tammy yanked down until she felt her finger sinking deep into flesh and heard a tearing sound like Ms. Fernandez tearing chicken apart in the kitchen.

Stone yelped again, but this time it became a howl, deep and only barely human. He kicked away from her and came to a stop against the door, both hands covering his face. Blood trickled between his fingers. He made noises that could have been crying or laughter, maybe even both. Despite the obvious pain, he was still erect, throbbing.

Tammy got to her feet and ran for the doorway. She was almost to it when Stone reached out with a foot and tripped her.

She went to the ground clumsily, banging an elbow hard on the floor.

Stone was on her again, his wounded hand now held out to his side. A patch of flesh as big as his thumb hung from the side of his face. One of his eyes was a bloody ruin. "Look whut y'all done t' me! Lookit!" Spittle flew from his mouth with each shouted word. He shook his good fist at her, as if he were ready to beat her to death.

"It's an improvement, asshole."

Stone nodded angrily. "Oh, yeah? An improvement? Ya wanna see what it's like gettin' under my skin, bitch? Ya wanna see what's up in there? Hmm?"

Stone dug his ruined fingers into the tear in his face and growled in pain. Once again, the growling moved from remotely human to beast. By the time his fingers had completely disappeared beneath his flesh, Stone was shaking from the pain, and the growl rose until it sounded like something primal, something more terrible than humans were ever meant to hear.

"Ya wanna know what's comin', hmm?" His voice became deeper and raspier as he spoke. He tore away a sheet of flesh, leaving nothing but wet, glistening bone on the left side of his face and a loose, dangling flap of flesh. The jaw, the cheek, the bony ridge over his eye—they were all visible. "Ya wanna see what's in me?"

Stone gripped the flap of dangling flesh with his good hand and peeled it up and around until his head was nothing but a terrifying, bloody skull. Blood and wet pieces of flesh fell onto Tammy like a gentle rain. Stone leaned back and howled, a sound that shook the room and knocked dust free from the ceiling. When he leaned forward again, his flesh had been replaced by something old and gray and evil, a shrunken, desiccated mask that was only vaguely human, something crafted from nightmare, or something that actually defined nightmare.

"How ya like me now?"

Stone leaned in and snapped his mouth an inch shy of her face, exposing rows of dagger-like teeth, like a human shark. His breath was cold and rancid and ancient, like something that might bubble up from the deepest ocean depths.

He tore her shirt open and stared for a moment, hypnotized by her heartbeat, then he looked into her eyes and winked. "It's such a purty sound."

Drool spilled from his mouth and pooled on her chest. She screamed, but only for a second. He bit into her chest, shearing through ribs and muscle and tearing her heart in two with those wicked, wicked teeth.

Tammy woke to a pounding sound. Someone was banging on her door.

"Damn it, girl, you fuckin' up everything!" Tessa sounded pissed and rattled. "Quit with the screamin'."

"Tessa?"

"Who the hell else you think would be out here? Fuck. You drink that shit you cooked up at your home? I thought *I* was all kinds of fucked up, but you didn't hear me screamin' like I was in some shitty horror movie?"

Once Tessa had stomped away, Tammy slipped out of bed. Her baby blue Thundercats T-shirt was soaked and clinging to her, exactly as she remembered from her nightmare. She worked the arm she'd fallen on. It was stiff and sore, like maybe she'd slept on it awkwardly.

The nightmare had been vivid, as real as the moment she was feeling right then. She could still feel and smell—even taste—Stone's rancid, cold breath. Just the memory of it was enough to make her gag.

Fingers. Shit.

She ran her tongue over her teeth and gums. She couldn't feel any flesh, but she touched her lips just to be sure. In the room's darkness, she couldn't tell if she came away with spit or blood. The idea it might be blood drew a soft chuckle.

Oh, fuck, I'm losing it.

What could she do to prove to herself it had been a nightmare, and the nightmare was over? She thought of checking the bedroom door, but she knew it was locked. It had to be. She always locked doors whenever she was in new places. Always.

But she hadn't in the nightmare. Sympathetic magic came to mind, lessons taught by William Big Bear. Not his own beliefs, but what he knew from previous members of...what were they? A cult? They officially called themselves "The Circle," and to her and Elliot they were "the Elders," even when they were young, like Neda and Praveen. But what *were* they?

Fuck it. They were mystics. Real mystics. *That's all that mattered.*

Sympathetic magic. She could actually remember that, because it was something she'd seen before in her own life. Grandma Grace had a kitchen witch in her shack and a whole bunch of other little talismans. She was all about making something happen by imagining it happening, and that was sympathetic magic right there.

So if the dream seemed real, was it meant to be real? Was Stone somehow getting into her head and shaping a reality he wanted?

A fucking neo-Nazi mystic? Seriously? "Goddammit."

She sneaked to the bedroom door and traced her fingers over its surface until she found the lock. She held her breath until she confirmed it was locked. Finally, she relaxed and let out a quiet, relieved sigh.

It was somehow almost disappointing she wasn't still stuck in a nightmare. That meant she was just having vivid dreams, something she wasn't really used to since—*Daysi's concoction. She said it was special. Just for me.*

The coma Tammy had fallen into when she was thirteen had changed everything in her life, some for the better, some for the worse. That wasn't surprising, what with it technically being lethal and all. Until now, losing vivid dreams or even memories of dreams had never bothered her. To have them back and at the sort of intensity she remembered from childhood…

She laughed and turned on the light, then made her way over to the nightstand. The small vial with Daysi's concoction was still sitting there, still half-full, next to an empty can of Coke. The combination had done its work, knocking her out and twisting the world around her into a completely new experience. Remnants of the effect lingered, with the room lights giving off strange, fluorescent gold and sapphire halos. It would make for an interesting night out on the town.

A quick rummage through her new luggage, and she found a dark blue tank top. She swapped it out for the wet T-shirt and headed into the sitting room. Tessa was sitting on the sofa, wearing one of her skimpy T-shirts, a pink number that left her midriff exposed.

"Sup, screamer?"

Tammy flipped Tessa off and walked to the window. The sun was blinding, the shadows just beginning to stretch.

"Shit. My head's still achin'." Tessa rubbed at her eyes, already bloodshot and puffy.

"I didn't scream that loud."

"Oh, you keep tellin' yourself that, but I was talkin' about the shit I took."

Tammy pulled out her phone and brought up the display. Just after three. It wouldn't be dark for hours yet. Her stomach gurgled. She looked at the table that Stone had knocked over in her nightmare. There should've been leftovers there, but everything was gone, the containers in the garbage can. They'd ordered enough for three or four people the night before, but Tessa had apparently gotten the munchies in the wee hours.

"You ate the fried mushrooms and cheese sticks?"

Tessa patted her stomach. "And the zucchini and those slider things."

"You're lucky you didn't throw up technicolor grease."

"When I woke up, I wanted to. It's all good now."

Tammy watched the buildings across the street for any sign of Stone. She could feel him out there, somewhere. Watching. Waiting. Inhuman.

"Are we still on for tonight?" *Please say no, Tessa. Please.*

"Friday night? Mm-hm. Ain't no way I'm missin' that." Tessa hopped to her feet and began to dance. Even as clumsy and uncoordinated as the drugs had left her, she managed to get the jiggle going.

Tammy didn't bother to silence a derisive snicker while admiring the display of fearlessness. It was like the X Games, but with indoor furniture challenges. "You're gonna break something if you keep that up."

"Yeah, some horny boys' hearts."

"Look, I'm cool if we call it off." Tammy dug through the refrigerator, trying to ignore the absurd prices of the "courtesy" drinks. The damn things weren't even really cold. "I mean, we partied pretty hard last night, and you're looking like shit today. I mean, is your period coming on or something? Can you even fit into your outfits?"

Tessa stopped dancing and stared at Tammy, then slowly clapped her hands. Tessa laughed loud enough to be heard in the hallway outside, a sure sign she was still having a party in her head. "Oh, don't you even! We are goin' out *tonight*! I'm thinkin' it's time we get your cherry popped."

Tammy winced and shook her head. "Not happening."

Tessa put on her best dramatic shocked look. "You afraid of sausage, girlfriend?"

"I just don't feel like it." Tammy had successfully avoided Tessa's hookup attempts since they'd become friends. "Too much shit in my life."

"A little love take yo mind off the worst things in life. Mm-*mm*."

120

"I'm not feeling it, okay?" She was suddenly regretting coming to St. Louis or ever having left the safety of the mansion that Memorial Day night.

"Oh…shit." Tessa ran her hands over her body and thrust her hips at Tammy. It was awkward and nearly sent her to the floor, but it was still funny. "Is you a lesbian? For reals?"

Tammy laughed despite the dark mood that had settled over her. "Fuck you."

"See? I knew it."

"Dream on."

Tessa danced around and spun in circles, seemingly always on the edge of falling over. Deep down, Tammy did have an undeniable curiosity about Tessa, but it was just that. Not some lesbian thing, just a wonder what it would be like to touch such a fantastic body.

Or to *have* such a fantastic body.

"You want *this*!" Tessa spun and shook her curvy butt at Tammy. At the last second, Tessa grabbed the table to keep her balance and she let out a little squealing laugh. "I'm so fucked up."

"That's what I keep saying." The sensation that Stone was out there, waiting, hunting became stronger and Tammy thought back to the nightmare. She shivered. "Why don't we just hit a couple bars nearby and get lit up? You can pick up some young stud and break his spine or whatever."

Tessa's face reddened, and she put her hands on her hips. "We come all the way up to the Lou for *you*, and now you tryin' to fuck up the one thing *I* want to do while we here? Am I hearin' that right? Is that what you sayin'?"

"I'm just saying you may have pushed yourself too far, and there's no need to—"

"Pushed myself—? I'm the one slept in all day and woke up screamin'? Was that me? 'Cause in my fucked-up state, it seemed like that was you!"

Tammy could tell right off it was pointless to go on. Tessa wanted her rave, and there wasn't a damned thing anyone could say or do to deny it.

"Whoa. We'll go. I just wanted to be sure you weren't pushing yourself too hard."

Tessa jumped in the air and pumped her fists, as if she'd just won the lottery. "You know, I could give you a big, wet kiss."

"Save it for the poor sucker you're gonna hook up with." Tammy almost laughed at calling someone else a sucker. Tessa was playing the martyr like a master, turning everything against Tammy. They'd come to St. Louis *for Tammy.* They'd blown all that money on drugs *for Tammy.* The expensive food? *Tammy.* Now Tammy won't let poor Tessa do the *one* thing she wants out of all this?

Seriously?

"Hells yeah! I'll be the screamer tonight." Tessa stopped jumping, her face suddenly dead serious. "Yo, wait. And I mean it, okay? I don't want you fucking everything up with any more of your nightmare shit, right? If you need me t' get you something that's gonna knock you out cold, you say so right now, okay? Hotel security gettin' up in my face about your screamin'? Uh-uh. A'ight?"

Tammy took a long drink of Coke, then she nodded. Daysi's brew had kept the nightmares away that night at Tessa's trailer, but something told Tammy that had been a truly *special* concoction, something meant to keep her away from the slaughter at the mansion. Daysi had saved Tammy's life; she was sure of it. And if she wanted Stone to stay out of her dreams, she might very well need something to knock her out hard, same as that night.

Then again, she wasn't so sure she wanted to be completely out of it with Stone still out there.

"I'm gonna shower and get ready. And even if you ain't goin' after some salami, you need to shower up, too, know what I'm sayin'?" Tessa jogged to her bedroom, doing her best to throw in an extra dash of hip wiggle. She turned at the door. "Hey, you hear anything more about your grandmother?"

"Not since the call about her diabetes complications. I guess it's worse than they thought. She's not that old, but, well, y'know."

"She still might move up here, though, right?"

"Yeah. I don't know for how long, though. I guess they're talking about amputating something?"

"You can't catch a break, huh?"

"I just need someone to watch me until I'm eighteen, you know?"

"Yeah." Tessa went silent for a moment, as if she were searching for some other plan to engage Tammy. "So we gonna have enough money to stretch this out to Monday?"

"Sure." They wouldn't, though, not if Tessa kept buying enough drugs to kill a horse every night. Tammy needed something to survive on, and if they checked out Sunday morning and the drive back to Arlington went without complications, Tammy figured she might have half of the money left. It was slowing sinking in that wasn't much.

"We doing grub before we go?" Tessa chomped her teeth.

Tammy twitched at the sight. She half expected Tessa to explode in a bloody, slow-motion display that left only Stone behind. She shook the image out of her mind. "Yeah. Let's hit someplace affordable, okay? We're burning through the money too fast."

Tessa hesitated at the door, her lips stuck out in a pained pout. "Sure, but goin' all cheap?" She spun and shook her butt again. "That ain't no way t' get a piece o' my juicy ass!" She danced out of sight, and a minute later, she ran naked to the bathroom, laughing and clutching her toiletry bag and clothes against her.

Tammy shook her head and chuckled, then she stood and checked the buildings across the street again, peering into each corner, each recess, watching every face in the crowd. Stone would stand out in a crowd. The people she saw below were nicely dressed business folks, or they were tourists—families with children or white-haired, elderly …

She'd almost done it again, almost called them fossils. Like she had Jeddo and Daysi and William Big Bear and Ms. Nakama.

Stone had killed with violence and brutality, but she felt like she had taken away a small piece of everyone's life with each act of disrespect. She walked back to her room and closed the door. She stopped in front of the mirror on her dresser and stared.

It was hard truly seeing the person staring back at her. Was she seeing her *real* self, or was she seeing something Daysi's concoction had produced? Tammy had a slight violet shimmering around her, a field of energy Daysi had now shown to her. What mattered, though, was the person shrouded by that energy. Was that a decent, kind person, or was it the sort of selfish, spiteful person Elliot seemed to see?

"Mirror, mirror …"

She stared hard, looking from dark eyes to bronze skin to the layers beneath. Stone had shown her what he had inside—a beast, a terrible level of wickedness and hate and violence.

What about you? Are you any different?

Her hands shook with fear. What if she wasn't any better than Stone? No. She knew better than that. She had her flaws, and they were easy enough to see, but she was no Glen Stone. She had her humanity. She cared about other people. Some of them. She loved Tessa. She'd loved Jeddo and the folks at the mansion, at least the ones who had treated her like their own daughter.

She still hurt from the loss of family. She still felt fear, something Stone was apparently immune to.

But is that enough to say you're really different? Seriously?

Real or imagined, induced by drugs or the product of mysticism, Stone felt close now. There was no denying Daysi's drugs, and it would be hard to argue with what she taught, so why disregard what Jeddo had taught, or what William Big Bear had taught, or what any of the others had taught? Everything they'd said made just as much sense as something invading her dreams. *Djinn, baraka, manitous, kami*…it wasn't so silly once she had a look into the heart of a killer like Stone.

Elliot had seen something in the folder he'd looked at, and she'd felt it. Horrific images, absolute terror.

She had felt it as well as if she'd looked at it herself.

What the hell did that drug do to me, Daysi?

It was too late now, but Tammy wished she had Jeddo's *takoba*. He'd always sworn the sword was magical, crafted by an *énhæd'*, a master blacksmith and powerful mystic in his own right, someone who knew the secrets of iron and silver and spoke the magic words of power. She wondered if, before the illness struck him, Jeddo might have stood against Stone with that blade and tested its magic against Stone's hate.

She knew he would have. Any of the Elders would have fought Stone. They had probably tried. They had to have tried; she was sure of it. And if they were all dead, what did that say about Stone? Could the dream have had another meaning? Could there really be something inside of Stone?

Maybe Elliot could fight Stone? Maybe wielding the takoba, *he would have a chance? Elliot had always been pretty excited to swing the sword around, and* Jeddo *seemed to be pleased with what he saw when training Elliot.*

She remembered how it felt, having Elliot there to hold her when she found out everyone was dead. The cops had played a dirty trick, but in the end, it had meant she wasn't alone when she heard the news. Elliot had been there, supporting her the whole time, giving her the strength she needed.

But he had been alone when he'd heard. And he'd been worried about her. Really worried. She'd felt that. He still cared. Not enough to stay with her, and not enough to keep her from foster care. But he *did* still care.

Tammy let out a frustrated sigh.

There was simply no understanding Elliot. Good-hearted, naive, sincere...*asshole*. Totally self-centered, oblivious, loving, and loyal jerk.

He was all that remained of their family. Without him, she was completely alone in the world.

Alone. With Stone out there, hunting her.

Chapter Eleven

Elliot sighed and shifted anxiously in the chair set in the corner of the hotel room. Even in the wee hours of the morning, the room's air conditioner was struggling to deal with the miserable humidity, the worst the desk clerk said he could recall in twelve years in Bangalore. To Elliot, the room was a cluttered oven, its droning television, faux fireplace, and spring-green wallpaper struggling to distract him from the fact that he was slowly being cooked alive. He sucked in the warm, conditioned air and wondered how everything could smell like someone had poured bathroom cleaner on top of a Chinese food buffet.

Do they even have Chinese restaurants in Bangalore?

Elliot was ready to throw his phone at the wall in frustration, but he couldn't. He needed it if he ever wanted to get his belongings back. He squeezed the loose skin of his face until it hurt.

He needed the pain to think clearly. After more than thirty hours of travel, any thinking at all was nearly impossible.

More than anything, he just wanted a resolution. He wanted the call to end. He wanted the room to cool down. He wanted a hot shower to wash away the travel grime.

He wanted sleep.

But first, he had to deal with airport security.

How is it even possible for them to lose boxes like this? Isn't this stuff automated?

Quiet Hindi echoed from the television set. Elliot had meant for it to be background noise, but it was distracting instead of calming, and it made it harder to follow the airport security person's words. Elliot toyed with the idea of muting the television, but he knew that wasn't the problem; it was the fatigue and stress.

He was physically ready to collapse, but he was too wound up to sleep. And then there was the humidity.

And Simirita.

Elliot slowly turned to look at the bed. Simirita was busily pulling clothes from the suitcase she'd opened on top of the bed. She only occasionally looked at him. Each time they locked eyes, she looked away, easily as frustrated as him, and then she would carry another set of clothes to the dresser or the closet.

Elliot felt himself grinding his teeth. He opened his mouth to stop it, took a deep, quiet breath, then worked his jaw to relieve the stress.

The security person's rambling suddenly stopped. "You understand, yes?" It was the thousandth time he'd asked that same question.

"I understand you've lost my luggage. I also understand you're willing to pay the insurance I had on it once I go through the proper process. What I don't understand is *how* you managed to lose that luggage. It's extremely valuable, but it's not something someone could sell easily. Do *you* understand that?"

"Yes, of course, Mr. Saganash." The security person managed a calm that Elliot was sure could only be attained through deep meditation or deeper medication. "The problem was with the extended delay in Paris. And we do continue the search even now. There is a very good likelihood the bags will be located before long."

"How long is *before long*? I'm scheduled to fly out Monday morning." Elliot gave himself a mental kick for such aggressive scheduling. He was already sluggish from the travel, and this was merely the first leg of the journey. "Can you find them by tomorrow? I have an obligation to deliver some items tomorrow afternoon."

"Of course." The way the security person spoke, Elliot imagined the man smiling pleasantly, as if there was no worry here. "We have people working even today and Sunday, you understand, yes? If the luggage is to be found, we will find it."

Simirita says the odds are better things will turn up if they don't have any real value, but that assumes this was incompetence or simple theft. What if someone saw the insurance I bought and figured they could ransom it back to me? "Okay. Please call me the moment you have any sort of update."

"Yes, of course, Mr. Saganash. Please do try to get some rest."

Elliot disconnected and stood. He stretched until the pain in his shoulders and lower back faded. He'd already burned through a good chunk of the prepaid SIM card's minutes. He debated taking a taxi back to the airport and searching for another SIM card, but he knew the odds of finding a shop open at such a late hour were not good.

I do need to get some sleep. I'm not thinking straight. He remembered suddenly meaning to send Tammy a warning about Glen Stone; he began composing a quick text.

Simirita stepped from the alcove outside the bathroom, arms akimbo, toothpaste foam at the corners of her mouth. She held a toothbrush in her right hand. Her blouse was undone except for a single button above her midriff. "Well? Did he sound authentic, or do you think he's in on this?"

Elliot stared distractedly at the shadow of flesh the blouse revealed. "Um...I think he's authentic." He forgave himself the *um*, considering the moment, but he still pulled his glasses off and rubbed his face. Hard. "There's nothing of real value in there. I can't believe someone would steal urns with ashes. They're not even expensive urns." He turned his attention back to the phone. He sent the text without even proofing it, then switched the phone to vibrate and set it on the nearby nightstand.

Simirita disappeared into the alcove, and the sound of her brushing floated back out for several long seconds. She stopped. "There are thieves and criminals everywhere. They're so pathetic."

"Not everyone is bad." Elliot winced at how weak his words sounded. They weren't even his words. *I've had these discussions before. I can't believe I can only repeat Grandpa William's words instead of voicing my own. What's wrong with me?*

Water ran and she rinsed and spat, then she came around the corner again and pulled her blouse off. "It's one of the things I hate about coming back here. It's so embarrassing to see where I came from: corruption, squalor, barbarity. It spoils the beauty that's otherwise there."

Elliot froze as she unzipped her skirt and rolled off her pantyhose. When she'd spoken about the embarrassment of returning home, his first thought had been the conditions of his own people and, worse, the conditions of Native Americans he'd seen in the United States. However, the sight of her undressing shoved all other thoughts away. She was glorious to behold— dusky cumin skin, dark hair, and dark hazel eyes, a slender frame with firm, shapely breasts.

Once again, his fantasies of Neda came to mind, and his excitement faded.

"Simirita, I ..." He stopped as she turned to stare at him, unconcerned about her nakedness. She pulled her earrings from her ears, pushing back her luxuriant, dark hair. The earring stones sparkled hypnotically in the lamplight.

"Is there going to be a problem?" She walked to him quickly, her perfume and musk filling the tight space of the corner. She took his hands and gently pulled them to her belly, then guided them up to her breasts, all the while watching his eyes. "Are you concerned about all the looks we received?"

"N-no." Elliot was used to the occasional strange look, but the hostility he'd seen from people at the airport and on the street outside the hotel *had* been slightly unsettling. Ultimately, he knew they didn't matter. What mattered was the fact he was alone with Neda after wanting to be with her for so long.

Neda? Simirita! I am such an idiot. I need to get hold of myself.

"Don't be. They're little, unimportant people. Small minds, small thoughts. They don't have any power. Not like me. Not like us." Simirita smiled and ran her tongue over her teeth.

The room grew even warmer, and Elliot found himself breathing heavily; his heart raced.

"It's just, things are moving so fast. The flight, meeting you, now my luggage—"

Simirita's hands moved to his chest and worked their way in the opposite course she'd led his, sliding into his jeans. "You obviously find me attractive, Elliot, so what's wrong?"

Elliot turned slightly at the sound of his phone's vibration.

Simirita squeezed him insistently. "Elliot?"

"Noth—nothing's wrong."

"You can lie to yourself, but don't lie to me." Simirita's hands dove deeper, her nails not quite so tender and soft as her body. "Is it the woman? The Iranian you told me about? Neda?"

"Y-yes." Elliot's breath caught as much at the harsh ecstasy of Simirita's hands as at the accusation. *She's not concerned I'm comparing her to a dead woman. I can't understand this. Any of it. How can someone so beautiful and confident see something in me?* His hands began to roam, despite his discomfort, trailing down her back to the hollow above her butt.

"I told you how I feel about shame and guilt, Elliot." Simirita's hands came out of his pants, taking his glasses off and dropping them to the floor before seizing his belt buckle. She undid the buckle with powerful, rapid tugs that left him feeling overwhelmed. "You need to seize life and frame it in your desires. If you don't do that, you're not really living."

Elliot's higher order thoughts began to slip away, smothered by Simirita's passionate embrace. She had his pants around his ankles before he realized what she'd done, then she managed a few buttons on his shirt before simply tearing it open. He tried to resist her, muttering quiet protests in between kissing her breasts and nibbling on her earlobes.

It was futile.

The next thing he knew, they were on the bed, entwined, growling and groaning and thrusting, both making animalistic sounds, and all he could think of was the moment, the intense power behind her needs and his desire. It was exquisite, a sensation beyond anything he could have imagined: fevered and wet and bestial in its complete absorption.

When they finished, Elliot rolled onto his back, as exhausted as if he'd been on his dirt bike for an entire day. He was covered in sweat, and he stank not just from the long flight but from the exertion. His limbs ached, and a weakness he'd never known before was settling over him. Thoughts—of the killer, the victims, and of Tammy—were there, so close to the fore, so near that he could almost grasp them and bring them in for closer examination. Examination of his troubled thoughts was exactly what he needed to do. He knew that.

But he couldn't. He needed to sleep.

He turned his head to look at Neda. She was beautiful, glowing. A fine sheen of sweat covered her head to toe so that her hair was plastered to her forehead and the sides of her face, framing it in a rich, sumptuous deep reddish-brown. He touched her, running his hand gently up a damp thigh to her soft, curved belly, finally coming to rest on her glistening breast. Her heart beat powerfully, as he imagined a tiger's might. She smiled at him, her eyes still closed.

For a moment, she wasn't Neda, but someone—something else: a wolf, or a coyote, or some beast he'd never seen before, with wicked teeth meant for tearing chunks of flesh free.

Elliot's heart skipped a beat, and he thought about jumping clear of the bed and running for the hallway. Then the beast was gone, and Neda was gone, and he was looking at Simirita, and the vicious teeth were just the slightly oversized pearls that gave an element of exotic beauty to her.

"Sleep," she whispered, and she licked her lips so they glistened like the rest of her. She twisted, her eyes barely open enough so that the lamplight reflected off them yellow-white, and her body almost glowed as she rolled on top of him again and began rocking and grinding until she was once again in control.

Elliot tried to resist, but he was even weaker than before. Almost immediately, he found himself mindlessly grunting and groaning, too tired to even look at her magnificent beauty, even though he wanted to.

She gave him other commands, verbally and with her powerful touch, and he did as she wished. Finally, he couldn't do anything more, and he collapsed.

And dreamed.

He was on a narrow, wooded path, the ground leaf-strewn, untouched except by animals. He could make out their prints—deer, rabbits, squirrels. Fog hung low, not thick enough to obscure but enough to limit how far he could see. A great, dead oak loomed before him, its trunk leaning against a large boulder.

One of the trails down to the creek.

A twig snapped as something moved in the woods. Elliot tensed. He knew the path well enough to make a run for it when the thing, whatever it was, revealed itself.

"The path offers you safety. That is why you have come here." The voice echoed off the trees. It sounded as if it drew energy from the surroundings.

It sounded like Grandpa William.

"Grandpa?"

A coyote stepped clear of the fog. "Appearance is what you wish it to be." A raven stood where the coyote had been a moment before. As the coyote's snout had moved when Grandpa William spoke, so now the raven's beak moved in time to the words. "Deception is a powerful force. You were always strong of will, immune to deceit. This was also a weakness. You cannot appreciate the world for what it is until you can see what it is not. Ms. Nakama tried to teach you this."

Elliot closed his eyes and willed himself awake. He'd had dreams many times as a child, usually terrible ones about the loss of his parents. They were impossible, despite their seeming authenticity. He'd only heard details about his mother's death years after the fact, and his father had died alone in the woods near their home. Tammy had helped him deal with the dreams shortly after they'd met. It had been something she'd had a natural affinity for, at least until the mysterious illness had nearly killed her.

Tammy. So much of this just came natural to you. Why didn't you embrace it?

Try as he might, Elliot couldn't break free of the dream.

"Elliot, remember how I told you I could never see the path you were on?"

Elliot opened his eyes; the raven was gone. In its place sat Praveen, eyes closed, face serene. He wore his white silk dhoti and jeans. His legs were folded in one of the yoga positions Elliot could never remember the name of.

"Praveen? You're in my dreams, too?" Elliot stepped forward, sensed another presence—this one menacing, terrifyingly powerful—in the fog; he froze.

Praveen didn't move. "This is not your dream, but your memories. Your dreams belong to another, what you sense in the fog. You are in a very dangerous place now. You must choose your path wisely."

Okay. Praveen's dead. So that's not him. It's my projection of him.

Or it's a projection of Praveen sent by whatever that thing out there is.

Praveen laughed excitedly, but his face remained neutral, his eyes closed. "Exactly! Perception is reality, and what you face now is a paradox. Have you ever thought you might have failed in your training not because of your adherence to logic and science, but because you failed to grasp that your training *was* logic and science? Your situation now: Dream? Illusion? Drugs? How can you know?"

Drugs! I hadn't thought of that possibility. Daysi used hallucinogens all the time for her trips. She had some lethal mixtures in her little lab. Praveen used that Soma mushroom. Peyote, mescaline…mind-altering drugs. But would they produce something so real?

"Excellent!" Praveen clapped once. "The logic! The scientific approach! Problem-solving! Why can't you wake from this dream? Break the situation into its smallest components, Elliot. No challenge is so great it cannot be broken down and attacked one piece at a time."

Break the situation into solvable parts. Okay. So, what do I know? I was with Simirita, in Bangalore. We had sex, and I fell asleep. I don't remember waking up, I don't remember traveling, so this is a dream, or a drugged state, or …

Magic.

I'm not ready to accept magic as an alternative. So, just assume I can't wake up because I'm under some sort of influence.

What do I know about the influence?

"You know it's coming from that thing in the woods." Praveen was gone. In his place stood Neda, dressed in a bright orange and dark red silk outfit trimmed in gold, one of the magi robe ensembles she wore during their times at the mansion. She was surrounded by a pure light, untouched by the gloom. "Eli, you must truly use your logic, that sharp mind of yours that none of us could reach."

"Neda—" She was the only one to call him Eli when he was young and their relationship was simple. It was special to him.

Neda waved him silent with an abrupt, dismissive snap of the wrist. "Ask yourself—how could it be drugs? When did you last eat or drink?"

"I could have breathed something in, or you could have had something on your...skin." He blushed. *On her skin. Simirita could have had something on her skin.*

Neda shook her head sternly, and her brow wrinkled as she urged him on. "You kissed her. She breathed the same air. She would have been affected. Eli, don't reject my teachings. Not now."

What were your teachings? Fantastical, beautiful nonsense about the stars and numbers and earthly spirits, about the power of the magi to interpret and divine and control the spirits, about the ability to find wisdom from helpful spirits and how to bind malevolent spirits to your will.

Neda bowed her head in disappointment. "Didn't I teach you the logic behind the magi process? Or did you view me as nothing other than an object of desire?"

Elliot's cheeks burned. "No! I listened! I tried to learn! I just can't!"

"*Won't*, Eli, not can't. You learned the science your school taught. You can learn anything." Neda leaned forward and raised a hand, irritated, as if she might slap him, then she drew back, relaxed. "For just a moment, set aside your skepticism."

"Neda—"

"Please." She tilted her head slightly, and the sunlight caught her round, soft cheek. When she did so—when she had done so before her death—she'd made his heart burn with lust that left him full of shame.

If not drugs, then a dream. Or magic. But Tammy taught me how to rise from a dream, and I can't rise.

So, for the moment, think of it as magic. Just for argument's sake. What do I know? What did they talk about?

Illusions? Bindings? Charms? Enchantments? Divinations? Wards? I can eliminate enchantments and divinations and wards; none of those apply. Charms are subtle; they leave the victim unaware.

That leaves illusions and bindings. Either could apply. An illusion would affect all senses and would be totally immersive.

But what's the use of an illusion that made you aware it was an illusion?

No, set that aside for the moment. So, bindings. I…I can't believe I'm even giving this a second of thought. This is insanity.

Neda crossed her arms in frustration. Her eyelids fluttered as they did— *as they had*—whenever she'd lost her patience with him. "Don't sabotage your own success. If logic takes you down a path, pursue it."

Elliot chuckled nervously. *Could me being stuck in this dream simply be some sort of reaction to everything that's happened? My mind succumbing to stress?*

"Eli!" Neda flared brightly, a trick she'd pulled on his first day of study with her. He'd later figured out it was a matter of mirrors and positioning.

No mirrors here in the woods. Or my memories. Or this binding.

Okay, a binding. Fine. I'm stuck in this dream because someone has used a binding spell on me. What bindings are most effective? Sexual ones, of course. Ms. Nakama made—claimed to have made—a living off that. Seduction, even rape. Especially rape. If a man raped Yuki, the resulting binding was even more powerful. It was all an intricate web of deceit, though. The subject was always drawn in during times of weakness and further weakened by sympathetic words and appeals to desires and regrets.

"Oh." Elliot shifted and reached for Neda, wanting nothing more than to apologize. The thing in the woods shifted with him, moving closer. "Neda—"

"Don't move." Neda bowed her head again, this time in concentration.

"But what I did, how I got myself stuck in this dream …"

Neda raised her head again. She seemed to be crying. "You're almost there. Understand why you're stuck in this dream, or you will not escape it. It is a binding. How do you escape it?"

Elliot wanted nothing more than to wipe the tears from Neda's cheeks, but he couldn't move without drawing the thing in the woods to him. "She seduced me, she tricked me, playing on my weaknesses and vulnerability. Showing me what I wanted to see."

"Did you want her?"

"Yes." Elliot couldn't deny Simirita's beauty, but he wasn't so sure the beauty was real. She had used illusion to appear as Neda. "Or she made me think I wanted her. She looked like you. Sometimes, she was you. And that's what I wanted, Neda. I'm so sorry."

Neda shook her head subtly. "I always knew what you wanted. It simply couldn't be. You're a young man, Eli. You have urges. That's normal. But now someone has shown you the way those urges can be exploited."

Elliot thought about that—deception, manipulation, exploitation. He felt used, and although he feared seeing Simirita as she truly was, he realized that was only one of the things that troubled him. She'd taken him without truly giving him a choice in the matter. Magic or not—and he still felt there was a more likely explanation than magic—she had forced him into an intimate experience.

"How do you break the binding, Eli?"

"It was crafted from deceit."

Neda whispered, "Yes."

"I've seen through the deception now. I have the power to undo this."

"Yes." Neda's voice was softer, barely perceptible.

Elliot studied Neda and saw that she was fading as she spoke. *Is that the price of freedom from her binding? To lose you?*

"Yes."

Elliot swallowed and ground his teeth. "Then you're free, Neda. And so am I."

He woke, not as if he'd awakened from a half-dream but as if he'd been in a deep slumber, completely oblivious to the world. He was shivering, the air conditioner having finally managed a wintry chill.

Suddenly, he remembered the dreams, or memories, or the spell, or whatever had happened. He looked over at Simirita, flinching, ready for her to attack him, ready to see the sort of haggard old witch he'd heard of from some of the Elders.

Simirita was as she had appeared before—young, pretty, vibrant. The sweat had dried from her body, but it still seemed to glisten. *Like Neda's light trick; maybe that's not her true appearance?* Her eyes moved rapidly beneath her dusky lids, and her head jerked left and right, her lips moving as if she were searching and calling.

Elliot recalled that a powerful spell could backfire when it failed.

He climbed out of bed as quickly as he could without disturbing Simirita, barely missing his glasses with his footstep. He caught a whiff of himself and realized he was every bit as dirty as he felt. He looked down and saw dried blood—on his hands, on his belly and groin. He searched for any cuts, wincing when he found a shallow, fairly wide one on his neck.

He hastily moved to the alcove and ran the hot water, poking his head out to be sure Simirita was still asleep. She hadn't changed: still searching through the woods in the dream, still calling for him. He was amazed to realize her nakedness no longer affected him like it had.

He washed his hands, then moved to the side of the bed, collecting his glasses, clothes, and carry-on bag. Once again, he returned to the alcove outside the bathroom and set the bag on the floor. He turned on the shower, again popping his head out to check if Simirita had stirred.

He wanted a long shower, something that could burn and scrub away the layers of his corrupted skin, but he couldn't risk it. He settled for scalding water and two vigorous passes with different, soaped-up washcloths. When he shut the water off, he listened for any noise that might indicate Simirita was awake.

There was nothing.

You're paranoid. You thought you heard noise in your hotel room in Rolla, and that turned out to be nothing.

He dressed hastily, tossing his ruined shirt in the garbage, then pulling his last fresh one on. He checked his phone, saw he'd been asleep for nearly six hours. The shower had helped, but he needed more sleep. And food. Message notifications rolled in—one from Lieutenant Henriksen, another from airport security.

Nothing from Tammy.

Elliot squeezed his feet into his shoes as he read the message from airport security. They'd found his luggage, and they would be sending it to the hotel. The message had arrived nearly an hour ago. They would be arriving any minute, probably calling on the hotel phone. *Will that wake her?*

He extended the travel bag's handle and prepared to exit the room, but first he opened Henriksen's message. They'd found DNA on Ms. Fernandez, and they'd had a hit in their DNA checks.

A phone rang.

Elliot froze. It wasn't the hotel phone on the nightstand. It was closer to him, in the alcove. But there was no phone there. *It's hers! She has a cell phone somewhere.* He glanced at Simirita. She wasn't searching anymore; her neck was craned toward the ringing, but her eyes were still closed.

The phone rang again. Elliot hissed and shoved his phone into his pants. He searched for Simirita's phone. The sink countertop held her toiletry items and bag. And another, smaller bag.

The phone rang again. Elliot desperately dug into the second bag, saw the glow of a phone display.

"Elliot?"

Half-asleep. Still in the spell. Or drug. He fumbled for the mute and wished fervently that there were a single, standard, universal design for all phones.

The phone rang again; he switched it to mute mid-ring. It vibrated in his hands, then the call ended. He set the phone down on a towel and glanced at Simirita.

She was slipping back into sleep.

The phone vibrated. A voicemail. Elliot relaxed. He wasn't sure what Simirita was capable of doing aside from raping him, but he remembered she was stronger than she looked.

I need to get out of here.

The phone vibrated again, and Elliot cursed the fool who had come up with the damned things. Then he saw it was just a text message. He leaned down to read it, jumping when the hotel phone rang.

Elliot slammed Simirita's tote bag down and hefted his travel bag, then he ran for the door.

Simirita stirred behind him. "Elliot?"

He slammed aside the locks and pulled the door open. Simirita stood by the bed, lit by the lamps, her shadow a distorted monstrosity that nearly reached him.

"Come back, Elliot. *Now.*" She took a step, but Elliot was already in the hallway, running for the stairs.

All he could think of was the text message he'd seen on her phone: *Have you consumed him yet?*

Chapter Twelve

The dress Tammy had bought to go clubbing left her feeling naked. It was black, tight, and low-cut. It would've looked completely wrong on Tessa, but on a skinny—slender, Tammy corrected herself—young woman like Tammy, it emphasized the strong points: her shapely legs and toned arms and her graceful, long neck. Plus, it went with the black, strappy shoes she'd purchased, as well as the little black clutch.

And yet, with Stone out there somewhere, watching her, she felt naked, exposed.

The sun was almost completely gone by the time they reached the neighborhood where the rave was being held, and the street they were walking was poorly lit and lined with abandoned, brick buildings. Everything around them was gray, indistinct, and shadowy. Clumps of people—young women, fewer men—were making their way down the street. Like Tammy and Tessa, everyone was dressed to party. A few wore simple T-shirts and jeans, the sort of thing Tammy preferred, but most wore "appropriate attire"—expensive and showy.

As the clumps came closer together, Tammy caught the familiar club scene sensations: perfume and cologne, excited chatter and laughter, and gathering heat. She took a few steps with her eyes closed, enjoying the company.

"Oh, my *God!*" Tessa pinched Tammy's butt. "Check that boy right there, in that purple shirt. I want some o' that. You think he straight?"

The young man Tessa had pointed out was walking just a couple strides ahead of them and halfway across the empty street. He looked like a Greek Adonis: bronze-skinned, light brown curly hair, and a beautiful face that was long and angular. His shirt was open enough to reveal a toned, waxed chest, and his pants were tight enough to answer any questions anyone might have about, well, what mattered to Tessa. The guy next to him seemed more like a blue-collar workout stud, still cute, but a completely different vibe from what Tessa went after.

Adonis turned at Tessa's comment and, after looking her over, shook his head while giving her the saddest pout. Tammy noticed that his eyes lingered on Tessa's breasts for a moment. That was surprising for a gay man.

"That ain't right, y'all." Tessa let out a wild laugh and booming clap. "You should let Tessa take you out for a test drive, see if she can't change yo' mind."

Adonis gave a dramatic, naughty wink. "Oh, I've been on a few test drives. I've got everything figured out just fine. Thanks, though!"

Tessa wrapped her arms around Tammy's neck and sniffled. "Just look at those shoes. I bet he's in dental school. Why can't I get what I want? Huh, baby girl?"

Tammy hugged Tessa back. "Maybe you're looking for the wrong thing."

"You know I'd've been fine with Elliot. Mm-hmm. I can't believe you ain't gone after that. You know you want to. That's a fine slice o' meat."

Tammy felt her face flush. "I don't want to talk about El." *Or you humping him. Or me humping him.*

"Ain't gotta be no drama."

Tessa pulled away and they walked in silence, the clumps eventually forming a line. The press of flesh and the sight of so many excited and happy people quickly drove thoughts of Glen Stone from Tammy's mind, but only until she saw the bitter, resentful look on Tessa's creased face. Her eyes were still bloodshot, and they were now heavy-lidded.

A couple of men in line ahead of them caught Tammy's attention. They were cute enough, dressed in unassuming T-shirts and jeans, and they looked like simple college kids out for fun instead of supermodels. Tammy pointed them out, but Tessa just rolled her eyes and crossed her arms.

Tammy groaned, but not so that Tessa could hear her. "What is your deal?"

Tessa glared at her with simmering hatred. Her eyelids were squeezed so that in the dark, it almost looked like they were closed. "Oh, mm-mm, don't you start in on me. My dealio?"

"Is this about El?" *Or is this because you smoked a rock before we left the hotel and you can't keep your head straight?*

"Ain't about a thang." Tessa continued to glare. It was as if they'd been bitter enemies going back to kindergarten. "Nuh-uh. Just go on and have yourself a great time. I'll be fine."

"Are you gonna be like this all night?"

"Me? Like what?"

"All *Miss Mighty Mood Swings.* Like you refuse to have a good time. Because if it's gonna be like that, let's just go back to the hotel."

Tessa managed to find eleven on the simmering hatred dial. She could find eleven on any dial.

"I mean it. You're the one who wanted to go to the rave, not me. I'm completely fine with—"

"We came here to dance, a'ight? No need to try and turn this into 'Wassup With Tessa?', okay?" Tessa rocked her head side to side as she talked, and her eyes went wide and wild every few words.

The line shuffled forward, but those behind them waited for the drama to play out. Tammy moved forward. A second later, Tessa joined her.

Tammy watched the cute college boys and wondered why Tessa couldn't just find satisfaction in *good.* Everett was a gym rat, a stud, but he had turned out to be the one-night jerk Tammy had suspected he would be. He was just one of dozens who Tessa had thrown herself at over the years, only to be used and abandoned. Tessa seemed drawn to self-absorbed jerks. She didn't seem the least bit interested in giving regular guys a try.

Except for Elliot. He wasn't really self-absorbed, and he wasn't all about image, and he wasn't a total jerk.

Tammy rolled her eyes, furious Tessa had made it necessary to stick up for Elliot. Tammy shot Tessa an angry look and got back more of the same. Once again, the line moved forward, and the two of them hesitated a moment.

Someone deeper back in the line shouted for them to move up.

Tammy took a step forward, now both angry and embarrassed. Tessa stepped up, glaring angrily at some imaginary point deeper back in the line.

"Oh, I *ain't* believing this. Girl can't even get her grr on." Tessa shook her head and adjusted her dress. The fury had completely disappeared from her eyes, as if it had never even been there.

"You sure you want to do this? Seriously. We could go back to the hotel bar and get smashed and have just as much fun." Tammy searched Tessa's eyes and tried to understand the thoughts churning inside her head.

Tessa stared back, for a moment, seemingly ready to explode. Instead, all the tension seemed to just evaporate, and a bright smile lit up her face. "I told you already, there ain't no way I'm missin' out on Friday night dancin'!"

Tammy concentrated, trying her best to establish a connection with Tessa to see beneath the mercurial surface.

Tessa was a complicated person, with layer upon layer of conflict raging at the moment. She had a fierce love for Tammy, the only friend in a sad, lonely life, but there was also a big bundle of resentment. Tammy could sense some of the roots: the comfort and security of the mansion, the big family with all their love for Tammy and the way she didn't even appreciate it or acknowledge it, and…the discipline and structure, the clear lines and expectations. Tessa actually longed for those, and Tammy rebelled against them.

There were other elements to the internal turmoil. Lust and a need to be wanted fought against a desire for happiness and fulfillment. A desire for a better life and a certainty that it wasn't deserved. Even the concept of happiness seemed fluid and full of contradictions.

Tammy realized it wasn't just the drugs messing with Tessa, it was a lifetime of problems, starting with Emmanuelle's fucked-up *no expectations, no conflict, no problem* approach to mothering.

Suddenly, Tessa jumped up and down and pulled Tammy along. "We up!"

And without so much as a cursory ID check, they were inside. The tickets Tessa scored when she'd bought her goodies were all they needed. They weren't in a nightclub or bar that had to worry about losing its single biggest moneymaker—the liquor license. The rave was a temporary operation, its money mostly made from admission. That opened things up for a completely different approach to entertainment.

Immediately upon entering the building, they were assaulted by the music and the lights. Booming synthesizers and sequencers, heavily processed vocals, bone-shaking bass, all served up in near-darkness cut through by banks of strobe lights that illuminated billowing fog. The dance floor was already crowded, with people breaking off into pairs or little groups. Fluorescent light strips lit up areas where people gathered—a bar, a corner where things passed quickly from hand to hand. The building itself was just an open space, probably some sort of industrial building in a former life. Where lit up in glowing blue and green and magenta, everything was aged brick. There were still rusted iron beams holding things together, and here and there rusty machinery hung from the walls. Blinding LED lights flashed from the girders overhead at random intervals.

Tammy searched around and finally spotted a tower of black speakers. The DJ booth was there. More than the dance, she had wanted to actually hear this DJ's work. The song that was playing when they entered wound down, and the DJ switched to a quicker electronica piece. Tammy loved the song, but she had to split her attention between it and keeping tabs on Tessa.

And watching out for Stone. He was out there; she was sure.

After a few minutes of getting the feel of things, Tammy decided the best thing to do was to keep moving. She wanted to stay close to exits and keep away from the darkest recesses, and she wanted to be ready to run at the first sign of trouble. With or without the black strappy shoes, she wasn't going to outrun anyone, but getting some distance might buy enough time to get someone to help her.

As she did a few circuits around the building, she developed boundaries for the zones in the building. The dance floor was where the serious ravers were, with the ones who'd come to sweat and get lost in the event in the area closest to the speakers. Their dancing was intense and nonstop. There were islands on the dance floor of semi-serious ravers who were actually a little more interested in hooking up than just dancing. They weren't like the ones operating outside of the dance floor, prowling and attacking potential victims at the first opportunity, but before the rave shut down, these people would be heading back to their apartments or dorm rooms for a little action. And then there were the poseurs who came to the rave to look like they were part of a scene. They wore the clothes; they might know some names or terms, but they weren't *real* ravers.

Tammy wasn't sure where she fit in, but she guessed it was uncomfortably close to poseur. She liked the music and the dancing, but she was starting to question the whole dance all night on ecstasy concept. It seemed too high-risk and immature.

Immature. She laughed at that. Suddenly, dancing and recreational drug use were immature.

She really, really hated Glen Stone just then.

During one of the moments where she took in the music and scanned the crowd, she spotted a whole new sort of predator: *lyingshitus dickheadicus*. Near one of the smaller bars, Adonis was talking to a couple young ladies, both of them somewhat attractive, if a little generic and forgettable. One was a bottle blond, the other a bottle black hair.

The blond was shorter, chestier, and—on a day when Tammy wasn't feeling charitable—almost chubby. The black hair was a little taller, almost athletic in a way. She wouldn't win any beauty contests, but Tammy had to admit the girl's look probably would catch most guys' eyes. But they seemed way outside Adonis's league, assuming he was even straight. They were tossing back their hair and pushing out their chests and doing all sorts of other things to flirt with him, and he seemed to be responding.

Uh-huh. You've got everything figured out all right.

Tammy gave the room another quick glance, then she made a beeline for Adonis.

As she approached, she heard him offering the blonde a drink, a red plastic cup with ice in it. He held another drink in his other hand. Tammy grabbed the offered cup from behind and stepped in between him and the blonde.

"I thought you said you were coming back for me?"

Adonis turned, momentarily speechless.

"Where's the other guy?" Tammy took a swig of the drink, wincing at the cheap liquor and watery soda. "Mm, are we still on for the three-way, or are they joining us?" She pointed at the blonde and black-haired woman.

The blonde threw up a hand. "Oh, um, yeah, no? Sorry, not my thing." She puffed out her cheeks and backed away, then she turned and headed toward the dance floor.

The black-haired girl seemed to seriously consider the proposition for a moment, then she caught the blonde watching her angrily from the dance floor. She gave Tammy a regretful look, then looked back at Adonis. "I'd—" She glanced back at the dance floor, then at Tammy. "You're both so hot, and I'd really like to, and I mean *really* like to, but Lisa's all kinds of protective and picky, y'know?"

Adonis flashed a charming smile. "Sure. Maybe next time?"

The black-haired girl bit her lip nervously, then she leaned in and kissed Tammy on the cheek. "I bet he's wild," she whispered. "I bet you'd be wild, too. Next time?"

Tammy took another swig of the crappy drink, unsure what to make of the moment. She'd just wanted to fuck up Adonis's night after he'd blown Tessa off. Getting propositioned had been…unexpected.

Adonis waited a second, then he raised the remaining cup in a toast. "Well done." He took a drink and looked back to the dance floor. "So, I guess that sort of makes for a different kind of night, doesn't it?"

Tammy looked Adonis up and down. "I hate to disappoint you, but I was just fucking with you after the way you treated my friend. I saw the way you looked at her."

"The butter face?"

Tammy leaned into Adonis's space. He wasn't much taller than her, and his muscles didn't seem the sort to come from a boxing ring or working the fields or anything *real*. His hands were soft, and he didn't have a hint of scars anywhere on his exposed flesh.

"Yeah, see, that's the *last* thing you want to say at a time like this."

Adonis put up his hands in surrender. "Whoa. Wait. Let's pull it back in there, okay? I don't know her name, so I went with a bad nickname. Bad decision. I get it. And you were getting some revenge for a friend. I get *that*. And I actually like it. I mean I really respect the hell out of someone who will stick up for a friend. Most people wouldn't."

Tammy leaned back and tried to read his body language, but he seemed all Zen, like he'd mastered mellow and laid-back. When she tried to get a feel for his thoughts, she couldn't get anything off of him other than…excitement? Hope? Not sexual, though. At least not yet.

That was as disappointing as the black-haired girl's proposition had been flattering.

Adonis looked into the people twisting and grinding on the dance floor. "So, what about me apologizing to your friend? I can make it up to her. I can at the very least buy her a drink. Maybe more?"

"Oh, yeah." Tammy swirled the ice in her cup. "Great peace offering."

He chuckled, and it came across warm and friendly. "I know. I can only buy what they sell. You, um, you think you might be able to ask her to come over here? In that crowd—" He indicated the dance floor crowd with a jerk of his head, then he shrugged in defeat. "Unless you want to wait all night?"

Tammy pulled her phone out of the little clutch she'd picked up with the party dress. Everything in the clutch was a tight fit, and it made getting the phone out an annoyingly long process. She felt like a klutzy idiot in front of—

"Hey, what's your name?"

"My friends call me Eric."

After flubbing her password a couple times, Tammy pulled up the message app and texted Tessa: *Adonny wants to buy u drnk. Over near bar. Flashlite.*

She turned toward the dance floor, fumbling around in the dark to bring up the flashlight setting. Once the phone's LED lit up, she swung the phone over her head three times. She waited a few heartbeats, then she swung the phone again. A second later, the phone vibrated, sending magical tingles up her arms. It was more than she'd felt when she'd entered the building.

Tessa's text read: *On my way.*

"She's …"

"Coming, yeah, I see her. Why don't you stay here, give me a moment to try to make it up to her, okay? That's only fair, right?"

Eric gently guided Tammy over to the nearest wall and leaned her against it. His grip was soft and pleasant, and he smelled nice, like a gentle, sweet musk cologne or something, and it was sad seeing him leave for—

Tammy realized she wanted another drink, but when she looked down, the cup was gone. She stared at her empty hand for a second, trying to recall what she'd done with the cup of watery soda and nasty, cheap liquor. A second later, Tessa was there with Adonis—Eric. She was laughing like a maniac and grabbing onto him like she thought he was going to make a run for it.

She took a long drink from a red cup that looked a lot like the one Tammy had been holding…some time ago.

"Oh, baby girl, you don't look so good." Tessa's voice was insanely loud and far away, like she'd found a whole new, impossible setting. Her words became one with the music system, but then they completely took over and made the music a servant.

Eric gave Tammy a really sad look. "She said she wasn't feeling good. Maybe that's why she worked up the nerve to chew me out? You said she can be really shy, right? And, hey, I deserved to be chewed out, I know."

Tessa laughed again. Her eyes were wide, and in the fluorescent glow, they seemed filled with an evil glee.

"Don't drink the fucking alcohol." Tammy was sure she had managed to get that out, but then she realized she was sliding down the wall, so maybe she didn't after all.

"Whoa!" Eric reached out and gently grabbed Tammy.

"Tammy?" Tessa moved in close. The alcohol was heavy on her breath.

"I think she needs some air." Eric slowly hauled Tammy up and threw her left arm around his shoulder. Tessa took the other arm.

Tammy struggled to break free, she twisted her head around to warn Tessa that Eric was a Rohypnol asshole creep rapist, moving to the top of the list of creeps, a Creeposaurus Rex leaping over Beanpole back at the Holiday Inn Express.

Tessa seemed to hear her, because she turned her head and looked worried.

"That's right!" Tammy shouted. "Run!"

But there wasn't any shouting, not even a little squeaking.

"Hey, I think she might get sick." Tessa shifted her grip, as if she might be angling Tammy for a launch onto Eric. "Mm-mm, not on this outfit, you ain't."

Tammy was ready to claw Eric's pretty green eyes out at Tessa's signal. It was going to be the ultimate …

Something.

"Whoa, you okay?" Eric reached across to grab Tessa.

No! Don't let him grab you! Get up, Tessa! Get up! Goddammit! I'm gonna scratch his—

Someone stepped out of the crowd. A guy, a little bigger than Adonis. Eric. Whatever the fuck the sick ratfuck bastard's name was.

"Hey, everything okay? They look pretty smashed." The guy got up in Eric's face. "What happened?"

Eric froze, like he might be considering just dropping them and making a run for it. Tammy lifted her head.

Fuck you, Eric. Fuck you! Fuck him u—

She recognized the other guy. Fairly muscular, sort of a blue-collar vibe, somewhat cute. She wanted to scream, she wanted to kick and claw and punch and bite. She wanted to take dull, rusty kitchen utensils to their testicles.

"They kind of ambushed me," Eric said. He grunted and nearly lost his grip. "Why don't you carry the big one."

You better be talking about Tessa, goddammit!

Eric seemed to regain his footing and grip suddenly as Blue Collar took Tessa's weight on his shoulder. They started moving again, the bodies between them and the door parting without challenge.

Tammy couldn't believe people didn't care. She was floating on an all-new high, being carried out by a rapist asshole, and no one even cared.

What is wrong with my life? One minute Stone's coming after me, the next I'm being hauled off to be raped?

They were almost to the door when Eric pulled up suddenly. Tammy opened her eyes, even though the lids felt like they'd been superglued shut. One of the cute college boys from the line stood in front of them. He had brown hair and eyes and the cutest little button nose. He was saying something, leaning in and shouting into Tammy's ear. She could smell the alcohol on his breath. It sounded like he might be asking if she was okay.

Fuck no! Don't drink the alcohol or he's gonna rape you, too!

Eric shoved Button Nose in the chest, and then, like magic, they were in the street. Bright lights blinded her as a car pulled up. It was big and black and its back seat was fairly comfortable. Then again, Tessa was shoved in first, and her breasts provided a lot of cushion.

Tammy heard snippets of shouting and she was pretty sure she heard someone saying something about 9-1-1.

She hoped it was Button Nose and that Adonis and Blue Collar were on their way to indoctrination into something that would force them to completely reset their understanding of horror. But then the car's massive engine rumbled, and they accelerated away.

And even through the Rohypnol haze, Tammy could feel Glen Stone. He was watching with his inhuman thoughts, and he was close to acting.

Chapter Thirteen

Elliot twisted around in the taxi's rear seat. Behind him, State Highway 58 disappeared in the shimmering morning heat and the whorls of dust kicked up by the little white Suzuki. Bangalore was just a bad memory. A terrifying memory.

What had happened with Simirita and how…Elliot wondered if he'd ever know.

Metallic pops, muffled scrapes, and rusty squeaks were the music of the road. The driver seemed to find every pothole, crack, and crease. At least the air was breathable away from Bangalore's clinging smog. The car wasn't going to outrun much of anything, but it was good enough for a drive down the surprisingly open highway.

He watched the road for a moment longer, trying to reconcile the cracking soil, wilting shrubs, and dust clouds with the smothering humidity. He turned around and saw the driver was watching the rearview mirror. Elliot smiled sheepishly.

"Everything is okay for you, sir?" The driver gave a gap-toothed, yellow grin. His head bobbed slightly as he spoke. "Your neck, it is okay?"

"Yes." Elliot absently rubbed at the bandage on his neck. Simirita had been sloppy, actually taking a slice of flesh when she'd cut him. He'd need to see a doctor before flying out. "I was just thinking about the traffic back in the city."

"Oh, yes." The driver chuckled good-naturedly, no doubt a routine he had for dealing with tourists.

"It's amazing people can deal with that." Elliot nearly laughed at his own paranoia, his near-panic while they had been stuck in the metal-and-glass prison of rush hour traffic. Even now, miles from the city, he felt like a rabbit fleeing an invisible wolf.

"It is quite bad, but we manage. It is worse on the workdays. Much worse." The driver turned his attention back to the road.

I forgot, it's Sunday! I've been making a fool of myself for so long now, and it's affecting everything I do. What was I expecting when we were in Bangalore? Was Simirita going to come jumping after me, leaping from car roof to car roof naked? Maybe she would have punched in the rear window and yanked me out of the car? I've watched too many action movies. She's not even concerned about me anymore.

She got her money.

He squeezed his carry-on bag tight to his side. The dollar bills she'd swapped for hundreds were an almost physical sensation through the sturdy material, a painful reminder of the need to be cautious when dealing with strangers. A high-class prostitute would have cost less, and there wouldn't have been any ridiculous drama about her being in cahoots with some sort of mystical enemy.

She had some sort of hallucinogen on her skin somewhere, and then she planted a suggestion when I was vulnerable. And I fell for it. I bet they're still laughing at the hotel. I bet they were in on it.

"Have you consumed him yet?" He had never felt so stupid in his life.

"This place you are going to, they are taking all of this you carry?" The driver's voice was conversational, pleasant.

"Not all of it, no. I'm bringing home a friend of mine to be with his family."

Elliot's eyes jumped from his bag to the boxes he had in the back seat with him. There were more in the front seat, and the trunk was full of them. Airport security had recovered everything. Just cheap urns and ashes, trinkets and clothing. The boxes held nothing with any real intrinsic value.

The value of the people those remains represented? Elliot suddenly wished he had acknowledged *that* when they had been alive.

The driver's head bobbed again, and his features softened and creased in sympathy, but he seemed uncomfortable carrying the boxes. He stroked a strange charm of green peppers and a small lemon dangling from his rearview mirror. "We should be there before much too long."

"Thanks." Elliot gently patted the box that held Praveen's ashes. It was plain white, wrapped with similarly white tape, and it sported a label with Praveen's name and the mansion's address, plus the address of his aunt's house.

Elliot wondered if Harrison Mansion had ever truly been home to Praveen. Elliot shoved away the thought and let his mind drift with the taxi's rocking.

He had hoped to sleep—truly sleep, not some drug-induced effect (in the light of day and wide awake, he was sure the whole thing with Simirita had been drugs, not magic)—before the drive. Instead, he felt drained, weakened. The countryside's peaceful and pleasant openness—pale brown soil, the occasional patch of shrubs, the less frequent but healthier groves: It all held a certain appeal. Praveen's calm and gentle personality seemed a natural byproduct of such a place, even though he had hinted at problems.

Bangalore seemed chaotic and far too busy to attract someone like Praveen, but the countryside was welcoming enough.

Elliot wondered what could have driven Praveen away. It could've been a single event, or it could've been the accumulation of years of anger. Of course, there were the scars on Praveen's hands, and his reluctance to discuss his youth in India was one of those cases of silence being every bit as telling as words.

There had obviously been violence. More importantly, Praveen had implied he'd been an outsider until he'd reached the mansion.

A memory came to Elliot, and he dug into the pouch of his carry-on. It held three pendants on simple gold chains, the pendants of those he was taking to their homes. He'd thought them lost as evidence. Discovering them at the bottom of the last box had been a pleasant surprise.

The pendants were the same: a gold circle with twelve equidistant, colored quartz crystals. Each pendant had a different, larger stone set at the top, each associated with a specific shaman. Neda's was a cool sapphire, Ms. Nakama's a pink topaz.

Praveen's stone looked like a ruby.

Stone had taken the time to break each of the chains, but he'd left them, even though the gold was easily worth two hundred dollars. It was the only valuable item on any of the bodies.

Elliot examined Praveen's pendant. He had intertwined his own simple, brass necklace around the gold chain. It was simple, functional work, not some sort of masterful jeweler's handiwork. The brass necklace held an even cruder, polished stone.

After a final glance at the polished stone, Elliot stuffed the chain into his shirt pocket and set the others back in his bag.

Grandpa William had once said Mangas had envisioned the mansion someday being home to twelve mystics from around the world. There had even always been fourteen rooms, although they had never been full. It was an ambitious plan, even at the turn of the century. Even then, the belief in magic was dying out. It was just getting worse now.

With Grandpa William's death, Mangas's dream would never be fulfilled.

Elliot pulled his glasses off and took his handkerchief from his pocket, then he slowly cleaned the lenses and the frames, rubbing away the last residue of Simirita and the humiliating incident at the hotel.

Before, caution had always been his watchword, something he'd been proud of. He had a future, a career, and he wasn't about to risk that. There had been a chance once with Tessa, and he'd chickened out at the end. All he had been able to think about was what would happen if he got her pregnant or if they got caught? And now? One foolish night, one imprudent act, and he had come close to losing all of his travel money, possibly the belongings of his friends, maybe even his life.

Of course, the fact that Simirita somehow knew to target him, knew about his association with magic, somehow sensed his attraction and emphasized her similarities to Neda—all of that still bothered him.

The taxi slowed, and a moment later the driver turned off the road and onto a private dirt path. Elliot took in what he could of the property. In the near distance, he could make out a large, wooden house. It looked old but solid, and it was surrounded by groves—areca nut, mango, and eucalyptus, according to Praveen's Aunt Rabia.

Elliot had never heard of areca nut until Praveen had described them and their importance in India, so Elliot knew what they looked like. He'd even tasted one, surprised to find it wasn't a nut at all, but similar to a mango.

A sharp pang of sadness hit as he suddenly realized he would never have another afternoon of sitting around the dining room table discussing Indian food with Praveen.

So much had been lost.

The taxi slowed. The driver seemed agitated, his brow wrinkled, his eyes darting. His face quivered, and his mouth began to move soundlessly. Finally, he stopped.

Elliot looked around for any sign of something amiss. "Is the address wrong?"

Everything looked pretty much like he'd expected based off the description Rabia had given over the phone. Here and there, ribbons of bright cloth fluttered in a gentle breeze, most marked with familiar symbols: swastikas—Hindu, not the corrupted Nazi form—and cross potents. He even saw an ankh.

What set him off?

A small lizard scurried across the windshield. The driver seemed transfixed by it.

Elliot leaned forward to examine the lizard more closely; it was unremarkable, but it held the driver's complete attention.

"Is there something wrong?"

The driver shook his head emphatically. He was shaking, his eyes bugging out. "I cannot go any more." He pointed to the lizard and the ribbons blowing in the breeze and muttered something under his breath.

"It's at least a hundred yards to the house," Elliot protested. "I have to carry three boxes." It wasn't the boxes or the walk that worried him, but the possibility the frightened driver might take off with the rest of the boxes.

"I am sorry." The driver's shaking continued; his eyes widened.

"But—"

As if sensing Elliot's suspicion, the driver held up his hands, then pointed to the ground beneath the taxi. "I will wait. Here. You can put your things from the boot onto the ground if you want, but I will not leave without you."

Even through the fog of fatigue, Elliot could see there was no changing the driver's mind. "All right."

They quickly unpacked the trunk and set the boxes carefully on a patch of dry soil. When they were done, Elliot offered the driver half of the fare, but he would have none of it.

"I will wait here. You will not pay until I have returned you to the city." The driver crossed his arms for emphasis.

Elliot sighed, resigned to another moment of seemingly random, incongruous, and inexplicable strangeness and the inevitable aftereffects. Even the lizard, the apparent source of the driver's near breakdown, had disappeared. Elliot hefted his carry-on bag and the three boxes and began the slow walk to the house. Sand swirled up from the path in a pale, brown cloud as he walked, for a time matching his course, then disappearing.

Elliot remembered the dust devil at the mansion the morning he'd left. Watching the trailing cloud, he felt like he was being observed somehow. The notion sent a shiver down his spine.

Halfway to the house, Elliot saw someone exit the front door. It looked like a woman, her long hair whipped around in the breeze. She wore a bright coral robe, a *ghagra choli*, from what Praveen had described—a long, pleated skirt that seemed thicker and heavier at the bottom, with a lighter, short-sleeved, low-necked blouse and what amounted to a loose vest.

Elliot picked up his pace and glanced back to confirm the taxi was still waiting for him.

As the woman neared, Elliot could see the wrinkles on her face, the way she carried herself: confident, proud. She reminded him of Praveen.

She stopped and allowed Elliot to cross the last few steps. "Elliot Saganash." Her voice was dull, her accent less noticeable in person. When he set the boxes down and extended a hand, she took it. She looked at the taxi in the distance, then she looked back at Elliot, her expression unchanged. "I am Rabia, Praveen's aunt. We talked."

"Thank you for letting me come by so early." He pointed back at the taxi. "The driver refused to come—"

"Superstitions." Rabia picked up the box with Praveen's ashes, everything about her almost dismissive. "Thank you for this. You could have shipped these things."

These things. He was your nephew. "I thought it would be safer to bring them."

Rabia glanced at him skeptically; it was the first reaction she'd shown. "Was it?"

Elliot shivered at the awareness that flashed across her eyes. "I don't really know. I guess. Anyway, I also wanted to offer my condolences for your loss. Praveen told me you let him stay here several years before he moved to the United States. He spoke highly of you. I'm not sure why he would leave. He always sounded like he missed you."

"Praveen was a good young man. He was an even greater mystic." Rabia gathered up the other boxes. "This place is nothing like Rajasthan. That is his home state—where he grew up. He was never happy here. To achieve *moksha*, it was necessary for him to go there, to the United States. To meet you."

"*Moksha?*" Elliot looked back at the taxi, wondering what the driver was doing and what superstition kept him from coming any closer to the house. *He couldn't possibly have picked up the strange vibe Rabia was giving off from so far back, could he?*

"The end of the cycle of the spirit being reborn."

"Oh. I didn't realize he was Hindu." Elliot shrank as Rabia stared at him, somehow managing to judge him without showing the slightest emotion. "Reincarnation, right?"

"There are ways much older than any of the Hindu traditions," Rabia said after a time. "Hindu is not a single way. It is from many old beliefs, many of them forced together by a desire to create a unified system. *Moksha* came before any of the religions that use it—Hinduism, Jainism, Sikhism. I would have thought Praveen would discuss this with you."

Elliot licked his lips and adjusted his glasses, suddenly feeling awkward and unwanted. "He might have. Honestly, I've never had a head for religion. I'm sorry if that offends you. I mean to get better about it. Losing Praveen helped me to appreciate the value of that sort of thing."

Rabia's wrinkles deepened and settled into new patterns, signaling the slightest hint of disappointment. "Praveen had said he was seeking someone to learn his ways. I thought you were the one."

Elliot thought back to the lessons Praveen had taught him. They certainly could have been leading him down the path to whatever Praveen's beliefs were, but the focus had always been on process, logic, and knowledge. "Praveen had been trying to get an apprentice for a few years, but…I think he was having a hard time with it."

Rabia shrugged her shoulders; the discussion was over. There may have been the slightest hint of sadness in her eyes. "Those in power resist the old ways. Praveen knew it would be hard to find someone from here to follow him." She studied Elliot intensely for a moment. "You said he was killed by a man who hated him for being from India? Why?"

It was Elliot's turn to shrug. He couldn't hope to explain the heritage of some of his mother's European people. "Not because he was from India, but because he wasn't white. The killer is a Nazi, I guess." Elliot pointed to one of the fluttering ribbons, where he could see a swastika on the material. "The picture I saw of him, he had a swastika tattooed on his chest. A Nazi one, not like yours. He killed my grandfather, someone from Africa, someone from the Philippines, someone from Japan, another person from Peru, and someone from Iran. It's just a sickness, I guess, a hatred for anyone different."

The sadness earlier hinted at became clearer on Rabia's face. "That is a troubled one, but he is just a vessel. They are always nothing more than vessels."

Elliot's mouth dropped at the realization that Rabia felt sorry not for the loss of Praveen but for Glen Stone. "There's no reason to feel sorry for him. He's not a vessel—he's a murderer. When they find him, they'll put him away."

"Not this one. Not the one you know. No. He is the result of what we are becoming. He cannot be put away."

"The result …" Elliot suddenly wondered if Rabia was even sane.

"We have turned from the old ways. We claim we have turned our backs on false gods, but look around you. The gods we worship are money, power, status, *things*." She held up a hand and made a strange sign. "And while people worship their false gods, the powers of old move among us unseen: *daevas, raksha—*."

She stopped suddenly and stepped away from Elliot, looking to her left at a patch of shadows beneath a eucalyptus tree. Elliot turned to see what she was looking at, but he couldn't make out anything.

"Rabia?"

Rabia's face became rigid, completely unmoving other than her trembling mouth. She slowly bowed toward the tree. "I will have no part in this struggle." Her voice was raised, as if she spoke to someone else, someone he couldn't see.

Good grief, she's insane. Elliot dug in his shirt pocket for Praveen's pendant. "I have to get going, but I wanted to give you this. It meant a good deal to Praveen."

He might as well have held up a grenade with its pin pulled.

Rabia backed away, her eyes bugging out. "I will have no part in this struggle." She looked at the eucalyptus tree again and shouted the words at the shadows, louder than before, then she shouted at the tree in Hindi. She hastily set the boxes down and ran for the house, more animated than at any time during the discussion.

Elliot watched her go, stunned. He turned to make sure the taxi was still waiting. The driver was leaning against the vehicle. When he saw Elliot looking back, the driver waved excitedly. Elliot stepped toward the vehicle, then stopped for a moment, curious what Rabia could have seen in the eucalyptus tree that so disturbed her. He stepped toward the tree and froze when something moved in the shadows beneath it.

Thirty, maybe forty feet separated Elliot from the tree, but the shape of the thing was distinct and unmistakable. A cobra reared up; its hood flared wide.

It watched Elliot's every move.

Elliot edged toward the taxi, and the cobra matched his movement. Elliot stepped back from the tree, and the cobra moved toward him, stopping at the edge of the shade. Elliot stepped back again; the cobra didn't move.

The gentle breeze intensified, and the leaves above the cobra rustled, plucking the shadow cover from the cobra's head. It backed up, but not before Elliot saw its head clearly.

Elliot ran for the taxi, only risking a single glance back. When he was close enough, he shouted for the driver to load the boxes. Elliot never took his eyes off the dirt road until the taxi was packed and they were back on State Highway 58. He watched the highway until they were well away and the house had faded once again into dust and the heat shimmer.

The whole time, all he could think about was the *impossibility* of the cobra.

The cobra's face had a vaguely human shape to it, and the eyes in that face had been Simirita's clear, hazel eyes.

Chapter Fourteen

S ensations came at Tammy in random bits and pieces. The car ride was darkness and movement and Tessa's candy-like perfume. It was the only pleasant memory Tammy could recall. After the ride, there were bad smells—musty and moldy, the pungent stench of urine and vomit. And there were sounds—crude voices, harsh laughter, pathetic crying, a distant engine running. And there was the heat and humidity and the hard surface she slept on.

Her eyes opened a few times, and she managed to get the vaguest look at things in the darkness: a small room, bands of black mold in dim, indirect light, stained blankets.

Once again, she couldn't get her brain to put things in any sort of meaningful order. Sometimes, she became aware, and she was being carried across a dying, weed-covered lawn. Sometimes, Blue Collar was there, squatting next to her, holding her clothes bunched in his hands, just staring, like he was some sort of ultra-creep robot. Sometimes, Tessa was beside her, sometimes Tessa was a pillow, but most of the time, everything echoed like a weak transmission from another world.

Tammy imagined she saw two other people besides Adonis and Blue Collar. One was a skinny, acne-faced, tattooed rat with thinning, dark, greasy hair that was pulled back in a ridiculous ponytail. He was pierced everywhere, and his eyes were a pale brown that reminded Tammy of the amber of a rich, colorful honey. His outfit consisted of a fraying, black T-shirt, tattered jeans, and scuffed-up combat boots rigged up with small chains that jingled cheerfully when he walked. He was shorter than Tessa, and if he weighed a buck-fifty, it was because he was carrying rocks in his pockets. The other guy was a terror. He looked like one of those computer animation creations— taller than anyone she'd ever seen, bulging, vein-covered muscles, and a broad forehead with a jutting eyebrow ridge. Tammy could almost see the guy in a superhero movie, knocking over buildings and throwing cars around. He had blond hair, also greasy and pulled back into a ponytail, but combined with small, gold, hoop earrings in each ear; the ponytail really worked for him. Tammy guessed he was fairly old, probably in his early thirties. He gave off that vibe of roid rage danger while also being sexually alluring.

Sort of. For an old guy.

At one point, Tammy finally had a moment of lucidity. There was a sudden sense of time passing, moving as normal, and she became more aware of her surroundings. The moment of lucidity stretched into several, then it stretched even more. Someone had put her clothes back on. She was thirsty and needed to pee.

And she was bound. Something thin bit into her wrists, keeping them pinned behind her. She guessed it was a nylon restraining zip tie. After all her run-ins with the law, she knew what those felt like.

She opened her eyes and looked around without moving her head. There was more light around her now than she remembered from before, enough to reveal a bare, wood floor with protruding staples and nails. She was lying on a bed of stained blankets, the source of the vomit and urine smells. Her eyes lazily moved around, and she made out a doorframe that led into a hallway mostly lit by something bright and next to the blankets, what looked like an older LED camping lantern. On the wall opposite the doorway, there were two windows taped over with something black and heavy. Her feet were pointed at a third window. Weak light leaked around the edges of the blocking material.

She didn't know if that meant the next morning was approaching or if she'd lost more time than that. What she did know was that she needed to escape.

She closed her eyes and drifted off for a short period. Or longer.

When she woke again, it was darker. The big guy came into the room. He was a giant, dressed in a T-shirt that seemed to have been painted on and a Speedo. Somewhere behind her, Tessa moaned. The giant stared at Tammy, as if she were a piece of meat. In the Speedo, Tammy couldn't help but notice that the giant actually *was* a giant. He was hung like a horse. He sucked on his bottom lip and nodded appreciatively. "Hey, Eric! Good selections this time around. Great body, great face on this one."

Adonis stepped into the doorway. He now wore a tan-colored T-shirt that had a faded logo on it. So close to the giant, Adonis—Eric—seemed small, his muscular body minuscule. "She's the one who made this happen. I thought Butterface there wouldn't be ..." He shrugged uncertainly.

The Giant snorted dismissively. Whether from the drugs or real, his voice and every sound he made seemed deep and gravelly, like thunder rolling through a cave. "We'll get buyers, don't worry. Hey, when you do the credits? Make her Big Momma." He reached past Tammy and slapped Tessa's butt hard. "That's catchy, huh? And this one can be Amazon Queen. Tell Darren I'll be ready for them in a few minutes. The little one's comin' around, so might as well shoot her up now, too."

Shoot me up? Tammy cast a groggy glance at Tessa. Her lids were open, but only barely. It was enough to see the glazed, faraway look in her eyes.

Fuck! Probably heroin.

Tammy looked at the giant and muttered, "I'm only sixteen, asshole."

Or at least that was what she tried to say. It came out all wrong, although *asshole* was intelligible.

A smile slowly slinked across the giant's face, and he squatted until his face was close enough for Tammy to slap had her hands not been bound. His breath was foul, like he'd completely forgotten how to brush his teeth somewhere in his twenties. "You just call me an asshole? You got one with spirit, Eric?"

"Yeah, she's got spunk." Blue Collar stood in the doorway next to Eric now, still wearing what he'd worn from the kidnapping. He was chewing on a fingernail, staring at her curiously. "She took the cup right out of Eric's hand when he was picking up a couple other sluts."

"Worked out for the better." Eric knelt down to examine Tessa. The way he looked at her was clinical, detached, without any hint of concern. "Shit, Leighton, I think she's on cruise."

The giant—Leighton—flexed his huge shoulders and thick chest as he stood. "Yeah. They'll both be a while coming down after we're done. I'll drop them downtown t'morrow."

Eric raised an eyebrow as if to say, "Seriously?" He glanced at Blue Collar. Blue Collar didn't seem to catch the look.

Tammy tried to push away the fog from whatever Eric had given her at the rave, but it clung to her. Eric's reaction was the first hint she'd picked up that something more was going on than just a kidnap and rape, as if that weren't fucked-up enough. "I'm sixteen, goddammit."

This time, she made sense. Mostly. Her tongue was coming around.

Leighton laughed. It wasn't necessarily taunting, but it stung. "Okay, we'll go with Little Amazon Queen. You'll be a good change-up. Those fuckin' college girls can be loose, y'know? Your friend here know you're sixteen?"

"Her—" Tammy nearly choked on saliva. She coughed, then swallowed. "Cops are…looking for us."

Leighton smirked at Eric. "They always are, aren't they?"

"No. Serious. The Memorial Day …" She lost her thread for a moment. *Fuck! Memorial Day. Memorial Day…we went dancing. Things went to hell.*

"Big party, huh? Lots o' cops there?" Leighton patted himself. "We'll have a party soon, don't you worry. No cops, just the three of us. And Eric 'n' Walt here behind the camera. You like cameras, Little Amazon Princess?"

Tammy shook her head in frustration. She was getting a stronger vibe off of Leighton now, even through the haze of the drugs, and it was big-time creepy. Worse than creeposaurus rex. Creepzilla-level creepy. She already knew everything was fucked up in the situation, but she didn't think being shot up with heroin and filmed being raped would be where it ended. Not with the impressions she was getting from him. "Memorial Day…Killer."

"Fuck." Eric looked at Tammy, *really* looked at her. "I thought I'd seen her somewhere before."

Leighton shrugged uncertainly. "What?"

Walt finally pulled his finger from his mouth. "Yeah! That *is* her. I *knew* it!"

Leighton glared at Walt. "You *knew* what?"

Walt stepped back, intimidated. "That I'd seen her before. It was all over the news a week ago. Somebody wiped out, like, I don't know, ten people?" He gave Eric a pleading look.

"Nine." Eric stood and brushed his hands on his pants. "She's older than in the photograph they showed on the news, but that's her."

"She killed nine people?" Leighton let out a booming laugh. Suddenly, he stopped laughing and became deadly serious. "Don't fuck around with me, y'get that? A skinny thing like that don't kill nine people."

Walt held up a hand to calm Leighton. "N-no. Shit. She's one of the survivors. There were two of them."

"Both foreigners, Leighton." Eric looked her over slowly, once again purely clinical and detached. "I would have guessed she was Mexican just looking at her last night. Apparently, she's African."

"So?" Leighton seemed to really be working his way into a serious fury, but he wasn't directing it at anyone yet. "Why's that matter?"

"One of the news reports speculated the case might go to the FBI because it was a hate crime. You know, lots of pissed off foreign embassies."

Walt pointed a shaking finger at Eric. "Yeah. FBI."

Leighton seemed to consider the idea that the FBI might be looking for Tammy, and his mood seemed to sour even more. After a minute, he began pacing the enclosed space. Walt and then Eric took the opportunity to move closer to the door.

Finally, Leighton exploded, abruptly punching the nearest wall. His fist easily broke through the moldy plaster and drywall. He pivoted onto Eric, mouth pulled back in a snarl, his thin lips connected by a spiderweb of spit. "Why the *fuck* did you get the FBI involved?"

Eric shrank back.

Tammy could feel fear radiating from Walt, but Eric just seemed to be…pragmatic? Like he knew provoking Leighton was stupid, but he wasn't necessarily frightened of him.

What the fuck, Eric? You all kung fu master?

The dynamic between the three—something she could never have perceived before Daysi's concoction—was slowly unfolding. It would have come to her easier without the drugs in her system, she was sure, but even what she was getting was helpful. The Three Creepos weren't a simple alpha and two subservient puppies, and there was a fourth out there somewhere— Darren? The acne jingle chains guy? She could barely sense him, but that was all she could do at the moment.

"Why not ..." Tammy's head throbbed, and her tongue and lips simply refused to cooperate. "Why not just...let us go? Just...walk away and...leave us here?"

Leighton turned his fury onto Tammy. "You stupid cunt! Stupid!" He reached for her as if he intended to lift her by her throat.

"We don't have good enough makeup to cover serious bruising," Eric said. His voice was calm, matter-of-fact. "And I doubt you have necrophilia fetishists lined up. Right? Leighton?"

Tammy shivered at what Eric's tone implied. She still couldn't get a good read on him, which might very well say a lot. *What do they call that? Psychopath? Sociopath? Psychotic? Fucked up, that's for sure.* Leighton's emotions and body language were raw and oversized. Roid rage wasn't the only thing driving him. She could sense desperation just beneath the surface. Not fear of arrest as much as ...

What? If he got caught, he was looking at dozens of years, easily. Rape, kidnapping, based on the way he was pegging out the Creepometer, murder. Injecting someone with heroin against their will? That had to be some time, too.

If he's not afraid of all the time he'd be facing, then what the hell has him so scared?

She didn't need Daysi's drugs to know how to push buttons. She'd always been good at that. "You can't...make money in...prison. That's what you...need. Right? Money?"

"Shut the hell up, bitch." Leighton cocked his hand back to slap her, but he stopped himself. He looked at Eric. "Fuck it. Get the credits done. I'm ready. Darren! Darren, get your fuckin' needle!"

The needle. I can't let him shoot me up.

Leighton shoved past Eric and Walt and stormed into the hallway outside the room. Tammy listened to his booming footsteps until a door closed somewhere down the hall.

Tammy tried to focus on Eric's face. Everything she was picking up off of him—the clinical detachment, the complete lack of empathy, and even reasonable fear—left her confident she couldn't easily reach him. She hoped not to have to.

"Guys, your friend…he's crazy."

Although a knowing, almost evil smile slipped over Eric's face, Walt's eyes said everything Tammy needed to know. He was well aware of the risks he was taking being around Leighton. And possibly Eric.

"You think…you think he's gonna…let you live? You could …" She couldn't remember the word. *Identify? Imply? Implicate!* "Implicate him in…how many murders?"

Eric gave a casual shrug. "He owes us money."

Walt licked his lips. "She's right. It's the coke and whatever he's shooting up."

Tammy heard the cheerful jingling of chains.

"That's his cocktail. He—he don't do smack." The grimy junkie—Darren Jinglechains—said from the doorway. *The guy with the fucking needle.*

Darren had a small jar about a quarter full of clear liquid, what looked like a stovetop burner cover, and a small box in his hands. Walt moved out of the way, and the junkie settled on the floor next to Tammy. After putting the burner cover over the small jar, he looked up at Walt. "He hates needles, see? So—so, I have to give him his in—injections."

Eric gave Walt a long stare, then looked out into the hallway; Walt stepped out of the room. Eric looked back at the junkie. "HIV?"

HIV? He's got AIDS? Shit! Can this get any worse? She looked over at Tessa. Tammy couldn't even tell if Tessa was breathing.

Tammy turned back to Darren. "Drugs…can interact …"

"S-sure, yeah!" The junkie leaned in close to Tammy and laughed manically, exposing bleeding gums and rotting teeth caked with yellow and brown stains. His breath was like rotten eggs. Closer in, a dozen small, black abscesses and a few more scabs were visible on his forearms.

"Hey, Darren? Is it HIV?" Eric was putting on his charming, friendly act now, all smiles and warmth.

It made Tammy's skin crawl, but it was effective, and she needed something effective.

"Y-yeah. Got it shooting a porn down in Rio. Waited three years t-to get into the b-business. Some b-big break, huh?" Darren shook his head, and it suddenly became clear: the ponytail, taking care of Leighton, the admiration in every word…he was in love with the giant.

Tammy wondered just how blind Darren was to what was going on. "You're his nurse?"

"Yeah! S-see, he lets me have some of his m-medicine. T-to take care of me and p-pay me back." As he talked, Darren set a spoon on top of the contraption, then adjusted the strange, metal lid on the jar. The smell of rubbing alcohol became noticeable. "W-we go way back. I helped him in chemistry back in h-high school. B-biology, too."

"So…you're friends?" Tammy looked at Eric, who seemed to be taking a lot of entertainment from the exchange. Where Darren was suddenly excited about discussing his closeness to Leighton, all she could feel from Eric was the same detachment.

"Oh, g-great friends, yeah." Darren pulled out a Zippo and tried to light the alcohol. "He g-got me laid. In h-high school."

Tammy watched Eric for a reaction, but he just seemed to take everything in as if she and Darren were lab rats. "That…means a lot…that first time."

"Y-yeah." The alcohol vapor caught fire. Darren set the lighter on top of the box and became caught up in adjusting it to a relatively narrow, blue flame.

"You…would do anything…for him?"

"W-we're bros. Yeah."

Darren was giving off gushy, overpowering feelings. Leighton was a big brother, maybe even a father figure. He wasn't going to turn against Leighton, not all at once.

"Darren…I gotta pee."

"S-sure, after I g-give you the shot."

As she tried to think everything through, Darren opened the box and pulled out several things: a long rubber hose, a grimy silk scarf, a syringe, a small squeeze bottle, a rusty modeling knife, and a zip bag with a dark, brown paste in it. He carefully set the syringe and knife on the silk scarf, then he unzipped the bag and squeezed a small amount of the paste onto the spoon, severing the paste with the knife. He resealed the bag, set the knife down, then squeezed a little fluid from the squeeze bottle onto the spoon with the paste.

Tammy stared at the syringe with fascination and dread. As far as she could tell, it was just a common disposable, the sort used for vaccinations. It was covered in brown stains she imagined were blood.

"Don't you have…another needle?"

"J-just Lucky here."

Lucky? Are you fucking kidding me? Probably the one he got AIDS off of. I can't let him stick me with that. "Well, maybe…you could sterilize…it?"

Darren nodded enthusiastically. "W-with the f-flame."

Walt reentered the room, a small, black gym bag in his hand. He walked past Darren and set the bag down in the far corner.

Eric seemed to take sudden interest in everything Darren was doing. "Hey, Darren, maybe you should use bleach. I doubt that flame is going to get hot enough to sterilize anything."

"D-don't got bleach."

Eric gave Tammy a sad smile and shrugged his shoulders apologetically, then he stepped back to stand beside Walt. Tammy could sense Walt's excitement and anxiousness, and she thought she could see him pass something to Eric. Eric's calm demeanor never changed.

There's something seriously wrong with him. Walt's acting like it's about to go nuclear, and Eric's all mellow. If they're going to mess with Leighton, they better have a flamethrower hidden somewhere.

Tammy strained to watch the spoon. She could see the fluid bubbling now, turning brown. She'd never actually seen anyone inject heroin, but she was pretty sure it wouldn't go into the vein while it was still bubbling. That meant she had a little time yet—however long it took for the spoon to cool.

"Darren?" She shifted so that she could get an elbow beneath her and look into Darren's eyes. The room stank now with so many *wrong* odors, that she was surprised she didn't throw up. "You ever wonder…what it might…y'know, what it might…well, to be cured?"

Darren looked at her, for a moment just staring into her eyes, then looking at her body. It amped up the creepy factor, but it was a little late to get freaked out about having him check her out. She'd almost certainly been naked around all four of them while unconscious, and as far as she could tell, they hadn't violated her. She didn't offer any sort of mystery anymore.

"Y-yeah."

"Wouldn't…you like that? Get off…the junk." She wished with all her might she had learned how to do a binding. Praveen and William Big Bear both had tried to teach her how to interact with the spirits, but she had just never *felt* it. Jeddo had promised her she would one day feel the *baraka* instinctively and learn to use them against *djinn* and people, but that day had never come. "Maybe you could…start today?"

A door slammed open somewhere, and Leighton's voice boomed down the hallway. "Darren! You stick that skinny bitch yet? I can hear her talking, and I don't need that. You know I hate it when bitches talk!"

"Jus-just a few more m-minutes." Darren shuddered as Leighton's footsteps echoed down the hallway again.

Leighton stopped at the doorway and leaned against the doorframe, gripping the sides with his massive, powerful hands, and he fixed Tammy with a furious stare. "I'm gonna need you t'shut up. You think you c'n do that? Or am I gonna have to smack you around?"

Tammy returned the glare, furious at her impotence. It was as if every dysfunctional man in the world was bound and determined to fuck with her. "Can't get it…up with a…without …" *Fuck!*

It didn't matter. She got what she wanted.

Leighton stomped into the room. "Listen up, you little cunt. Unless you shut up, I'm gonna make a *special* video of you, okay? Go for a very special market that pays good money. And you ain't gonna like it. So how 'bout you shut up and maybe it won't be so bad?"

"About that video …" Eric sounded so calm and threatening, even Leighton froze.

Leighton straightened and turned on Eric. Veins bulged on Leighton's forehead, and his skin went a brilliant red. "Are you fucking threatening me, you little—" He took a step forward, then stopped abruptly when Eric and Walt pulled pistols from behind their backs. The pistols were black and squarish and scary as hell. Tammy guessed they were Glocks of some sort. That seemed to be the universal handgun.

"As I was saying, about that video…" Eric gave a smooth, polished smile.

"Yeah?" Leighton's face contorted, and the color lingered, but his feet didn't budge.

"We'll need our cut of the money before we help. No more fucking around. If you're buying HIV drug cocktails, you're burning through a *lot* of money. That means you can pay us."

Leighton turned slowly to glare at Darren, then turned back to Eric. "I told you before, *Eric*, I ain't got the cash yet. A lot of this stuff I gotta sell on commission. It takes time to move. You gotta be careful about your buyers."

"You're buying drugs, okay. That's money right there." Walt stepped closer and pushed his gun up into Leighton's chest.

"You're fuckin' pissing me off, kid. Your hands are shaking. Gun might go off. Then what? You got no money."

"Walt, back off." Once Walt had stepped away from Leighton, Eric shifted to his left slightly, getting some distance from both Walt and Leighton.

Tammy felt a change in the tension, as if a threshold had been crossed and decisions made. Leighton was shaking with rage, but he had two guns pointed at his chest. Walt was on edge, terrified, but ready to finish the whole thing.

Eric? He just seemed calm, cold.

Tammy figured she had about a 50/50 shot if Darren or Walt came out of the situation alive. Walt seemed sweet on her. Sort of. Mostly, he seemed to be a follower, not a leader. She could manipulate him. Same with Darren. She couldn't make heads or tails of Eric, but she was leaning toward him being some sort of serial killer wannabe, like Leighton's understudy.

And Leighton? Leighton was a desperate businessman who wanted to shoot her up and violate her on video. She was pretty sure the end result of that was a shallow grave somewhere.

"I want my money, Leighton, and I want it tonight." Eric's voice was cool.

Leighton slowly flexed his muscles. "I'll have to—"

A booming knock echoed down the hallway. Tammy started to scream, but she saw Eric point his gun at her and shake his head.

A smirk slowly spread across Leighton's face. "Looks like we got a decision t' make."

The knock came again, louder than the first time.

Leighton tilted his head and looked at Eric. "You're makin' the calls now, *Eric*. You got the gun and all."

Eric pointed at the wall. "Back up against that wall. Darren, go invite our visitor in. If it's a cop, our decision's made for us. Agreed?"

Leighton nodded.

Eric crossed his arms, hiding his gun in his left armpit. Walt did the same. After a minute, Darren's voice came down the hallway. Tammy could hear another man's voice: deep, raspy, tired. She imagined an older man, probably a chain smoker. Not Elliot. Not the kind of person who could rescue her. She could sense it from the others; they felt the same.

Darren stepped into the room, and a shadow filled the hallway behind him. "Th-this guy wants t-to cut a deal with you. For the pretty one."

Eric cocked an eyebrow at Leighton, who seemed ready to burst out laughing at the absurdity. "Sure," Eric said. "Bring him in. We'll listen to any offers."

The shadow stretched, and a man stepped into the room. He wore a gray cotton hoodie and loose jeans, and what looked like generic sneakers. He seemed about Elliot's height and build, and for a second Tammy hoped Elliot had somehow made it back from his travels and found her.

She knew better.

The man's hands were shoved into the hoodie's pockets, pockets too small to hide a meaningful weapon. He slowly pulled those hands out and showed them, palms forward, to the others. "It's a good offer, y'all can bet on it."

Tammy nearly peed all over herself at the sound of the man's voice so close. The voice from her nightmares.

The man reached up and pulled the hoodie down revealing his shaved head. Tattoos covered his neck.

Glen Stone had found her.

Chapter Fifteen

Bandar Abbas International Airport baked in the early afternoon sun, threatening to boil the asphalt of the tarmac. Elliot's flight had arrived in the late morning, the plane's passengers spilling out in *chador, burqa,* and *thobes.* Seen through the shaded glass of the terminal, the outside world seemed to shimmer and ripple. Inside, the airport terminal was a choking mixture of accumulated filth and sweat, and the sound system blared distorted, headache-inducing recorded messages in Arabic and Persian and broken English. Even before exiting the plane, Elliot was ready to simply collapse for a day or two. Now, he wanted Tylenol and a tall bottle of cold water, maybe a cold shower.

He was processing through customs, leaning against the luggage cart his boxes were resting on, when two uniformed men—airport security—approached him. One was nearly as tall as Elliot but chubby; the other was short and thin. Elliot couldn't be sure, but it seemed like the short one had a greater sense of authority, or maybe the taller one didn't care.

The short one considered Elliot's luggage cart for what seemed to be at least a minute, then fixed his dark eyes on Elliot and said, "You will come with us."

They wandered the steaming halls until Elliot was ready to collapse. When they reached the airport security office on the eastern side of the terminal, it immediately became clear that the two weren't airport security; they were Revolutionary Guard.

Posters of the Revolutionary Guard fighting godless infidels covered the office walls. Black-framed sheets of paper covered in Persian script—Elliot was pretty sure it was religious exhortations—filled the open gaps.

Neda had talked many times about the horrors the revolution had brought to Iran, stories she'd heard from her mother and other minorities.

Elliot was living through one of those horrors now.

The two guardsmen told Elliot where to set his belongings, then they settled behind gray, metal desks and stared. Sweat stains and salt rings provided a bizarre camouflage pattern for their faded, olive drab uniforms. They were unshaved, as ragged looking as their uniforms.

The office was miserably hot and cramped, its furniture vintage World War II surplus: dull, torn green-gray vinyl held together with duct tape. A single, ancient computer terminal blinked its white cursor at Elliot.

At the guardsmen's direction, Elliot carefully set out Neda's and Ms. Nakama's boxes and his own luggage, then he sat in the only other chair. It was an uncomfortable wooden thing bristling with splinters.

The chubby guardsman stood and pulled a pocketknife from his pants. He opened the blade slowly and held it so that Elliot could see it, then cut the boxes open and unzipped the luggage.

The whole time, the short one watched Elliot with hopeful eyes.

After an exchange of looks with his short partner, the chubby guardsman roughly rummaged through the luggage and the boxes. When he found Neda's urn, he opened it and tentatively sniffed the contents.

Elliot nearly lunged at that point.

The short one seemed to sense they'd found a limit with their guest. He said something, and his partner returned the urn to its box, struggling for a moment with the lid's catch, then settled into his desk chair to watch Elliot.

The two guardsmen spent several long minutes just looking at Elliot, then occasionally looked at each other before looking back at Elliot. Their faces were blank, emotionless. When they had their fill of that, they lit cigarettes and blew smoke at Elliot. He coughed, but he said nothing. When the cigarettes were done, they spoke to each other in Persian or Arabic—Elliot couldn't be sure.

It was a passive, lazy form of harassment.

"Um, do you think I might be able to go soon?"

There was a tense discussion between the two guardsmen, then the chubby one wheeled his squeaking, groaning chair back to the computer terminal.

The short one angrily turned back to Elliot. "You are American spy."

Not a question. Not a tease. It was an accusation.

Elliot blinked hard and gulped. He wasn't used to insanity from law enforcement types. Henriksen and Traxler had their annoying games, but they were rational, almost reasonable. "I'm Canadian—a member of the Cree First Nations—and I'm not a spy." *Damn it, I'm traveling on my Canadian passport. Why this harassment?*

"You flew from United States." The short one picked Elliot's itinerary up from the desktop and waved it accusingly before slapping it back down onto the desk.

"I came to deliver the remains of Neda Abadi to her mother, Iryana Abadi."

The short guard gave a dismissive wave. "Iryana Abadi is a spy and a *Kaffir*."

Kaffir. *Infidel. This place is just like Neda described it. It's overrun with religious intolerance, and not the haphazard, amateur crap practiced in America. That's just clueless arrogance. This is institutional and dangerous on a personal level.*

The chubby guard sneered.

"I have no political connections to anyone or anything or any nation." Elliot nodded at the boxes—his boxes—sitting a few feet away. "I'm returning the remains of my friends to their families. You've seen my passport and tickets."

"American spies, very clever." The short guardsman sat back in his chair and propped his scuffed and dusty boots on the desktop. The chubby guard said something Elliot couldn't understand, and the short guard wagged a finger. "And thorough."

Elliot sighed heavily. "Maybe a quick call to the Canadian embassy would clear this up?"

The short guardsman crossed his arms over his chest. "Phone lines are down."

"American drones," the chubby guardsman said in halting, barely understandable English.

Elliot sank in his chair and let his head drop into his hands. Even without the need to catch the next flight back to Dubai, he just wasn't in the frame of mind to deal with two clowns trying to intimidate him. "Well, then keep my luggage until I come back. I'll take nothing more than Neda's belongings and my carry-on bag."

The short guardsman looked at the ceiling, apparently considering the idea. "All right." He rose from his chair, which seemed to sigh in ecstasy, then stooped to inspect Elliot's carry-on bag. After digging around inside the bag for several seconds, the short guardsman pulled out the envelope that held Elliot's cash, holding it up in plain view. A toothy smile spread across the guardsman's face as he pulled several bills from the envelope and stuffed them in his left breast pocket.

Elliot seethed, but he said nothing.

The short guardsman patted his bulging pocket with smug satisfaction. "To be sure you return for your things."

A hushed conversation ensued between the guardsmen, then the chubby one escorted Elliot to an exit on the northern side of the terminal. The chubby guardsman stuck close by Elliot's side the whole time, twice grinning stupidly, but otherwise not reacting. Elliot couldn't help but wonder if Neda's experiences had been along the same line, if that might not have been a part of her motivation to leave.

Are we all outsiders, no matter where we live?

It hadn't cooled any during the interrogation. If anything, it was hotter than Elliot had imagined. A breeze hit him, and he understood what a convection oven must feel like.

They crossed a sand-covered parking lot, eventually coming to a stop beside a rusty, off-green Mitsubishi sedan with grime-smeared, sand-coated windows and bald tires. The driver's side window was open, and his head was down, as if he were napping. Despite being parked in a narrow strip of shade, the driver's brow was sweat-soaked.

The guardsman opened the rear passenger-side door for Elliot, and the driver jerked awake in his seat. The guardsman said something to the driver.

Whatever had been said, the driver nodded nervously. He started the car, gave the coughing engine a moment to catch, then put it into gear.

Elliot turned and watched through the grimy glass until dust and white clouds of exhaust blocked the chubby guard from view. In no time, the afternoon sun was baking the car's gray interior. The engine was a loud, erratic whine and rattle, a wall of noise accompanying the blinding sunlight. Combined with the rhythmic jostling and the occasional squeal of the struts, it was enough for Elliot to start nodding off.

Too quickly, Elliot was being shaken awake.

The driver was standing in the rear passenger-side doorway, leaning into the car. He said something, and Elliot saw they were at a house, a modest-sized, wood and mud brick building, almost an oversized shack. It looked simple, rundown. Gentle waves lapped the shoreline not fifty feet away. Small fishing boats were visible here and there, some pulled ashore, a few anchored in the relatively calm water.

A thin man in loose-fitting jeans and a bright-colored shirt stood in the front doorway. He was younger than Neda, but with a masculine slant to the same round face.

Caspar, her younger brother. Caspar angrily glared at the car.

And at Elliot.

Elliot shifted his carry-on bag onto his lap and clumsily slid out of the car. He pulled the two boxes that held Neda's remains and possessions from the backseat, then gently set them on the sandy ground. When he tried to offer the driver one of the remaining hundred dollar bills, the driver held up both hands and retreated back to his car.

"You have Neda?"

Elliot turned at the broken English, saw the anger still on Caspar's face. Elliot picked up the white box and reverentially handed it to Caspar. The anger turned to sadness as Caspar took the last of his sister, then he turned and disappeared into the house.

Elliot gathered up the box of Neda's belongings and stepped back as the car lurched forward and turned back onto the dirt road. It sped away in a cloud of dust and exhaust.

How am I supposed to get back to the airport?

He took an uncertain step toward the door where Caspar had disappeared, then halted at the sight of Neda—older, thinner, worn down by time—standing in the doorway. It was Neda's mother, Iryana. She was dressed in faded jeans and a blouse.

No burqa. No robes. *So much like Neda.*

"Mrs. Abadi?"

Iryana gestured for him to enter, then she too was gone, leaving only Elliot baking in the afternoon heat.

He stepped through the doorway.

The building exterior was deceptive. The interior was clean, relatively modern, and attractive. A small foyer led to a hallway that ran to Elliot's left and to an open doorway on his right. Sunlight lit the interior, revealing shelves lined with trinkets and astrological charts and walls lined with iconic symbology—an ancient swastika, smooth stones arrayed in a star pattern, a gold cross potent.

Elliot followed Iryana into the room on the right, a kitchen with simple wooden countertops, a small metal sink, a gas stove, and a small refrigerator. Instead of cabinets, the kitchen walls held shelves. Cups, dishes, glasses: everything was visible. A counter separated the kitchen from a small dining room with a bright wooden table and four matching chairs. To the left of the dining room was a larger room with pillows, an older television set, and a couple cloth-covered chairs.

Iryana came to a stop in the middle of the kitchen. "You look like you could use some tea?" She indicated a tin kettle next to the stovetop.

"Thanks." Elliot's sense of being an invader intensified. Iryana wasn't making him feel unwelcome, but the alien nature of the environment and the situation at the airport had combined with the fatigue to knock him off his center.

"Sit." Iryana pointed to the dining room.

Elliot settled into the chair facing the kitchen and sagged, and Iryana turned to watch him. She looked at the box Elliot had set on the tabletop, and after a moment, her hand went to her forehead. She pulled a cloth from her jeans and wiped her eyes.

"She said you would be the one," Iryana said around sobbing. It didn't help her accent.

Elliot straightened. *The one what?* "I'm sorry?"

"My Neda. She said *you* would bring her home to me." Iryana blew her nose and tried to regain her composure. Finally, she rinsed her face in the sink. That seemed to help. She turned and leaned against the counter. "She could see…things—the future, the true nature of a person. She saw her role and fate: to teach you. In America. And you…she saw who you are and what you will be. She was *magi*."

Iryana's words, the simple conviction behind them, made Elliot's skin crawl. *She could see the future and she knew her fate. Is it even faith when it's stated so matter-of-factly?*

He reached inside his shirt and pulled out the leather pouch he carried with him always. The cross behind the panel of leather anchored him for just a moment. "Neda was an exceptional person, Mrs. Abadi."

"Iryana. Neda told me enough; I know you like a son."

"Did she tell you I don't believe? In what she believed." Elliot blushed, but he had to know what Neda had told her mother.

Iryana nodded once, eyebrows arched. "You don't still, or do you?" She turned at the tea kettle's mournful whine. "She said you like mint tea."

"I—" Elliot flinched. He'd loved the tea Neda had made him, but he'd never actually told her that. It was the day she'd caught him staring at her legs in the Daisy Dukes. He'd been too embarrassed to talk with her when she'd tried to reach out to him, and they'd never really had the same sort of private moment again. "Yes."

Somehow, the tea's aroma settled Elliot's nerves. He waited until Iryana was seated and had taken a sip from her cup before he sipped his. Iryana watched him in silence for several seconds, then closed her eyes and smiled with a melancholy Elliot had never seen before, even after seeing so many lose so much. He thought she might simply collapse and die at that moment, but she didn't.

"When Neda was young—before she was a beautiful woman—" Iryana gave Elliot a knowing look at that moment. "She told her father one morning

180

he could not fish that day. She was ten, maybe eleven. It was hot, like this. Miserable. Her father laughed and kissed her on the head. He did not believe in her gift. His family was Muslim, and he thought our ways were silly. She cried when he did that, and she begged, but he went out. He almost took Caspar with him, but I would not let him." She glanced toward the other end of the house. "Caspar was just a baby."

"What happened?" Elliot breathed in the tea's aroma and recalled Neda's gentle, patient eyes. Iryana had the eyes, but the twinkle, the energy that so clearly defined Neda, wasn't there. *Had it ever been? Was it snuffed out when Neda died?*

"A storm came from nowhere and took him and two other men." Iryana bowed her head. "Neda felt when he died."

"I'm sorry." Elliot wondered if magic always carried such a price: Everyone seemed to lose family and loved ones if they took the path. *And for what? To what end? It's as pointless as me coming here. I'm not helping them. I don't know what I was thinking taking this trip. There's no healing to be done. I need to get back to the airport, catch a nap, deal with the security goons.*

Iryana brushed aside Elliot's concern. "It was nearly twenty years ago." She poked around in the box of Neda's belongings, looking at jewelry and other trinkets Elliot had packed.

"I wasn't sure what you would consider most important to remember her by." Elliot felt horribly embarrassed. What he'd packed was mostly what carried memories for him: fancy earrings, a pretty platinum ring with a sapphire stone that Neda seemed to treasure, a tray of makeup, a simple gold necklace he had given her one winter holiday. It all seemed so impractical and selfish sitting there with her mother.

"These are all Neda's favorite things." Iryana held up the ring. "She said Praveen gave her this. He had feelings for her, too. She wanted to be sure she did not lose focus on her reason for traveling so far from home. She took the ring, but not his love." She set the ring back in the box. "He was handsome?"

"Very." Elliot did his best to hide the pain. He had confided about his feelings for Neda to Praveen; Praveen had never said anything about his own feelings for her.

"There is no shame you were attracted to her." A bittersweet smile touched Iryana's lips as she picked up the simple gold necklace Elliot had given Neda. "She gave her life for this. She found it comforting and a compliment."

A wave of pain hit Elliot then, and his breath caught. So long as he kept his thoughts of Neda just distant enough, he could deal with her death. To know that she'd known of his feelings and to know she wasn't offended, and worse, to know she'd traveled to Harrison Mansion fully expecting to die while trying to teach him? He pulled his glasses off and wiped away hot tears. "I'm sorry. I—she shouldn't have died for me."

Iryana reached across the table and took his hand from his face. It was a gentle act, but there was a force to it. "She did what she had to do. Now it is your time. She said you would refuse to believe. It is the way you are, and it is what makes you special. Your little friend, the pretty Berber?"

"Tamment?"

"Yes. You cannot be her. Neda said this one is special. She can see, but she is frightened and bitter. She will need you, though. Even with what she can do, she needs you." Iryana squeezed his hand hard for emphasis. "You see, but you refuse to accept. You will. My Neda did not die for nothing. She died for this." She held the necklace up with a shaking hand. "You see?"

Fatigue and the intensity of Iryana's misery combined with the immensity of what she was saying, and together they brought down Elliot's last resistance. The pain was a crushing force that drove the breath from his lungs in a silent, agonized exhalation. He gasped hard and released a great, pathetic wail. The tears flowed, not just for Neda but for Grandpa William and for Praveen. For all of them.

And Tammy. All alone, abandoned. He had abandoned her, just like everyone else in life had. The realization burned nearly as intense as all the death.

He had betrayed her when she'd needed him.

Iryana let him get it out of his system, once or twice joining him. When the worst of it was past, she brought tissues from the kitchen and let him clean himself up, always ready to take his hand into hers when he needed to hold someone. "It is not good to hold these things in," she said, finally.

Even though he disagreed, Elliot nodded. It seemed the right thing to do, and he felt obligated to Iryana after what she'd suffered. Still, the pain he was feeling at that moment was so intense, the sensation he had betrayed those he loved and had failed them was so raw; he wasn't sure they shouldn't have been kept bottled up. He could accept the responsibility he'd been shirking, but not the faith and belief, and those seemed essential to Iryana.

Iryana released his hand with a gentle pat. "Before you go, there is something Neda sent to me. To give to you."

Elliot pushed his glasses up his nose. "Sent to…to give …"

Without even acknowledging Elliot, Iryana strode to the larger room and dug beneath a pillow, producing a small wooden box, which she brought to him. "Open it."

Elliot wiped his hands on his jeans, then took the box and set it on the table. He opened it cautiously, afraid it might contain something fragile.

It held a pendant, Neda's main focus, a trinket of gemstones and gold that she had considered powerful and treasured even more than the one William Big Bear had given her. Neda could somehow make the trinket's gems glow, a trick she had never shared with Elliot and one he had never figured out. He'd thought the pendant had been lost to the police evidence boxes.

"Take the necklace you gave her," Iryana said, handing him the necklace. "She said it belonged on there."

Elliot opened the necklace and slid the pendant onto the chain.

He looked at the stones, wondering if he might ever figure out what made them glow as they had. Radiation of some sort? Chemicals? He would have to figure that out one day. For Neda. For everyone. Neda had always felt his focus on logic and science was what made him special. What better way to honor her than to get to the bottom of one of her tricks?

"This is very pretty." He held it out for Iryana.

She shook her head. "It was her request for you to keep it." Iryana kissed him on the forehead, then took the chain from his hand. She looked at it once, kissed it, then fastened it around Elliot's neck.

Elliot stood, and they hugged for a few minutes, each drawing strength and comfort from the other. Elliot took in her warmth, the brine of her tears, her simple scent that reminded him of the sand and the sea.

It was Iryana who pushed away, finally. "You have much ahead of you. This moment, remember what was done for you. Be there for your friend. This cycle of sacrifice and duty, you will see it and understand it. Neda knew this." She smiled again, and there was the slightest hint of healing, a look of true happiness beneath the years of misery and loss.

She's lived with the knowledge this day was coming since before I met Neda. Even if I don't believe in this, she does, and I need to accept that her belief—other people's belief—is just as important as my own disbelief.

They walked to the front door, and Elliot wondered what he would do now. His phone was in the airport security office. The driver had left him stranded at the house. Iryana opened the door to reveal Caspar sitting on a motorcycle in front of the house, waiting.

"You take strength from today." Iryana placed her hand on Elliot's back.

"I will." Elliot walked toward the motorcycle, adjusting his carry-on and taking the helmet Caspar offered him. When Iryana approached, Elliot put on his bravest face. "Thank you. For everything."

Iryana reached into his shirt and pulled out the gold necklace. "You will see. What we see, what you see, what makes you special. Like her." She held the pendant up so that it reflected in the handlebar mirror.

The glowing stones dangling from small golden bars held together by fine gold wire caught the sunlight at that moment. The glow intensified. The brilliance of the stones magnified until they appeared as vibrant and beautiful as any gem Elliot could imagine. The pendant not only looked beautiful, it looked powerful, as if caught in one of Neda's illusions he had never quite figured out.

"It's beautiful," Elliot murmured.

"Are you so sure of what you see?" Iryana somehow managed a small smile and pointed to the motorcycle mirror. "Or of what everyone else sees?"

Elliot stared in disbelief. There were no radiant stones, merely a few small pieces of wire-pierced, polished wood slowly spinning from the end of a gold necklace.

Chapter Sixteen

Even over the stench of the musty room that was Tammy's prison and the soiled blankets and all the body odors and the funk of sex, Stone's rank odor was powerful now that he was so close. There was a strong layer of cheap aftershave, as if he'd maybe bathed with it, but very noticeable beneath that was an animal stench, like a dog that had rolled around on top of a rotting corpse.

Tammy looked the room over, hoping for a miracle escape route to appear, but there was still only what had been there before: the windows and the door Stone clogged up with his bulk. And then there were the plastic restraints on her wrists and the fact that Tessa was near-unconscious from heroin.

There was no escape.

Eric took a moment to look Stone over, bald head to booted toes. Tammy considered Eric and Leighton and Stone to be the only people of concern, and there was a physical hierarchy among them. Leighton was a terrifying, muscle-covered giant; Stone, although smaller than he'd appeared in the prison photo and smaller than he'd sounded from Henriksen's description, still managed to give off a menacing aura; and then Eric, who was shorter and more male model than gym rat.

But Eric had a gun; Leighton and Stone didn't.

Finally, Eric casually pointed his gun in Stone's general direction. "I missed your name."

"Probably 'cause I di'n't give it. Glen."

Tammy hated the smugness in Stone's voice. It was a cold, irritating reminder that she'd let him sneak up on her. She consoled herself that she couldn't have done anything about it even if she had known, but that wasn't the point.

Eric bit his bottom lip, and Tammy felt the cold detachment replacing curiosity. "You're brave coming out here and contacting us like this, Glen. I almost want to know how you even knew to come here. We were in the middle of a business discussion, so you're introducing a new variable."

Leighton's face screwed up, all wrinkles and bulging veins and squinted eyes. "Variable? What the fuck? A minute ago, it was all about wanting your money."

Stone let out a snort. "This bitch is givin' y'all all kinds of trouble, but I've been lookin' for her all day, followin' her phone. I'll take her off yer hands and she'll never be no more trouble for no one."

Following my phone? I guess that sounds better than "I'm in her head."

Leighton threw up his hands in exasperation. "What the fuck kind of deal is that? She's worth thousands of dollars to me. *Us.* Eric, fuckin' think about it. Someone like her, she's exotic, pretty. Maybe when everything's said and done, that's one hundred big. You can't let that kind of money go."

"It's the kind of deal y'all walk away from with yer arms and legs intact." Stone gave Leighton a smoldering glance that finished the sentence with a clearly implied *shut the fuck up.*

The tension, the probing and establishment of boundaries combined with the unspoken challenges almost flooded Tammy's somewhat diminished awareness. Leighton was on edge, ready to snap, and Stone was becoming the target of his anger. Stone actually seemed to be provoking Leighton, and it felt like this was a natural alpha challenge. Oddly, it didn't seem to be bothering Eric at all. Instead, he seemed pleased with the exchanges. Walt and Darren only watched, each occasionally swallowing, Walt constantly shifting the grip on his Glock.

There was no good outcome, as far as Tammy was concerned, but the conflict was buying her time. She wanted to extend or complicate it, but the only thing she could think of was to undermine Stone's apparent credibility with Eric.

"He's the Memor…Memorial Day Killer!" She hated how long the drug was taking to get out of her system.

Eric arched an eyebrow. "No shit?"

"All I can say is, boss man wants her alive when I bring her to him. After that…?" Stone gave an inscrutable shrug.

Tammy could feel Stone's joy; he was toying with them. But there was something more than Stone's devious little mind at work, something beneath it all. Tammy could feel it, but she couldn't understand it beyond its primal power. It seemed to be an influence of its own.

Walt shook his head anxiously. "I don't like this, Eric. I say we waste them both."

"Shut the fuck up, *Walt*." Spittle flew from Leighton's mouth as he shouted.

Stone gave Eric a squinty-eyed smile. "Big boy's right. Might want to tell yer bitch to shut it."

A contented smile spread across Eric's face. "Walt's just providing another perspective. You're suggesting we give her up, *gratis*, and the upside is no drama."

Stone bowed his head slightly. Leighton leaned forward until Eric shifted his gun back to Leighton's chest.

"Leighton here has a point, though. She's worth a lot of money, and that's my main motivation," Eric said. When Stone tensed slightly, Eric shifted his pistol to the space between Stone and Leighton. "I do value the offer, mind you, but I think this is the wrong place to negotiate. Too much like a tinder box. Why don't we move out to the studio?"

Tammy's heart leapt. She could feel the tension rise. Leighton and Stone were staring at each other, their energies like two wolves snarling over a bloody chunk of meat. It felt like Stone was aware of Eric's manipulation and was going along with it, but it also felt like a part of Stone just wanted a physical confrontation, and everything the other part of him was doing was a frustrating set-up. Tammy wasn't sure if Stone had a split personality, or if he

187

did, which part of Stone was the dominant part. The two sensations coming off him were simultaneous and completely different.

Eric didn't seem to be aware of the undercurrent of animal rage warring with the cold manipulator in Stone, but there was a definite design to Eric's behavior. He was sure he was the one pulling the strings, but after getting a better sense of the inner turmoil driving Stone, Tammy wasn't so sure.

Eric smiled sweetly at Darren, and said, "Help her up and bring her along."

Darren hooked his bony hands beneath Tammy's arms and got her to her feet. She looked back to see if Tessa was reacting at all, but other than a slow eye blink, she did nothing.

Darren put a hand on Tammy's right elbow and maneuvered her into the narrow hallway. Tammy held her breath until she was past Stone. It was less the odor of death and more that she half expected the animal rage to win out and for him to simply tear her head off and end the standoff.

Time was the key to survival. She needed more time.

Once in the hallway, she did what she could to slow progress—stumble, lean against Darren, swoon. It was only a dozen or so steps, but she milked it.

Her efforts paid off in at least one way: She got a fairly good sense of the building. It was a house, small, wood, old. There was a big room across the hall from the smaller one she and Tessa had been in—the master bedroom from all appearances. It had a door—open—and she could see taped-up windows, an open door she guessed was a bathroom, and what looked like some sort of operations center—a laptop, a pile of women's clothes next to maybe ten purses and clutches lined up in a shallow box, another LED lantern, a pile of shoes, and a stained mattress covered with blankets. And car keys.

Any attempt at escape was going to go through that room.

Ahead on her left, there was another small room without a door, a twin bedroom to her prison, and shortly beyond that on the right was another door, also open. An ancient bathtub—white, stained—occupied most of the room, leaving a little space for a small toilet and sink. Beyond that, there was an opening into a small kitchen opposite a closed door that was probably a closet or larder.

The hallway opened into a large room by the house's standards. Tammy could see two LED spotlights fashioned to poles and a small camera attached to a tripod. Beyond those, the floor was covered with what appeared to be a huge, brand-new, white comforter. A thin sheet of clear plastic sat on top of that, and on top of the plastic was a bundled-up, bloodstained white sheet. The room was like a big L, with the shorter leg by all appearances a dining room just off the kitchen. There was a door to her left, probably the door Stone had come in through. All the windows were taped over, just like in the bedrooms.

Their rape and murder studio. Awesome.

Tammy tried not to show her revulsion, but Stone looked at her and licked his lips as if he could sense her thoughts.

If you're feeling my thoughts, asshole, I want you to know, I'm going to kill you.

Stone laughed suddenly, and Tammy shivered. He was in her head.

"Okay, I think this is fine." Eric stepped out of the hallway and leaned against the shared closet wall.

Walt stopped halfway between the hallway and the film studio. Darren pulled up a little bit ahead of Walt, still gripping Tammy's elbow. Leighton and Stone continued on into the heart of the main room, separated only by about five feet; Leighton's right foot was actually resting on the comforter.

In the larger room, Leighton truly seemed to loom over Stone. It really emphasized how diminished Stone was compared to the image Tammy had built in her head.

Tammy didn't like how close she was to the two big men. She stepped back, and Stone's eyes seemed to grow larger. He let out a sound that could have been a deep gust of wind or a cough. Even Leighton recoiled slightly.

Stone looked Eric in the eyes. "So, what you got in mind? This room don't change nothin' but how far I gotta go t' git to you."

Eric's eyebrows arched in acknowledgment of Stone's understanding of the situation. "I think we can all agree we've come down to final presentations? The extra space gives me some room to consider my options."

"Fuck that." Leighton stepped forward until he was looming over Stone. "You want the money, and you know it."

"You might want t' step back, *Leighton*. I ain't some drugged-up bitch you c'n choke to death fer one of yer snuff videos." Stone smirked and coolly glared at Leighton.

Leighton's body shook, and his face went a deep red. He flexed and balled his hands into huge fists. "I think I've heard enough bullshit."

"I don't know, Leighton." Eric shook his head. "If you've been making snuff films, you've been cutting me out of some of the money you've made off my work. Right, Walt?"

Walt seemed disturbed by the idea he'd contributed to snuff films, but after a second of thinking it through, he nodded. "No more fucking us over, Leighton."

Eric lazily waved his gun at Leighton. "I don't know. I'm beginning to think she's right and you planned to kill us and not pay us at all."

Stone snickered and swept a gaze from Darren to Walt to Eric. "That's the way it is, boys. Yer just bitches to him. Those guns don't change that none. Big dog always needs bitches to do the work and take the fall."

Tammy shivered as Stone's seeming calm nearly collapsed and the animal raging beneath flared in intensity, ready to burst out. She took another step away from the big men, and Darren, possibly sensing something was about to happen, released her elbow. She wanted to make a run for it right then, to get away from the sickness and wrongness surrounding her. She'd always known there were bad people in the world. A day didn't pass without hearing about a little kid being murdered or a public place being attacked by a gunman, or atrocities being committed somewhere in the world, but those were all things affecting *someone else*, and the killers were…well, fucked up, but in a different way.

Leighton's face contorted into a snarl, his eyes wide, his nostrils flared.

Stone's calm side just seemed to draw strength from Leighton losing his composure. Stone's eyebrows rose and fell in a taunt. "Ain't that the way it is, *Leighton*? Always gotta be bitches?"

Leighton roared and launched into Stone, first shoving him, then bringing a huge fist down with terrifying force. Stone stumbled back, arms flailing as he tried to keep his footing, but he fell against the front wall, his head cracking a taped-over window before he slid to the ground. His nose was a flattened, bloody mass.

Tammy squealed and backed up a step. "Darren, he's going to kill Leighton!"

Darren shot forward, boot chains jingling, and began stomping on Stone. Leighton was right there at Darren's side, the two of them kicking and stomping. At first, Stone seemed like he might ward them off, at one point knocking Darren down with a glancing backhand and nearly standing. But Leighton was always there, punching, kicking, stomping. Once Darren rejoined the attack, it became academic. Stone collapsed, and once he was down, there was nothing but the meaty thud of boots and fists crashing against him. Occasionally, a bone snapped, flesh ripped, and blood spurted wet and heavy.

And over Leighton's furious roars, Darren's chains jingled cheerfully.

For the first time, Tammy felt Eric grow excited, aroused. He was engrossed in the brutality, but not so that he didn't notice when she tried to sneak back into the hallway.

Without taking his eyes off the attack, Eric pointed his gun at her and shook his head. "Why not stay for the conclusion?"

Walt backed off from the brutality, finally looking away. Tammy tried to do the same, but she couldn't. There was something wrong about the moment, like a train wreck happening right in front of her.

Stone was a murderer, a butcher. He was the threat that had invaded her dreams, but he was being destroyed by people every bit as inhuman.

Then, the frenzied attack simply stopped. Like two sharks tearing away at a body until there was nothing left and then calmly swimming away, Darren and Leighton simply stepped back. Little droplets of blood covered both of them, dripping from their skin and seeping into their clothes. Strips of flesh clung to Darren's boots. A wild, primitive look filled their wide eyes. They were panting from the exertion, shaking with exhaustion and elation. Stone was a broken, bloody heap on the ground, only a thready, gurgling wheeze away from death.

"You fuckin' see that, Eric? You see that? Fuckin' with the big dog, huh?" Leighton flexed his arms like a wrestler working through one of his rehearsed routines. He took a step toward Eric.

Eric casually pointed the pistol at Leighton, and the giant froze.

"Goddammit, Eric!"

Tammy flinched, expecting the roar of a gun, but Eric was still caught up in the thrill of the moment. And more. He was taking some perverse pleasure from something beyond toying with Leighton.

Then Tammy saw what had Eric's attention. Behind Leighton and Darren, Stone was slowly getting to his feet. Even with a shattered leg, he managed to stand. He tried to pull off his blood-soaked hoodie despite his broken arm, but it kept getting caught on protruding bone.

Walt looked up to see what was going on and muttered something unintelligible.

Once again, Tammy could sense the arousal strong in Eric's thoughts. A whimsical smile lazily crept over his face, and he casually motioned for Leighton to look behind him.

Leighton and Darren turned as Stone finally hooked a mangled hand in a tear in the hoodie's front and ripped the bloody thing the rest of the way open. There was a wicked burn mark on his chest, a charred area as big as Tammy's palm. It was open to the rib below, which looked discolored. Bone protruded from Stone's left forearm and hand, and from his chest. His right lower leg was bent noticeably above the ankle. His right ear hung from his jaw by a ribbon of flesh, and his lips were torn in spots, burst in others. And yet, Stone was chuckling.

It was a wet, quiet chuckle, but it was real. Stone dropped his hoodie to the floor and said, "It's 'bout time y'all learned who the bitch is."

Darren didn't even wait for Leighton, instead charging for a kick at Stone's ruined leg. Stone caught the kick with his good hand and squeezed Darren's ankle, then gave an effortless twist that snapped the leg at a ninety-degree angle. Darren screamed, but only for a second. Stone's broken hand swept across Darren's throat, and he fell back, unable to even whimper, his throat completely crushed.

Tammy felt the change at that exact moment. The beast, the thing raging inside Stone, was alive and in control. Stone was little more than a giddy passenger in his own ruined body. Leighton and Eric sensed the change, too, the unnatural and the impossible.

For Leighton, the change was something not consciously noted; he roared and swung at Stone with desperate intensity. For Eric, the clinical detachment returned, replacing arousal.

"Walt?" Eric aimed at the wrestling forms, suddenly unsure who the threat really was.

Walt stepped forward, gun raised. "Who do we shoot?"

And Tammy was gone, padding down the hallway and into her prison as quiet and quick as she could. She dropped to her butt next to Tessa.

"Oh, fuck, Tessa. Fuck! You've got to get the hell up!" Tammy contorted until she had her arms below her butt and riding up the back of her legs. "Tessa, c'mon."

Stone's roars echoed down the hallway, more energetic and clear than before. "How y'all like me now?"

Leighton's roars had a different tenor to them: the first sounds of terrible realization, the hyena discovering the lion he attacked is the apex predator.

Tammy needed to get her arms in front of her. She crunched her torso until her face was pressed against her knees and worked her arms the rest of the length of her legs, and finally up to the front of her body, gasping at the pain as blood began to flow and muscles came out of the strange position they'd been held in. She searched Darren's box, finally spotting the knife and Zippo. She grabbed the Zippo and tried to burn through the plastic restraint with it, but she quickly abandoned that idea after burning her wrist. She shoved the lighter into her pocket and grabbed the knife. The blade was surprisingly sharp. It took two nicks before she got the blade onto the restraint and began the slow task of cutting through the plastic.

A popping sound floated down the hallway.

"Fuck! Oh, fuck!" Leighton's roar was closer to a disheartened plea. "Eric, this guy's on PCP or something!"

Stone's answering laughter dropped from a taunt to something almost demonic.

The blade finally sawed through the final piece of the restraint. Tammy shoved the handle into her back pocket and grabbed Tessa. Her body was still warm, but not as warm as it had been before, and it felt damp.

"C'mon, Tessa, we have to go!" Tammy managed to get Tessa up with a fireman's carry, then set her against the wall. "Tessa!"

Tammy slapped Tessa twice. Not hard, but enough to get through to her. Tessa's eyes opened, heavy-lidded. "Oh…baby girl…I ain't feel so good."

"Can you walk?"

"I just wanna sleep." Tessa's eyes closed again.

Another popping sound came from the hallway, and Leighton screamed in pain. Stone's voice sounded like a snarl, drowning out Leighton's screams for a moment, then Leighton's screams rose higher and higher.

Stone was killing Leighton, and not quickly.

Tammy threw her left arm around Tessa's hip and dragged her into the hallway. Once again, Tammy felt compelled to look to see what was happening. Eric stood at the end of the hallway, watching, waiting for her, gun raised. Tammy bolted forward just as he fired, and Tessa jerked in Tammy's arms. Tammy pulled Tessa across the hall and into the master bedroom, slamming the door behind them and twisting around to lock it. She let out a relieved sigh when the lock actually worked.

"Tessa, you've gotta hold on. I've got to find the keys." Tammy set Tessa down on the mattress and began desperately searching through the little operations center she'd seen before. The laptop gave off enough light that the search went fairly quickly. She gathered up her clutch, a pair of bright, cheerful pink sneakers that were her size, and the keys, then took a moment to transfer the knife and lighter to the clutch and to pull on the sneakers. She was relieved to see they hadn't taken anything from her clutch yet. She kept the keys in the same hand that held the clutch.

Leighton's high screams finally stopped, and Tammy felt his thoughts just…end. Stone was done with him.

"Tessa, we've got to—"

Blood bubbled up weakly from a huge hole in Tessa's chest. It was the sort of hole only special bullets could make, the kind of bullets that fragmented. Tessa's eyes were open and staring at the ceiling. Her breathing was shallow and weak, and bloody foam collected at the corner of her mouth.

"Oh. Fuck. Tessa."

"Tammy, I—" Tessa's eyelids fluttered, then closed, and her breath became a shallow whisper.

Tammy wanted to just curl up next to Tessa and wait for the end, but gunfire roared from the other end of the house.

Stone was going for Eric and Walt now. The end would be…

"Tessa? Tessa?" Tammy shook Tessa, but she didn't react. Tammy kissed Tessa softly on the cheek. "I'm sorry."

Tammy ran for the bathroom door, pulling it shut behind her and locking it. Then she turned to examine the bathroom window. She didn't wonder how she'd known it would be there; she just accepted that it was.

It was a small window, wood-framed, with brass fixture. She tried to unlock it, but the fixture seemed frozen.

No fucking way.

She tried again, nearly screaming when the fixture swung free and her fingers banged hard against the glass. The wooden frame had a brass handle at the bottom; she grabbed that with both hands and yanked up. It froze a little over halfway up. She squatted and tried to push with her legs. The window wasn't budging.

Whoever lived here before, I hate you. Seriously. Assholes!

She squeezed into the tight area and almost immediately got stuck. A whimper slipped out of her tight-squeezed lips, then she shifted and twisted and tried again. Her head was through. One shoulder was partway through. It was doable.

In her head, seconds ticked by.

She got her shoulder through and twisted again, bringing her body around so that her back was resting against the sill. Contorting was a matter of patience and practice. It was best done without a bladder ready to burst.

Another push, another twist, and she was out, falling onto her hands.

She jumped up and ran along the back of the house, dragging her left hand along the wall, head cocked to listen for what was going on inside the house.

The moonlight was dim, the ground flat and unfamiliar. There were clumps of grass, but there were also areas of dirt and weed vines. She flinched with each gunshot. They roared as if the guns were close by instead of somewhere inside the house. Then, as she approached the kitchen door, she saw why: the top third of the door was a large pane of glass, and there was a hole in the near bottom corner.

The guns suddenly went silent.

Tammy slowed until she was standing at the hole in the glass. The engine she'd imagined she'd heard before was nearby, a generator from the sound of it. She wanted to run, to get as much distance from Stone as she could, but she had to know what was going on inside the house. *Why hasn't Eric run yet? What's Stone doing? How much time do I have?*

She peered into the hole and simultaneously reached out, trying to sense Eric and Walt and Stone. She could see part of the kitchen, including the opening into the hallway.

She felt Eric's thoughts first, shifting from his signature cold detachment to absolute terror. Shadows flashed across her vision, and then Eric came into view, his torso crashing against the wall, the lower half of his body blocked by the kitchen wall. His gun dropped and he grabbed at his throat, which was held by Stone's mangled hand; it was now thicker, more brutish, and covered in dark hair. She could feel Eric's terror rising, and at the same time, she felt his arousal returning. *What's his deal? Is he suicidal?*

"Y'all was one sick group of fucks, y'know that?" Stone's voice was strong, deep, and gruff. He was past whatever the injuries had done to him before. The brutish hand squeezed, and Eric blew snot and spit out in a desperate gasp. "Normally, I focus on the niggers and spics, but you? Dayum! I thought you was queer. I was gonna give you somethin' special. But you just get off on violence, don'tcha? That's some kinda fucked up. But here, I'll getcha what yer lookin' for."

A tearing, cracking sound suddenly filled Tammy's ears, and she could see Eric trying to scream. Whatever noise he made was drowned out by the cracking noise and Stone's demonic laughter, then there was just a wet sloshing sound, and Eric's torso slumped against the wall. It took Tammy a moment to realize what had happened, then she heard Stone drop Eric's lower half to the ground. A second later, Eric's intestines began to slowly unravel and fall to the floor.

Tammy gagged, and Stone peered around the edge of the kitchen wall and stared at her. "Got one last one t'take care of, then I'm comin' for you."

She turned and ran, shuffling past the door and the kitchen window. Abruptly, Eric's thoughts just...ended. He was dead, and only Walt remained, and he was a bundle of fear somewhere at the other end of the house, waiting for Stone.

Tammy reached the edge of the house and saw that it connected to a covered carport. A generator rested flush against the house wall, and a boxy sedan sat at the opposite end of the carport. The car was an almost glossy black in the moonlight shadows.

It was the most beautiful sight Tammy had seen in some time.

She ran for the driver's side door and tried the keys. On the second try, she got the key into the door lock, popped the door open, and slid into the driver's seat.

What moonlight made it through the smeared grime on the windshield was gray. The interior stank like the house: musty, dirty. Terrible things had happened in the car. Cracks spiderwebbed across the dashboard, and foam bubbled up from tears in the vinyl seat covers. The torn vinyl dug into the underside of her thighs.

Tammy ignored the distractions and stabbed the key at the ignition. When the key slammed home, she started the engine. She almost screamed at the horrible sound—throaty, sputtering, arrhythmic.

There were no other options. She searched the dashboard display for the lights and turned them on, then she popped the car into reverse. She didn't have time to adjust the rearview mirror, so she pivoted to get a good look at the area behind her. She could see the gray glow of a driveway, and beyond that she could see a field as sickly and weed-riddled as the backyard. Beyond the field, she thought there might be a road curving past.

She hit the accelerator and backed out, tires chirping on the carport concrete. The car's heavy rear end swung around to point back to the house, and Tammy froze.

Walt was running toward her, and Stone was close behind him.

Stone didn't even look completely human anymore. Where he'd appeared to have a waxed chest in the photograph, he was covered in thick hair now, and his upper body was hunched over. His gait was closer to an animal's than a human's.

"Don't leave me!" Walt nearly stumbled as he sprinted. He waved his arms over his head. "Please!"

Tammy straightened in the seat, put the car into drive, and floored the accelerator. She instantly lamented her lack of experience. All she'd ever managed was a little tooling around Arlington in Tessa's Cavalier, which probably weighed half as much as the tank Tammy was trying to maneuver. When the car's engine finally responded and the bald tires had enough traction, it felt like a minor tremor had hit the area. The car nearly fishtailed, and when it did move, it rocked side-to-side.

The headlights revealed a line of trees at the end of the driveway. The driveway passed through a gap in the trees and intersected the road she'd seen. Tammy slowed as she approached the gap.

Walt's screams caught her attention. She risked a glance back.

Stone had Walt suspended in the air by the back of his neck and hip. Stone was bending Walt's spine backward and already had him in an awkward upside down *U*. Walt's screams rose to a high pitch, then Stone completely snapped Walt in half; Walt's screams just stopped. Tammy never had the chance to look away.

"Holy fuck." Tammy squeezed her eyes shut, but she couldn't un-see what she'd seen.

She opened her eyes as the front of the car bounced on the road. With no idea of where she was and no time to dig around for her phone, Tammy just turned left and punched the accelerator.

The engine sputtered, then it died.

Tammy tried to start the car again, but it just coughed and growled. She looked back and saw Stone charging toward her. She had opened a good distance between them when speeding away from the house, but he was closing that gap in no time.

She turned the key again, and this time the engine started. It didn't take a genius to realize Stone would catch her if she turned left. The car was just too slow, and its engine too unreliable. Instead, she put the car into reverse and pressed down on the accelerator, cutting the wheel just enough at the last second to clip Stone in the hip.

He went airborne, flying over the front of the reversing car. His head caught on the edge of the hood, then he landed hard on the dirt driveway.

Tammy spun back to look out the front windshield, braked, and put the car into drive. Stone scrambled up to his knees, but Tammy had the car moving too fast for him to get out of the way. She caught him square in the chest with the front of the car. He somehow managed to get a hand on the hood and hung on until she cut the wheel sharp to the left just before the tires hit the road.

Stone disappeared beneath the car.

Instantly, she felt and heard him bouncing off the undercarriage, and then the car's rear popped off the ground when a tire caught him.

It was a sickening sensation, feeling the car run over someone. As bad a beating as Leighton and Darren had delivered, it couldn't compare to such a big car first hitting, then dragging, then running over Stone. Tammy was sick at the thought of what she might see if she looked back, but she had to know what she'd done to him. She had to.

The road ahead was empty. Tammy braked and glanced back, then she screamed.

Stone's body was a twisted, bloody ruin, but he was slowly propping himself up and turning to look at her.

"Y'cain't get away from me, bitch!" Stone's voice was raspy and weak, but it carried far enough.

A sense of utter hopelessness hit Tammy at that point, and she began to cry. There was no escaping Stone, not forever. There simply wasn't. He wasn't even human. Not anymore. Not after all that had happened to him.

She needed a way back to Harrison Mansion, but she didn't have time to check her iPhone for a route. Not yet. She needed to get some distance from Stone. Now.

Stone was slowly resetting bones and peeling off flesh. The whole time, he just chuckled. Tammy shook her head to clear his sick noises from her thoughts, then she put the car in drive and pulled away.

She took a last glance. Stone was waving at her.

Chapter Seventeen

After the brutal heat of Bandar Abbas, Elliot had a greater appreciation for the cool, stale airplane air, even on a smaller, commuter model like the one he was on. The jet was just wide enough for four small but relatively comfortable seats across, divided by a narrow center walkway. It was clean, proudly displaying the bright, cheerful red and white of Japan Airlines. The turboprops provided an almost hypnotic backdrop, a white noise that approached annoying without actually becoming uncomfortable.

Elliot swallowed, trying to work the worst of the rancid taste of travel from his mouth; a quick, cleansing tug from the small bottle of water he'd purchased at the Osaka airport helped, but he knew his breath was damned close to lethal at the moment. He wanted nothing more than for his trip to be over and to enjoy the comfort of a hotel room—a long, hot shower; a thorough flossing and vigorous brushing; fresh clothes; then a sleep to rival Rip Van Winkle's.

Tanegashima was his last stop, this time without the pain of meeting with family. Ms. Nakama's directions about what to do after her death had been clear: Take her belongings to the Kumano shrine on Tanegashima.

Tanegashima was a small island, one of a handful that was at the southwestern end of Japan. As far as Elliot could tell, it had a small city and very little else.

The plane vibrated slightly, and Elliot shifted in the confining seat, trying to position himself so that his knees weren't crushed against the unforgiving seat back in front of him. It was difficult, but he finally managed to find an angle where he could relax in something approximating comfort without touching the passenger beside him.

Bright afternoon sunlight filled the window Elliot leaned against, but its heat didn't touch him. Henriksen had sent an email while Elliot had been in the air between Bandar Abbas and Dubai. He had skimmed it once, but the words had been too hard to fully take in.

He dug out his phone and read it again, this time fortified and ready.

Elliot, we have confirmation on the DNA. Glen Stone is our man. Other DNA being re-tested, possibly tainted by animals. We worried about that when we got a look at the bodies.

Although DNA puts Stone at the mansion, even if we could get him for rape, which isn't likely, it wouldn't be enough. Major Case Squad wants Murder One. This guy needs to be off the streets permanently.

Email me if you can think of anything of value he might have stolen. If he fenced something, we'd also have the breaking and entering angle to pursue.

It would be even more helpful if you recall ever seeing him in your area. He stands out. You should remember him. Hope the travel is going ok.

Lt. Paul Henriksen

Elliot's heartbeat picked up as he read the email for the third time. He visualized those who had been his family. He visualized Stone. Stone was a violent racist, someone who wore his hatred in ink for all to see, someone who took pleasure in hurting dark-skinned people, people who had committed the crime of being different.

He calls us less than human, but look at him, covered in hate messages, head shaved, eyes empty except for hatred. If I could believe in souls, I would see that he doesn't have one.

Unfortunately, there were no sightings of Stone to recall, despite Elliot's wish otherwise. Seeing someone like Stone left a mark, an unpleasant memory that didn't fade quickly. Even the photo Henriksen had shown was enough to make the skin crawl.

I want him put away just as bad as Henriksen, but they have nothing on him, nothing other than...what...circumstantial evidence? Possible DNA that puts him at the mansion? That's it. Nothing that will hold up. He's a free man when it's all said and done. At least this shows the enemy for what it is: a man. A sick, hate-filled, broken man who is closer to beast than human. There's solace in that.

The man in the seat next to Elliot's got up and shuffled out of sight; Elliot barely noticed. Even on such a tight-packed plane, there was too much going on in his life to spend time on something trivial like a person who would share his space for a couple hours.

Elliot turned his thoughts back to the idea Stone might have fenced something from the mansion, something that could tie him to the crime scene.

The religious weapons and totems? There's nothing. I had the most valuable item to steal. They won't get him without witnesses, and everyone who saw him is dead.

Elliot shook his head angrily and scolded himself.

Self-pity, frustration, loss—they were all combining with the fatigue, making it impossible to think clearly. There had been other valuables in the mansion, but they weren't obvious or flashy. He realized he might be missing something that would catch an outsider's eye.

Despite the fatigue and distractions, Elliot tried to think through what a potential burglar would see.

Looking at Harrison Mansion from the private road, Elliot guessed it might appear tempting to a thief. It was three stories tall, all stone, built solidly and aesthetically pleasing. From the outside, it probably looked like it was home to wealthy people.

Elliot had never thought of that before.

Seeing the mansion through the eyes of someone visiting it the first time, there would be a lot of disappointment. The front door opened into a foyer, and that into a large, open space with the stairs at the center. The foyer held a table and a pretty but cheap vase. There was a framed painting on the foyer's east wall of the Black Forest, and a painting on the west wall of Mount Fuji. Pretty, but not worth anything. The open space was filled with chairs and sofas and a divan. The trophy room, library, kitchen and dining room, tea room, Ms. Fernandez's room, and a couple other empty rooms were all off the sitting room.

The tea room had some china, some silver settings—useless outside of antique or niche shops. The trophy room had its useless trinkets. Even Mangas's medicine bag would only hold value to museums and collectors. Would silverware be worth stealing?

No. None of the rooms on the first floor had anything of significant value.

Looking up the stairs, nothing flashy would be visible, either. No expensive artwork or pottery or…anything.

Everyone in the mansion lived a simple life. There were personal items— Neda's ring, Daysi's drugs, Praveen's heirlooms, Driss's *takoba*—but they weren't in plain sight. They almost certainly weren't visible from outside the mansion. Praveen's heirlooms, mostly crafted from precious metals, were the most valuable, but they rarely left the basement.

The mansion had always been *home* to Elliot since he'd moved in. He'd never accepted that, but in the back of his mind, it was there. Grandpa William was Elliot's family, and where family lived was home. And even with all its quirks and the seeming antiquity and the folks who hadn't at first been family, there had always been a sense of comfort in the mansion. Nothing drove the point deeper and harder than Elliot's stays at hotels during his trip.

When he considered what might motivate a thief, he came up with the standard goodies: a high-end TV, computers, stereo.

They didn't have any of that. The only person who watched a lot of television was Ms. Nakama, and that was on the old television in the study next to Elliot's room. She spent several hours a week watching Japanese soap operas and things Elliot thought of as pornographic. There was no stereo system, and the only computer of any worth was the MacBook Pro he'd received as part of his going-away haul.

Elliot took off his glasses and rubbed his eyes.

Face it. We didn't really live large. Aside from the things we all shared—the mountain and dirt bikes, the hunting weapons, the old minivan Ms. Fernandez tooled around in—there just wasn't much of real value. It was all personal value, like Neda's pendant, or Grandpa William's medicine bag, or Daysi's mortar and pestle and masks.

None of that was missing.

After a quick glance to be sure the seat was still empty and the man wasn't on his way back, Elliot opened his carry-on bag. The envelope was still there, the money—minus what the guardsman had stolen, which had included all the one-dollar bills—was still there. Elliot hastily closed the bag again and carefully set it under the seat in front of him.

The airplane tickets had cost thousands of dollars. The taxi to Rabia's was more than two hundred. That was dwarfed by what they had been spent on the going-away presents.

Elliot swallowed, embarrassed.

They'd probably spent more on him in the last two months than on everything else combined his entire time there.

He flipped through older emails, vaguely acknowledging the dozen or so unopened messages he simply hadn't had time for in the last few weeks. None of them were from Tammy, and that's who he was most worried about.

He finally found the email he was looking for and opened it.

The subject—*Settlement of the Estate of William Big Bear Saganash*—provoked a flinch, but whether because of the fatigue or because of time passing, the pain was less intense than before.

Elliot scrolled through the message until he reached the attached document; he opened that. More scrolling—impatient, almost frantic—until he found what he was looking for: the projected post-tax value, not including the mansion and its associated dozens of acres.

Twenty-two million and change. I'm sweating spending thousands of dollars to see these people receive the dignity of safe travel to their rightful resting places, and the estate I have to take care of when all is said and done is worth over twenty million dollars, and that doesn't include trusts set up for me and Tammy. We're millionaires ourselves, or would be if we were to stay at the mansion. Investments, money stashed away: I guess Mangas planned for everything, all those years ago. Everything but someone killing every member of The Circle.

Reconciling the life and death of every one of the people Stone had killed was beyond Elliot's abilities. It just didn't compute, whether as a burglary gone bad or a hate crime. He'd been the one with the biggest footprint: his laptop, the

GLK, his college tuition. Grandpa William had cut back on his travel significantly in the last few years, so even Elliot's travels seemed outsized.

Elliot flushed with guilt at another memory: talking with Grandpa William about the possibility the others—even Tammy and Driss—might simply be taking advantage of Grandpa William.

It hadn't been an accusation. It hadn't been a fight. It had been a cynical observation Elliot had made as Grandpa William talked about another possible occupant, another child mentioned in a vague report in a newspaper half a world away. A gifted healer this time.

Another mouth to feed.

Another room in the mansion given over to someone fleeing violence in their homeland, or an outcast, or a spectacle.

Elliot wished he could blame the words on a heated exchange.

He shrank inward, hating himself for what he'd said. Grandpa William's reaction—not anger, not pain, but shame—hurt more now than it had at the time. It wasn't shame in Elliot, but self-shame, a sense of failure in how Elliot had been raised.

How much of your wisdom was wasted on me, Grandpa William?

You should have found someone more worthy. You were wrong to put any effort into someone like me. Iryana was wrong to have let her daughter throw her life away on me.

The man who'd been sitting beside Elliot since they'd left Osaka settled back in his seat, never so much as making eye contact with Elliot.

He was a middle-aged Japanese businessman with slicked-back black hair, gold wire-framed glasses, and a wrinkled face. He was dressed in a charcoal gray business suit, white dress shirt, and blue tie, all very professional looking and a little bit standoffish. Once settled, he pulled an iPad out of a small laptop bag and began to flip through documents of Kanji script.

Elliot felt underdressed in his jeans and button-down Tommy Hilfiger shirt. He guiltily closed the attachment and slid his phone back into his pants pocket. He didn't worry that the man might see the document of the estate. The man probably barely noticed anything outside his own world.

There was, however, what the document brought out in Elliot: shame and guilt, enough that Elliot feared they might consume him completely.

What was someone supposed to feel, Elliot wondered, when they've so thoroughly misjudged everyone and everything for so long? It occurred to him that even the trip back to Manitoba might have been a lie, not the first step in his return to help his people, but an excuse to escape Harrison Mansion.

The same thing Tammy wanted. The same thing he had condemned in her.

It wasn't enough that he had to condemn someone who'd been his friend through some of the hardest years of his life. No, he had to be a hypocrite in the process.

So, now what? I drop off Ms. Nakama's possessions at the shrine, and then? Am I supposed to toss a ring into a volcano? Blow up a Death Star? Return to Missouri and tell Tammy I'm sorry? Head straight for Manitoba and bury myself in the books and hope I can become a better person? I certainly can't become any worse.

Or what? Stay at the mansion? Study what they left behind for me? For us? Try to replace the Elders and keep the Circle alive, or at least try not to disappoint everyone too greatly?

But replace them at what? Guarding two snot-nosed, unappreciative kids? Providing a haven for charlatans?

Except they weren't charlatans. He realized that now. A charlatan sought to take someone in for gain. Daysi, Ms. Nakama, Neda, Praveen, Driss—they had all believed. They had shared their knowledge. They had left behind foci and documentation that showed the depth of their belief.

And maybe more.

There was *something* to their beliefs, something real and tangible and undeniable. What that was, Elliot couldn't begin to guess. And even though he could never truly believe, he could at least respect the others' beliefs, maybe even try to understand them somehow. Codify them. Resolve all the contradictions and inconsistencies…

The question was whether that would be enough for him to take on Grandpa William's old obligations—watching the news for another candidate; reaching out to the potential candidates; traveling to the farthest corners of the world to see for himself if the candidate believed he or she was gifted; working with the legal team to go through the hassles of immigration, seeking political asylum, or working some other angle.

It was a tremendous burden meant for a mature person.

And there were other obligations he would probably have to take on—assisting law enforcement, working with well-meaning but misguided witches and others. Elliot was now privy to a lot of the things Grandpa William had shielded him from.

Even if Elliot didn't pursue the same role Grandpa William had, any existing contracts would be valid until Elliot could find a way to get out from under them.

*That was millions more already allocated. Multi-year, open-ended contracts—*with legal firms, with associated businesses.

Grandpa William knew what was coming, just like Mangas did when he set the estate up in the first place.

The businessman next to Elliot jerked suddenly, setting his iPad down in his lap. Elliot followed the man's eyes, looking forward until he saw a cute stewardess angrily storm past them on her way to the rear of the plane. The businessman leaned across the aisle and exchanged a few whispered words with a young woman sitting in the seat opposite his. She wore a professional business outfit—charcoal gray skirt and jacket and white blouse. They separated when the stewardess returned, stomping to the front of the aircraft with two small bottles of alcohol and a bottle of water.

The businessman looked at Elliot, eyebrows raised, dismissively snorting. "Trouble passenger."

Elliot suddenly wished he'd paid attention to the other passengers. Coming out of Dubai, he hadn't relaxed until they'd settled on the runway at Osaka. Out of Osaka, he'd never even considered the possibility of trouble. It was such a small plane, with so few passengers going to an obscure little island; he hadn't considered it a target for terrorism.

The businessman continued to stare up the aisle. No one seemed to be moving to help the stewardess. The passenger was probably just rowdy or drunk.

He probably touched the stewardess inappropriately.

Elliot sat up straight in his seat and tried to see who was causing the trouble. The stewardess was at the first row, leaning across the opposite side of the aisle, handing the water bottle to whomever sat in the aisle seat. One of the bottles of alcohol was in the passenger's hand, already empty.

It was a female hand, delicate but large, cumin-colored.

A voice sounded over the drone of the propellers at that moment, and the stewardess angrily stormed back down the aisle.

Elliot froze at the sound of the voice.

His eyes locked on the seat where the troubled passenger sat. Simirita's head popped around the seat edge, her beautiful face framed by the same luxurious hair Elliot had run his hands through. She looked at him defiantly, taunting him.

Elliot looked around in a panic, but everyone had gone back to whatever they'd been absorbed in before the distraction.

Simirita laughed. The sound was an icicle plunged into the small of his back. He shivered, and he realized his mouth had gone dry. No one else had reacted to the laugh. Simirita stared at him from her seat not twenty feet away, and no one seemed to notice.

Elliot pulled his Evian bottled water container from his carry-on bag and cracked the seal. He stopped before taking a drink.

Blood swirls spun lazily in the water.

He resealed the lid, and Simirita laughed again.

This isn't happening. His throat ached where she had cut him. Elliot pulled the two necklaces from inside his shirt, first feeling the warmth in Neda's focus, then unbuttoning the leather strip that protected his mother's cross.

"You thought I was done with you?" Simirita's voice echoed in the enclosed space, but once again the other passengers didn't seem to notice. She licked her full lips seductively, but because of the sneer on her face, the end result was something closer to hunger.

How is this even possible? How could she have known where I was going? I never told her the itinerary or dates. How can I hear her and no one else can?

"Oh, Elliot. You are so cute. I really mean that. But I have tasted your flesh now, so you are mine. Today, tomorrow, at the shrine, or at the mansion, it doesn't matter. You are mine, and I will collect."

She laughed again, and this time, people around her looked up. She flashed an angry, impatient glare at everyone, finished off her water bottle, then disappeared around the seat, only the slightest hint of the crown of her hair rising over the seat back.

Elliot shivered, suddenly terrifyingly aware that the plane's comfortable confines were actually a trap.

Chapter Eighteen

T he road was dark and silent, a narrow stretch of asphalt running between what Tammy was sure would soon be corn or soy fields. At the moment, though, they were just moonlit dirt with shoots rising from low rows. The shoulders of the road were covered by knee-high grass and weeds. Across the field and to the west stood what looked like a housing development. To the east, woods.

Tammy checked her phone again. The map said she was on East Simon Boulevard. It might as well have been Fifth Avenue in Manhattan.

She turned the key again. Nothing. Except for crickets, the night was quiet.

The car was dead.

She smacked her head against the steering wheel in frustration, then she turned off the lights. Despite having the window open, the interior was stuffy and had taken on a truly unpleasant odor; she sniffed herself. She wasn't particularly pleasant smelling, but she wasn't the problem. There was something *wrong* about the car.

She opened the door and slipped out. After a moment, she checked her phone and zoomed out the view of the map. According to the route she'd taken, she hadn't even managed 150 miles—on a tank she'd filled before leaving Granite City in Illinois, where Leighton's little hideout had been. It didn't make any sense.

Her plan had been to shoot west on I-70, then south on Highway 54 before circling back east to Rolla. She had used back roads wherever she could, and now that was going to cost her. It was a mile to the nearest house, unless she cut through a field, and even farther to the highway.

When the hell is something going to go my way?

She stomped her right foot in frustration, fought off a crying jag, then reached back into the car and pulled the keys from the ignition. The most important thing she could do was figure out what she had available to her. Her clutch held her prepaid debit card, some cash, her hygiene napkins zip case, some lipstick and lip balm, a small mascara, a stale piece of gum, an old condom, and Darren's Zippo lighter and modeling knife. None of those were likely to get the car running, and none of them would kill Stone.

She walked to the back of the car and unlocked the trunk.

It hit her after a few seconds: part of the smell was definitely coming from the trunk. Not much, but definitely a part of it. It was part gasoline, part…something.

It took several long seconds for her eyes to adjust to the dim light, then she began rummaging through the accumulated junk: a hefty tire iron; a sour smelling, stained blanket; a small, stained segment of rope; two emergency flares; a nearly dead flashlight; an old, yellow Chilton's maintenance book for a 1985 Chevrolet Monte Carlo; and dark stains at the bottom of the well where the spare tire should have been. Those stains made her shiver in revulsion. She eyed the maintenance book in the moonlight; at least she knew what the car was, for all the good that was going to do her.

Once again, nothing to fix the car, nothing to destroy Stone. She needed one or the other. Or both. She'd be cool with both.

Just call the cops. Deal with the fallout. A foster home's better than being killed.

But a foster home wasn't going to be the end of it. She could *feel* that much. Stone wasn't going away, and the cops couldn't stop him. Only she could.

Standing around and feeling depressed wasn't going to get anything done, she realized, so she set to work. She started by tossing the blanket and rope into the tall grass at the side of the road, then she pulled out the tire iron, maintenance book, and flares. The rest stayed in the trunk.

She returned to the open driver's side door and searched around for the hood release, all the while hoping she might find something easy to fix, like a leaking radiator or a disconnected battery cable.

When the hood popped open, she brought her haul from the trunk up to the front of the car and set everything on the ground. The latch gave her a hard time, but she finally got the hood up and secured. Unfortunately, no obvious problems presented themselves. No steam rose and no water hissed from the radiator cap. No battery cable hung loose.

Fiddling with visible cables and hoses produced nothing.

Sickening as it was to consider, it was quite likely she had simply pushed the old car too hard.

A sound echoed in the night air, and Tammy straightened and strained to listen. After a second, the sound resolved into a car engine. A powerful one. She peered around the hood, rocking back on her heels when she saw bright headlights approaching.

Stone. So quickly?

She fought off panic and tried to concentrate. Leighton's screams, the sight of Eric being torn in half, the sight and sound of Walt being snapped in half: They filled her thoughts and made concentration nearly impossible. Tessa's face—drugged, dying, so abused.

I left her to die. I left her there to die. Alone. After everything they'd done to her, I just left her.

The car drew closer. It was accelerating.

Tammy thought about running, sprinting across the field to the housing development. She remembered Walt trying to get away from Stone and failing.

There was no way she was outrunning Stone.

She grabbed the modeling knife from her clutch. It was sharp enough to cut a nice, deep slash, maybe in Stone's face. Maybe she could take out one of his eyes.

She had to do *something*.

The car slowed as it approached, its engine spitting thunder stolen from the heavens. It passed the Monte Carlo, and Tammy felt the occupant. A man, but it wasn't Stone. The man was curious. Suspicious.

The tail lights brightened. The car stopped. It was backing up.

Fuck. Why does this keep happening to me?

The car stopped, and the passenger side window lowered. She could see a man, big in the low car, middle-aged, with puffy, white hair, a beak nose, skin burned red, and a thick neck. "Excuse me, Miss. Is everything okay?"

Tammy looked at the Monte Carlo's engine. She didn't know if the guy was trustworthy, but he sort of seemed like it. Even if he was, though, she worried he might engage the cops. Cops meant being stuck in one place, just waiting for Stone to come. There was only one place she could be safe: Harrison Mansion.

Blowing the guy off seemed like the best option.

"*¿Habla inglés?*" He seemed determined to get through to her.

Tammy could feel the first hint of hostility in the man, a simmering anger. "Um, I'm not actually very good with Spanish."

The hostility faded immediately. "You can never be too careful. We get illegals in these parts all the time, sneaking around on back roads and such. You having car problems?"

All worked up because I looked like an "illegal" on a night where I watched five white fucks fight over killing me? Wonderful. "Yeah. It just stopped on me."

"You mind if I give it a look? It's a pretty old car. 1984?"

Tammy held up the Chilton's manual. "This says 1985."

The man chortled, then pulled past the Monte Carlo again and swung wide into the other lane. He made a tight turn that brought the front of his car close to the Monte Carlo and came to a stop a few feet from Tammy. She could clearly see the Chevrolet emblem on his car.

"She's a beauty, isn't she?" He slid out of the car and gently patted the hood. "Not even a year old yet."

"She is. What is she?"

He straightened and smiled proudly. "Camaro. Get her on the open road, she can outrun all your troubles."

"How much did you spend?"

"Too damn much." The man laughed hard at that and brought a beefy hand up to scratch his chest.

Tammy could make out a big, black tattoo on his forearm. He followed her gaze.

"Twenty years in the Corps." He pointed to the tattoo. "Another twenty-five in the highway patrol. Name's Larry, by the way." He offered her his right hand. It reminded her of Stone's hand: big, hairy, but the hair was white. "Larry Sargent. Friends call me Sarge."

She nodded, unsure what to make of that. His hand engulfed hers, but the shake was gentle and friendly.

"That's a joke. Larry's fine. Let's take a look at what we got here." He hunched over and repeated what she'd done earlier, fiddling with cables and hoses. "What sort of symptoms did you have?"

Tammy shrugged, perplexed. "It just died."

Larry stopped fiddling and looked at her. "No noises or smells or anything like that before it died?" He stepped back from the Monte Carlo and hitched his pants up. He was a solid man, big and intimidating, maybe as big as Stone in the photograph, without the bodybuilder part.

"Well, sure. I guess. It was making a lot of noises, like knocking and skipping. And it was shaking. And there was a smell, like something might be wrong with the exhaust."

Larry leaned in close and looked her over. "You're dressed up awfully pretty for a stretch of cornfield. Is there something you want to tell me about, Miss…?"

"McPhee."

"Miss McPhee."

"No. My boyfriend and I had an argument, that's all."

"This his car?" Larry jabbed a thick thumb at the Monte Carlo.

"Yeah."

"Well, it's a piece of work. Someone took care of it for a while, but not recently. Looks like a little vandalism on some of the wiring. That could cause the engine to cut out on you." He hopped around to the back. "You smell that?"

Tammy froze. "No. I mean, what?"

"Like maybe you ran over something?" He dropped from sight, and she could hear him moving underneath the car. "Yup, right there. Looks like you got a gas leak, and your exhaust is all torn up. You take this thing off road or something? You're probably looking at a few gallons on the ground back here, and it's still dripping. You didn't smell that?"

Tammy held her breath, incapable of doing anything as Larry stood back up and brushed himself off. He made his way back to her, nibbling on his bottom lip. "Look, Miss McPhee, if you're in any trouble, I know some folks. There's a state trooper station just across the river. They can help you."

Tammy shook her head without hesitation. *No cops.* "No, thanks, though. The kind of trouble I'm facing, cop—police can't help."

"People say that all the time, but you might be surprised what law enforcement can help you with." Larry gave her a warm but stern smile. "The law protects folks."

Tammy clenched her jaw against saying anything to that, but she wanted to know where the hell the law had been when Jeddo had died and William Big Bear and Praveen and Tessa and Daysi and…and…damned near anyone who had ever been there as family or friend.

"Miss McPhee?" Larry touched her hand. "You okay?"

"No." Tammy finally accepted she was holding herself together by anger and denial and not much else. She wrapped her arms around Larry and squeezed him hard. "There's a man after me—"

Larry hesitated for a moment, then he softly patted her on the back. "This your boyfriend?"

"No. This guy…he's a murderer. He killed Jeddo—my grandfather—and he killed the people who were taking care of me, and then he killed my best friend."

"Whoa whoa whoa!" Larry gently pried her away so that he could look her in the eyes. "You mean this man really *killed* people, or do you mean something else?"

"Killed. Murdered. He's a killer." Her voice cracked and she almost began to cry, but she held it together. "It was in the news. The Memorial Day Killer?"

Larry's eyes were white saucers in the headlights. "Son of a—" He looked past her at the sound of an approaching vehicle, then looked back at her. "If there's someone trying to kill you, we need to get you some protection. Let me make a call."

He took a step toward the Camaro and Tammy gasped. She could feel Stone, more primitive beast than man, more…alien than human, but it was certainly Stone. She turned in time to see the approaching vehicle—it looked like a decked-out pickup truck—pull to the side of the road, pinning the Monte Carlo against the Camaro. Even if the Monte Carlo were working, she wouldn't be able to pull out with it now.

"Larry?" She grabbed her clutch and walked to the Camaro's driver's side door. Larry was standing back up, cell phone pressed to his head. He covered it with his right hand. "Larry, he's here."

"Who's that?" Larry looked past the Monte Carlo at the blinding headlights. He uncovered the cell phone for a second. "Hold on, Mike, I think our perp's right here."

"Could you…could you get me out of here? Now?"

Larry leaned back into his car, grunting with effort, then he stood again, a huge revolver in his hand. "Just stay calm, Miss McPhee. We've got a unit on the way."

"No, you don't—"

Larry gave her a reassuring wink, then he was past her, revolver held high. "All right, sir, I'm going to have to ask you to stay in your vehicle!"

Tammy looked from Larry's back to the Camaro. She couldn't remember the jangle of keys or anything like that when Larry had stepped out the first time. Even a key fob like what Elliot had with his GLK would probably be on a chain. She wondered if Larry had left the keys in the Camaro.

"Well, good evenin', Marshal Dillon."

Tammy shuddered at the sound of Stone's voice. It was about a fifty-fifty mix of evil and menace layered with a deep subvocal of loathing. She spun. "Larry, keep back! He's dangerous!"

"I've dealt with criminals before, Miss McPhee."

"Miss McPhee? Izzat what she got y'all callin' her now? Miss McPhee? Y'all lettin' an A-rab boss you 'round?"

Larry showed his cell phone to the truck driver. "I've got state trooper dispatch on the line with me. They have a unit en route. You just stay calm and keep your butt in your seat, and everything is going to be fine."

"Oh! I best be quick, then, huh, marshal?" The driver's side door opened, and Stone stepped out. He seemed smaller than before, less intimidating. He was wearing Walt's clothes, and, although they were tight, they should have been stretched to bursting. The hair covering his body was even more visible now, and his brow ridge was noticeably heavier.

"Hold it right there!" Larry cocked the revolver and leveled it at Stone's chest. "This is a .357 Magnum, and I don't care how badass or stoned you are, this *will* put you down."

"Big gun! Big man!" Stone pretended to take a step forward, stomping the road.

Tammy could feel Stone's hostility, his desire to break Larry, to…devour him. *What the fuck? All this time, that beast mind, that's been* hunger? *It had to be more than that.*

"I said hold it!" Larry's tension was easy to sense. It was in his voice, in the way he stutter-stepped away from Stone.

"Maybe y'all don't really got the Highway Patrol on the phone at all, huh? Maybe that's yer wife, hoping you didn't get your dick stuck up in someone's crack who's gonna break it off?" Stone stepped forward, hand extended. "Lemme talk to 'em. You really got 'em on the line, lemme talk to 'em."

Larry held the phone out. "I'm passing you to the suspect. Tell him—"

Stone darted forward, but not quick enough to avoid a shot from Larry's pistol. The roar of the shot seemed to expand out and fill the open sky. Stone lost his footing.

"Holy—! He charged me! He tried to take my gun!" Larry took a step toward Stone. "Are you—"

This time, Stone moved too fast for Larry to react. Tammy saw everything in the glow of the truck's headlights. Stone's furry, oversized hand had Larry's gun hand clasped in a crushing grip. Larry squeezed off another shot, and it must have grazed Stone because he snarled, then there was a snapping sound clear in the night and Larry gasped. It was a sound like air being released from a balloon. The snapping turned to a wet tearing, and Tammy saw something dark land on the road a few feet away.

It was Larry's hand, the pistol still gripped tight.

Larry screamed, and Stone pounced. He pulled Larry to the ground between the Monte Carlo's trunk and the truck's bumper and began…it wasn't pummeling. It was more like tenderizing. Just brute, overhead pounding. The sound of bones snapping alternated with squishy rupturing noises.

Tammy ran for the gun.

She pried it from Larry's warm, detached hand, and stepped out onto the road. Larry held up shattered, bloody arms to try to fend off Stone's attacks. Blood dripped down the front of the truck, streaking down the headlights and grill. Larry coughed up more as Tammy tried to sight in on Stone. Stone was so close to Larry's savaged body, it was almost impossible to get a shot off.

She fired, and Larry went limp.

Oh, fuck!

Stone stiffened, and she ran for the gap between the Camaro and the Monte Carlo. She dropped to the ground and closed her eyes.

Oh, fuck! Oh, fuck! Oh, fuck!

"Hey, A-rab bitch! You shot yer protector!" Stone howled with laughter. "You shot him deader'n a doornail!"

Tammy wanted Stone to just die. Just *die!* All she could think of was the brutal murders he'd committed, the senseless one she'd committed, and the smell of—

Gas. Under the car. She looked around for the maintenance manual and spotted it just under the front of the car. She pulled it to her, made sure it was as dry as it looked, then dug the Zippo lighter out of her clutch.

"You think you can hide from me, bitch? I can fuckin' see you."

The manual caught fire easily. She looked the length of the undercarriage of the car, straight into Stone's eyes. They were barely human anymore.

"Like what I did to this ol' hunk o' junk when you run me over?" Stone flashed a terrifying, toothy smile. Even his teeth had changed, grown sharper and more wicked looking.

Tammy skidded the burning manual toward Stone and flipped him off.

"Oh, look out, she goin' try to set me on—"

An explosion drowned out Stone's words. The Monte Carlo's rear end lifted a few inches off the ground.

Tammy grabbed the pistol, leapt to her feet, and ran for the Camaro. She slid into the driver's seat and tossed the pistol on the floor beneath her, then she searched the steering column and dash. She spotted the ignition in the console's bright blue light.

Key fob.

Something had finally broken her way.

She turned the fob, and the engine roared to life. The power running through the vehicle was almost orgasmic. She popped the car into drive and punched the accelerator. The car bucked, and then she was thrust forward when it hit the Monte Carlo. Even without any room to build up momentum, the Camaro had enough power to push the Monte Carlo back and then some.

Stone stood just as the Monte Carlo started moving. He was on fire, his clothes burning, his skin burning, his hair burning. He screamed something at her, but she didn't care. He was pinned between the Monte Carlo and the truck. It was all she needed for the moment.

She looked out the rearview mirror and saw distant lights. Police lights. Too far away to matter. She threw the Camaro into reverse and again punched the gas. The car's speed was intoxicating, the lack of control even more intoxicating.

She braked, and the car nearly flipped. She gripped the steering wheel and shivered.

Stone shoved the Monte Carlo forward, then gingerly stepped clear of it. Tammy licked her lips. She reached down and found the pistol, pulling it up and pinning it between her left thigh and the seat. She slowly backed away from Stone.

He started to run toward her.

It was slow and awkward at first, but then he began finding his stride. She gave the Camaro a little more gas and opened the distance some more, watching the road behind her. The police car's headlights were still almost a single point, but they were coming head-on after approaching at an angle before.

She braked and let Stone get closer, then she popped the car into drive and floored the accelerator again. Her eyes were on the speedometer as she closed the gap. The Camaro was approaching fifty when she hit him square in the thighs.

Stone went airborne, bouncing off the windshield, then over the car, then hitting the road with a meaty thunk.

Tammy braked hard.

When she came to a stop, she threw the Camaro into reverse again and accelerated until she felt the car bounce off Stone.

The sirens were close enough to hear over the Camaro's engine now. Tammy stopped and got out of the car, the .357 in her hand. She walked up to Stone, the pistol held up where he could see it.

Stone was a mangled mess, his flesh charred in spots, his hair burned away. Bones jutted out of his flesh or bulged noticeably beneath his skin. His jaw was shattered and dislocated, and blood trickled from the place where his nose should have been. One good eye watched Tammy as she approached, and somehow Stone still managed to laugh his brutal, inhuman laugh.

Tammy pressed a pink-sneakered foot against Stone's mangled jaw and wrapped her other hand around the pistol. "I don't have to be a marksman for this, asshole."

He grunted, and his jaw worked beneath her sneakered foot.

"For Jeddo." Tammy fired a shot straight into Stone's good eye, destroying it and tearing off a chunk of his skull. The gun kicked in her hands, but not that much worse than the pistols she'd fired before.

"For my family." She fired again, blasting away another chunk of skull.

The siren was deafening now, as was the sound of rubber skidding across asphalt.

"For everyone you've killed, you monster."

She fired again, and the top of Stone's skull popped off. His body convulsed and blood and brain fluid leaked from the holes. Tammy kicked a piece of brain from her sneaker top.

A door popped open somewhere behind her. "You! Drop the weapon! Drop the weapon!"

Tammy dropped the pistol and slowly raised her hands.

"Get to your knees, hands behind your head!"

Tammy did as directed. Whoever it was, they'd seen her execute Stone. They were running forward, and they would see the damage done to Stone's body and the Camaro. They could see the burning Monte Carlo and the pickup truck.

The trooper slapped cuffs on Tammy's right wrist and jerked her arm behind her back. She didn't resist. She didn't care. As the trooper cuffed her other hand behind her, she kept telling herself that whatever came, she'd done her part. She'd killed Stone. She'd avenged her family.

"You have the right to remain silent …"

Tammy couldn't remember even being told she was under arrest, but there were going to be gaps in her memory after what she'd gone through. She was running on fumes, and things were moving quickly now.

Except for Stone. Even the convulsions had stopped for him.

The trooper's voice came again. "Ma'am? I'm going to lift you to your feet."

Tammy did what she could to help.

The trooper turned her around, and she got a decent look at him: big, white, young, blue-gray uniform, dark Smoky the Bear hat. Troopers always seemed to be white.

"He killed Larry," she whispered. Or at least it sounded like a whisper after the gunfire.

"Sarge?" The state trooper turned to look at the scene.

"Yeah, he said that's what everyone called him."

"You still can't just execute someone like that, ma'am. That's murder."

"Self-defense. He killed my family. He's been trying to kill me. I saw him kill four people across the river, in Granite City. But they deserved it. They killed my friend, and they were planning to kill me."

The trooper just looked at her for several heartbeats, then he looked back at the crime scene. He never showed the slightest emotion. "You Tamment McPhee, ma'am?"

"Tammy, yeah."

"All right, Ms. McPhee, I'm going to put you in my cruiser, and we're going to wait for some other units to show up."

"Sure."

He led her to the cruiser and carefully helped her into the backseat, then he grabbed his radio and began a back-and-forth with a couple people. Tammy couldn't work up any interest in the conversation. Her mind's eye saw only one thing: Stone, dead.

"Why the hell didn't I just tell you no, Tessa? Why?" Tammy sniffled and leaned forward in the seat. She looked up and saw the state trooper, a dark silhouette by the distant pickup truck. Something passed between her and the silhouette, something low to the ground and awkward and slow.

"Oh, fuck." Her heart pounded and she squinted, trying to see past the Camaro, where she imagined Stone's corpse should be.

It was gone.

Chapter Nineteen

The plane bounced on landing, then it recovered and set down gently. Elliot shifted in his seat. It felt tight and stiff and rough to the touch where before it had been moderately comfortable. His eyes never left Simirita's chair. At any minute, he expected her to charge him.

She didn't move.

He sucked in a deep, long breath, felt the dry air against his throat. The fear that had been gnawing at him since spotting her had left him damp and pungent. His thoughts were filled with the memory of her taste—beastly and rotten.

She's already in my mind.

Braking thrust him forward in his seat, the drone of the propellers changed, and still Simirita stayed in her seat.

Elliot relaxed. If all she'd wanted was to kill him, he'd be dead. That meant she wanted something from him. That meant he had something valuable— knowledge, a possession…something.

What? Not something of Praveen's, since she didn't attack me at his aunt's house and she's still after me. She never showed up at Neda's. If Simirita could find my flight to Tanegashima, she could certainly have found my flight to Bandar Abbas. So is it something of Ms. Nakama's?

Or is this just the right place to take whatever it is from me, out in the middle of nowhere? What if I don't have it on me? Yet. Something not in my carry-on bag.

The plane slowed and turned, taxiing to the terminal.

Elliot imagined a grid of possibilities: Simirita wanted something physical that he had; Simirita wanted some knowledge he had; Simirita wanted to kill him, but in a special place; Simirita wanted to take him captive and eat him, but she had to do that away from prying eyes.

He winced at the last two.

If she wanted something physical, she would either immediately attack him in the terminal or she would attack him at the baggage claim. Waiting longer than that didn't make much sense. She was strong. She could apparently make herself forgettable or unnoticeable, although there were apparently limits to that; the passengers had looked up during one of the times she had laughed at him.

If she wanted knowledge from him, she might try the drugs or the binding or whatever it was again.

He shivered at the memory of what she'd done to him before.

She had limits to that as well, or she would have simply affected him while they were still in the air. Maybe the cabin was too big for her drug to work. Or maybe it was something to do with being in the air in the first place.

Whatever it was, she seemed likely to wait until they were off the plane.

Killing him would be harder. She might be strong, but he was young and in excellent shape. She couldn't simply overpower him, so she would need to come up with something more clever. Poison seemed like a good idea.

The same idea applied to eating him or some variation of it. She couldn't just do that out in the open, or she would've done it already.

So I'm safe until I get into the terminal. Maybe.

The plane slowed again and entered into a turn. It felt slow, precise, as if it were trying to negotiate a small area. *The terminal. We're already there.*

Simirita looked back as the plane came to a halt. She smiled archly: the hunt was on.

The plane came to a stop. Elliot desperately wanted a drink to wash away the bitter taste of fear in his mouth, but the water bottle now looked like it held blood—real or illusion, it still made the bottle off-limits.

A soft sucking sound caught his attention. He looked up from the blood-filled bottle.

The door was open. They were lowering the steps.

The stewardess thanked everyone for flying Japan Air Commuter and wished them a pleasant time on Tanegashima. People stood and opened the overhead bins and gathered their bags.

Simirita waited and watched, shifting so that Elliot could see her in profile.

She wore a silky cream blouse with a low neckline and chocolate brown skirt cut to mid-thigh. Elliot realized that if she'd intended the outfit and pose as a reminder of what he'd lost, it didn't work. Regardless of whether she had used drugs or something else on him, she was too dangerous a threat for him to see her as anything other than a hunter and him as helpless, confused prey.

The feeling irritated him. As a hunter, his kills had always been for food, not sport. Simirita was playing him for sport.

He weighed the benefits of trying to wait her out versus aggressively going for the terminal. Everything about the plane screamed dead-end, and if she wanted something in his bags or Ms. Nakama's boxes …

No. I've got to get ahead of her.

Getting into the terminal meant crossing the apron, and that would be its own particular moment of terror. It was an open space, there were no security cameras, and there wouldn't be any security personnel. She could kill him in front of everyone, and there wouldn't even be that many witnesses. Escape would be possible through the terminal or simply by running away from the airport.

But simple killing didn't make sense. If she'd wanted him dead, she could have done it in the hotel. So it wasn't just killing him.

She wants to consume me, whether figuratively or literally. Whatever it is she's doing is driven by something more than just my death. But what?

The businessman beside Elliot stepped into the aisle and bowed slightly, waving him out. Elliot moved, awkwardly bolting into the aisle. He nodded at the businesswoman across the aisle, then twisted slightly and began edging forward until he was even with Simirita. The arch smile returned to her face, and her eyes once again reflected the light.

Animal eyes.

Suddenly, she leaned toward him, almost lunging, and he could smell something bestial and foul on her breath, emanating from her body.

He recoiled, and for just a moment Simirita was gone, replaced by something large and inhuman, something fanged and clawed and fur-covered, with bloodshot, feral eyes filled with animal longing and need.

Neda's focus burned against his chest, and Iryana's words echoed in his head: *Are you so sure of what you see?*

Elliot regained his composure, licked his lips, and moved beyond Simirita and down the steps. He turned back as the businessman and businesswoman appeared at the exit. Simirita was behind them, once more pretty and feminine and perfectly normal and pleasant.

Except the illusion was finally shattered. Elliot knew that no matter what she was, she wasn't pretty little Simirita who had drawn him into her arms against his will.

She would never be that to him again.

He moved quickly through across the concrete, sucking in the warm, humid air, ignoring the sweat collecting at the small of his back. He tried to control his stride, to beat back the urge to run, but each time he glanced over his shoulder, Simirita was there. He did his best to ensure she never had an easy run at him, keeping the businessman and businesswoman in between. They were caught up in a conversation, totally oblivious to the threat.

When Elliot entered the terminal, Simirita was a few steps behind him, still on the apron. He relaxed slightly. She had passed on a post-landing attack, and she had passed on an attack out in the open.

His reasoning was holding up.

He quickly scanned for a sign, hoping there would be something universal about baggage claim: an image of a bag, maybe even English text. The stewardess had said something about baggage claim being just off the waiting area.

He finally spotted it, a baggage claim sign with an arrow pointing straight ahead. Even if Simirita gave serious thought to attacking him in the terminal, there would be security guards and the other passengers. It would be too risky, assuming she wanted a clean getaway.

It was a big assumption, but his assumptions were holding up. So far.

The baggage claim sign pointed him down the length of a short corridor. He passed an opening onto a waiting area. Elliot stayed close to an elderly couple in relaxed attire who shambled slowly along. They passed through the doorway that opened onto the baggage claim area. He could see the baggage conveyor to his left, several feet into the room. A middle-aged, uniformed woman stood a few feet beyond the end of the conveyor, watching the people entering the terminal. An elderly man swept the polished floor between the conveyor and two doors labeled with men's and women's icons.

Bathrooms.

Everything was immaculately maintained. The conveyor was a stainless steel apparatus that could have been assembled just before their landing, it was so shiny. Only by truly staring at it could someone hope to make out scrapes and dents from constant use.

Elliot took up a spot at the point where the system turned back on itself, a spot that offered him a good view of the conveyor while keeping his back to a wall.

Simirita settled at the spot exactly opposite him.

"So close, yet so far away." She bit her lip and bounced on the balls of her feet in anticipation. She looked down the length of the moving stainless steel plates, then she turned back to Elliot. "It's so interesting to see what surprises it holds, isn't it?"

Elliot stayed focused on the conveyor belt. *She's toying with me. She wouldn't do it here, not with so many people around. Would she?*

"You like surprises, don't you, Elliot?" Simirita flashed her oversized teeth; her canines looked like something straight out of a vampire movie.

The warning klaxon sounded and Elliot jumped. "Shit!"

Several of the people from the plane who had gathered around the conveyor looked up from their phones. The spinning light over the conveyor came to life.

A portly, round-faced little boy at Elliot's side gave him a surprised look. Elliot blushed. "Sorry."

The boy looked away, satisfied.

Simirita giggled, apparently entertained by something even so trivial as embarrassing him. Elliot wished he could manage the silent talking trick

Simirita was pulling off. He wanted to say something to her that wasn't fit for public consumption.

He turned his attention back to the conveyor. An internal clock began ticking off the seconds before the first bag appeared.

Like Neda, Ms. Nakama had only needed two boxes, one for the urn, one for her belongings. Other than the bills the guardsmen had taken, airport security had returned everything to him when he'd returned to the Bandar Abbas airport. They'd even re-taped the boxes. That meant there was no way to simply grab his belongings and make a run for it. He easily had thirty pounds to haul, and the boxes made the idea of running a joke. He needed a cart.

"I've told you, Elliot, you can't escape me. This is where our little game ends. I will fulfill my obligations and be done with you." Simirita scratched the corner of her mouth with a pinky nail that looked razor-sharp.

Elliot's stomach flipped, and for a moment he thought he was going to vomit.

Excitement began to build among the other passengers as the first bag shot through the chute, black rubber flaps dragging along its surface. It was a battered, deep-gray carry-on piece.

Not Elliot's. Not the boxes.

Elliot shifted anxiously.

It's got to be the foci. She'll go for the boxes, or for the box with the belongings, and then she'll come for the foci I have. Will she know which one is the urn and which one is the belongings? Did I even bring Ms. Nakama's focus? Is it packed, or is it on me?

Elliot blinked as he realized he didn't even know Ms. Nakama well enough to identify what she'd used as a focus. Her training had been so different from the others, and it had been so limited. She'd spoken of the power of deception and guile, using someone's weaknesses—lust and greed and envy and so many others—against them, and she'd spoken of how her people had mastered nonviolent conquest.

Sexual. Blackmail. Put your target in a compromising position. No. Let them put themselves in a compromising position, then take advantage of the weakness that followed.

Charms. Bindings. Minor enchantments. It was all a form of charlatanry built into the belief system.

Why didn't any of them teach me something offensive, something I couldn't ignore or challenge? Blowing up a glass jar, making someone slip, crushing someone's skull—I couldn't have been skeptical about that.

Simirita's abilities seemed similar to Ms. Nakama's teachings in some ways. She had operated off illusion, certainly deception. She had used sex to put him off his game and turn him into a prisoner. Drugs or magic, human or beast, he wondered if there could be something in Ms. Nakama's teaching he could use against Simirita.

Why use the charms and bindings in the first place? Why not something more direct? Had Ms. Nakama ever said there was power tied to the weakening of the victim? Not just gaining advantage over, but gaining power from? I think she did. So if the charms and bindings—the illusion—are shattered, is that power stripped away?

Another piece of baggage rolled onto the conveyor, followed immediately by a third. Elliot flinched when he recognized the third piece. It was bright blue trimmed in pale green. A young woman standing in line in front of him had checked it in. There weren't many other check-ins before him or after.

It didn't seem like Tanegashima was the sort of place people stayed. Not for long, at least.

I'm running out of time.

"Not much longer now." Simirita shifted, taking on a bolder stance, her right foot now resting on the edge of the conveyor platform. She wore modest, black strappy heels with asymmetric straps that ran above her ankles. They were very elegant, and when her skirt slid back to reveal her toned legs, she drew numerous stares.

Vanity. Deception. Illusion. Just like Ms. Nakama's teaching. The weaknesses must be the same. Or similar. Like elements—there can be differences within a family, but they share basic properties. I have to try something, operate off those assumptions.

Elliot waved at Simirita's exposed thigh. "They're fairly nice looking, but trust me, she's got a real cellulite problem." His voice rose above the drone of the conveyor. He blushed slightly when everyone turned to look at him. He had never been comfortable with attention.

Simirita stared at him, suddenly more confused than confident. "What do you—"

"No, really." He pinched the back of his leg, just below the butt and above the hamstring. "Right here. A big clump. Hideous. Like cottage cheese."

Simirita withdrew her foot from the conveyor platform.

"And she doesn't…well, she needs to work on her grooming." He looked at Simirita, shrugging and opening his hands hopefully. "I mean, seriously, just a little effort."

He turned to the nearest Japanese woman, a short, squat, middle-aged woman in bright shorts and pullover top; she was collecting the second bag from the conveyor. "Ma'am, maybe you could help me?"

The woman shook her head and backed away nervously, nearly dropping her bag.

Elliot pointed at Simirita. "I mean help her. She just has this …" He looked back at Simirita. "It must be so embarrassing for you. I mean, I can't even discuss it, and it's not my problem. There are products, you know."

Simirita's face spasmed so that her long canines showed.

Elliot took in everyone around him. Most seemed transfixed by the drama, but several were doing like the woman who had nearly dropped her bag: stepping away, eyes wide, mouths gaping ever so slightly. What little he knew of Japanese culture, his whole display was very bad form.

Shit. It's not working. They think I'm the dangerous one.

"Just look at her teeth." Elliot pointed at Simirita again. "Sure, she looks pretty, until you get up close." He looked at the businessman who'd been in the aisle seat. "Right? Something like that? You'd get that fixed, wouldn't you?" Elliot turned to the businesswoman, his voice rising. "I know I would. I've got big teeth, right? But they give me personality." He smiled so that his incisors showed clearly. "My girlfriend told me they were cute, actually."

Simirita stood rigid, her head lowered so that she looked at him from beneath her brow.

It's working. I think.

"Did I forget to tell you that? That you weren't the first? And certainly not the best? Oh, wow, not even good. I—"

Simirita jumped, a terrifying, improbable leap that carried her over the conveyor and straight at Elliot. It was eight feet, easily, nearly half as high and not with some sort of lean or bend in the body or arm swing, just from standing still.

Elliot had a moment to react, and all he could think to do was to hold up his carry-on luggage to take the blow.

It probably saved his life.

Before her body smashed into his, Simirita slashed furiously at his chest. Her hand instead caught the bag.

The blow easily tore through the heavy material and the top zipper, spraying Elliot's spare underwear and his ruined toiletry bag onto the floor. The miniature shaving cream can, gouged open by her nails, sprayed its contents in a wide spiral as it spun.

The impact of Simirita's body was greater than Elliot had expected. He'd seen through her illusion, so he knew she was no hundred-pound dainty, but the impact was what he would expect from a football lineman running into him at full sprint.

It took the wind out of him and sent him skidding across the floor and into the wall.

Simirita was on top of him, knees dug into his chest. Her face was gone, replaced now by the bestial thing he'd seen on the plane. Her beautiful, dark golden skin was deep brown fur. Hot, foamy drool dripped from wicked fangs that slowly separated until there wasn't a mouth, but a chasm lined with ivory spears. He could see in her eyes that she was ready to strike, that he'd served his purpose and become an annoyance to boot.

The sound of running feet and the jangle of metal somehow broke through the deep, guttural vibrations rolling up from the depths of Simirita's chest.

"Up! Get up! Get off him!"

Simirita froze, the bestial, rotting smell intensified.

Oh, shit! She's considering going all out, killing everyone.

The smell disappeared, and the mask returned. The drooling monstrosity was gone, but not its work. His carry-on bag was tattered, his toiletries scattered across the floor. He looked past her at the two airport security guards standing, legs spread, weapons held in shaking hands, eyes wide in fear and disbelief.

What did they see? Enough to know she's the threat, obviously.

Hands raised, Simirita slowly got to her feet.

Elliot rolled over and finally managed to drag in a breath. He nearly gagged from the reek of the saliva coating his face. Out of the corner of his eye, he saw one of the security guards pushing Simirita against the wall, kicking her legs wide, legs that had moments before easily launched her into the air and across the luggage claim area as if she were a steroid-enhanced track star.

Elliot began gathering his belongings, never fully taking his eyes off Simirita. He wondered what the threshold was where she would simply kill everyone around her. He'd seen what she'd done. He'd felt her power. She could kill with ease.

Is she bulletproof? Of course not. She can't be bulletproof.

The security guard closed handcuffs over her wrists.

It doesn't matter now. She's letting me go. Just like in Bangalore. She knows she can find me.

The second security guard holstered his weapon and took a step toward Elliot. The security guard's face was red, and his eyes were blinking rapidly. "You okay?" His voice shook, making his accent a little harder to understand; it wasn't from exertion. He'd definitely seen something, and it had rattled him.

Elliot tried taking a deeper breath. His ribs ached, but not so bad that he thought they were broke.

"Yeah, thanks." He pointed at Simirita. "She's crazy. Did you see what she did?"

The second security guard nodded enthusiastically, as if he needed to convince himself he had actually seen what had just happened. "Your friend tell us what was going on. Save your life."

"My friend?" Elliot looked past the guard and the crowd that had nervously started to move back toward the baggage claim conveyor.

For the first time, Elliot saw a pretty, young Japanese woman. She was fairly tall, with large breasts and wide hips rather than the more slight women he'd seen in Tokyo. She had a round, youthful face and eyes that seemed much too old and wise. She wore a Western outfit, the sort of thing Elliot might expect to see while walking around in Rolla near one of the campuses: a clinging top and tight jean shorts.

The second security guard stepped past Elliot to grab one of Simirita's arms. "Someone clean up mess. Don't worry."

The security guards hauled Simirita away, stopping after a few steps when she planted her feet and prevented them from going any farther. She glared at the young Japanese woman, then turned back to Elliot. The look she gave both of them was withering, terrifying, and absolutely clear.

She would deal with them soon.

Elliot tried to salvage his ruptured toothpaste tube and toothbrush, but he quickly gave up; they looked like someone had taken a big knife to them. He gathered up his razor and the few other things that had survived and wrapped them in a T-shirt. A moment later, he found his carry-on bag. It had survived, but he would need to replace it once he got back to Osaka.

When he looked up again, the young Japanese woman was standing in front of him, holding the box that contained Ms. Nakama's ashes. Elliot's bag and the box of personal effects sat on the floor behind her. Elliot looked around the baggage claim area; everyone was making a serious effort to avoid meeting his gaze.

How about that? I'm an Ugly American.

He stood. He badly wanted to wash the spit off his face, but he had to thank the young woman. He had to know.

She handed him the ashes—slow, reverential.

"Yuki?"

She nodded once, her eyes suddenly sad. "You must be quick. They are just men. They cannot hold it long."

"*It.* What is it?"

"An Ancient. A *kami* of great power, a *rasetsu*, a *rakshasi*. It is in the service of someone very powerful."

Rakshasi. Rakshasa. *Neda and Praveen had mentioned those.* Rasetsu...*I can't recall that.*

Elliot blinked; Simirita was more than imagination. "How did you...?"

Yuki tugged at a piece of material sticking out from a pocket: Ms. Nakama's silk scarf.

Illusion. Transformation. Or delusion? No, she looks sort of like Praveen described, although I thought she'd be smaller. Am I seeing what I *want to see?*

"What do I do?" Elliot looked around, wondering what he could possibly do now that his enemy had so brazenly revealed itself. *How do I deny this? I can't. It's not like the dream. It's real. Others saw it.*

"Clean yourself, then go. Hurry."

Elliot hauled the luggage and boxes to the bathroom at the end of the baggage claim area. He turned to ask Yuki for any tips or suggestions—anything.

He wasn't surprised to find she was already gone.

Chapter Twenty

The highway patrol car was built to hold prisoners, and the backseat's rough cloth and stuffy air certainly held the lingering odor of sweat and grime from Tammy's predecessors, but there was no sense of safety or security in the car. A prison shouldn't just smell like desperation; it shouldn't just have the faint impressions of vulgarity. It should impose on its occupants a sense of hopelessness and impregnability.

After what she'd seen Stone do, nothing would ever feel impregnable again.

The lone trooper who had cuffed her still marched the perimeter of the crash scene, flashlight running from the road to the grass, and then to the fields beyond. Flares marked a clear demarcation point: *inside here, something terrible happened.*

Larry's murder happened here; she had failed to execute Stone here. Her breath caught, and she shivered despite the car's thick, hot air.

Even after the second patrol car arrived at the scene, she couldn't relax. It just meant two guns should Stone attack. Eric and Walt had had guns, and they'd had fragmenting bullets. They were dead, and Stone was still alive.

He's out there, hiding somewhere in the darkness, waiting for his chance to strike. I can still feel him, or what's left of him.

She glanced out the window, searching the early morning sky. She was terrified that clouds might start to gather and block out the slight fingernail sliver of a moon. Fortunately, for an early summer night, there was still little wind to speak of, and the clouds were nothing more than occasional silver, thready tufts.

If Stone attacked, it wouldn't be in complete darkness.

Tammy leaned back and tried to clear her mind. She needed to understand Stone, needed to make sense of the insane situation.

She'd shot Stone point blank in the head three times with Larry's revolver. The bullets had torn away flesh and bone and brain. *Brain.* But Stone had survived. No, he hadn't survived, he had…gotten better? Well, he'd *recovered*, at least.

The photo Henriksen had shown her and Elliot at the police station had been of a big, terrifying man, but the Stone who had shown up at the abandoned house in Granite City had been smaller, not that much taller or larger than Elliot. And the Stone she'd run over with the Monte Carlo had seemed smaller still, and his face and body shape had been different—hunched, wider, withered, almost more animal than human.

With each round of violence committed against him, Stone seemed to be changing. His jaw and brow seemed to be growing more prominent. Even his body seemed to be growing thicker, at least at the joints, and maybe the bones themselves were getting bigger, wider, possibly harder. Considering the way he'd handled the car hitting him—

The door Tammy had been leaning against suddenly opened, and she recoiled with a surprised gasp, half-expecting Stone to be there.

"Sorry, Ms. McPhee." The trooper's voice didn't make it sound like he was sorry. "We just got a call that Major Case Squad wants you down in Rolla. I've been asked to transport you."

Moving. We'll be moving again. That's safer than sitting here, waiting.

"Do I have to stay in these cuffs?" Tammy shifted so that she could raise her hands and wiggle her fingers.

For a second, the trooper looked like he was ready to punch her, as if she'd just hurled a really effective insult at him, then he relaxed and the emotionless mask returned. "I've been advised that you're not under arrest at the moment. No body, no crime." He winced at the last statement.

He helped her out of the cruiser and uncuffed her. As she took in the crime scene, she realized two more cruisers had arrived. She wondered if there was a limit to what even Stone would attempt. The trooper led her to the passenger-side door and stiffly opened it for her. His body language was clear: There would be no BFF texts, no visits to the mall to talk about boys, no sharing music between iPods; he was all business.

Tammy settled into the seat and buckled up, and the trooper closed her door. Stone was gone now, or his impression was too weak for her to pick up. She didn't know what to make of that, and once they finally got going, she wouldn't care.

The trooper got in and closed his door, then he set his hat on the dash and radioed in to dispatch that he was en route with *the package*. It wasn't just the way he said it that bugged Tammy, but the terminology itself. The sound of it, the meaning behind it—were they hoping to use her as bait or something?

The cruiser's engine roared to life, and the trooper backed them up and brought the front end around. Every second of maneuvering felt like an eternity. They were moving slowly, safely, and that meant they were vulnerable. She wanted to put her foot on the accelerator and push it to the floor. She wanted to be away from the murder scene, to be on open road and *going*.

It was the fugitive's life, she realized. The prey: always running and hiding.

A stop sign loomed around a bend, and Tammy realized it would be the perfect spot for Stone to attack. They were a half mile or more from the crime scene. He could be waiting in the darkness near the sign, charge out, shatter the window, and kill the trooper with a single blow.

"You okay?" The trooper kept looking from her to the stop sign. He was braking, but it was a gentle, granny brake, not something hard and aggressive. They came to a complete stop, and his big left hand slowly moved from the steering wheel to the left bar on the steering column. The blinker kicked on; even the pace of the blinking seemed slow.

"I just want to get moving, that's all." She did her best to not make it sound accusatory, but the way the trooper sucked in his lips, she knew she'd blown it. "I mean, my friend drove dangerously, you know?"

The trooper relaxed slightly, then he checked the road they were turning onto for traffic.

Highway 54.

"The one who died?"

"Yeah. Tessa. She was my best friend." The last few words caught in her throat.

"I'm sorry about that. It sounds like things got rough in Granite City. You're lucky to be alive." He turned south onto the highway, the same route she had been planning to take.

No ambush, no Stone. Yet.

"Did the police get there already?" Tammy sniffled and wiped a tear from her eyes.

"Apparently. Dispatch said they were describing a war zone. Blood everywhere."

"Aren't you bothered by that?"

The trooper shrugged ambivalently. His face was expressionless, his eyes empty. "I've been at this for a few years now, and I've seen some pretty terrible things. People think they can just carelessly drive a car around, but you get a ton of metal moving sixty, seventy miles per hour, the human body inside it is going to be pretty broken up when things go wrong."

"I saw Stone tear a guy in half." She sliced across her abdomen with the edge of a hand.

"With what?"

Tammy looked the trooper over. He didn't look old, not even thirty. She guessed he was probably twenty-five or twenty-six. He had short, almost red hair, pale pink skin, and big blue eyes. The way those eyes locked on, they almost seemed vacant sometimes. Freckles were sprayed across the bridge of his broad nose. Everything about him seemed youthful except his attitude. "What do you mean with what? Stone tore Eric in half. Bare-handed."

The trooper shot her a skeptical glance. "Are you high or something?"

"What the fuck, dude?"

"Hey—" The trooper held up a warning finger. "Watch the language!"

"Whatever. I'm telling you, Stone tore this guy in half."

"You saw him do it? You were clean and sober, and you saw this Stone guy tear another guy in half?"

"I—" Tammy suddenly realized she hadn't been completely sober, and she hadn't actually seen Stone tear Eric in half. She knew Stone had done it, but that wasn't going to get through to the trooper. "Didn't you see Larry's hand? Stone tore that off, not fifteen feet from me."

"And you saw that? You saw him tear the hand off?"

"Fuck! Are all cops so close-minded?"

The trooper squinted his eyes. "Are all teenagers so disrespectful and foul-mouthed, or do some of them just settle for being self-absorbed, spoiled whiners?"

"Self-absorbed?" Tammy's ears burned like hot coals. "Do you have any idea what I've *gone* through?"

The trooper looked her up and down quickly, then returned his eyes to the road. "You've got your arms and your legs. You're breathing. I don't see anything seriously broken. I'd say you're doing okay. A lot better than your best friend and your family and Sarge. That makes my point, doesn't it? You're yapping about what *you've* gone through, but it's everyone around you who's dead, not you. That's the definition of self-absorbed, right there."

Tammy crossed her arms over her chest and wrestled with whether she wanted to slap the trooper or...or...or punch him. Twice. Hard.

"Hell, you want to hear a sob story?" The trooper glared at her with a barely suppressed anger that told her it was a rhetorical question. He was going to have his say. "What about kids born in a war zone, or they lose their parents before ever knowing them? Or what about kids born blind or with no legs? Or, I've got one, I have an older brother whose firstborn was diagnosed with some crazy disease while still in the womb. The best case they could hope for was the kid being stillborn. If it was born alive—it would die within hours and be in agony the entire time. How about that? Those are sob stories. Those are people who have it bad."

Tammy's chin jutted out as the cruiser accelerated along Highway 54. She suddenly remembered Elliot telling her not long after they'd met that "her little pout routine" made her look silly. That had, of course, caused her to pout, and he had laughed like a chimp. He had probably meant for that to happen. He had always been such a jerk to her. Like everyone else in the world.

After a few minutes, the trooper turned to consider her again. "Okay, that was out of line and unprofessional. We're trained not to let a situation get out of hand like that, to de-escalate stressful confrontations. That's on me."

Tammy glared at him.

"Why don't we start over?"

Tammy relaxed slightly. She wasn't sure if he was trying to set her up for another unprovoked insult, or if he was sincere, but she unfolded her arms from her chest and straightened in the seat. There was no reason not to give him a chance. "Okay."

"I'll start. My name's James, but you need to call me Trooper Murkofsky in front of everyone else, all right?"

"Sure."

"So, you survived the Memorial Day Killer? That's a pretty big accomplishment."

"I guess. I don't think he wants to kill me, though."

The skepticism returned to Murkofsky's face. "Really? What makes you say that?"

"He told the guys who'd kidnapped me that someone hired him to bring me to them."

"Is that why this Lieutenant Henriksen wants you so bad? Body or not, I saw you shoot a man. This Henriksen seems to be willing to overlook that right now."

"I think he just wants to use me as bait to get Stone. If I'd managed to kill him, Henriksen would've probably been okay with you taking me off to jail."

Murkofsky seemed to chew on that for a minute. They were driving through the outskirts of Jefferson City now, heading east on Highway 50. Quiet, peaceful, well-lit suburbs rolled past to the north and south, and ahead they gave way to small clumps of trees and farmland.

Few cars traversed the highway, and there were fewer the farther out they got from the city.

Tammy had been to the area once before on a field trip to the wineries, and she remembered the impression she'd had that it had been squeezed up from lowlands by the fingers of the Osage and Missouri Rivers. It was pretty enough, and it was undoubtedly peaceful in its own way, but when she looked at things now, she saw risks and threats. Pretty trees and tall grass were now potential hiding places for Stone, potential ambush sites that would leave her vulnerable.

"Sun'll be up by the time we get to Rolla," Murkofsky said, as if he were reading her mind. "You'll be safe there."

"I don't think I'll ever be safe anywhere again."

"They'll get this Stone guy, eventually."

Tammy sighed and let her head sink to her chest. "It's not just Stone. It's everything. Ever since I was a little kid, everyone I've loved has died: my mother, my father, now Jeddo—my grandfather. And it sounds like my father's mother isn't doing all that great, either."

Murkofsky covered his mouth with his left hand and winced. "I'm really sorry about that. That's really tough, especially on a little kid, but this is different."

"You think so?"

"Yup. You're a teen, and you come across pretty self-reliant. Major Case Squad, they can call in whatever resources they need. I mean, they're supported by so many agencies, and if someone calls Major Case Squad in, they aren't going to say no to what they ask for. I've never heard of them this far south, so this must be big. When they've got you under their protection, you're safe."

Tammy rolled her eyes, not out of some cynical need to blow off what Murkofsky was saying, but because she was frustrated that she couldn't get across to him just how deadly Stone was. "James, I saw Stone take a beating from a guy who had to be six-six, maybe six-eight. A bodybuilder. He and his friend stomped Stone until...I could hear bones snapping. An ear was hanging off his head by a little piece of skin. And then I saw Stone get up, stand up on a broken leg, with the bone sticking out, and I saw him kill those guys." When Murkofsky turned to look at her, she stared back into his dull, blue eyes. "Don't even ask, okay? Yeah, I *saw* it. I know what happened. I wasn't strung out on some crazy drug. The guys who kidnapped me probably slipped me a roofie. They shot my friend up on heroin. I saw what I saw."

Murkofsky sighed, apparently equally frustrated. "I don't want to fight, okay? We've got more than forty-five minutes of drive ahead of us, and I'd prefer we keep that time civil."

"But?"

"No, it'll just make you mad."

Tammy thought about letting it go, but she had to know what Murkofsky was thinking. It would be wrongheaded and stupid, but she had to know. "Go on. I need to hear." *How dumb you are.*

"Have you ever listened to yourself?" Murkofsky shook his head and snorted. "Seriously, have you? This guy killed a house full of—no, *two* houses full of people—and he let you live because someone hired him to bring you in? And he tore someone in half, then he tore Sarge's hand off?"

Tammy decided she didn't like Murkofsky at that exact moment. She crossed her arms again and stared straight ahead, wishing the highway would fly beneath them quicker.

Murkofsky leaned forward to push his hat deeper into the crease of the dashboard and the window. It was an embarrassed, anxious move. "Come on, now. You said you wanted to hear. I wouldn't have said anything otherwise."

"No, you're right. It does sound stupid." Tammy uncrossed her arms again. "Did you report me shooting Stone?"

"Yup, I told you I did."

"So they think I'm a killer?"

He snorted angrily. "Apparently not."

"But that's how you ended up getting stuck driving me, right?"

"What?" His dull, blue eyes went wide. His expression was the same an animal might make in the fraction of a second between hearing a spring trap trip and feeling the metal jaws bite.

"You called in that you saw me blow his head off, right? You told them I'd murdered somebody, but then there was no body. Blood and chunks of skull and probably some brains, right? I kicked brains off these sneakers. Yeah,

I can see it in your eyes. So, how's that feel? Being ridiculed by everyone around you when you just tell them the truth? That's gotta suck, right?"

Murkofsky slowly licked his lips. "That's good. That's real good."

"Stings, doesn't it?"

He nodded slowly. "Yup."

"You believe me now?"

He chuckled self-consciously. "Let me think—"

Murkofsky braked as the cruiser's lights caught something on the road ahead; he flipped on his brights and turned on the searchlight. The road sparkled like a sea of diamonds. Beyond the asphalt, the lights were covered by twisted strips of metal—car trim—and bits of red and clear plastic.

Tammy felt the cruiser slowing, felt the tires slide off to the shoulder. "What are you doing?"

Murkofsky put his hat on. "That's an accident." He grabbed the microphone and started rambling about a 10-52, which Tammy assumed was code for walking into an ambush with your head stuffed up your ass.

She could see the cars in the grass median ahead of them, both with collapsed roofs and crumpled sides. One looked as if it had been hit right in the middle, T-boned.

"No. We need to get out of here." She grabbed Murkofsky's shoulder. "It's him. He did this."

Murkofsky pushed the microphone away. "What?"

"It's Stone. He did this." She reached out and tried to sense Stone.

"Stone did this?" The radio squawked, and Murkofsky gave another code to the dispatcher and then rattled off more information. He looked back at Tammy. "How do you know he did this? It's nothing like attacking people in their homes."

"Neither was killing Larry. Right?"

Murkofsky surveyed the wreckage through the front windshield. "Those cars flipped. A lot of times, that's a spinal injury. Time really matters when it comes to saving lives."

"No! You can't just stay here! He's out there, waiting."

Murkofsky slowly blinked his dull eyes. "I'll leave the engine running, okay? You can even get in my seat. If he is out there, you just get the hell out of here."

"You promised to take me to safety!" Tammy was nearly in tears at that point, and her voice had risen to a panicked scream. She fought back the panic as well as she could and clutched at his hand. "Please?"

Murkofsky opened his door and flinched at the soft alarm tone. He chuckled nervously. "You've got me on edge, all right." He unbuckled and slid out, then leaned back in. "I need to check whether we've got any survivors, okay? There's an ambulance en route, but we might need more. You're going to be just fine. Trust me."

He turned and jogged toward the closest car, the one she was sure Stone had been driving. From where she sat, it was pretty obvious the driver's side door was gone. The car looked like some all-steel tank from a century before, probably once painted a pale, metallic blue. It had hit something that looked like a cross between a minivan and SUV, once cherry red, now just crumpled metal streaked with red.

Tammy didn't need to see Murkofsky's reaction when he reached the blue tank. It was empty. She was sure now. She scanned the woods along the side of the road, watching for a shadow or movement or anything that would give Stone away.

Something flashed at the edge of the dark woods to her right. She squinted and leaned forward. Yellow eyes reflected the cruiser's lights.

She could feel Stone now. He had come for her again.

Chapter Twenty-One

A gentle breeze blew across the stone path that led to the *Kumano* shrine, setting the trees on either side to swaying. The wind blowing through those trees brought a fresh, woodsy scent to the warm, humid air. Soft sunlight and dancing shadows played across the gray stones so that each step might be a step into darkness or light. Spaced at regular intervals on either side along the path, red posts supported what looked like miniature, steep-roofed houses, what Ms. Nakama had called lanterns.

Elliot followed the path down, feeling the way the land sloped as it dropped toward the shoreline.

The whole place was definitely serene and peaceful; the perfect resting place.

Rustling leaves, the occasional bird whistle, and the ocean's distant whisper barely drowned out his heartbeat and breathing.

Elliot tightened his grip on the boxes that held Ms. Nakama's ashes and her personal belongings. He was close to completing his objective, even though he still wasn't sure what that objective really was. He didn't have any religious beliefs of his own, and he wasn't even sure the others had, at least not in the conventional sense. Yet he had gone seeking peace for them.

Or maybe it's just closure.

The taxi driver had given excellent directions, and Elliot still had the sense the driver had traveled the path himself many times before. That only reinforced Elliot's feeling he was an intruder.

The path turned, and Elliot slowed. Ahead, he could see a raised stone. The stones were huge, gray-green blocks that marked a clear path to the steps of the shrine. More of the red lanterns, these close-spaced, lined the stone path. At the front of this area stood a *torii*, a stone gateway, about eight feet wide. It consisted of two posts that rose easily a dozen feet from the stone foundation. The posts supported a heavy stone crossbeam and a smaller support beam beneath that. A heavy rope was anchored to the posts at the same spot the smaller support beam joined the posts; the rope hung like a hammock at the center of the *torii*.

Elliot stopped at the base of the raised stone, admiring the massive *torii* and marveling at the shrine beyond.

The shrine consisted of a modest wooden building, simultaneously rustic and sophisticated. Wooden steps rose to a modest porch, and beyond the porch, wooden sliding doors with glass pane inserts revealed a small inner chamber. It was guarded by a pair of white lions that sat on large stone blocks with Kanji symbols etched into them.

The temple was isolated in a wooded area, largely hidden from sight. It wasn't even really advertised as a tourist attraction, not like the island's space center and gun museum. It was only accessible by the stone path.

Ms. Nakama had requested her ashes brought to the shrine, and Elliot had expected…

What? What did I expect? Monks? Chanting? Incense?

There was a tranquility about the place that seemed unearthly, especially in light of the horrific way Ms. Nakama had been killed.

Elliot stepped up onto the raised, gray-green stones and set the boxes that held Ms. Nakama's remains and belongings on the ground. He carefully pushed the personal belongings box against the base of the *torii's* left post, then he balanced the box with her ashes on his thigh so that he could retrieve the urn.

His eyes ran up and down the *torii*. It was imposing yet simple, its lintel elegantly sweeping upward at the outer edges. Ms. Nakama's notes indicated it was a *Nakayama torii*, whatever that meant. There was a primal power to the thing.

The whole thing felt like a mountain to him: solid, immutable.

Elliot focused on the distant sound of waves crashing against the shore. He wasn't 200 yards from the shoreline. He closed his eyes and concentrated. The ocean's roar, the energy and power, almost shook the ground he stood upon.

My imagination is running loose. The ground here is solid. There haven't been any tremors reported.

Whitecaps had been visible from the parking area. The beach was on the island's southeastern shore. According to the taxi driver, despite its pretty white sand, the beach was actually dangerous. There were a lot of rocks, many of them hidden and slippery. Surfers seemed to like the challenge, though.

Gusts of wind tossed his hair around his face. The air was cooler than before, and he could taste the salt—every bit as much a discernible taste as a scent. Once again, there was the pleasant and peaceful sensation, the calm of the trees surrounding the shrine and the strength of the *torii*.

How did she know about this place? Did she grow up here? Maybe that's why she wanted to be brought here? A return journey home?

Looking back the way he had come, the ground climbed toward the inland, sometimes steeply. The taxi driver had shown a welcome sense of reverence toward the shrine rather than the hackneyed superstition the driver in Bangalore had exhibited when they'd reached Praveen's aunt's house.

Hackneyed? Am I going to deny that I saw Simirita there, either possessing or shifted into the form of a cobra? Is that how I'm going to view things now?

Elliot stepped forward, the urn containing Ms. Nakama's ashes held before him.

She left no prayer to be spoken, no words or spells to utter. What makes it right for me to speak about her? What did I know about her, really? What did anyone know about her? That she was old. That she was very knowledgeable.

That she was brutally murdered.

Elliot thought for a moment, recalling the words of both his grandfather and Praveen. Ms. Nakama had come to America despite feeling unwelcome, giving up a good—or at least rewarding—life in Japan. She had reached out to Elliot early on, but her knowledge was subtle and...sophisticated...and it eluded—frightened, really—his young mind.

It had been very hard on her.

I was wrong to judge her. She was right about the power of sex and deception. I can see that now.

A quick glance around confirmed he was alone. He momentarily knelt at the *torii's* base, still feeling foolish for what he was considering.

This isn't about me. This is about finishing this, finding peace.

For Ms. Nakama and everyone else who died.

He stepped through, passing from the profane to the sacred. Something—a whisper of energy—tingled at the base of his skull.

He opened the urn and held it high over his head and pointed the urn toward the top of the shrine. Rocks and shells had been left in a short pile at the foot of the steps leading up to the main building, like stone sacrifices made to a mountain god.

Mountain god. That felt right to him. There was supposed to be a *kami,* a mountain spirit, associated with the shrine, connecting it with other shrines.

He licked his lips slowly, nervously, then he spoke. "Great mountains, I ask you for just a moment of your time." His voice was weak, faltering. His arms shook, as much from nerves and embarrassment as from the fatigue weighing on him. He cleared his throat and tried again.

"Great mountains, I ask you for just a moment of your time. In the eternity of your existence, ours is just that: the slightest of moments." He bowed slightly and leaned forward, presenting the urn.

"And in her moment of time, this woman did what she could. She tried to teach a young fool wisdom, as a mountain might warn a pebble about the sea smashing it into sand. She tried to show the path to tread, even though she knew doing so meant her death. Even though she knew the young fool would never *hear* her words, she spoke them."

Elliot turned around, trying to see the shrine for what it was and for what he imagined it should be. It was neither, at least at that moment. Neither old planks of wood nor the ear of a mountain god listening to the tale of the works of a servant.

What he saw was something else: elemental, ancient, tranquil.

There was peace there and healing of a sort.

The shame slipped away, carried off on the back of a breeze.

"Sacrifice, putting others before you…believing…in others. And yourself." Elliot shifted his weight and inhaled deeply. "Isn't there honor in that? The hopeless, thankless struggle to help others?"

He shivered at the thought that there might not be honor in the sacrifice. The shivering continued, and a wave of weakness and nausea coursed through him. *What if they all died for nothing? What if we're not good enough? Too weak or too flawed or too stupid to let go of our own doubts in the face of such overwhelming evidence that there's more to this world than…us and what we want it to be?*

The wind gusted, nearly knocking Elliot off his feet. The gust became a sustained wind that he had to brace against. It was cooler than he could have imagined for a June day.

It felt less like a wind and more like the breath of a giant, preternatural beast.

Or a mountain.

"I believe there's honor in her sacrifice. In all their sacrifices." He was shouting now. He was completely free of concern anyone might see him yelling at a wooden building, his back braced against one of the *torii* posts. "And if there isn't honor in what they did for us, there should be."

It was nearly impossible to keep his grip on the urn. The wind became a howling beast, and Elliot felt the slightest worry Simirita's hand might be behind it. He shook the worry away and brought the urn to his chest, plunging a hand into the ash within. It was improbably hot to the touch, as if it might have only recently been scooped from a great fire.

"Some of my people say we're cut from you—from clay or stone. It doesn't matter whether that's literal or figurative, not any more than it matters where we come from, or how we look, or who our ancestors were."

Elliot released the ashes he held and watched them rise up in the wind, holding together for several long seconds instead of immediately dissipating into nothing.

"What matters—what I *think* matters—is what we do."

He pulled another handful of ashes out and released them into the wind.

He blinked a few times as the ashes seemed to join what had already been released, collecting in the air a short distance above his head.

"What we do for others. It's easy to do for yourself. And in the time I knew her, this woman sacrificed for others. And now, when it's probably too late, I can see what she sacrificed for. Like I said, I think that matters."

He hurled the urn upward, letting the wind take it.

It should have dropped to the ground almost immediately, burdened as it was with so much ash. Instead, it rose, spinning, rotating, the wind reaching in with ethereal hands to release the last of Ms. Nakama's mortal remains. The ash continued gathering, climbing upward, then edging out to sea.

It's done. Real or imagined, it's done. She's found peace.

I can return.

Elliot watched until the ash was gone. The wind dropped once more to a cool, gentle breeze.

As quick as the wind had blown itself out, dark clouds began to form over the sea. Elliot shivered as lightning slashed and crawled across the belly of the clouds. The wind shifted direction, blasting his face with a cold sea mist that carried with it a foul stench that brought to mind something dredged up from a shipwreck in the ocean's darkest depths.

It smelled like Simirita's spit.

I need to go. Elliot turned and nearly stumbled.

Yuki stood before him.

"It is too late to go." Yuki's pretty, wise, old eyes drooped sadly.

She still wore the sheer top and short shorts she'd been wearing in the airport terminal. They were damp from the mist and clung to her. Elliot could hardly take his eyes from her. Even more than Neda, she was perfection.

I'm tired and weak. This has to just be my imagination.

He touched the bandage covering the wound on his neck, the wound Simirita had left him with.

Yuki looked past him, to the sea, ignoring the mist that was now becoming a cold rain. "She would have liked what you said, my *majyo*."

"Ms. Nakama?"

"Yes." Yuki blinked. It was her first reaction to the rain pelting her.

Elliot wasn't sure if Yuki was crying or not, but he knew he was close to it. Her words had touched him. The thought that he had honored Ms. Nakama after years of pointless friction was a huge relief. Even with death approaching, he found himself blushing and looking to the ground. He forced himself to look at Yuki's sad face.

"Thank you."

"Do you believe them?" Yuki stepped closer, stopping only a foot away from him. Her eyes stared into his, probing with an unsettling intensity. "Do you have faith in her teachings?"

Elliot's eyes dropped to her body. Her breasts were full and firm and shapely, her hips wide; she was much more developed than he would have imagined based off Praveen's descriptions. He closed his eyes and concentrated, then he opened them again, hoping that might free him from whatever the fatigue was doing to him.

She was a black snake now, head raised barely a foot off the ground.

Elliot knelt to look her straight in the eyes. "How can I not believe?"

She lunged at him, stopping less than an inch from his face. "Fool. You could have believed long ago; you could have learned and been there for her, and she would be alive today, and we would all have a chance."

The wind intensified, and the temperature dropped. Thunder pounded overhead, blasting the area with its booming voice. Everything around them was energized: the air, the sea, the ground beneath them.

"I'm sorry for my mistakes." Elliot slowly bowed his head.

Despite his effort to see her for what she was—the black serpent—Yuki, the young woman of his desires, stood before him again. She was naked, whether by her design or his.

"It is coming to kill you now." Yuki seemed resigned to the inevitable. She let the rain wash over her as if it were nothing.

Elliot shivered in the chill. It should have helped him shrug off some of the malaise gripping him, but it didn't. He was sure the lethargy affecting him was part of Simirita's magic. He waved a hand to indicate Yuki's nakedness. "You don't need to do that, Yuki. My focus is here. Her beauty doesn't work on me anymore. Her magic is shattered. I know what she is. I saw her. I felt her."

"It is not for you. This is who I am. It is my magic."

Elliot wiped hair from his eyes. "You'll fight her? It?"

"The fight is for your kind."

Your kind. Humans? Mystics? "I'm not ready for something like this. I'm close to passing out. I think she might have broken a rib when she attacked me at the airport."

"The greatest battle never comes when you are most prepared." Yuki glanced up the path Elliot had taken to reach the shrine. Foxes gathered there, at least a dozen. "We cannot defeat her."

The foxes: companions, familiars. Like Yuki. Spirits. What had Ms. Nakama called them? Kitsune? *Fox in Japanese. All foxes were spirits.*

"Can...can I defeat her?"

Yuki rested a hand on his cheek. The sadness was in her eyes again. She didn't answer.

She didn't have to.

"So I die here?" Elliot was surprised there wasn't any fear in his voice. All he cared about was failing, leaving Tammy alone and unprotected.

"Probably. This is Surpanakha, one of the ancient powers. It acts only when ready, it uses only the greatest of tools. It is a corrupter and destroyer. It has waited for years to strike against your grandfather and those he was connected to, and it has now been given the opportunity. There is a desire to destroy you all. And it is close."

She stepped back to the *torii* and placed a hand against one of the pillars. "There are so few of you left. Not like long ago. If only you had believed. You were such a promising student. You could have protected the other one. She is alone, and she is not ready for the threat. Not so soon. Even with the permanence of your home, she cannot stand against what is coming for her. Another Ancient."

Tammy! Whatever this is, it wanted us out of the mansion. "Is she still alive? Can she be saved?"

Yuki bowed her head slightly. "She is alive."

"Wait. Yuki, I think my grandfather realized at the end he'd made a mistake. That's why he let me go. I'm not the one they were looking for." Elliot lit up at the realization. *I'm not the one they were looking for! There's still someone out there who can protect Tammy! There's still a chance Grandpa William's dream can carry on, despite my screw-ups!*

Yuki's brow wrinkled. She shook her head once, slowly. "No. He released you so that you would survive. You are the learner. He hoped you might have time to remember what you know, to see the truth you have held all this time." She lowered her head. "It should have been your father."

Elliot shook at the words. It stung to have failed. It burned to have failed his grandfather. It was a terrible wound to have failed Tammy.

But to have failed his father as well?

"H-he wouldn't have been like me. He was strong. He would have embraced this. He would've become greater than even Grandpa William. And you know why he didn't go when Grandpa William asked him to? Because of me."

"It comes." Yuki looked at the *kitsune* again. They scurried away from the path, dancing, leaping, then disappearing into the woods.

"Why?" Elliot closed his eyes, wishing away the threat, the inevitability of his doom. With time, with rest, with study, maybe he could find some way to deal with Simirita. *Why did it have to strike now? What did it want?* "Yuki, can't you give me some sort of help? Some sort of guidance? Didn't you share your knowledge with Ms. Nakama?"

"She was my *majyo*. We had a special bond. You and I do not."

Elliot opened his eyes and Yuki was gone. The *kitsune* were gone.

He was alone against an ancient force.

The storm intensified, hurling rain at him and buffeting him with cold blasts. He struggled to keep his feet. Lightning flashed, and when the thunder came, its voice was a bestial roar from his deepest, darkest nightmare.

Another flash of lightning, and Elliot saw the creature on the trail where the *kitsune* had danced only moments before. It crouched low and looked down on him as if it might conclude the matter with a single leap. It watched him for a moment, muscles bunching beneath wet fur, jaw working open wider and wider until its viciously curved teeth were far enough apart it could swallow Elliot's head in a single bite.

Elliot gasped and staggered forward, through the *torii*.

And then the beast leapt, arcing high into the dark, thick air.

Chapter Twenty-Two

C louds obscured the weak moonlight that had moments before washed Highway 50 in the faintest silvery glow. That moonlight and the Missouri Highway Patrol cruiser's headlights had been enough to reveal the wreckage of two vehicles before Trooper Murkofsky had driven into the debris. Murkofsky was moving among the wrecked vehicles now, a blue-gray form in the white search light.

But Tammy's attention was on the woods bordering the highway, where she'd spotted a yellow glow, a reflection of the cruiser's headlights off an animal's eyes, an animal watching her.

She knew immediately what it was: Glen Stone.

When she tried to shout a warning to Murkofsky, Tammy's voice failed her. She could see him moving from the crumpled metallic blue husk of the car to the crumpled red husk of the SUV.

She could wave at him, but she couldn't scream.

The yellow glow moved, and so did she, shifting into the driver's seat. Instantly, she became aware of Murkofsky's faint imprint—his almost herbal cologne and his salty sweat, the heat that hadn't yet faded from the seat's fabric, even the slightest hint of his shape in the seat. She felt small and powerless in that shape.

The glowing eyes broke from the shadow of the woods, and Tammy saw a hunched form that was only vaguely human. It was broad-shouldered and deep-chested, but it was closer to a gorilla than human in its proportions and the way it moved.

It was what Stone had become after she'd blown his head off.

She honked the cruiser's horn and pulled the door closed. Stone froze for a second, then he charged toward her, a loping shadow silhouetted against the dark woods. Tammy popped the cruiser into reverse, gripped the wheel tight, and pushed the accelerator to the floor. The seat was still pushed back, adjusted for someone Murkofsky's size, so she had to stretch and slide down to get her feet far enough to push the accelerator to the floor.

With a deep growl, the cruiser shot backward, its tires spinning madly and kicking up clumps of grass and loose pieces of asphalt.

She hadn't been ready for the engine's power. It was a struggle to keep the steering under control as she angled the rear end off the shoulder and back onto the highway. Almost immediately, the car began wildly snaking across the road.

When you're losing control of a car, don't brake!

If nothing else, at least she remembered that lesson from her Driver's Ed class. She took her foot off the accelerator and just tried to ride the moment out. The cruiser popped up on two wheels, and she was thrown against the door for a second, then it settled back onto all four wheels and slowed.

Fuck!

Losing control had been terrifying, but it had also been exhilarating. She braked and scanned the darkness for Stone. He was closer, still sprinting toward her.

Once again, she hit the accelerator, but this time she didn't push it all the way to the floor. The cruiser was much faster than Stone. She didn't need to be so aggressive. Once she was sure she was opening up some distance on him, she glanced up at the rearview mirror.

No lights were approaching. The highway was hers.

She kept the speed up, drawing Stone toward her. He was running on the road now, occasionally dropping so low she expected him to run on all fours. The headlights revealed a truly deformed man who only vaguely resembled the humongous skinhead from Henriksen's photo. The jaw, forehead, and cheekbones were all prominent now. In fact, Stone's whole head seemed larger than before. His eyes definitely were. They were huge, with no clear delineation between pupil and oversized iris; it gave the eyes an almost black, hollow look. Dark, heavy hair and whiskers covered the top of his head and face. Thin lip slivers peeled back to reveal wickedly sharp teeth that snapped in frustration, and huge, powerful hands swiped at the air. Even with thick, knobby joints, he was running faster than any human could hope to.

Tammy shivered at the thought of the inhuman thing hunting her.

Hunting.

It sank in at that point. The sensation she was getting off Stone, the vibe that she had never quite understood: it wasn't just hunger. It was more complicated than that. He was a hunter, a famished, desperate hunter struggling to survive. And she was his prey.

But he can't eat me. How fucked up is that? That must be torture.

She smiled and popped a middle finger at him. "How you like *that,* dickhead?"

Stone's pace increased as foam dripped from the corners of his mouth. It could have been fury at her taunting; it could have been the intense, ravenous thoughts so close to his victim, his prey.

Either way, Tammy took solace from his suffering. She'd found a way to make him suffer, and at the same time, she was keeping him away from Murkofsky.

Stone slowed, then he stopped completely.

Tammy took her foot off the accelerator and checked the rearview mirror. The road behind her was still clear. She looked back at Stone in time to see him turn back. There was nothing behind him but the wreckage he'd created.

And Murkofsky.

Shit!

Murkofsky was running toward them as fast as he could, arms occasionally waving wildly. He was a small figure, barely visible at the extreme edge of the search light. The cruiser's lights were probably making it hard to see anything else. If he saw Stone at all, there was no telling what might be made of him.

Animal? Someone from the wreck?

Stone looked back at Tammy, tilted his head inquisitively, almost teasingly, and then he sprinted toward Murkofsky.

"No!" She slammed the brakes and put the cruiser into drive. "No you don't!"

She stretched down to the accelerator; the cruiser shot forward. Murkofsky seemed to hear the change in the engine's roar, or maybe he saw the cruiser coming closer. Whatever it was, he stopped and sidled off the road.

Tammy quickly closed the gap with Stone, but rather than run him down, she just clipped him. Even that was enough to jerk the steering wheel around in her hands. Stone went airborne and disappeared from her sight, and then she was past him, wrestling to pull the cruiser back under control. She braked hard when she was parallel with Murkofsky and popped open the door.

"Hurry up!" She waved him toward the car as she slid back over to the passenger seat. "He won't stay down for long!"

Murkofsky pointed back down the highway toward Stone. "What is *wrong* with you? First you execute someone, then you deliberately hit someone? With *my* car?"

"It's Stone!" Tammy shook her head, exasperated. "He came charging out of the woods!"

"It's probably the driver of that car back there, and he was probably too banged up to even know where he is. And you ran him over!" Murkofsky began walking along the shoulder. "No wonder everyone thinks you're trouble."

Tammy slid back into the driver's seat. Murkofsky was marching to his death, and she didn't see any reason to hang around to watch it. She popped the car into drive, then she leaned out the door and shouted, "He'll kill you."

"He's not Stone, and I doubt he's even alive anymore. You hit him doing close to forty."

Tammy bunched her hands into fists and pounded the steering wheel. She put the cruiser into reverse and backed up until she was parallel with Murkofsky. "Can't you just trust me?"

Murkofsky stopped, and she braked. For a moment, he considered the body sprawled at the edge of the road, a huddled red clump in the brake lights, then he looked at Tammy. His dull eyes were alive and twitching, as if he were wrestling with some complex puzzle. "I do trust you. I think you believe everything you're saying."

"So, what? You think I'm crazy?" The look in Murkofsky's eyes answered her.

He broke eye contact, then walked over to the cruiser. He reached through the window and adjusted the searchlight until it lit up Stone's form. It was twisted awkwardly on the asphalt less than one hundred feet away, face hidden from view; man or beast, it wasn't moving.

It didn't look the least bit threatening.

Murkofsky pointed at the twisted shape. "Stone's listed as six-three, two-fifty. He's a skinhead. Does that match the description?"

Tammy looked back. As far as she could tell, Stone hadn't moved since she'd clipped him. She could still feel him, his insatiable hunger, the devilish, beastly mind within a mind. She was sure it was him. "I'm telling you, that's *him!*"

"Okay. Look, just back up slowly, and keep the searchlight on him. Can you do that?"

"James, right? James, this is going to sound crazy, but you've got to believe me. Stone caused that wreck. He set this up to kill you and get me."

"Tammy...Ms. McPhee, please, just back up slowly!"

"Damn it! He knew we were coming this way the same way I know that's him and he's alive and just waiting to kill you. He's in my head, and I'm in his, okay? He knew you were bringing me on this route. He—he's not even...there's something inside his mind. Like another person is driving him. Or like a *djinn* possessed him."

Murkofsky's brow wrinkled in confusion. "A what?"

"A demon, whatever. What matters is, he's not human. He's not—"

Flashing lights lit up the western sky.

The ambulance.

Whatever connection she had hoped might have been established with Murkofsky was broken. He waved her to back the cruiser up, then he jogged forward. "Sir, are you okay?"

Tammy hesitated. Stone—the body—wasn't moving. Stone would have been up with his target so close. He was perfectly positioned to strike, but he didn't move. His presence, the beastly thoughts that made him so distinct, it was still there.

Fuck! Could *I have been imagining all of this?*

She backed the cruiser up, slow and cautious.

"Sir, we've got an ambulance on the way."

The searchlight was moving off of the body, the near edge barely lighting the head. The head lifted suddenly, and Tammy felt Stone's mind come alive.

Another ambush.

Stone flashed a toothy grin at Tammy. "Ever'thin' goan be...jus' fine, offi-officer." Stone leapt to his feet with a gurgling laugh.

Murkofsky's dull eyes went wide, and his mouth became a shadowy chasm as the realization settled in. He drew his pistol as he skidded to a stop. "Holy..."

"James, come on!" Tammy waved for Murkofsky to run for the cruiser, but she didn't have to struggle to feel the hopelessness coming from him. There was no way he could get into the cruiser before Stone got there.

"Go!" He stepped backward and waved his gun over his head. "You! Look! Over here."

Stone let out a wolf-like snarl, then he dropped into a crouch and turned on Murkofsky. "Sh-should sh-shut yer mouth...boy."

Tammy hit the accelerator, but Stone jumped out of the way. She braked when she saw Stone charging Murkofsky, who was backpedaling as quickly as he could. Tammy's heart sank as she realized she'd gotten into Murkofsky's line of fire, fouling any chance he had at getting a shot off at Stone.

And then, Stone was on Murkofsky, and there was nothing she could do but listen to his screams.

"Go! Aaaa! Go!"

Tearing, snapping sounds filled the darkness, and Murkofsky's screams became high-pitched wails broken only by the need to breathe. The world blurred, and Tammy realized she was crying for someone she barely knew, someone who had pissed her off and admitted he hadn't trusted her. He had been a typical authority figure, the sort of people who had made her life miserable for so many years, and his agonized screams were like body blows: staggering, painful, the sort of thing that would wear her down.

Another tearing sound filled the night, and Murkofsky's screams stopped.

Stone turned to glare at Tammy, then he turned to watch the approaching ambulance. Blood covered his face, and a wet, fleshy strip of meat dangled from his mouth.

"N-no." A chunk of meat fell from his mouth as he growled in pain. "M-my kill. Hungry."

The conflict between Stone and the thing inside him was primal, with it directing him to do something, punishing him with pain, and him refusing its commands. There wasn't much left of Stone, but what was there was base and almost immune to the influence.

The transformation from human to...whatever he was...was nearly complete.

Yellow eyes reflected the cruiser's lights, and even without the reflection, Tammy felt she wasn't looking at a human, but at a shell that had once been human, although not by much. She could feel the thing inside Stone consuming him as much as he was consuming Murkofsky. Stone desperately needed the food his prey offered, but the thing inside him both pushed that hunger as punishment and drove Stone to ...

What? Whatever Stone had agreed to? Whatever it had agreed to?

They want me. The thing *wants me, but it needs Stone.*

"R-runnin' ou-outta people, b-bitch."

Tammy blinked away hot tears. The ambulance was nearly up to her position, but there was nothing she could do to stop it. If she drove back to warn it that a possessed human was lying in wait, the paramedics would either ignore her or subdue her, then Stone would kill them and take her.

She slammed the cruiser door. "I've got something for you, asshole! You want me, you've got to come and get me! And I'm not going to make it easy!"

Stone casually tore one of Murkofsky's arms off and stood, eyes trailing the cruiser as Tammy accelerated away. There was no sense of panic and he didn't even feel an intent to pursue her, at least not immediately.

She slowed and pulled off the highway as she approached the wreckage, sobbing and screaming in fear and fury that she couldn't make Stone do what she wanted him to do. She had always been good at pushing people's buttons, making them do stupid things that put her at an advantage. Only a couple people had ever gotten the upper hand with her or been immune to her manipulation, Bitchley and Jeddo. Well, and Tessa, who had been the queen of manipulation.

As Tammy passed the last of the wreckage, she looked back. The ambulance had already stopped, and now she could feel Stone the hunter waiting to strike. More death, more pointless violence because of her, or because of the people who wanted her.

Maybe I should take away what they want, just end it all right now?

She pulled the cruiser onto the highway and accelerated, taking it up to sixty, then seventy, then eighty miles per hour. She kept pushing the engine.

How would you like that, Stone? How would you like it if I took away what you wanted, dumbass?

She had the cruiser up to ninety and climbing. A quick jerk on the wheel would flip the car and probably send her tumbling around, maybe throw her out of one of the windows. Murkofsky had said people died horribly at much slower speeds. It would probably be instantaneous and even if not, probably less painful than anything Murkofsky or Larry had suffered through.

Something about Stone shifted, changed. It was like the thing possessing him had finally won control for a moment.

The ambush was off.

Tammy took her foot off the accelerator. "Can you hear me, whatever the hell you are? I think you can. So let's keep this personal. No more innocent lives. This is between you and me. You tell your little Nazi bitch to come get me, if you can."

Stone exerted his will again, and she could feel his thoughts clearly. She got her wish.

He was coming for her.

Chapter Twenty-Three

Lightning ran like white thread across black clouds, and for a split second, the monstrosity that had seconds before been Simirita—now clawed and fanged and fur-covered—seemed frozen as it arced through the air. The terrible power of the beast's frame intensified the chill of the air. Its roar harmonized with thunder and wind. The stench of death and corruption that followed it drowned out the Kumano shrine's comforting natural scents: the fresh, sweet trees; the earthy soil; the salty ocean.

Elliot's stomach convulsed as horror gripped him, spraying bitter bile into the back of his throat and up into his sinuses.

With Yuki and the *kitsune* gone, he was alone and helpless.

The lightning faded, the moment passed. The thing that had been Simirita fell toward him again. Its giant chimp feet curled as if to clutch Elliot's throat. It had leapt unerringly fifty, maybe sixty feet.

The desire to live overrode his fear, and Elliot dove to the side. Too late. He was always too late.

The thing hit him. Only one foot, only a glancing blow off his left shoulder, but it was enough to knock him off his feet and send him flying and twisting. He landed awkwardly.

A loud pop ran through his body. Elliot gasped, a sound that tapered off into silence.

The thing's stench—a rotten, ancient musk—was overwhelming. Memories from the night in the Bangalore hotel, from what Simirita had done to him and had him do to her, flooded back into him, nearly drowning out the physical pain from the attack.

The thing—Simirita, Surpanakha—hit the ground with an unnatural, thunderous boom, a bass so deep it vibrated through the giant stone and into Elliot, shaking him.

Elliot struggled to get his feet under him, but they were heavy and clumsy, and the stone was slick from the rain. He managed to get to his knees; that effort nearly drained him. He hoped the awkward blow had knocked Simirita off-balance, even for a moment. Without some respite, there was no way he could get any distance between them, and Simirita would close and finish her bloody work.

A clawed hand touched Elliot's shoulder, and he knew he was doomed.

The claws dug into flesh, the hand—inhumanly strong—grabbed him and Elliot immediately realized what had popped. He nearly passed out as the dislocated shoulder bone ground against the socket. He wanted to scream, but the pain was too intense.

Simirita turned him so he could see the finishing blow coming. She drew an arm back to slash him across the throat. Elliot threw his good arm up to block the blow, to buy just another second of life, to show that Elliot Saganash was no coward to go down without a struggle.

But the blow didn't come.

Elliot forced his head—so heavy now—up to see what Simirita was doing. *Taunting? Salivating? Fantasizing?*

Simirita's bestial face contorted and twisted. Her eyes bulged in fury. Five of the *kitsune* clung to her arm, another three to her groin. More danced in and snapped at her heels.

Elliot felt as if he might pass out. The sight of the *kitsune* made him wonder if he already had. It was fantastical, surreal. The *kitsune* were small, one minute no more than oversized dachshunds, the next, lithe, slender young women, naked as Yuki had been. Finally, they were nothing more than bright, pale cyan and teal streams of light, inconsequential wisps—energy, *spirits*—somehow binding Simirita's giant beast form.

For a moment.

Ripples of frustration rolled across Simirita's face. Her muscles flexed and bunched, bulging until Elliot thought they would burst. She let out another roar, again drowning out the rain and wind and thunder, sounds Elliot had completely lost in the moment.

Then another sound replaced the roar: snapping, tearing.

Elliot recoiled as one of the young women clinging to Simirita's huge arm split in half. Her eyes rolled up in her head as her lower half fell to the wet stone, pulling pink, ropy intestines with it. Simirita bit into the neck of another of the women, yanking her from the arm she'd held. The woman squealed in agony and writhed, shifting to *kitsune*, then to ethereal spirit, then back to a fragile, little woman, but she couldn't escape Simirita's deadly jaws.

The other *kitsune* fled into the woods.

Simirita bit deeper into the second woman's neck until wet, popping sounds echoed and the woman's head fell from her body. The torso of the first woman relaxed and slid free of Simirita's arm. Simirita caught the torso and shook it in her powerful hands until the last of the body's viscera slipped free and fell to the stone.

Elliot let out a barely perceptible gasp, and Simirita's fury faded, replaced by an unholy satisfaction. Her musk intensified, drowning out the natural, pleasant scents that had returned while she was distracted with the *kitsune*. Elliot remembered Simirita's reactions in Bangalore, the way she had seemed excited to control him. She was exhibiting the same reaction to the slaughter and, maybe more importantly, to Elliot's horrified reaction. What must have been a smile spread across her hideous face, a face of fangs and flaring nostrils and bulging eyes.

It was a face meant to produce despair, not to express innocent pleasure.

Simirita hurled the bloody torso at Elliot, knocking him off his knees. He held the ruined woman, unsure what to do: comfort her, scream in horror, thank her. Her mouth worked, and her eyes blinked slowly, then they dimmed.

Elliot set her down gently and closed her eyes.

Simirita was moving in a wide circle now, stalking the *kitsune*, watching the surrounding trees. She snarled and growled, sounds that would have shamed the largest of tigers. A *kitsune* appeared next to a tree several feet behind Simirita and shifted into a naked woman. The woman laughed, and Simirita turned and leapt, crashing into the tree.

Although she shattered the tree and managed to claw the woman's legs, Elliot realized that Simirita had been fooled, lured by the *kitsune*.

The *kitsune* had shown him something he would never have believed.

Even an ancient power isn't infallible.

Simirita regained her balance and charged into the woods after the wounded woman for a second, then stopped suddenly. She craned her neck to look at Elliot, then lowered her head and snorted, once again absorbed in the hunt.

"Elliot, you must go." Yuki was squatting by his side. She shivered as the creature stepped from the woods and shook its powerful shoulders, spraying Yuki and Elliot with steaming spittle and bloody threads of flesh. "Elliot. Please. We cannot stop it. We have done all we can."

Elliot tried to get to his feet, but he couldn't, not with his dislocated shoulder. He accepted Yuki's help. Once on his feet, he pushed her away. "Go, Yuki."

They're too weak. They've already died for me. I need to buy them time.

He turned so that his ruined shoulder was behind him, then he staggered back as Simirita advanced on him.

I need a weapon. A spear, a sword, a machine-gun.

There were only the woods and the shrine. He backed toward the *torii*, trusting stone over wood after seeing the way Simirita had so casually destroyed the tree.

Simirita advanced toward him, speeding up at first, then slowing.

Elliot came to an abrupt stop, his shoulder banging into the sturdy stone of one of the *torii's* pillars. Tears filled his eyes and were quickly washed away by the rain. With his good hand, he felt along the pillar until he had a sense of his position. He was braced against the westernmost pillar. It felt like a cliff wall rising up from the ground: ancient and unmoving.

Yuki hovered near the edge of the woods, watching angrily, her wet hair hanging down, resting on her chest just above her breasts. Water dripped from her face and body. The image made Elliot think of a baptism: his mother's god, the symbolic purification.

Simirita circled Elliot, closing, then backing away, then closing again. Elliot saw Yuki moving in, trying to sneak up on Simirita. Yuki's beautiful human form was gone. She was a snake now, slithering, sliding through water puddles, moving fast, one second a slithering, black shape, then quickly disappearing into the grass. She slid up onto the stone, disappearing among the ripples of rain puddles that had formed.

What's she think she's doing? I can't let Simirita see her.

He looked Simirita in the eye. "So this is it? You kill me now, and what? You get the focus? And then?"

Simirita lunged at him, stopping a few feet away, transforming into pretty human flesh. She did her best to appear as Elliot had fantasized—Neda, Simirita, Neda, then the beast again. "I could have the foci anytime I want. No cage of man can hold me. But why bother with the inconvenience? I can gather them from the families. I can take them off you. All in good time."

Then why wait until now? "But that's not what you want. Not all of it. Is it?"

Simirita leaned in. Behind her, Yuki slowed her approach and shifted position, lingering only a few feet away. She was silent, and she was almost invisible. She was directly behind Simirita, who was staring at Elliot.

"Things are never so simple." Simirita tried to shift forms again and failed. A small waterfall of drool splashed into a puddle at her feet.

"I saw the message on your phone. Consume me? Is that what you have in mind?"

"It's what my employer promised me as part of the deal." She sniffed at him and smiled. "Human flesh can be so tasty."

Elliot stayed focused on Simirita, but he couldn't stop wondering how Simirita hadn't seen Yuki yet. She was so close, Simirita had to at least feel a presence. Unless Yuki could deceive an Ancient? The idea that Yuki had such power was unsettling. Ms. Nakama had always said deceiving humans was just a matter of using their true nature against them, but Yuki had never been able to affect him when they were living at the mansion. Being able to affect something like Simirita seemed improbable. It had to be something else.

He shifted away from Simirita slightly. "So? You want revenge? You want to make me suffer?"

Simirita matched his moves but didn't come closer. "Yes. Suffer."

The smell hit him again. She was aroused by his pain and suffering and fear. He wondered if that might be it: Simirita wanted to keep him around, torture him for some extended period to get one huge orgasm.

Even assuming huge appetites for huge powers, that didn't seem likely. "Your master—"

Simirita hissed, furious, and she leaned in ever so slightly closer. "I have no master! I do the bidding of those who can serve my needs."

"Your ally? Your partner? Whatever. Used a cell phone?"

"Don't mock, Elliot. Ignorance only makes you look foolish. The phone was practical and simpler than magic."

"I'm just trying to understand all of this. It's so much larger than me. You and your ally, able to do so much, so quickly. Now it's just me and Tammy."

Simirita shifted back to her human form, a form that had once rendered him stupid. But the illusion was shattered. Even Yuki's illusion was stronger, her appearance more appealing.

Simirita licked her lips and chuckled; it was a strangely seductive sound for someone ready to kill him. "Just Tammy soon, until she has served her purpose."

"Why?"

"You were just in the wrong place at the wrong time, and she...?" Simirita shrugged, something almost certainly meant to be teasing. It came across forced. "She isn't my concern, though. Only you."

I don't need Yuki's powers to see Simirita's true nature. She wants power. She sees me as a...threat somehow. "Then go ahead. Do it. Get it over with."

Simirita shifted back to the beast form—her natural form—and moved forward. Yuki shot across the stone, stopping inches from Simirita's leg, mouth open, fangs bared. Simirita stopped not a foot away from Elliot. Stretched to her full height, she towered over him. She hunched down so that her face was level with his.

Her breath nearly knocked him out.

"Don't you miss me, Elliot?" Her tongue shot out, stopping short of his face. Foamy globs of saliva fell to the wet stone. "Wasn't it good for you?"

She made noises like she had at the hotel in Bangalore, shivering and shaking as if she were still caressing him in the bed.

Just like Ms. Nakama said: sex, seduction, deception, manipulation. Even an ancient power like this must think it's all about indirect control, knowing the true nature and using it against them. "It was good. Sure. But it wasn't what I wanted. What I wanted couldn't be had: someone I loved giving me something of her own will. No trickery. No magic. It must be terrible never to know something like that."

Neda was there again, touching herself, closing her eyes slowly, moaning with pleasure, licking the rain from her lips. "Oh, Elliot, please. Please!"

Simirita stood before him again, once more the beast, but now another step closer.

"Oh, *please.*" Simirita ran a clawed finger along the base of his throat, never quite actually touching his skin. "Your people were hairy little apes when I first wandered this world. You think your simple minds can appreciate what I think? What I desire? Are all your people so arrogant?"

Elliot leaned back against the stone pillar, doing all he could to escape the threat of the claws. His neck still throbbed where Simirita had taken a slice from him. "So what do you want?"

"The medicine bag," Simirita purred, still trying to seduce. "Give me the medicine bag!"

Mangas's medicine bag?

"You...You went through all of this, killed all of these people, for a bag of ash and trinkets?"

"It's not just for me, and it's not just for the silly trinkets." She reached for his face again, a clawed finger hovering just short of his eye. "It's what it represents. It's what we despise."

We. The person who texted her? The killer? "Sure. It doesn't mean anything to me. I'll give it to you."

"And the foci. The chains."

Elliot shrugged. "Sure."

"And I'll kill you quickly, with no pain." She tried to smile again, but her musk gave away her true intent.

"Okay. Th-thank you." *She could have just tortured this out of me. I don't understand.* "I have the foci here." Elliot fumbled in his shirt pocket. "One condition." His hands shook, but it was from the cold now. The fear was gone. Mostly.

Simirita slowly reared back; Yuki shifted behind her. "I don't bargain, Elliot."

"Actually, you already have. You promised me a quick and painless death." Elliot held up Praveen's necklace. "Unless you were lying?"

Simirita gave a devilish laugh.

Elliot tried to return the laugh, but he couldn't manage more than a dry, raspy rattle. "Yeah. Well, at least we know where we stand." He held the necklace up for her to see, saw the lustful look in her eyes intensify. "You can see these. Pretty, pretty foci." The necklace rocked side-to-side, bright even in the darkness, shimmering with a fire that burned in the rain.

Neda's lessons about hypnosis had been pretty clear, even if Elliot had always argued with her about them. She'd said that reaching a level of comfort and trust with an audience—the target—was the key. He wished desperately he had paid more attention, listening instead of arguing. He'd been bothered by the inconsistency in her words: authenticity, honesty, integrity. That they were wrapped in chicanery—smoke-and-mirrors, lights, and other ploys— had troubled him even more. Grandpa William echoing Neda's points had only made matters worse.

Honesty is the greatest ally of deception. Who can believe such a thing?

"The foci," Elliot whispered. His voice was a soft drone, something he was barely even aware of. "The foci. So pretty, but so useless."

"The foci," Simirita repeated. She reached for the necklace, stopping just short again. Foam gathered at the corners of her mouth.

"So powerful, so deadly." Elliot's whisper dropped so that it was just audible above the dying storm. *It is dying. The wind is fading.* "The foci. You want the foci."

"Yes." Simirita blinked slowly, transfixed.

"But you can't just take it, can you? You can't just take the foci. The pretty, powerful foci." Elliot pressed as hard as he could against the stone, readying himself for the fatal blow he was sure Simirita was about to deliver. "You can't just kill me. Even though you want the foci."

"No." Simirita's breathing had leveled off. She was looking at something far away.

Elliot looked up at the stone *torii* that rose above him, then around at the piece he was pressed against. They didn't feel like separate pieces; they felt whole, like an anchor deep into the Earth.

For the first time, he saw—and felt—the *torii's* ancient energies. Spirits— wispy white, but radiant—flowed around and through it. It didn't just feel as solid as the mountain; it *was* the mountain. The mountains. The *torii* was a gateway, a passage connecting the lands to the great mountains.

And their spirits.

Those spirits flowed out from the *torii*. Elliot felt them moving through him, slowly entwining Simirita's limbs. More flowed through him and wrapped around her waist and chest.

She stood frozen, staring at the focus's pendulum.

Mountain spirits. What could be stronger than that? He laughed at himself, but only for a second. *It's all real. All of it. Everything I've denied. And here I am, alive because I believed. Because I let it flow through me.*

Yuki slowly circled Simirita, watching her for a moment, not afraid of her, not even hating her. Yuki then turned back to Elliot. "You see now?"

"Yes." He glanced around the shrine, saw the *kitsune* again. They were watching now, some women, some foxes, some just spirits. The corpses were gone. He looked back at Yuki, suddenly able to admire her beauty while knowing it was an illusion. "How could I do that? Against an ancient power? A *rakshasa*?"

"*Rakshasi.* Just one of its names." Yuki bowed toward the shrine. "You did not do it. It is bound by the mountain, not by you. You let the mountain flow through you. You opened to it, and it sensed your need."

Elliot looked at Simirita, at the creature he called Simirita. He could feel the power radiating off of her: heat, pressure, energy.

But it was contained.

"No spells, no chanting, no ritual?" He waved his good hand in front of the creature's face and groaned; his dislocated shoulder ached.

Yuki said nothing.

Elliot slipped the focus back into his pocket. "Why does it want Mangas's pouch? Why can't it see it like it can these other foci?"

Yuki looked down at the ground.

"Can you at least tell me if Tammy is safe? Simirita said they were going to take her."

"She is alive, but neither of you will ever be safe." Yuki looked at him hopefully—eyebrows raised, eyes wide. "But you can see now."

I can see now. Wonderful. "If I step away from this shrine, how long will the binding hold?"

"A while. Days. Probably weeks. Do not be long, though." Yuki was a snake again, tongue flickering. She watched him for a moment, then she slithered away.

Elliot stared at the creature for a moment. He could feel Simirita inside the furry form. He wanted so badly to hit it, to find a branch and poke its eyes out, to wait for the rain to dry, and then to set it on fire. "Won't others see it?"

"No. Like this, it is just a spirit to them."

It's a spirit, a force. I can't destroy it. Not permanently.

He took a step, stopped and gasped. His shoulder ached worse than it had before, the pain ignited by the single step.

Is it the movement, or is it moving away from the healing of this place?

Instinctively, he hunched down and started forward again, sticking to smaller steps, sucking in the cool air, trying to draw what healing he could from the peaceful surroundings. It wasn't enough to stop the pain, but he didn't care anymore.

The pain would have to wait.

Tammy was in danger and only he could help her.

Chapter Twenty-Four

Trees all along the road swayed in the pounding wind, their leaves thrashing loud enough that Elliot could hear them through the GLK's closed window and over the hammering rain that had greeted him at the airport. The wind was more powerful than any he could remember in his years at Harrison Mansion. Combined with the dark, boiling clouds overhead, it created the sense of a precursor to a massive storm, an imminent threat of a tempest seeking land.

It reminded him of the Tanegashima shrine and Simirita.

Elliot's mouth went dry and became overwhelmed by a bitter tanginess. He smelled the rancid musk of his own fear. He worried it would never leave him.

The mansion's main entry came into view. With only one good arm to steer, Elliot struggled to keep the GLK on the road. The turn onto the mansion's driveway was even harder, not because of the storm or his bad arm being in a sling, but because of the memories of those he'd lost here.

He pulled past the front porch on the mansion's west side. The garage, shed, and now-empty stable were on the eastern side of the mansion, hidden from view by the storm. He wasn't interested in those. He wanted to see the mansion, his violated home.

He shut the engine off. Without the air conditioner, the interior quickly became warm and stuffy, even though clouds hid the late afternoon sun.

He had greater concerns.

Most importantly, he needed to find Tammy.

Entering the mansion would take strength and courage he wasn't sure he had. He closed his eyes and concentrated, gathering his resolve.

He got out of the vehicle and jogged for the porch, squinting and hunching in a futile attempt to avoid the rain. The wind battered him as he tried to jump up on the porch. It took his mind back to the day he'd left, the dust devil that had spent itself against the north wall.

The mansion had survived for decades. It would survive the storm.

Will I? Will we?

When he reached the front door, he paused to again calm himself. He breathed in the air, hoping to find some respite from the lingering dread that had followed him back from Japan. Instead of a hot summer day refreshed by the storm's winds, the air reeked with a moldering rot, as if a great, festering wound had split open and sprayed pus onto the mansion and its surroundings.

Elliot tore evidence tape from the doorframe and gripped the doorknob, testing his good hand against the brass knob's strength.

The knob held; real, tangible, unlocked. He turned it and opened the door.

It was dark inside and musty, like a crypt. There was something more, a lingering putrescence, as if he'd stepped into an abandoned slaughterhouse.

There was enough light to pick out details—the foyer, the sitting room beyond, the dining room entry. Dark smears on the wall caught his eye. Blood from the slaughter. The smears seemed to slither. It was a trick of the light, the clouds opening and closing, twisting and reforming.

He wanted—needed—a flashlight.

Furniture, untouched by the chaos, still lined some of the walls; the police had left it. It was jarring, the mundane mixed in with the macabre. Glen Stone had been in the mansion. He'd raped and murdered. His taint was everywhere.

How could they just leave it like this?

Elliot shivered and scolded himself. The traces the beast had left were a personal matter, not a matter for the police. Elliot convinced himself that he would deal with everything by and by.

He stopped and blinked away rain and tears. "By and by" had been one of Grandpa William's sayings.

Things will come to pass by and by. We'll find peace by and by.

It was as if Grandpa William were right there beside him.

If there was an opportunity, Elliot swore to himself there would be a cleansing and a restoration. The mansion would endure, and the foul stain would be erased.

He pulled out his phone and punched in Luis's number. Too much time had passed, and it was no longer reasonable to expect him to just hang on the edge of his seat, waiting for a call.

"Hello?" Luis's voice sounded weak and tired.

"Luis? *¿Cómo estás, amigo?*"

"Is *Señor* Elliot?" There was the slightest hint of excitement in Luis's voice.

"*Si.* I need to...*hablar con usted.* About what happened and the future."

"*Si. ¿Estás en la mansión?*"

"Yeah, I just got here. But don't come out here. The storm...*la tormenta no se ha roto.* Still blowing, you understand?"

"*Si.*"

"So let's plan on...what is this? Wednesday? Let's shoot for Saturday? *¿Puede venir el Sábado?*"

"Oh, yes. Saturday. I will see you then, *por la mañana.*"

"Not too early. It'll probably be a week before I get over this jet lag."

"*¿Qué?*"

"Um, *necesito...dormir.*"

"Oh, is sleep. *Si, si! Buenas noches!*"

"You too."

Elliot disconnected and put the phone away. He owed Luis better than he'd given him and better than he was going to give him, but it was a matter for another time, a delay so that he didn't have to deal with the inevitable.

He closed his eyes and exhaled, then he stepped into the sitting room.

Three steps, then four, listening to the floorboards creaking, remembering the voices from happier times. Elliot had never really thought of it before, the way everyone had their own little laugh—in Praveen's case, a big, deep laugh—even at the simplest of things. Even Ms. Nakama had laughed occasionally, although it was always restrained and quick, like she didn't want to compromise her mystery.

He walked to the right, past the tea room, and stopped at Ms. Fernandez's door. It was open. A terrible pain hovered beyond the doorway.

Just my mind. Only in my mind.

Stone had…taken her in there. The photos…

How does someone like Stone reconcile raping a nonwhite with his beliefs? We're just subhumans to him. Maybe it's no different than what Simirita did to me, the means to an end? Or just an attack and not sexual at all?

Elliot walked to the kitchen entry—Ms. Fernandez's kingdom. Light that momentarily broke through the clouds filtered through curtains still drawn; Ms. Fernandez would have closed them once dark set in.

The light of day. Stone came in the light of day! Fearless. Brazen. But how? This place was warded. I've seen the power of magic now. I can't deny it. If the wards truly were there, how?

Elliot stepped into the kitchen and looked around. There was a lingering smell, something he couldn't place at first. He dug in one of the drawers that held flashlights and batteries, something that was always there for when the mansion lost power. There was only one flashlight left and only one spare set of batteries. Elliot tested the flashlight, then slipped it and the batteries into his pants pockets. He turned, spotted something in the sink, and leaned in closer.

A cigarette butt. *Traxler? Stone?*

Elliot gathered the butt up and crossed the dining room to the veranda door. He hunched over against the wind and took the butt outside, dumping it in one of the garbage cans. The cans were rattling around in their metal cart, empty, the contents probably seized as evidence. The sheds and garage caught his eye, and beyond them, he imagined he could see the stable. They were vague forms in the falling rain, but they were real, a part of the mansion.

He went back inside, closing the door behind him. He held the handle, felt the solidity of the door. To his right, the glass door that opened onto the veranda's east side stood intact.

Stone gained entry somehow. That's the weakest entry point. That almost proves it wasn't just physical. The wards must have worked to some extent. But how did he get in?

A thought came to Elliot, a memory of the shrine and the spirits there. The shrine's antiquity and the spirits it held, they felt like the mansion— eternal and changeless. Simirita hadn't been able to pass through the shrine's gateway. She'd always circled the *torii* wide; she hadn't even been able to touch him when he was pressed against the pillar, and Yuki had said the *rakshasi* was an ancient power.

What did that say about Stone? Yuki had said he was also an Ancient.

Elliot winced at the realization he was considering that Stone might be something more than an ultra-violent racist, maybe a man possessed by an ancient spirit. Elliot knew he was letting his concern for Tammy cloud his judgment.

Or, he wondered, was that oversimplifying things? Could he just be stubbornly refusing to accept what was plainly in front of him?

Yuki had been real. Simirita had been real. He'd told himself that on Tanegashima.

Why change now? Flying a few thousand miles undoes everything?

He closed his eyes and reached out, trying to feel what he'd felt at the shrine: the *kitsune*, the *kami*, the *torii's* raw power.

Nothing came to him.

He blew out the breath he'd been holding in and tried again. He thought of the trees blowing, the rain, the cold, the path between the trees. There was a power there, just as there was here. It was something he could feel, physically feel, like the time he'd stood near a transformer station. It...there was nothing.

No. There was something, but he couldn't connect with it.

Why won't it come to me? Is it Stone? Is he somehow able to suppress the power?

Elliot sighed, frustrated. He had hoped to settle in quickly and to establish a connection, possibly to understand what had transpired the day of the massacre.

Even if he *was* more than human, Stone had a weakness, Elliot was sure of it. There had to be something that made Stone special, but there also had to be something that made him weak. He was a skinhead. It wasn't like hate organizations drew in brilliant people. They catered to the damaged and insecure.

It was all convoluted, contorted. There was no getting at the information, and that was exactly what finding answers required.

Elliot shook away a shiver.

There was only so much time, then the threat—Stone or someone like him, maybe even Simirita—would be at Elliot's throat, ready to finish the job.

I should be able to figure out an answer. It's what I do. It's just like anything else: break it down, understand it. Ask the right questions!

His shoulder throbbed, and his head hurt. He dug a bottle of Tylenol out of his shirt pocket, ran some water into the sink, and swallowed a couple tablets. There were too many distractions, too many imminent concerns and threats. He needed something to clear his mind, to let him focus.

The sweat lodge!

Elliot passed through the sitting room, stopping just a moment to stare at the trophy room. Only Mangas's pouch was missing; Elliot promised to return it.

The door next to the trophy room stood before him: four panels, solid oak, painted white. Elliot pulled it open and stepped into the dark room. He dug out the flashlight and turned it on, then he closed the door behind him. Steep stairs—too old to be safe, but still sturdy enough—led down to the basement.

He descended.

The flashlight beam bounced along the walls and steps. He lost his footing, catching himself only by pressing hard against the wall, stabbing at it with his flashlight hand; the flashlight slipped from his hand and bounced the rest of the way down the stairs, flickering out for a moment, then coming back to life with a weak, yellow glow that barely lit the stairs.

What's the saying? Haste breaks necks? Well, at least that's what it should be.

Elliot made it the rest of the way without trouble, carefully scooping up the flashlight at the base of the stairs.

The basement was mostly committed to storage, largely of the possessions of those who'd died in the mansion. Just off the stairs, there was a relatively small area dedicated to food storage—shelves stuffed with cans and jars, a broken deep freezer that had been converted to dry bean and nut storage. Deeper in and along the east wall was a door to a finished room: the sweat lodge.

It was normally a challenge to open the sweat lodge door. He shifted the flashlight to his bad hand and gripped the knob with his good hand, then he set his good shoulder against the door and readied for the push.

The door opened easily.

There was a small table just inside the door. He set the flashlight down there, then he hovered anxiously when the light threatened to wink out again. It slowly gained strength.

Even with renewed brightness, the flashlight barely lit the small room. It was deeper than it was wide, anchored by a sturdy, river stone fireplace that was built into the east wall. Other than that, there were a few old chairs in the corners, a stack of Army surplus wool blankets, and a large, orange, clay jar that seemed as old as the stone floor.

Old as the mountains.

Elliot crossed to the fireplace.

Wood stood in a neat stack at the hearth's left edge. Elliot slid the screen aside and gathered kindling and tinder from an open box. Once he had those stuffed beneath the grate, he set a few logs atop it. He plucked a long match from a copper urn standing next to the kindling box.

A quick strike and the match hissed to life.

With the flames slowly flickering around the wood, Elliot moved to his next challenge: disrobing. Sliding out of the sling was the worst of it. Dressing easily took twice as long as it had before. Had it been his right shoulder that had dislocated, unbuttoning his shirt and jeans would have been almost impossible.

He stood naked in front of the fireplace, his clothes tossed onto a corner chair.

The door opened, and he spun. A dark form stood in the doorway, holding a shotgun level at Elliot's chest.

Elliot held up his hands. "Wait! This is my home!"

"Elliot?"

"Tammy?"

"Fuck! What are you doing sneaking around down—? Oh, shit. Grab a blanket or something."

As much as she wanted to, Tammy couldn't look away as Elliot awkwardly wrapped himself in one of the blankets. He grabbed two more and returned to the hearth, where he dropped them. He began the slow process of spreading first one out and then placing the other on top and spreading it out.

"I just got back from Japan."

"Uh…what's wrong with your arm?" She cradled the shotgun with her right arm and pretended like she wasn't looking at him, pointing vaguely in his direction with her free hand. She felt…not uncomfortable, but maybe a little awkward being so close to him while he was naked. She'd been alone in the house for a few days, so she'd taken to wearing tank tops and shorts. Skimpy ones.

He snorted, but it sounded as if he were laughing at himself. "You wouldn't believe me if I told you."

Tammy quit pretending to look away. She gave him a hard look. "Try me."

Elliot froze at the edge in her voice. "No, I'm serious. You'll think I've gone crazy."

"And I'm serious, Elliot. Tell me."

He considered her for a moment, saw she was serious, even anxious. "Okay. You mind closing the door? You're letting the heat out."

Tammy hesitated for a moment, then she closed the door. That made it even more awkward: being in a small *closed* room with a naked man, especially Elliot. It was doubly awkward—annoying, really—that he wasn't as uncomfortable about it as she was, like he didn't consider her sexually relevant.

"I met a lady on the flight over to India—"

"Shit, if this is going to turn into some sort of kinky sex story, forget it."

"No, no." Elliot waved energetically, then he stopped. "I mean …" *How do I tell her about Simirita without talking about what happened?* "There was—"

"You know what, El, forget about it. I thought you might be talking about something more important."

"It *is* important. It's just that, things happened. I saw things I didn't believe existed. Tammy, I saw Yuki. As a human. And I was attacked by this thing that Yuki claimed was a *rakshasi*."

"Like in the stories Praveen and Neda told? A *djinn*?" Tammy set the shotgun against the wall. "Seriously?"

"I know. I told you it would sound insane." Elliot clutched the blanket he was wrapped in with his left hand and set more logs on the grate. Once they caught, he moved over to the clay jar. "I keep asking myself how much of what I saw could be explained away—drugs, hypnotism, a blow to the head. It's getting to the point I—"

"Fuck. What is it with you and your refusal to accept what's right in front of you?"

He propped the clay jar's lid open, dug out the wooden ladle within the jar, and scooped out water. He carefully poured the water into shallow troughs built into the fireplace walls, then he returned the ladle to the jar and sealed the lid.

"Things have to make sense for me, okay? They just do. It's the way my brain works. And now—" He stiffened suddenly and looked up from the clay jar. "How'd you get here? Aren't you supposed to be in a home or something?"

"Yeah, great to see you too. Kind of hard to be in one of their fucked-up little families when you're on the run for your life." She smirked when she saw the realization hit him.

"Stone? Yuki said he was coming for you, that he was an Ancient, just like Simirita."

"Okay, hold it right there. One, so you had a snake tell you Stone was coming for me, and you didn't warn me?"

"She just told me yester—um, today, sort of. And I did text you a couple times."

"Mm-mm, I'm not done. Two, what the hell is an Ancient? And three, who is Simirita?"

He settled onto the blanket. "Okay, give me a second, all right? You have no idea what I've been through."

Tammy considered clubbing Elliot with the shotgun a few times, maybe knocking him out. *No, you have no idea what I've been through, moron.* "Is that why you came down here? To try to find some peace or something?"

"Understanding, I guess." He turned to watch the fire for a moment. "All I could think about was how I was going to get to you. Yuki said the ancient was coming for you. I guess I assumed you were safe for the moment. I wanted to—" He lowered his head, ashamed.

"What?"

"To reach out to Grandpa William and the others for guidance. I know that sounds stupid coming from me, but I had a dream in India, and it's how I escaped Simirita—the *rakshasi*—the first time. My memories of Neda and Praveen and Grandpa William, they helped me. And I was hoping they'd help me understand things and lead me to you."

"Do the dreams work like that?"

"You were down here once. What was it like for you?"

"Uncomfortable. Wrapped in itchy blankets, naked, stuck between a couple naked old guys and Daysi chanting? Not high on my list of things to do again."

"So you didn't dream?"

"I was too freaked out. It was like that time Ms. Nakama wanted to explain to me all the ways a man could be pleasured and how that would weaken him for future control. I mean, come on! I was barely thirteen, y'know?"

Elliot winced. "I think she said her training began when she was seven."

"Yeah. Too bad no social services people were around. Too busy protecting spoiled rich girls from their victims when they bite back, I guess."

"So what about you? Did Stone attack you?"

"Yeah." Tammy shrugged, noncommittal.

"But you escaped. What happened?"

"Well, Tessa and me—" Tammy's voice cracked, and she covered her face to hide her tears. "Goddammit, El. We fucked up, okay? We snuck off to St. Louis so I didn't have to go into the stupid state system you abandoned me too, and we got into a mess, and now Tessa's dead."

"Oh." Her words were like a kick to the stomach. "I'm so sorry. Stone killed her?"

Tammy shook her head and wiped away the tears. She thought she'd cried herself out, but there was still too much pain in her to talk about Tessa and not feel something. "We fell in with some fucked-up guys, they drugged us, they were going to…kill us, but Stone showed up."

Elliot blinked and swallowed. Tammy had gone through so much after he'd left her. His run-in with Simirita suddenly didn't seem so horrible. "Stone *rescued* you?"

"Looking back on it, I think he let these guys kidnap us for him, then when he sensed I was in trouble, he killed them. They'd done their part. If they hadn't taken us, he probably would've killed Tessa and taken me for himself. I *dreamed* he was going to do that, so I think it was his plan, or it was *a* plan or something."

"So how did you escape?"

"While he was killing them, I slipped out of the house they had us in. When Stone tried to stop me, I ran him over."

"With a car?"

"It sure as hell wasn't a golf cart. Yeah, with a car. A big-ass car. I fucked him up good. After what I saw him live through, I wasn't going to take any chances. Leighton and Darren beat him to death, but he got back up."

"Leighton was—?"

"The…sick guy who was going to kill us. He was huge, bigger than Stone—and, by the way, Stone keeps shrinking and changing."

"Wait, he's shrinking? Like in that movie where the guy has to fight a cat and everything?"

Tammy shook her head again. "No, it's not like that. I mean…he's…changing. Transforming. You saw what Stone looked like, right? Tall, bodybuilder? Well, now he's not tall, and he's different, hunched over. And his head's all fucked up."

"Fucked up how?"

"I don't know. You'd have to see it. He's got hair now—dark and spiky— and whiskers, and his cheekbones and jaw are heavy, and his forehead and eyebrows stick way out. And his teeth, they're like animal teeth. His eyes, too. And something's happening to his skin. He smells dead."

Elliot went back to watching the fire.

"And his shoulders, they're like really wide now. And his arms look longer, and his hands and elbows and…everything about him looks big and hairy, but he's not as tall, and all that bodybuilder muscle is gone. And he's eating people. I think there's something inside him, and it's making him feel hungry all the time, and—"

"Wendigo." Elliot sucked in a deep breath. "I mean, it sort of sounds like a Wendigo."

"Isn't that something your grandfather talked about?" Tammy could vaguely remember one of the more chilling and believable stories William Big Bear had told when she was young, some sort of giant that ate people.

"Yeah. Wendigos were bogeymen for our people, kind of a morality tale. To deal with hard times—a famine or a long winter or something—to keep people from reverting to cannibalism, the legend was created that eating flesh opened you to possession by a terrible *manitou* that slowly drained away your humanity. But they're supposed to be tall and look like an old corpse. What you're describing sounds more like, I don't know, maybe a Neanderthal?"

"Whatever."

"I believe you." Elliot winced at his own words. Believing in the supernatural was becoming too easy. "And I guess the Neanderthal thing makes its own sort of sick sense. Simirita bragged she'd been around since we were savages, and when I saw her true form, it was pretty hideous. Maybe this Wendigo's as ancient as her and looks like ancient humans. Maybe it's the first cannibal spirit or something."

"Seriously, El? Do you always have to try to make sense of everything? Who cares?" She felt like punching him in his bad shoulder. "It's out there. Stone is out there. He's been waiting. I can feel him. And I still have no idea how to kill him. I mean, I blew the top of his head off. Literally. Point blank, big-ass gun, pieces of brain fell out. And he got back up."

Elliot tried to digest that. "You hit him with a car—"

"I've hit him with three cars. Sort of. I've set him on fire. I've shot him.

I've seen him stomped to death and shot the hell up by other people. Nothing keeps him down."

Just like Yuki said—Simirita will eventually escape from that torii, *and then she'll come for me. These spirits can't be destroyed.* "I don't recall anything about how to destroy a Wendigo, but there has to be something. You said there's something inside him?"

"Yeah. And he's inside my head. I mean, he's always a step ahead of me. Until I got here. I don't think he can get through the wards."

"He got in before."

"I—" Tammy's head sank against her chest, and she looked away from Elliot's eyes. "I think the wards were down. Or weakened. They were definitely down when I got here."

"How?"

"Does it matter?" She stuck her jaw out defiantly. "What matters is he's out there now, and he's going to have to come for me eventually. The cops are going to find me here if I stay. I've hidden in the attic twice when they came looking, and I've hidden in here once, but they'll check everywhere one of these times, and when they do, they'll drag me out and I'll be fucked."

"Tammy, if we know the wards were down, that's important information. I tried to feel them when I got back, and I couldn't feel a thing. Not like the *kami* I felt at the shrine."

"*Kami?* Japanese spirits?"

Elliot glared at her. "Don't change the subject."

"Can't you just trust me, El? The wards're back up. I can feel them when I walk outside." She could see in his eyes that trust wasn't something he was going to give up quickly.

"I know you don't like me trying to make sense of things, but I need to understand what happened if we're going to have any chance against this thing. If you think you know how it got in, tell me."

Tammy thought about storming out right then, just telling Elliot to shove his need to ask questions and then taking her chance against Stone. But that wouldn't undo what she might have done. That wouldn't bring back the dead. She sighed, long and slow. "I've been thinking about it since I came back. The night I went out to the club, I sneaked out through my window. I left the window open and the screen off. I felt a strange tingle as I left the mansion, like something was different. Like I was never coming back."

"People left windows open all the time, Tammy. And I doubt the screen would have made any difference. You may have been a jerk for doing what you were told not to do, but I think you're beating yourself up over something you had no control over."

"But what if that was what let him in?"

Elliot shook his head. "You remember the way no one was ever let in without someone being sure it was safe? Even delivery people had to leave packages on the porch? Remember? They did that with the door open. I think it's like in those vampire movies. So long as there's someone here to protect, you have to get past the barrier. You have to be invited in."

"So someone let Stone in?"

"I think so."

"Is that the guidance you were looking for?"

"Yeah." Elliot gently snorted. "Pathetic, isn't it?"

Tammy suddenly straightened. "El, can the dreams be shared?"

"Shared?"

"Can you see what someone else sees in the dreams? Can it be a shared experience?"

"I...we never tried anything like that."

"Daysi whipped up a tincture for me. It really opened my mind and made me more aware, y'know? I have one vial left. If we split it, I think we might be more open to each other's thoughts."

"Tammy, you know what I think about drugs."

"Sure. Drugs: bad. Dumping Tammy off on state services: good. That about right?"

Elliot slumped. He was too tired to fight a battle with Tammy, especially one he knew he couldn't win. "Fine."

"Okay, so I'll get the Seer's Sage, you throw some more wood on the fire."

When Tammy stepped into the basement, she realized just how hot the sweat lodge really was. As Missouri summers went, the basement air was fairly cool and dry, but after standing around in the steamy air for so long, the basement felt almost arctic.

She reached into her back pocket and pulled out the flashlight she'd taken from the kitchen. It was small, but it gave off enough light to get her around.

She probably knew Harrison Mansion better than anyone else had, even William Big Bear. She'd always been curious about it, and there were times— too many times—where she had needed someplace to be alone and to think, especially after Elliot had cut her off and made her life one big, miserable mess.

As she climbed the stairs, Tammy wondered about her feelings toward Elliot. She wasn't so sure she was being honest with herself or with him when she framed him as the ultimate villain in her life. It was convenient, but was it real?

And if they did manage to share their dream, what would he sense?

She paused one step shy of the door at the head of the stairs and switched off her flashlight. There were more serious concerns, obviously. Like what if the Wendigo sensed her vulnerability when she took the Seer's Sage. Would Stone attack when they weren't capable of defending themselves? He seemed to be pretty clever. For a neo-Nazi. For a Neanderthal.

She laughed at that.

It was something they would simply have to risk if they wanted to know what had really happened the day Stone attacked. If they didn't have enough time to shake off the effects, any confrontation with Stone would be a short one.

Chapter Twenty-Five

O ther than the glow thrown off by the fireplace, the sweat lodge was dark. Steam floated out from slits in the water reservoir, slowly spreading throughout the room like a lazy fog. The pleasant scent of pine wood burning and the occasional pops and whistles from the fire mingled with the room's less pleasant musty notes and Elliot's body odor.

Tammy said nothing. She wasn't a walk through a flowery meadow at the moment. Time just wasn't there for comforts, not with Stone out there, just waiting for the perfect time to strike.

She handed Elliot a cup half full of Gatorade. "You're going to want to down the whole thing fast. It's pretty bitter, even with all the sugar in that drink."

Elliot sniffed at the cup and winced. "It smells like …"

"Fermented hemp and lemons rolled up in a compost heap?"

"I guess."

"Just drink it, okay?" She made her way over to the blanket pile. "And scoot over. I don't need to throw a bunch more blankets down when I can just share yours. Do it before you drink. That stuff hits pretty fast."

Elliot scooted over, grunting when he strained his bad shoulder. The doctor he'd seen at Seizan Hospital on Tanegashima had warned the shoulder might need surgery. Elliot hoped not. He gave the drink one final sniff, and then he downed it in a gulp that seemed to go on forever.

"Oh. Wow. That's...terrible."

Tammy rolled her eyes and sighed; Elliot could be so stubborn. "I told you to drink it fast. You don't have to argue about everything."

Elliot turned, ready to make the point he wasn't arguing. The words never came, though. Tammy was standing next to the blanket pile. She had already taken her top off, and she was pulling her pants down. She had her back to him, but her neck was craned so that her face was in profile, lit by the firelight. For the first time ever, Elliot realized she was pretty. Not just cute, but pretty. Really pretty. She was filling out, developing womanly hips.

And she was changing, taking on a fox form. *Is she a* kitsune?

Tammy turned to look at Elliot. "What are you doing? Elliot! Dammit, don't you look, creep!" She grabbed a blanket off the top of the pile and wrapped herself in it. "You're moving up the Creep Scale, jerk."

"You're a fox." Elliot blinked slowly. The orange embers reflected wetly in his eyes.

"Okay, now you sound like you're losing it. Who says foxy anymore?" She settled next to him on the blanket, her hip resting against his. She had miscalculated how much room there was on the blankets. Or maybe she hadn't. Whatever.

"No, not foxy. I mean, you're pretty, sure. I meant *kitsune*, but in the mystical sense. A fox—"

"A fox familiar, yeah, I get it. I remember Ms. Nakama's lessons, thanks." Tammy wasn't sure whether to feel disappointed or flattered. It was still creepy of him to stare at her and call her pretty.

Sort of.

She reached back and grabbed the cup she'd prepared for herself, staring at the red liquid for a moment before gulping the whole drink down. It *was* bitter, but she wasn't about to make it into an Elliot drama. *Oh, God, I think I'm dying, wah wah!*

Elliot stared into the fire, watching the flames flow across the chimney stones. It was a slow, red current, but when it struck a raised stone, the current frothed gold and yellow. It flowed up the chimney, where the hot air mixed with the warm, summer air and rose into the cool storm winds and eventually joined into the ocean of clouds above.

The storm was back now. It was a physical sensation. Not just the pummeling wind or the cold rain, but the storm *itself*, the energy behind it.

Like everything in the shamanistic world, it was all so *primal*.

Does that give Stone an advantage? Does our civility make us weaker?

"El? *Elliot?*"

Elliot turned at Tammy's voice. She was completely a fox now, only identifiable by her big, dark, blue eyes. They were such pretty eyes, even when surrounded by red fur.

The fox's snout moved, and Tammy's voice came out. "We need a chant now, right? Something to get our heads in the right place?"

Elliot tried to suppress a smirk. "It's so funny when you talk and the words come out of your snout."

Even as Tammy glared at Elliot, he changed, his face melting into a raven's head. The blanket had partly slid off him, revealing his thick shoulders and chest. They glistened with sweat. Ugly, purple bruises stood out against his coppery skin. The sight was disturbingly erotic, and it was hard for her not to reach out and touch him. It took a second for it to register that only his head had changed into a raven.

"Don't be one of *those* people, El, okay? It's not the first time you've taken one of Daysi's brews."

"This is just so weird. I'm hearing colors. You actually…taste pretty. How is that even possible?"

Taste pretty? That's another step up the Creep Scale. You're closing in on creepopotamus, El. "Just start one of the chants, all right?"

"Sure."

Elliot imagined Grandpa William's chants echoing in the room. They were pleasant sounds that Elliot repeated, sometimes smiling with pride as he remembered every aspect of his grandfather's voice—pitch, cadence, the raspy quality, the tone.

It was comforting and welcome, but that wasn't what he needed at the moment.

He continued chanting, the prayers and songs coming to him with surprising ease. It wasn't exact, and he didn't always know what the words meant, but he didn't think that mattered.

"That's it? It sounds like mumbo jumbo."

Elliot shrugged his shoulders and immediately hissed at the pain that shot down his left arm. "Yeah, I mean, everyone just repeated Grandpa William's chants. They're Cree prayers, but I think they can be anything. It's all about clearing your mind, embracing memory, and focusing. Think of those you've lost. Remember what they meant to you, what they taught you."

Tammy took Elliot's good hand in her right hand. "So we can find each other, okay?"

Elliot began the chanting again, and she started to catch the rhythm and the words. She echoed him as much as she could, and once she had a chant of her own, she concentrated on Jeddo and William Big Bear, Praveen, Daysi, and Neda. Even Ms. Nakama and her uncomfortable obsession with sex entered Tammy's thoughts.

She could feel her heartbeat as well as Elliot's; they beat in the same time. His senses were her senses, and suddenly she understood what he meant: she *did* taste pretty. Her mother had always been the bar for pretty to Tammy. Her father had said her mother had reminded him of a model from his youth—Iman. Tammy realized she didn't have to look exactly like her mother to be pretty. She was her own woman, and she was pretty. To Elliot, at least. That was something.

After a few minutes, time became less concrete and orderly.

Voices joined theirs: William Big Bear's raspy bass, Jeddo's softer tones. All the voices became one, its own sound of thunder. She felt their presence now, their spirits. They were all mingled in with the power of the mansion, rooted right there, in the basement, in the stone foundation.

It was stone from the mountains. Eternal, unbreakable, impassable.

And then she found herself alone, no longer surrounded by the mansion's protective walls. She stood in a sea of sand, a brilliant orange in the sunset. A large structure—round, with a roof that rose like a shallow cone, tapering to a fine point at the top. It was an ancient tomb, like one she'd seen when she'd visited her homelands with Jeddo. It had only been a few years before, but it seemed forever ago.

She shuffled across the sand, hating her legs and the awkwardness that would never leave her. Warm sand flowed over and between her toes, and with each footstep she sank a little deeper.

If Stone had been the hunter and she the pack's lame child, why hadn't they left her to appease him? They could have survived that way. It was just how nature worked.

Details popped from the tomb's long shadows as she approached: columns comprised of multiple, perfectly matched stone segments, stone segments outlined by dark creases, other stones pressed so tight against each other, they appeared to be a single piece.

And then she saw the doorway. Towering, rectangular, imposing. But open.

She entered the tomb, following the last of the dying sunlight until she reached the base of a stone slab. Despite it being a tomb, the air was pleasantly scented, as if someone had burned spices within. Her footsteps echoed in the open space.

Jeddo lay upon the slab, curled like a fetus and wrapped in a bright blue Berber robe. He was surrounded by trinkets—an ostrich egg, talismans he'd sworn by in life, and the greatest of his talismans, his *takoba*. The silvery pommel almost glowed in the shadows. Red ochre powder completely covered him, but even so, it was obvious that the sickness had gone from his body. He looked more like she remembered him when she first met him as a child: strong, pleasant, and wise.

She dropped to her knees on the tomb's cool stone floor.

Jeddo's eyes opened. Wise eyes, the eyes of a powerful and respected *marabout*, the mystical leader of a tribe, no longer full of frustration and fear. He was the wise man she had so adored as a child. He sat up and looked into her eyes.

"Why have you come here, Tamment?"

"I don't know. To seek your guidance, I think? And to say goodbye. I never got—"

"You said goodbye to me when you were born, *honey sweet*." He smiled sadly. "I will never forget your spirit and how you have overcome so much."

"Or how I failed you so badly?" She bowed her head in shame.

He took her chin in his hand—stronger than she had ever known it. "You think because I was hard on you that you have failed? Your mother failed. I failed. Maybe I failed her. She was so troubled and conflicted, in love with rebelling without knowing what she was rebelling against. I did not want that for my precious Tamment. Your father did not want that, either. You are the last of an important line."

"You *talked* with dad? I didn't know you two, y'know, got along."

"There are things you are too young to understand. Gordon was a good man. He brought *stability* to your mother."

Tammy tried to picture her father and Jeddo just talking instead of having heated arguments. She could remember times, but when she was younger, not when her father was going off to war and fighting against Jeddo getting custody of her.

"I need your help, Jeddo. This ass—" She saw the look of warning in his eyes. "This guy Stone keeps trying to kidnap me. Elliot and me, we need to kill this guy."

"You have survived the *djinn* when I could not. What help I could offer you, you already know." He reached behind him and hefted the *takoba* by its scabbard. He held it out to her, hilt-first. "You go into battle armed for victory."

Tammy took the sword. She drew it from the scabbard and felt its weight. It was lighter than she remembered. It had been that long since she had practiced with it. "It can slay a *djinn*?"

"Anything can be slain so long as it walks in a man's body. You cannot slay the *djinn*, but you can drive it from this world. One does not summon such a thing lightly. Those who summoned it will not do so again if you destroy its host."

Tammy admired the *takoba's* silvery blade for a moment, then she sheathed it. "I have to find Elliot. We were supposed to come here together, but he must have missed that."

Jeddo chuckled, and it seemed like just a little wisdom leaked out with the comforting sound. "Tamment, you must one day learn that not everyone has the patience to separate the vinegar from the honey. Even family has its limits."

THE JOURNEY HOME

"I'm sorry, Jeddo. I'll try. I swear."

He bowed to her, and she returned the bow. She stood and secured the *takoba's* belt to her slender hip, then she retraced her steps to the entry. It was dark outside, and much cooler than before. She took a step through the doorway, and the tomb was gone. She stood in a forest now. A pleasant breeze blew through the trees, filling the air with calming aromas—pleasant pine scents, the slightest hint of sweet meadow flowers. An owl hooted as Tammy came to a spot where the tree line thinned. She heard voices: Elliot and William Big Bear.

Pale, white moonlight lit a glade centered on a large boulder. William Big Bear carefully set twigs onto a small campfire burning a few feet from the boulder. Elliot sat, cross-legged on the opposite side of the fire. He was laughing, totally absorbed in whatever his grandfather had said.

"So he had set out to prove you wrong?" Elliot asked.

"Oh, yes. Achachak was every bit as stubborn as you when he was your age. He had to prove to his father that he knew what he was saying, so he moved out east and took a construction job in Montreal at eighteen. He ended up working at one of the banks your mother's family owned. That's where Achachak became *James*, and that's how he met your mother. Genevieve Cuvillier. Very pretty, and very sweet, and even more in control of her life. And then his."

"He...loved her?" Elliot looked into the fire, anxious, too afraid of what he might hear and more afraid of what he might show his grandfather.

"As much as a man can love a woman. I'm sure at first it was more a love of the body than of the spirit, but before you were born, he had matured and become a true man and had truly known what it is to love wholly." William Big Bear's eyes sparkled proudly at the memories of his son. "It was never for money. He introduced her to me as if she were a teller, because that is what he knew her as. It wasn't until he asked to marry her that she told him who her father was."

Elliot stabbed at the fire with a stick. "He's someone important?"

William Big Bear looked to the starry sky overhead and pursed his lips before grunting. "Your mother's family is extremely powerful, Elliot. They

293

have been in the banking business since there were banks among the white man in Canada. And Mr. Cuvillier disapproved of his daughter marrying one of our people, so he cut her off. Maybe it would have been different if your father had come from money himself, but he wore his hair long, and he was a laborer. It would have been too embarrassing for Mr. Cuvillier to accept."

"I'm sorry, Grandpa William."

"Never apologize for another person's shortcomings, Little Dove." William Big Bear's voice was stern, but it was also full of love.

"Why do you call me that?"

"Little Dove? Your mother insisted you have a name of your people as well as hers. For her name, she chose Elliot, which means *to believe*, maybe in the white man's god." William Big Bear laughed at that, a pleasant sound full of love and warmth. "Your father chose Hawk, which is not even a true name. I wanted him to choose *Wajiwa*, which is the strength of the mountain. When I saw that you were no warrior, but one who seeks peace, I took to calling you Little Dove."

"Did you want a warrior?" Elliot squinted as he looked into William Big Bear's eyes.

"Achachak was a warrior. He died before he was thirty. Maybe we should be seeking peace instead of war? You think more than most. Wisdom comes from thinking."

"I need your wisdom."

"My wisdom is yours already." William's voice was as patient as the mountain.

"You gave it, but I was too foolish to accept it." Elliot choked up for a moment. "I need it if I want to face this man who killed you. Glen Stone." Elliot blushed, ashamed that he hadn't been there to stand against Stone, and angry that he would have died had he been. It was a failure of his generation, a betrayal of the trust and the love of those who had come before.

"You have more wisdom than you accept. You know what this Stone is."

"A Wendigo. But why did it attack now?"

"Because it was time. Because we were weak. We never understood our enemies. We barely knew any existed."

"But the Wendigo, how do I kill it?"

"It is a foul aberration, a *gitchi manitou* clothed in a man's body. Cut it out from the body and burn the vessel, the heart. The man's body can be harmed while the *manitou* is inside it, but only what is pure—magic, silver, jade—wounds the body permanently."

That was all Tammy needed to hear. "Elliot!" She stepped from the tree line and waved for Elliot to come to her. She shared the pain his eyes showed, a pain derived from the love so visible in both Elliot and William Big Bear's faces. She wished she'd had that sort of relationship with Jeddo. "Come on!"

Elliot stood. "I'll return, Grandpa William. I promise."

"And I will be here, so long as the walls are standing. You are the Circle now."

Tammy waved at William Big Bear, then she hooked her arm around Elliot's good arm. In the dream, he actually seemed to be free of the injury. "We still need to figure out what happened. I don't know how long the drug is going to work or even how long it's been."

"I know. I-I guess I just needed to say goodbye in case—" The look in Elliot's eyes finished the sentence for him. They both understood they weren't likely to survive any run-in with Stone.

They walked back into the forest until it opened again, this time onto the mansion property's western lawn. Hay bales were stacked in the clearing not far from the woods' edge, lit by morning sunlight. Birds chirped happily, and the undergrowth rustled with the activity of animals of all kinds.

Even in the bright light, a sense of dread hovered in the air, weighing down the otherwise pleasant sensations and amplifying unpleasant ones. The exhaust from Elliot's GLK was pungent, even though it was nowhere to be seen. The garbage cans—sealed tight and cleaned every month—stank as if coated with years of grimy filth. Even the horses' manure—a normally modest annoyance that was at least testament to life—was thick and suffocating. To the naked eye, though, the mansion seemed normal.

They crossed the lawn and climbed the western steps to the veranda. Elliot tensed when he passed through the glass sliding doors. It was as if he were looking into the mansion minutes after he'd left.

William Big Bear sat at the dining room table next to Driss, who was shaking visibly. Daysi sat across from them, clearly troubled by Driss's condition.

"Driss, this is unnecessary. Something, anything, let me prepare help for you."

Driss shook his head defiantly and pulled his hands away when Daysi tried to take them. "All our times have come. Why fight what is?"

"He is right." Praveen stood in the doorway to the dining room.

Neda stood behind Praveen, her hands crossed in front of her. She locked eyes with Daysi for a moment, and then Daysi looked at William Big Bear.

"William, we should have those supplies."

William looked past Daysi and cleared his throat. "Ms. Fernandez, would you go to the grocer and collect our food? They're expecting you. You may as well go to Rolla to pick up some of the special things for Praveen and Neda's cooking while you're at it."

Ms. Fernandez looked them all over, then she pulled off her apron, folded it, and set it on the counter. She had learned early on not to argue about their quirky behavior. They all waited in silence until she returned from her room with her purse. She walked right through Elliot and Tammy, then she was gone, the minivan's engine a muffled whine a couple minutes later. By then, Praveen and Neda were fully in the dining room. Ms. Nakama lingered in the sitting room, watching, the outsider, even when the youngsters weren't around.

Daysi rose and joined Praveen and Neda. Daysi stood tall and closed her eyes. "Now is the time, William."

William Big Bear looked at each of them, then he bowed his head slightly. "So, we have the discussion? I will tell you what I think, then. I say whatever Neda has seen can be destroyed. The future is always a mystery, even when it seems clear. I thought my son would be here this day to lead us, but Neda said otherwise. Two who had visions of the future, but only one of us right. Maybe this time, I am the one who is right?"

Praveen bowed respectfully. "I think to wait for them to attack is pointless and dangerous. Whoever is behind the killing of all the young ones you have tried to bring to the mansion is almost certainly behind the attempts to break the mansion's defenses. If we destroy their assassin, that will not stop them. We must act against those who have started this fight. Take the fight to them. If we are destined to die anyway, why not make it worthwhile?" He held up a fist clenched so tight, the scars across the knuckles were nearly white.

William Big Bear looked at Driss beside him. Driss seemed to shake with fury now rather than just pain. William looked beyond Praveen, at Ms. Nakama. "Even in his weakened state, Driss would fight. What about you, Ms. Nakama?"

"Deception is greatest strength. How you strike what you cannot see?" Ms. Nakama's voice was clipped, and her face was strained.

Tammy remembered Praveen saying that Ms. Nakama was frustrated by her English. She seemed just as annoyed by being the outsider. Tammy felt Elliot squirm beside her and sensed his own embarrassment at having mistreated Ms. Nakama, whose teachings had been too sophisticated when he was young, too embarrassing when he was old.

He thinks Yuki has a right to hate him because he never gave Ms. Nakama a chance. Why should he care what Yuki think—Oh.

Without even meaning to, Tammy could feel Elliot's desire for Yuki.

"Power to deceive come from desire. Desire to be deceived."

"We did not choose to be deceived." William Big Bear sounded testy, and he seemed to realize it. "It was my fault."

"If I may?" Praveen bowed again, both toward Ms. Nakama and William Big Bear. "I think we should focus on our strategy to address our enemies? Starting with a seeing? Neda could perform a divination." He waved her forward.

"I've actually done a divination before, alone. I don't have the ability to see through everything they've put up to obscure—"

"They?" Driss leaned forward, sweat beading on his forehead. "You have seen their numbers, then?"

Neda blinked and licked her lips, looking for a moment to Praveen for assurance. When he gave the slightest signal with his fingers, she continued. "Only enough to know there is no single foe. Their numbers rival ours, as far as I can tell. As far as I can tell, there are some who are as old as this—"

A booming knock echoed in the sitting room. They all flinched at the sound.

After a moment, William Big Bear stood, chanting under his breath. He stopped at Praveen's side and whispered, "Be ready."

Praveen nodded, and they all slowly formed a wide semicircle around the foyer as William Big Bear moved toward the front door. Tammy and Elliot followed, now holding hands, dreading what they knew must come.

William Big Bear glanced back to be sure everyone was ready, then turned to the door. He opened it slowly.

A big man stood in the doorway. He wore a Cardinals baseball cap, stained jeans, and a red hoodie. Ms. Fernandez was cradled in his arms, a slight trickle of blood flowing from the corner of her mouth. "Oh, thank God! Y'all have a phone? Can ya call 9-1-1?"

Tammy tensed. She could feel Stone's sick energy, even before he had changed. "It's Stone," she shouted. "Don't let him in!"

William leaned out of the doorway to examine Ms. Fernandez. "What happened?"

"It's all my fault. I got lost and I was comin' up this chere road too fast, and I didn't see her comin' until it was too late, and she drove offa the road. Oh, God, I think she's hurt."

"Bring her in." William Big Bear stepped aside and waved Stone in. "Set her over there, on that divan. Daysi, please call the hospital."

Stone was quickly past William Big Bear, setting Ms. Fernandez down gently and stepping back. "I sure hope she's okay."

As the others turned their attention to Ms. Fernandez, Ms. Nakama shuffled up to Stone and stared at him with cold eyes. Yuki reared up at Ms. Nakama's side, as if ready to strike.

"Shit, lady! Is that thing poisonous?" Stone recoiled, but there was no fear in his eyes.

"It not poisonous." Ms. Nakama waved Yuki out the front door. Yuki hesitated for a second, then she slithered across the floor, only stopping at the front door for a quick look back. She and Ms. Nakama bowed toward each other, then Yuki was gone. Once she was out of sight, Ms. Nakama looked back at Stone, gracefully rolling her kimono sleeves up. "You look hungry. Like eat something?"

Stone looked at her skinny arms, then he let out a wicked snort and tossed aside the baseball cap. "Y'all goddamn slants are jus' too smart for yer own good. You done said enough."

Everyone turned in time to see Stone's hand shoot out and grab Ms. Nakama by her jaw. He jerked and twisted his wrist, and her jaw tore away with a horrifying tearing and cracking sound. She reached for her mouth, trying to stop the spurting blood, but it quickly coated her hands. She fell to the ground, mewling.

"The assassin!" Praveen stepped between Stone and Neda. "Neda, up the stairs!"

Driss staggered forward, muttering and raising his shaking fists. "It is a *djinn*! Praveen, my *takoba*!"

Stone tracked Praveen and Neda's climb up the stairs for a second, then tossed Ms. Nakama's jaw aside. It hit the floor with a meaty thunk. Stone wiped Ms. Nakama's blood across his chin, pausing a moment to taste it before taking a step toward Driss. "Fuckin' A-rab cancer patient thinks he's gonna take me down?"

Daysi stepped back into the sitting room, a vial in her hand. She nearly had the lid open, but her hands were arthritic and weak. The lid caught for just a moment.

That was long enough for Stone. He dashed across the room and grabbed Daysi by the wrist with his left hand. He shattered her wrist with a popping sound, like dry twigs snapping. "Lady, I jus' sell drugs, I don't take 'em."

He backhanded her with his right hand, and the sound of her neck snapping was louder than that of her wrist being shattered.

"It's a Wendigo," William Big Bear shouted. He fell back to the far side of the stairs, and Stone moved back toward the foyer to circle around and close.

Driss threw his arms wide and stepped in Stone's path. "*Mak—*"

Stone lifted Driss up by his throat. "Okay, A-rab, that's enough o' your shit. I was gonna leave yer scrawny ass for last, but y'all done pissed me off."

Tammy cringed and sobbed as Stone shook Jeddo from side to side. Bones snapped from the powerful motions, and Driss slumped like a rag doll. Stone dropped Driss's limp body and leapt up the steps, easily jumping past Praveen and stopping just behind Neda. Stone's powerful hand grabbed Neda by the hair and yanked her down.

"Okay, A-rab princess, no *takoba* takuba fer you 'n' Aladdin." He hurled Neda into Praveen, and the two fell down the stairs in a heap. He was on top of them with a quick leap. "Oh, hells yeah, boy. I c'n *feel* your lust for her. She sure 'nough is purty. For a brown girl and all."

Stone lifted Neda up roughly, clearly taking delight in her squeals of pain. "So purty, I could just eat you!" He lifted her to his mouth, a mouth that opened wider than should have been possible, and he bit into her left breast, tearing away flesh and muscle and bone. Blood spurted up from the wound and Neda passed out from the pain.

Praveen tried to get to his feet, but Stone tossed Neda down and closed quickly. He lifted Praveen and wrapped one arm around Praveen's back and chest, the other around his butt. Stone gave a hard jerk, and with a loud crack, Praveen was twisted so that his face was looking down on his butt. Praveen spat up blood, then his eyes rolled up in his head.

Stone howled in delight.

Stone stopped laughing, and his eyes squinted into narrow slits. "Where'd y'all go, Injun Joe?"

He leapt into the sitting room and sniffed the air, then he ran for the dining room, pulling up short at the last second. Tammy and Elliot followed, holding their breath, hoping somehow that things ended differently than they already knew.

William Big Bear held up a steak knife in his shaking hand. Sweat dripped down his brow. The knife glinted silver in the morning light leaking in from the glass doors.

"Oh, the big Injun got him a knife?" A glob of red foam fell from Stone's mouth as he stepped toward William. "Gonna scalp me?"

William Big Bear whispered, and a blinding bolt of lightning shot from the sliding glass door frame. He shouted, and the bolt was joined by another from the glass door's frame. Stone gasped and fell to his knees. Smoke rose from his burning hoodie where the lightning had struck.

"This is silver, Wendigo!" William Big Bear stepped closer to Stone and let the light reflect along the length of the blade. "Berbers won't touch steel, you understand? We had a silver set made just for Driss. And now I cut out your dark heart."

William Big Bear chanted, and the spirits of the mansion and those of the surrounding land began to coil around Stone's legs.

Stone writhed against the binding, furiously shaking his head side-to-side. Muscles and veins stood out along his neck and face.

William Big Bear took another step, then his eyes went wide, and he clutched at his chest. The knife slipped from his fingers, and his jaw locked. He fell to his knees, for a moment, eye to eye with Stone. The spirit binding broke, and Stone roared. He grabbed William Big Bear by the back of the head. Stone yanked, and again there was a tearing, cracking sound followed by the loud, wet gush of blood, then William Big Bear's headless corpse fell to the ground.

Stone stood at that point, working the pain from his singed chest. He quickly inspected the fallen, then he dashed up the stairs to the second floor. Tammy and Elliot followed, careful not to make any noise, even though they were just phantoms.

Stone hunched low to the floor, sniffing until he reached Tammy's room. He pushed the door open and entered.

It took him just a second to find what he was looking for: Tammy's treasure box.

No! What a fucking creepasaurus rex! I hate you!

She tried to suppress her rage so that Elliot wouldn't sense the importance of the treasure box, but he was caught up in his own suffering.

Stone pried the box open and began rummaging through it. Tammy seethed at the intrusion, the sense of impotent fury gripping her. Stone examined her father's dog tags and tossed them aside, then her mother's gold wedding ring. He tossed that aside, too.

No wonder the police took the treasure box!

Stone stopped and plucked out Tammy's pendant. The quartz stone glowed amber. He sniffed at it and let out a satisfied growl, slipping it into his pants pocket.

"Elliot, let's go." Tammy yanked on Elliot's hand. "We have what we need."

Elliot nodded. He'd seen the photos of the corpses. Stone wasn't through with them yet, and there was no need to see the gory drama play out in real time.

Tammy led them out of the mansion and back to the clearing on the west lawn and from there into the woods. The sunlight faded as they moved deeper into the trees, the canopy thickening. Before long, it was dark as night.

She did her best to stay focused, but the pain of seeing so much horror wasn't something she could easily shake off. Elliot was similarly affected; he seemed introspective, quiet. The path through the darkness was longer than she'd expected, and then she remembered it was all a dream, something she could control.

Her bitter laugh shattered the silence, and Elliot squeezed her hand.

"What is it? Are we lost?"

"More like clueless. Sorry about that, El." She willed them awake, and a moment later, the dream ended.

Glowing embers were all that remained of the fire. The room was still hot, and now it was thick with their sweat, a sweat rank with fear. The concoction's bitter taste lingered on their tongues, but it was an afterthought.

Tammy's blanket had slipped off, and she was vaguely aware of her own nakedness, her torso as sweat-slick as Elliot's. She wasn't bothered by it, though. She pulled her blanket around her shoulders.

Elliot was sluggish and clumsy getting to his feet. "How...long...?"

"The effects?" Tammy carefully pulled on her pants, leaning against a warm wall for support. "That was only a half dose. I don't think it'll be too long."

"Silver," Elliot said, nodding weakly. "And the heart."

"Yeah. We're cutting that mother fucker open with the *takoba*, then I'm setting his heart on fire. Then I may crap into his chest cavity."

Elliot finally pulled his jeans on. "We need to get ready. Lure him in."

"Yeah. I think we're both ready for a shower first, huh?" She made her way over to his good shoulder, throwing it over hers. She opened the door to the basement, then grabbed the shotgun, using its weight as something of a balance against his.

They climbed the stairs in silence, each step cautiously sought out in the darkness. They paused in the small room that opened onto the sitting room, trying to catch their breath.

Suddenly, the door to the sitting room opened.

"Well, well. What have we here?" Sergeant Traxler smiled at them from the sitting room doorway. He waved them toward the waiting Lieutenant Henriksen. "We've got a lot to talk about, you two. Like murder charges?"

Chapter Twenty-Six

After what Elliot had seen in the dream, he couldn't sit still at the dining room table. His back was to the kitchen, his chair only inches from the dark stain where Grandpa William had died. Even dimmed, the overhead light seemed to draw out the contrast between the dried blood and the stone tiles. Lieutenant Henriksen and Sergeant Traxler sat across from him, their backs to the glass door. Tammy sat at the end of the table that faced the sitting room doorway, also fidgeting. A warm breeze slipped through the partially opened sliding glass door; cricket chirps and the soft creak of the veranda's planks rode that wind. The creaks were a comforting reminder that two police officers were just outside, alert and ready.

Elliot imagined he could smell blood on the warm breeze, or maybe it wasn't imagination at all. His grandfather had been killed not a foot away. Either way, it was a constant distraction, even more than Traxler digging at his ear with his car keys. Henriksen drummed his fingers on the tabletop, occasionally looking from Elliot to Tammy, other times looking into the sitting room.

"Okay, could you not do that?" Tammy's face scrunched up as if she were about to vomit. "It's gross, and you might damage your ear."

Traxler froze, then he smiled warmly. "My daughter Sharyl says that exact thing. Is that something generational?"

"Oh, sure. We're the first generation born with common sense, I guess?"

Traxler put his keys away and looked at Henriksen. "I don't know if we're getting much more from these two, especially Miss Mouth here."

Henriksen quit drumming his fingers. He was apparently still playing good cop, although it had been his idea to settle down at the table next to one of the more gruesome murder scenes. "I'm not ready to give up on them just yet. What about it, Elliot? Can you help us out here? Major Case Squad's down to just me and Sergeant Traxler here, but we'd love to see the case closed. Stone's a real bad guy, and if Ms. McPhee here is right, we've got him on six more murders, one of those a cop."

"Or she could be lyin' to cover for herself," Traxler said, pointing a finger at Tammy. "She's already facing a Class A misdemeanor for throwin' that fake ID around up in St. Louis. That's a year in juvie right there. Plus you stood up the Department of Social Services, and that's not a good idea. I got pulled in on a case where this punk was running from Social Ser—"

Tammy rolled her eyes dramatically. "Oh, my God. I can*not* believe this."

"What sort of deal did you have in mind, Lieutenant?" Elliot leaned in and stared Henriksen in the eyes. "I can make a call right now, if you'd like. You've already talked with our attorneys. They can get us top-notch representation, if we need it. Tammy's a minor, and she's had a lot of terrible things happen to—"

Traxler threw his arms up in disbelief. "She ran from Social Services. She fled three murder scenes. She dumped a Highway Patrol car in the woods."

Elliot coolly turned on Traxler. "She was being pursued by a killer the police failed to apprehend, Sergeant Traxler. And I believe Mr. Stone is still on the loose?"

Henriksen signaled for Traxler to drop it. "We'd like you to consider protective custody. We put you up someplace safe, around the clock protection. We could work with the FBI to get you new identities. All we'd need from you is assurances that once Stone is captured, Ms. McPhee will testify against him. Her testimony alone will put him away for life."

Tammy slammed a hand on the table. "Stone's not going to jail. You won't even recognize him when you see him again. I doubt his prints even match anymore."

Elliot held up both hands, begging Tammy to let him do the talking. "I think what Tammy means is that Stone has gone through a lot. Like she said earlier, she saw the big guy at that farmhouse in Illinois really work Stone over."

Traxler let out a derisive snort. "You should see what the other guy looks like."

"Sergeant Traxler …" Henriksen shook his head, then he braced his beefy arms on the table and cradled his thick jaw in his broad hands. "Elliot, we understand there are going to be some complications. But DNA is close to airtight. Even if Stone has undergone reconstructive surgery of some sort, he can't hide who he is. And Ms. McPhee—Tammy here has seen him. She's an eyewitness."

"What if we can guarantee you delivery of Stone?" Elliot looked to Tammy for reassurance, to see if she was okay with that. The determination in her eyes said she was.

Henriksen and Traxler exchanged a look of curiosity. Henriksen leaned back in his chair, as calm as if he had already heard a dozen such offers earlier in the day. "Outside of protective custody?"

"Right here. We lure him to the mansion."

Tammy folded her arms across her chest, trying to hide the fact that her nerves were just about to fail her. "We give him to you with a bow on his ugly fucking face."

"And how do you propose to do that?" Henriksen seemed to be trying to hide his curiosity, but his poker face failed him.

"He already knows we're here," Elliot said with a casual shrug that made him gasp. He was overdue for some Tylenol, but he was afraid of how it might interact with whatever remained of Daysi's Seer's Sage brew. "He knew the second I drove up to the mansion."

Traxler waved at the ceiling and the room in general. "What, he's got some sort of camera hooked up somewhere? Our tech guys didn't find anything. He must be *real* good."

"Let's just say he's watching this place, and we caught him, okay? Tammy spotted him."

Henriksen drummed his fingers again for a few seconds. His brow was knit, as if he were weighing the odds. "All right. Let's say you've seen him and he's seen you. Let's also say you can deliver him to us. What do you want?"

"Tammy's juvenile record gets wiped clean. She does three months in a rehab clinic, not juvie, then she's released to the custody of her grandmother. If her grandmother isn't available for any reason, she gets released back into my custody."

"Your custo—"

Henriksen held a hand up to cut Traxler off. "Three months in juvie is about as good as you can hope for, Elliot. Tammy has a substantial record."

"Three months in rehab. All of her problems were drug related, and she was under the influence of Tessa Copeland, someone without any sort of adult supervision or guidance. Obviously, that influence isn't a concern anymore. We can also pursue counseling: anger management, life coaching, whatever."

Tammy shot Elliot a sour look. Even if he was just negotiating, it wasn't like she was strung out on heroin or wasting away on meth, and he was speaking ill about her best friend. If there was one person in the world who'd been dealt a crappier hand in life, it had been Tessa. She hadn't deserved all the bad things that had happened to her.

And there's no fucking way in hell I need anger management, El!

Henriksen rubbed his broad chin, apparently considering the offer. The kitchen was silent except for the occasional creak of the men walking the veranda and the reassuring sound of crickets.

"Let's say your representatives sign off on this." Henriksen once more braced his arms on the table and settled his chin into his cupped hands. "I still have to get my leadership to work with two district attorneys, various attorneys general, and a number of agencies."

"Like Social Services." Traxler leaned across the table and jabbed a finger at Tammy.

Henriksen closed his eyes and shook his head. "Like Social Services."

"Oh, you can act like that's nothing, but you haven't dealt with them." Traxler was seriously agitated. "There's no way they'd let you negotiate using a minor as bait like this. She's just sixteen!"

"If they're in protective custody—" Henriksen squeezed his eyes shut tighter.

The wrinkles on Traxler's face deepened as his agitation grew. "This guy killed four men, *Paul*. He bent Andre the Fucking Giant into a pretzel, and he tore another guy in two. Crime techs found thirty shell casings, and they only dug a dozen bullet fragments out of the walls. The bullets they found in the magazines recovered from the corpses were Hydra-Shoks. Now, you tell me, you think a couple U.S. Marshals are going to do much better than that?"

Henriksen's lips moved as if he were counting, and his breath slowed. "We already went over this. Stone has to be wearing some sort of armor."

Tammy's hand shot up. "Um, I shot him in the head? He was lying on the ground, and I was standing right on top of him. The top of his fucking head came *off*, okay? Off!"

Traxler snapped his fingers excitedly. "Trooper Murkofsky reported that. That was a .357 Magnum. And the forensics team said they found brain matter and skull fragments on the road."

Henriksen let out a long-suffering sigh. "We've gone over the evidence. Nothing recovered has been tied directly to Stone yet. It's also possible he suffered a freak wound that he somehow survived. Brain injuries aren't always fatal."

"Hmm." Traxler's eyebrows arched, but after a second, he shrugged and settled back in his chair.

Elliot focused on Henriksen, but Traxler's behavior was always there in Elliot's peripheral vision. Traxler's reactions didn't seem to be part of the good cop/bad cop act. He was having a hard time dealing with Henriksen's assumption of complete control, and the sticking point seemed to be Henriksen's willingness to put Tammy at risk. Elliot suddenly wondered if he'd been reading Traxler wrong the whole time.

Henriksen straightened and drummed his fingers on the table once, then he relaxed. "I would imagine you wouldn't be open to the idea of spending the night in a jail cell for your own protection?"

"So we can't run from Stone when he wipes out the people on duty? Seriously?" Tammy let out a frustrated groan. "No fucking way."

Elliot frowned at Tammy. She wasn't helping the negotiations. He tried to meet Henriksen's calm glare. They were both faking it, but Henriksen had years of experience, and Elliot only had the mellow buzz off the last remnants of the Seer's Sage. "That would be a deal-breaker, lieutenant."

"Without anything to legitimately arrest you for at the moment—"

"Other than the ID card and leaving the scene …" Traxler put his hands up in surrender when Henriksen glared at him.

"We can't really force you into custody. Yet. So here's what we'll do. We have a temporary command post about five minutes out from here. We'll leave you a radio. Tonight, we'll fully staff the command post—me, Sergeant Traxler, the tactical team we've got at our disposal. Whatever deal we finally reach, we all agree to stick to it. Agreed?"

Tammy nodded when Elliot looked at her for reassurance. She wanted Stone dead, and she wasn't going to get that by letting the cops dangle her as bait. Stone was like that robot in the movies that just kept coming, no matter what you did to it.

Except she had a few ideas to try on it.

The robot had a nuclear battery for a heart, and Stone had some sort of *djinn* or *manitou*. Whatever the name, it was something magical, and it was the only thing keeping Stone going.

She intended to correct that.

Elliot cleared his throat. "We agree to meet those terms."

Henriksen stood and offered his meaty hand to Elliot. "I'll make some calls once I get back to the command post."

Elliot shook Henriksen's hand. The guy was huge, intimidating, and powerful, but Tammy said he was nothing like Stone.

How the hell are we going to do this? I've only got one good arm. Tammy's skin-and-bones, mostly. I don't think Stone's going to give us a break just because we're determined.

Traxler whispered something to Tammy, then he looked back at Henriksen. "Lieutenant, you want to point out the stipulation?"

"Stipulation?" Henriksen's brow wrinkled and an eyebrow shot up.

"About Stone's condition."

"Oh." Henriksen turned to look Elliot straight in the eyes. "This is all contingent on us getting Stone alive."

Elliot froze. He'd hoped implying Stone would be captured was enough. Having it explicitly spelled out that they had to give Stone to the police alive to have Tammy's record wiped clean changed everything. He looked to Tammy for approval. She was the one who was getting the short end of any deal gone bad.

"Y'know, Lieutenant Henriksen, the cops have had three weeks to get Stone. Oh, wait, they've had *years* to get Stone. I forgot about that." Tammy screwed up her face as if she were completely clueless about what might happen. "I figure this is the time you finally get it right? I sure can't see a couple dumb kids doing anything to a guy who can evade police capture for nearly a month, can you? I mean look at us. He's got an arm in a sling, and I'm just a girl, right?"

She gave Elliot a look she hoped said it all. She wanted Stone dead; they could figure the rest out later.

"We just want Stone taken care of, Lieutenant. We'll cooperate fully." Elliot watched Henriksen and Traxler for any indication they might be reconsidering. Henriksen looked comfortable with the deal, and he was the one who would make the final call.

Henriksen rubbed his chin for a moment, then he grunted and unhooked a leather phone carrier from his belt and handed it across to Elliot. "All right. Here's the radio. Use the call sign *Harrison*. Communicate with the call sign *Command Post*, or *Lieutenant*. Let's try that now."

After fiddling with the snap, Elliot pulled the radio out and looked it over. It was black, rectangular, and fit in the palm of his hand. There was a stub antenna, a channel switcher, and a transmit button. It seemed pretty straightforward. He keyed the transmit button. "*Harrison* to *Command Post*. Um, test?"

The message came in loud and clear through Traxler's radio.

"All right." Henriksen rubbed his thick hands together. "We should have something ready for all parties to sign by the end of the day tomorrow, unless your lawyers become too stubborn."

Elliot looked up from examining the radio. "I'll do what I can to push for a quick negotiation, if the government is capable of that?"

Traxler snorted, then he followed Henriksen to the sliding glass door. A minute later, engines started and headlights came on. Elliot and Tammy watched the lights drift through the dark night and disappear beyond the walls, only to reappear, ghost-like through the trees lining the private lane.

"Anger management, Elliot? What the fuck?" Tammy stomped all the way to the foot of the stairs. "And I didn't appreciate what you said about Tessa, either." It sounded like a herd of wildebeests stampeding when she climbed the stairs.

"Gee, I don't know what I was thinking," Elliot muttered under his breath. He began pacing in the kitchen.

The pipes clanged as Tammy turned her shower on. The idea of a shower was extremely appealing, but it would have to wait.

They had a timeline now, and a plan, but they needed details, and they needed to get things moving immediately. It was a good starting point, nothing more. He needed to gather equipment.

He ran to the library and settled at one of the small tables with a pad of paper and a pen. Spontaneity and quick thinking were Tammy's thing, but everything had to be orderly and thought out for him. He stared at the paper for a second, trying to figure out where to start. He decided on separating known quantities from guesses. He drew a horizontal line the width of the paper and a vertical one the length of the page.

What do we know?

He labeled the top left square *Facts* and wrote down, *"Supernatural strength, fast."*

The top right square was labeled *Assumptions*; *"Impossible to kill, animal cunning, connection to Tammy's mind, heals quickly. Can be hurt temporarily by conventional weapons."*

In the bottom left square, he wrote *Conjecture* and listed, *"Can be hurt permanently by magic, silver, jade. Seemed afraid of whatever Daysi had. Always hungry."*

In the final square, he wrote, *"Must take Tammy alive"* and circled it.

Elliot underlined the point about conventional weapons. "We need some serious firepower. Things that don't care about his speed."

He started a list on the next page: *grenades, bombs, shotguns, fire, gas, fluids.*

Aside from their shotguns, they didn't have most of the items that would be effective against something like Stone. After a moment considering the list, he started another one below it.

Fire—Molotov cocktails. Grenades—improvised explosives. Gas—chlorinate. Shotgun—silver pellets.

They could build a modest arsenal that would give them a chance, but it meant going out to the garage. Unless Tammy was confident she could sense Stone, it was going to be risky. Very risky.

He jotted down another list: *gas can, screw jars, torch, tin snips, iron skillet, ball of twine, large standard screwdriver, hammer.*

If they pushed it, they could make it in a single trip. He wrote down *backpacks* and *towels*, then he sketched out the garage and where things were. They would need to go to three areas—the camping gear area on the left, the engine work table on the right, and Luis's general tool area at the rear. That meant being out of the mansion longer than he would have liked. After looking at the sketch and notes for a few minutes, he jotted down two lists, one for what he would gather, the other for what Tammy would gather.

He turned at the sound of bare feet padding around. Tammy stood at the base of the stairs, craning her neck to search the dining room. She wore a more modest outfit—skinny jeans and a bright red lycra shirt she used when she went biking. It was snug, but it was comfortable. She had Driss's sword scabbard strapped over her shoulder and a shotgun cradled in her arms.

"In here!" Elliot tore out the piece of paper with their lists.

"The library? What, are you going to read him a bedtime story? What's this?"

"We're going shopping."

"Yeah, not until you shower, stinkbag."

He nervously pushed his glasses up his nose. "Heading up now. But you need to look that over and see if I'm missing anything obvious."

"Wait, shopping where? And what do we need all this stuff for? I was thinking we just chop him up with the *takoba*."

"We'd never get a chance to swing that thing if he's as fast as you've said. We need to slow him down, like you did before you blew his head off." Elliot turned for the stairs, but he stopped at the doorway. "We should be able to find everything we need in the garage, but it's going to be risky. Are you *sure* you can sense him before he gets to us?"

"Definitely. Wait just a second, okay? I only ever stopped him by hitting him with a car."

"You mean the cruiser you stole and dumped?"

Tammy stuck her bottom lip out angrily and fixed a furious gaze on him, but only for a second. "After Stone killed James—"

"James?"

"The state trooper. After he died, it was steal the cruiser or die right there with him. Pretty simple choice, don't ya think? I brought it here to grab my dirt bike, drove out to the quarry, then came back here on my bike as fast as I could. No animals were harmed in the filming of this action sequence, okay?"

Elliot lowered his head. It wasn't worth fighting over. "I just want you to think about the implications of what you do? Is that too much? What's the use of getting your juvenile record purged if you're just going to get into trouble as an adult?"

"Way to back your friend up, El!"

"Tammy—"

"No, fuck you, okay? You haven't stuck up for me in anything. It's always, 'Oh, gee, golly, Tammy, you sure did get yourself into trouble again,' and shit like that. Feels just like family, huh?" She was seeing spots, a sure sign she was ready to explode. There wasn't much that set her off as bad as Elliot's holier-than-thou routine. "Why don't you just blame the whole Stone thing on me, hm? I mean, he came here for me; he killed everyone to get to me. Must be—" Her voice broke, and tears flowed down her face. She wiped them away angrily. "Must be my fault, right?"

"That's not what I meant," Elliot replied weakly. He turned and jogged up the stairs.

Tammy stared after him for an eternity, alternately trying to bring her breathing under control and letting out furious curses. Finally, she turned her attention to the lists he'd given her. They didn't look like much, but Elliot always had to have his drama. A small wipeout on the dirt bike meant a trip to the ER just to be sure nothing was broken; a small fire in the garden meant getting everyone out with hoses and shovels.

"It's not always the end of the world, El, and it's not all about *you* and your stupid, convoluted plans."

Plus, with his busted shoulder, he was all but useless now.

I can do this myself, no drama.

She ran to the kitchen and stuck the shotgun on top of the table, then she climbed the stairs as quietly as she could and walked to her room. She could hear Elliot stumbling around up in his room. She gathered up some towels and her school backpack, then she dug around in her closet for her camping backpack. It was sturdier, but it was also stiffer. She couldn't imagine the two of them being heavy enough to slow her down, even if they were full.

Lightning flashed, and a second later, the windows shook from the thunder. Rain began to fall, first with big, fat drops that banged against the windows, then with a machine gun rat-a-tat. She grabbed a windbreaker from her closet as Elliot's shower kicked on and ran back downstairs.

She stopped at the sliding glass door and popped it open to listen. There was nothing other than the whipping wind, occasional thunderclaps, and the pounding rain.

It was late, nearly midnight, and there wasn't even a hint of moonlight slipping through the cloud cover. The flashlight was squeezed tight in her pants pocket, an unzipped backpack hung off either shoulder. She counted the steps to the garage in her head. Run, slide the door open, get inside, flashlight on, gather the camping gear, gather the stuff from Luis's tools, gather the things from the engine area.

Five minutes, easy.

She slipped the windbreaker on and stepped onto the veranda. She tried to sense Stone. Nothing.

The wind shifted and blew rain into her face. For a moment, it felt like she was drowning. She leaned into the wind and rain. Every second outside the mansion was an invitation to Stone. At the steps, she jumped. Her feet went out from under her when she landed, sending her to the ground hard. She rolled to her feet and ran, or at least what passed as a run for her. Against the wind, with her head down and her eyes half closed, she had to move even slower than normal, and normal was pretty slow.

At the garage door, she tried to use her momentum to skid and drag the door open. It was a bad decision that once again sent her to the ground.

"Fuck *me*!"

She got back to her feet and slid the door open, but it caught after a few inches. She shoved an arm into the gap and leaned into the door. It slid open reluctantly.

With a muttered curse, she stepped into the garage and dug out the flashlight, annoyed at the time she'd already lost. She flicked the flashlight on and pulled the list from her camping backpack. The garage was generally well organized, and with the minivan gone, it was pretty spacious.

Camping gear. That was her first target.

She squeezed past her dirt bike and stopped at the tackle boxes and canvas bags where they stored less-used things. She checked the list again. *Ball of Twine, Iron Skillet.*

She found the ball of twine, but it didn't seem like enough. Whatever twine could do, nylon rope could do better, so she pulled a spool of rope from a hook on the garage wall, too. She grabbed a handful of glow sticks before taking the iron skillet from the shelf where she'd found it for the Celebrate Elliot the Dickhead Picnic.

She shoved everything into her camping backpack, then froze.

There was a small, disposable propane tank sitting against the wall. Propane meant fire. And noise. What could be better?

She tried to stuff the tank into her backpack, but it took a lot of effort. Finally, she tossed the towels out and the tank fit. Barely. But she'd wasted more than a minute. Plus, the backpack was pretty heavy and bulky now. She shuffled it out to the middle of the garage floor and settled it to the ground, then she moved to the back wall and ran her flashlight across Luis's precious tools.

Elliot's list was pretty simple: *Tin Snips, Screw Jars, Large Flat Head Screwdriver, Hammer.*

Screw Jars? Are you kidding me?

Eight jars of various sizes hung from a two-by-four that had been hammered between two studs at the edge of Luis's tool area. The jars contained an assortment of washers, bolts, nuts, screws, nails, and other things that probably gave Luis an erection.

She unscrewed the first jar and dropped it into her school backpack with a muffled thud. She did the same with the second, but instead of a thud, she heard a sickening shattering sound.

Fuck. That's what the towels were for! Goddammit, Elliot, cryptic much?

She emptied the broken jars out and ran back to where she'd earlier tossed the towels. It was seriously going to slow things down, unscrewing the jars and then wrapping them in the towels. She hoped it was worth it. She didn't waste a lot of time choosing the tin snips, taking the biggest one she could see; the screwdriver and hammer were the easiest part. Then she moved over to the engine work area.

Torch, Gas Can.

The only torch she could think of was the propane torch they used for welding. She carefully pushed that into the backpack, then hefted the backpack over her shoulders.

Shit! That has to be thirty pounds!

She put the flashlight back in her pants, then shuffled over to the other backpack and tried to slide it onto her back. It was pretty close to the same weight, and the arm straps were too tight to fit with the other backpack in place.

Brilliant idea, Elliot! Now I've got to carry it.

She shuffled to the door and checked the path to the veranda. The rain had picked up, and lightning was now a continuous, brilliant white flashing across the sky. She stepped out of the garage and froze. A second later, a lightning bolt arced down from the sky and danced along the mansion's east wall, lighting the night with a blinding white flare.

Tammy waited for her eyes to adjust again, then she waddled toward the veranda. Halfway there, she stopped. She'd forgotten the gas can.

"Son of a bitch!"

She dropped the backpack she'd been carrying and waddled back to the garage door. It was pitch black inside after the constant electrical display, so she had to stumble around a bit before her fingers finally skipped across the gas can's handle. She grabbed it, grunting at the weight, then staggered back to the door, where she had to wait for another lightning blast to run its course, this time dancing across the mansion's roof.

She waddled forward, stooping to pick up the backpack she'd dropped. She looked up at the sound of Elliot's voice, which was almost completely drowned out by the booming thunder.

"What?" *What the fuck, El? Maybe you could run out and help me?*

Elliot stepped out onto the veranda. "What do you think you're doing?"

"Going shopping." *Asshole.* She took a clumsy step forward.

Elliot sprinted toward her and took the backpack and gas can from her hands. He was all graceful and suave, grabbing them on the first try and turning, completely unaffected by the arm that hung uselessly in a sling. He was soaked by the rain, and the way his skin glistened, it reminded Tammy of some of the pretty boy porn she'd watched with Tessa. Elliot waved her to the porch, but his wave stopped abruptly.

Tammy followed his gaze and froze when a distant flash of lightning revealed what Elliot had seen: a hunched form, broader and taller than she remembered.

She didn't need to reach out to confirm her fears.

Stone had come for them, and they weren't protected.

Chapter Twenty-Seven

As quickly as if a switch had been flipped, the temperature dropped, and the wind shifted. Sleet intermixed with the rain, and lightning flashed in a dazzling, continuous series of forking streaks. With the wind's shift, Stone's stench became evident, an impure and foul assault on the senses, a mix of death and ruin. It seeped into the sinuses and became a nauseating, sour stain on the palate.

Stone took a step forward in the light of the storm's fury, and Elliot instinctively backpedaled. Stone was at least as tall as Henriksen had said, probably a good bit more. Although they were closer to the veranda than Stone was, Elliot had no confidence Tammy could make the door before Stone could.

She would need a distraction.

"Get inside, Tammy!"

Tammy ran. Her feet slapped against puddles and slid through mud, and the backpack weighed her down as if it were full of lead, but she didn't lose her footing. She felt like a gazelle. A wounded, pregnant gazelle with an alligator clamped to her ass, but a gazelle.

Elliot stepped in the opposite direction Tammy had taken and waited for Stone's attention to shift toward her.

"Hey, you ugly son of a bitch! Hey!" He wanted to wave his arms and bellow, but his good hand was weighted down and his throat was somehow dry.

What he'd done was good enough. Stone's oversized head tilted and he paused, mid-leap. Stone shifted, and the thin, tattered slivers of flesh that were supposed to be lips parted in a horrifying grin reminiscent of a Great White shark.

"Tonto! Guh...guh...gonna git me...a scalp!"

Elliot juked left and planted his foot hard, intending to cut back toward the veranda, but his foot slipped on the slick grass, and the weight in his right hand pulled him off-balance. Elliot managed to keep his feet, but only just.

Stone charged.

It was like watching a grizzly bear or a lion, with Stone's head dropping slightly and his shoulders dropping level with the ground. His hands—huge and misshapen—planted knuckle-first into the ground and he began an almost gorilla-like loping move. Elliot stepped back and to his right, but he was too weighted down and too clumsy with his arm in a sling. There was no way to avoid at least a glancing blow. Right into the same, damaged shoulder.

A thunderclap sounded as Stone reared up and stretched out his hands. They were as big as a rake head, and the fingers ended in jagged nails that looked capable of tearing through sheet metal.

Elliot flinched for the blow that very well might tear his bad arm off his body, but Stone somehow missed, his perfect, predator balance taken from him.

Time seemed to freeze. Elliot registered a flash of light to his right and turned to run for the veranda. He nearly stumbled when he saw Tammy standing on the porch with the shotgun in her hand. Smoke rose from the end of the barrel in the chill air.

"Get inside!" Elliot slipped and staggered in the rain, and he was certain Stone would close before anyone could get inside the mansion. Elliot was less certain the mansion could even protect them.

Tammy worked the shotgun's pump and sighted past Elliot, but not that far past. Stone was close! Elliot dropped.

The thunderclap sounded again, and Stone roared in pain.

Elliot got to his feet and scrambled up the veranda steps. Tammy was inside, calmly readying to slam the door shut. When Elliot fell through the doorway, she slid the glass door shut and locked it. Elliot twisted in time to see Stone land on the veranda. The wood groaned with the impact. Stone's dark form hunched so that his face was at Tammy's eye level.

"You gonna try the wards, fucker?" Tammy flipped Stone off. "You know you want to, you piece of shit."

To Elliot's surprise, Stone stepped back and rubbed at a charred circle of flesh on his chest. Ribs were visible inside the wound, and the flesh radiating out from it slowly transitioned from coal black to deep gray to a lifeless, pale gray.

"Gonna…gonna…g-get you, black cunt." Stone's voice boomed like thunder. He laughed, a twisted, improbable sound coming from his primitive, animal face. "Gonna…eat…Tonto."

Tammy slapped a hand against the glass door in fury. "Yeah, I don't think so. I think we're gonna fuck you up, that's what I think. And when I'm done with you, I think maybe I'll cut you your own sli—"

"Tammy! Let's…let's not piss off the Wendigo, okay? It's a bad idea."

Tammy stepped away from the door, and Stone leapt over the veranda railing and was gone. She settled on the floor next to Elliot. "That high-pitched squealing you were—"

"I banged up my shoulder again, all right?" Elliot got to his knees and began unpacking the backpack.

"Oh, okay. For a minute there, I thought Stone had stepped on a gerbil or something."

"What do you think you were doing out there?" He stared at the nylon rope before tossing it aside. "Is this 'Try to Get Yourself Mauled Day'?"

"I think it's called being productive, El. You got what you wanted, didn't you?"

"I didn't want the Wendigo hovering around our door while we were working on a way to kill him, if that's what you mean. I thought you said you could sense him?"

"He must have been just outside the range I can sense."

"What's that, six feet? He was at the edge of the mansion, Tammy."

"When I tried to sense him, okay? Before I ran for the garage. You saw how fast he can move. Fucking need to recruit him for the Olympic track team."

Elliot finished emptying the backpack, each motion stiff and loud. He set the skillet on the stone tile and walked to the kitchen to retrieve several dish towels and the big stainless steel sauce pan. He laid the dish towels down on the stone tile and set the saucepan upside down atop them, then he set the iron skillet on top of the saucepan. He began digging through the other backpack, stopping when he found the torch.

"You didn't get the torch striker?" He rummaged around in the backpack, but he already knew the answer.

"Was it on the fucking list?"

"Glow sticks weren't on the list. The propane tank wasn't on the list."

"Those were a bonus." Tammy flashed a sardonic smile. "You're welcome, El!"

Elliot sighed and closed his eyes. He tried to forget there was a giant, flesh-eating *manitou* somewhere outside, hidden by a storm he was pretty sure was supernatural. He tried to remember that Tammy had once been a sweet, loving kid who felt betrayed and abandoned and alone in the world.

It took a lot, but he finally found a place where he could do that.

He took in a calming breath, then he pulled the iron skillet from the top of the saucepan and set it on the stovetop's largest burner. He turned the burner to high, then turned around to look at Tammy.

"The propane tank and glow sticks were good ideas. Forgetting the striker is all on me. My bad. My fault. I'm sorry."

"Whatever."

"I'm going down to the basement to search around for a striker. I'm pretty sure Praveen had one down there with some of his stuff. Could you do me a favor and go to the laundry room and bring me the bottle of ammonia and the jug of bleach?"

Tammy stared at him angrily, then she got up and stomped off. He waited until he heard her rummaging around in the laundry room, then he scooped up the flashlight she'd left on the floor and headed for the basement. It took him several minutes, but he found the striker he'd recalled seeing. He shoved it into his pants and stopped at the small food storage section. There was a brown box beneath one of the shelves of canned food. He slid the box out, brushed away cobwebs, and hefted the box onto his hip. It jangled, a sound of glass and metal.

Climbing the steps with his hand full was a chore, but it gave him some time to think and plan.

They were probably running out of time. Definitely running out of time. Stone didn't look very human anymore, and it was almost impossible to recognize him at all. Eventually, the Wendigo would be the only intelligence remaining, and it would realize it had to get into the mansion to get what it wanted.

The wards might hurt it, but they wouldn't kill it. It knows that. It knows we're up to something, I'm sure of it. It'll come through soon enough, and it'll probably take the path it knows—the front door.

Tammy was waiting for him at the head of the stairs. She took the box from him without a word and carried it into the kitchen.

It was as close as she could come to apologizing.

"Bleach and ammonia." She pointed at the containers as if she were a game show hostess.

"Could you go through the jars you brought in and find any that can fit into the canning jars in that box?" As he talked, Elliot lit the torch and set the flame to just above the inverted saucepan. He grabbed the iron skillet with a potholder and set it on top of the saucepan, adjusting the skillet until the torch flame was striking the skillet dead center.

Tammy took the canning jars out of the box and emptied out the jars she'd taken from the garage. Only two were small enough to fit through the mouth of the canning jars.

"We've got two, Dr. Evil. What now?"

"Take one of those towels and cut pieces off big enough to fit over the opening of those small jars. Then get some aluminum foil and wax paper. Cover the opening with those—aluminum foil, wax paper, aluminum foil, wax paper—and then the towel. Fill the jars about a third of the way full with ammonia. Seal the jars with the foil and wax paper lids you made, then tie them up tight with twine and knot them, but leave some twine hanging on both sides. A couple inches each should do, but you be the judge. Then fill the two canning jars about halfway up with bleach. Put the little jars in the canning jars, but not all the way in. Leave some of that twine over the edge of the lid, then seal the lids shut as tight as you can, using the twine to suspend the little jars. Do it over the kitchen sink, and open that window up. Be very, very careful. If the little jar breaks, turn the water on and back away fast, okay?"

"Fuck, Elliot. What're you making?"

Elliot walked back to the kitchen and dug through the utensils drawer." What *you're* making is a bomb. A chloramine vapor bomb. If we get lucky, maybe hydrazine. They're both bad news. I figure at best they'll slow him down." He settled next to the iron skillet and dropped Driss's silverware to the ground. "For you, though, they'd probably be enough to ruin your day. Maybe forever. So be careful. Please."

While Elliot snipped the utensils into small pieces, Tammy carried the jars and the chemicals into the kitchen.

She set the chemical-weapons-to-be down and slid the window over the sink open. As she worked, she tried not to think about the jars she'd broken. They had both been small enough to fit into the canning jars. She also tried not to think about the potential for shit to go wrong.

Really wrong. She hadn't felt Stone's presence the entire time she'd been outside. That had been one of the things she'd been counting on. She was pretty sure Elliot had been counting on it, too.

The way he'd reacted when she'd admitted she hadn't sensed Stone…

"El, you think Stone's changed so much, I can't connect to him anymore?"

Elliot had his knee on the towel she'd left behind. He was cutting it into long strips with one of Jeddo's silver steak knives. "Probably. His skin was gray. Did you notice that burn mark on his chest?"

"No, but I saw one in Illinois. That's where the wards got him when he attacked the mansion?"

"I think so. I think it's where he started dying. And his sudden growth? Maybe the Wendigo legends got watered down over time? Maybe it's not until the host starts to die that the body starts to transform. The growth, I think that's supposed to be part of the curse—he eats, but instead of finding satisfaction, he just grows to the point where it's never enough. Primitive beliefs, so it had to make sense to them, but maybe there's something to it. As the host dies, it leaves behind the shell the *manitou* needs, and that shell becomes more and more reflective of the *manitou*."

"So we're dealing with something even more Wendigo than Jeddo did?"

"I think so."

"Fuck. Wendigo, now with fifty percent more Wendigo!"

"Yeah, I know." Elliot scolded himself for letting Tammy in on his worries. She didn't need to know how grim things looked.

Elliot set three of the disc-shaped canning jar lids on what remained of the towel. He hunched over one of the lids, the large screwdriver clenched in his left hand, the hammer in his right. He centered the screwdriver on the lid and tapped the screwdriver handle a few times before striking it hard. Another couple strikes, and he was done. His forehead was beaded with sweat, and his body shook from the pain shooting out from his shoulder.

He decided he could manage one more lid. The rest of the jars would need to be used for their grenades.

"You okay?" Tammy held the gas bombs out to her side. Her hands shook enough that the little jars danced on the twine.

"Pretty impressive work. Could you set those in the sitting room? Somewhere where we can lob them into the foyer."

After setting the bombs down next to the bottom of the stairs, Tammy called out, "You think he'll come in this way?"

"I'm hoping he's like an animal and sort of goes with the known, yeah. Plus, if we can get him while he's in the enclosed space of the foyer, that would be perfect."

"Will the glass break if we hit him with it?" Tammy took the screwdriver from his hand and settled to her knees beside him.

"Don't bother trying to find out. Throw it at his feet, or as close as you can." Elliot watched her pierce the lid. When he was satisfied, he turned his attention to the silver. It was melting.

"What're these lids for?"

"Molotov cocktails. Pull the towel down through, but leave about half of it sticking out. When we're ready, we fill the jars with gas and, boom."

"Boom? We set the mansion on fire?"

"If we have to, yeah. We'll have time to put it out. I think."

"And the silver? You making shotgun slugs?"

Elliot carefully tilted the pan so that the last few pieces of silver were exposed to the flame. "Pellets. They don't have to be perfect. Could you bring me one of the metal mixing bowls? Fill it with cold water."

After a moment, Tammy returned with the largest of the mixing bowls. She set it down to his right, then she stepped back. He hefted the skillet, turning it so that a slender stream of silver dripped into the water. He did his best to keep the flow down to drops and to move the pan around a bit so that the droplets wouldn't bump into each other before cooling. His good arm began to ache from the exertion.

When he was done, there were silver pellets at the bottom of the bowl. Not perfect, but better than he'd hoped for.

"Last piece. Shotgun shells."

Tammy disappeared, and a few minutes later she returned with a huge, pink shoulder bag covered with sparkling flowers. Neda had given Tammy the bag as a gift for her first birthday at the mansion. Tammy unclipped it and showed him the inside. It was full of shotgun shells. She pulled out a couple powder horns.

"It's not quite what you've cooked up, but my plan was to blow myself up if I didn't get him with the shotgun and *takoba*."

Elliot tried not to react to the grimness in her voice. She wasn't stupid. She'd known all along she probably couldn't kill Stone, but she'd come up with a big middle finger if she failed.

"I've got a Zippo in here, some waterproof matches, magnesium shavings, and a tin of lighter fluid. And now, I've got the propane tank. I figure if it didn't all go off in one big blast, it'd probably burn me so bad I wouldn't live. So, yeah, fuck you, Wendigo. And double fuck you to whoever hired him."

Summoned, but, yeah, fuck you, assholes. "It's a pretty good plan. Could I bum some of that gunpowder off you, though? I'd like to make those last few jars into grenades: gunpowder, pieces of silver, nails, and screws. We'll need to soak some twine in gas for fuses, poke a small hole through the lids for that."

"I get the idea. Why don't you give the gas bombs a look? They're over by the stairs. I'll put the grenades in my handbag, then I'll start on the shells."

Elliot wandered into the sitting room. The jars were in the perfect position for a throw into the foyer. "Perfect."

He paced the sitting room, trying to figure the best place to stand when the time came. There were only a few exits—the front door, the sliding glass door, and the glass door. That meant a run for the dining room.

After shifting the gas bombs slightly, he stepped into the foyer and listened for any hint of Stone moving around, possibly working up the nerve to attack. Unfortunately, any noise shy of the door being knocked in would be drowned out by the storm raging outside. It was still hurling lightning at the mansion, and pummeling the walls with wind, just like the dust devil he'd seen the day he left.

Elliot flinched.

That had been the day of the killings.

Praveen had mentioned something about attempts to break the mansion's defenses.

The storm had kicked up out of nowhere on Tanegashima right before Simirita's attack, a storm perverted from the winds that had taken Ms. Nakama's remains to sea.

Tammy couldn't sense Stone. What if that isn't Stone she's sensing? Or what if there's not enough of him to sense anymore? What if it's the Wendigo she needs to sense, and she can't sense it because it's protected by the storm, just like we're protected by the mansion?

"Tammy? Get everything bundled up!" He ran for the dining room and began pouring gas into one of the jars.

"What is it?"

"The storm. I think the storm is…I don't know, interference, protection, whatever. It's hiding the Wendigo from us. And I think it's trying to weaken the mansion's defenses." He sealed the lid and flipped the wick to the side, then he started on the second one.

Tammy was desperately shoving wadding into a shotgun shell.

"How many shells did you get out of that?"

A blast of lightning struck the mansion, and the lights winked off and on, then died. The thunder took her answer.

Elliot turned the flashlight on. "How many shells?"

"Three. I've got them loaded." She cycled a shell with the pump.

"Can you feel him? Can you sense Stone?"

Tammy reached out. "No. I—Shit! The glass door!"

She slung the handbag over her shoulder and stood. She brought the shotgun up and took aim at the glass door, the most vulnerable part of the mansion. As she tried to sight in on what she figured would be chest level for the Wendigo, the door burst inward, spraying glass everywhere. Tammy flinched, and the wards erupted in a brilliant azure glow.

The Wendigo dropped to its knees and let out a pitiful scream, its fur smoldering. Elliot stood, one of the finished Molotov cocktails gripped tight in his good hand. He threw it with everything he had, aiming for the floor beneath the thing's crotch. The glass shattered, splashing the thing with gas, which immediately caught fire.

"Get the gas bombs!" Elliot grabbed the second jar and hurled it into the same spot. The flames shot up around the Wendigo's torso. Its entire lower half was on fire, and flames crawled up its abdomen.

Elliot took a step back, and then another. The wards fizzled out. The Wendigo slumped, weakly swatting the flames. Its breath was weak, raspy.

It was vulnerable. Elliot reached out for the *manitous* to bind the thing.

He couldn't sense them.

The storm. It's cut us off from the manitous! *No* manitous, *no binding, no time to cut its heart out! We have to get out of this storm!*

He patted his pocket, just to be sure the GLK's keys were there. They were. "Tammy! Plan B! Get to the GLK!"

A burst of wind washed over the Wendigo, dousing him with rain. The fire slowly died off. Elliot backpedaled, then turned to run.

The Wendigo was getting to its feet, and it looked furious.

Chapter Twenty-Eight

Lightning reflected off the shallow puddles that covered much of the front porch, lighting the mansion front beneath the overhang. Tammy took a step back from the door and then took a step to her right, shivering against the cold, foul wind and rain that must have blown in from Shitsville Station in the Arctic Circle. She could still barely see into the sitting room, but she was closer to Elliot's GLK, their ticket out of what she'd originally considered her last stand.

The Wendigo's roar filled the mansion, and this time it was more fury than pain. Whatever Elliot had done to it, it wasn't happy.

Tammy tested her handbag's weight, just to be sure. They might need its contents.

Elliot's sneakers squeaked on the hardwood floor somewhere just beyond the doorway, and she sank a little lower, ready to run. He skidded into view and bounced around inside the foyer, finally grabbing the door jamb with his good hand for support. He stepped onto the porch and dug into his right pocket, producing the key fob for his treasured GLK. He tossed it without a word and ran back inside. Tammy caught it, barely.

His fucking precious gas bombs. Don't you die on me, Elliot, not over a stupid chemistry experiment.

She ran across the porch, nearly wiping out when she hit a particularly slick puddle. It took all she had to hang onto the shotgun and keys, and she banged her right hand hard against the cement, driving the key ring into her flesh. More importantly, the near-fall cost her seconds. She got her legs under her and stumbled forward, jumping to the ground with all the grace of a drunken sloth. Hoping for some idea of Elliot's situation, she turned.

He stood just outside the doorway, one gas bomb pinned to his chest by his bad hand, the other gas bomb in his right hand. The Wendigo's stomping feet echoed out through the front door.

"Fuck, El, come on!"

Elliot tossed the first jar, then he hastily dug out the second and dropped it just inside the doorway. He slammed the door closed, sealing the Wendigo inside, and ran to join Tammy.

As she ran for the driver's side door, Tammy tapped the unlock button. Nothing happened. She tapped it again. Nothing. Elliot splashed as he jumped from the porch, momentarily blinded by the sleet and rain. The wind was deafening, but he could still hear the Wendigo's roar.

Sturdy as it was, the mansion seemed to groan beneath the storm's assault. The tearoom's western window erupted outward, showering Tammy and the GLK with glass. The mansion released a sour belch, a bilious, sulfuric stench that settled into their noses and the back of their mouths.

Harrison Mansion did not like unwelcome visitors.

Despite all the enchantments, the mansion wasn't a place of sanctuary anymore, and it trembled in fury and despair at that realization. The Wendigo roared in return, and it crashed against the front door.

The door held.

Elliot saw the GLK, and he felt something he hadn't since waking in the hotel room in Bangalore: hope. The GLK was tough, powerful, agile. It would get them free.

Tammy tried the lock button. Again, nothing. "Elliot, battery's dead!"

Elliot stopped halfway to the passenger side door. *Shit! Did I leave the lights on? I probably wouldn't have heard it beep in all the wind and rain. We'll have to push it. How do we get inside with a dead battery?*

Lightning flashed and they both staggered backward, stunned. The GLK's hood was gone. Where there should have been an engine and battery, there was only shadow.

Elliot simply stared, unable to wrap his mind around the kind of force it would take to rip an engine out of a car by hand. The flickering flame of hope he'd been sheltering winked out. He wasn't Tammy. He couldn't keep up with something so strong and hard to kill and...clever.

Tammy ran around to the front of the vehicle and frantically waved. "Let's go! Plan C!"

Elliot stumbled forward, his resolve slowly kicking in. It was amazing to see how Tammy operated. No time wasted on pointless plans and contingency plans and contingency contingency plans.

She acted on instinct. She adjusted.

The Wendigo's shriek was deafening, and there was a note of frustration and pain to it. A loud boom sounded, a wrecking ball crashing into a mountainside, and the front door loudly slammed against something hard: the porch. Almost immediately the mansion lit up as the Wendigo tried to exit, and it let out a pitiful, agonized roar.

Tammy spun and ran, head down against the wind and rain. She could hear Elliot following behind her. She wasn't going to outrun him.

She sprinted past the fuse box, then past the veranda, and although Elliot closed on her quickly, he stayed back, letting her lead. The garage was a familiar dark, square bulk. It held what they needed: the dirt bikes. Plan C wasn't perfect, but it beat the shit out of Elliot's indecisiveness.

The garage door was still open, the floor inside surprisingly dry.

She carefully navigated the shadows, stopping at her Kawasaki, wishing as she climbed onto it that they would've paid a little extra to bump up from the KLX 140 to the 250. Considering they were being chased by a ravenous, mythological creature capable of snapping them like dry twigs, it would have been a small difference, but every little bit helped.

Elliot stood in the door. He looked ready to vomit.

Tammy hooked a thumb over her shoulder, pointing to Elliot's 140. "Let's go!"

Elliot shook his head. He had that look of surrender on his face. "Not with this shoulder."

Tammy smacked the seat behind her. "Get on, Precious."

Elliot snorted, spraying rain and snot into the air.

Tammy kicked the engine to life as he trudged forward, smiling the same doomed, hopeless smile he'd had when Tammy had convinced him to ask out Corrine Brooks, the school's most sought-after and untouchable beauty queen.

Elliot straddled the bike. "This isn't going to end well."

He'd said the same thing about Corrine. That had been a disaster that left him moping for a month.

"Probably not. You wanna hoof it?" She handed him the shotgun, then shrugged the handbag off her shoulder and handed that to him as well.

Elliot shifted the handbag onto his bad shoulder and over his neck. The shotgun remained in his good hand. He hooked the fingers of his bad arm through Tammy's belt. The bike felt like a toy beneath him. A wobbly, unsteady, fragile toy.

Tammy revved the engine; it sounded like a weed whacker on steroids. It wasn't the big stuff pro athletes used. She let out the clutch and the Kawasaki jumped forward.

Elliot yelped as the thrust jerked his bad arm.

"Sorry." *You've got to man up, El.*

They cleared the garage door and hit the muddy driveway. The bike wobbled, heavy in the ass, threatening to give out beneath them and bog down in the mud until they finally picked up some speed.

"We should have helmets." Elliot's voice was barely audible over the storm and the bike engine.

"Fuck that," Tammy shouted over her shoulder. "You want one, jump off and go back."

Elliot grimaced. *The downside of improvisation.*

Tammy anxiously glanced to their left, and the bike nearly wiped out beneath her.

"Watch the trail." Elliot gripped her belt tighter. She was a good rider, but she was dangerous, reckless. The idea that they might escape the Wendigo only to wipe out and have it catch them…

What could go wrong? A dirt bike at night, pouring rain, muddy road, no helmets: perfect!

He turned as they passed the glass dining room door the Wendigo had burst through. His glasses were a smudged, rain-streaked mess, but he caught a flash of movement.

He aimed the shotgun as well as he could and squeezed the trigger. Even braced, the force of the shot nearly knocked him from the bike. He shifted his grip, squeezing the pump and working it one-handed. It wasn't as graceful as the movies and video games he'd seen, and it damn near took him off the seat, but it worked.

A stroke of lightning tore across the black sky. The Wendigo was chasing them.

He fired again.

A howl—not the inhuman shriek, but a mixture of pain and fury—melded with the thunder and wind.

Elliot shivered; it wasn't the sleet or the wind. "I-I think I hit it."

Tammy released the left handlebar and flipped the bird in the general direction of the howl. "One of the silver shells?"

"Yeah." Elliot worked the pump again. He had one silver shot shell left. He looked behind them and wondered if he'd bought them any time. *Maybe I just pissed it off some more? It's still moving after everything we hit it with. I don't think we can kill it.*

"Shit! Cops! Did you call them?"

Elliot turned around; the bike wobbled beneath them again. He was getting used to it. His fear of the Wendigo catching them receded ever so slightly. Red and blue strobe lights flashed on the private road.

Police vehicles. Three of them, coming fast.

"Yeah. When I couldn't connect with the *manitous* to bind him." *Fastest five minutes I've ever lived.*

"Way to complicate things, El."

As the first cruiser pulled in through the gate, it skidded across a water puddle. Its spotlight kicked on, blinding Tammy. She braked and threw a hand over her eyes to shield out some of the glare.

Doors opened, and a uniformed cop in a rain slicker stepped out from behind the wheel; Lieutenant Henriksen stepped out of the passenger side. The second car pulled in through the gate and skidded to a stop at about a forty-five-degree angle to the right of the first cruiser. Another patrolman exited the second cruiser, followed by Sergeant Traxler.

The third vehicle looked like an ambulance—blocky, white, a single stripe down its side, red, flashing lights on the front. It braked hard before taking the turn and pulled up on the left side of the first cruiser. Tammy couldn't see the big vehicle's back end, but she heard it open. Heavy splashes sounded and men in dark tactical gear came around the side.

Henriksen's deep voice was clear and even in the storm, projecting supreme authority and certainty. "He's here?"

Elliot stood and pointed the shotgun back the way they'd driven. "Back there. He was chasing us a second ago. I may have wounded him, but it won't stop him."

"El, sit the fuck down." Tammy was furious. There had been an agreement: kill Stone, burn the heart, call the cops. Simple.

But nothing was ever simple with El. Nothing.

Elliot settled back onto the seat.

The uniformed officers drew their firearms; the men in tactical gear already held what looked like small assault rifles held ready. The signal was clear: they weren't fooling around.

"We'll take it from here." Henriksen looked at one of the men in tactical gear. "Let's get a line. Stay inside the lights."

The man signaled to his team, and they spread out.

Traxler stepped closer. He gave the handbag on Elliot's shoulder a curious look, then shook his head. "You better hope you didn't kill him, Mr. Saganash. After calling us like that, it would look an awful lot like premeditated murder."

Tammy laughed. The sound sent a shock through Elliot's body.

Tammy looked back through the bright lights. "Stone's still alive, or whatever you call the condition he's in, but you're not gonna stop him. Not with those guns." *At least I hope not. I don't even want to know how you'd react if I try to chop his head off after you take him down.*

One of the men in tactical gear pointed with his gun. "Movement! He's coming!"

Tammy twisted in time to spot something at the edge of the spotlights.

Glen Stone. The Wendigo. Running toward them.

No. Loping toward them on all four limbs, like a gorilla. Fast.

Elliot turned to see the Wendigo. "Holy fu—"

Traxler stepped forward, pistol held out slightly to his side. "Glen Stone, get down on your knees! This is your only warning." He sounded like a drill sergeant—crisp, loud, commanding.

The Wendigo kept coming.

Henriksen hesitated, but only for a moment. "Take him down!"

The SWAT team members each popped off several controlled shots. The weapons' reports were much more of a crack than the pop sound pistols made. The Wendigo came forward several more yards before falling in a heap and skidding to a stop in a muddy puddle ten feet shy of the Kawasaki.

"What the fuck?" Traxler looked from the Wendigo to Henriksen. "That ain't Stone."

"The hell it isn't." Tammy stared at the Wendigo's corpse for several long seconds, then she pushed the bike forward. When Traxler grabbed the handlebars, she met his determined glare with her own. "You better empty your guns into him before you go near him." Her voice was even, not the least hysterical. She revved the dirt bike.

"Do not try to run again, young lady. You hear me?"

Elliot found a voice finally. "The guy who killed our family is *right there*. You need to be focused on him, not us." His voice quivered with rage as he jabbed the shotgun at the Wendigo.

It was a bloody, battered mess that barely resembled a human at all. Three tightly placed scorch marks showed where the wards had struck; each had burned down to bone. The Wendigo's gray skin was pale in the floodlight. Bullets had deformed its already misshapen head. Elliot wanted to stomp over and fire the last silver shell into that head, but he knew better. If the Wendigo was still alive, it would come for Tammy. He could deal with it then.

Elliot pulled his legs farther away from the corpse. "Does that look normal to you, Sergeant Traxler?"

Traxler snorted and holstered his pistol. "Doesn't even look human. But we stopped him. I guess he's not as bulletproof as you thought."

Tammy's glare intensified. "I never said he was bulletproof. I said you can't kill him. But you just can't listen to me, can you?"

The SWAT team fanned into a semi-circle and approached the body, weapons trained on it, ready for anything. One of them leaned in closer to examine the corpse. "This guy's dead, Lieutenant Henriksen. No breathing. I've got five...six...six holes in the head, any one of them lethal. Several chest wounds where the rounds passed all the way through."

Henriksen's eyes locked on Tammy's for a long moment, then he sneered at her *takoba*. "Nice sword. Heading out for some Dungeons & Dragons?" He stepped up to Traxler and whispered something in his ear, then walked over to the corpse, each step an impatient stomp.

"Don't do it, Lieutenant." Tamment locked eyes with Traxler again. She revved the Kawasaki's engine. "He's baiting you."

Elliot spun around to watch Henriksen, who pulled a cigarette from his jacket and tried to light it, as if that might give him some sort of style points. All the while, Henriksen inched closer to Stone's corpse. Henriksen finally tossed the soggy cigarette aside and squatted next to the corpse. He winced in disgust and removed a pen from his jacket, using it to twist the Wendigo's head around for a look.

"If this turns out to be Stone, the FBI is going to be very disappointed."

Elliot felt something, an impossible-to-quantify tremor of dread. "Lieutenant—"

Henriksen shot Elliot an impatient glare. "Don't encourage her—"

The Wendigo's hand twitched.

The nearest SWAT officer jumped back. "Shit!"

Henriksen turned back to look at the Wendigo. Its hand shot out and gripped him by his left thigh. Its jagged nails dug in as Henriksen tried to stand and draw his pistol. Henriksen screamed, the sort of high, climbing, wavering scream that can only be managed in times of extreme pain. The Wendigo flexed, and a loud crack sounded; Henriksen's femur snapped. His mouth worked, but he couldn't scream anymore. His pistol dropped to the ground.

Traxler blinked in disbelief and pulled his pistol. He sighted on the creature. "Holy mother of—" His pistol roared, the round making the Wendigo's head snap sideways.

The Wendigo was on its feet, Henriksen now a slumping shield between it and the SWAT team. Traxler fired again and ordered the other patrolmen to fire. They aimed low, taking the Wendigo's legs out from under it.

The Wendigo laughed.

It grabbed Henriksen on either side of the collarbone and casually tore him down the middle. It flung the half with the head still attached at the SWAT team, knocking three of them to the ground, the other half it hurled at Traxler. It was a near miss; Henriksen's headless half crashed wetly into the windshield of the first cruiser, spiderwebbing the glass before limply bouncing off and disappearing on the far side of the cruiser, a mound of steaming viscera piled against the windshield marking the impact.

Traxler looked from the bloody windshield to Tammy. "Go!"

Elliot felt vomit rising; terror held it down. "Tammy—"

"Yup." Tammy worked the clutch, kicked the bike into gear, and opened the motorbike up. She nearly wiped them out in a spray of mud, but she got the thing under control as she passed Henriksen's half-corpse.

Elliot twisted as they skirted the cruiser's rear end. Even over the wind and gunfire and the whine of the dirt bike's little engine, he could hear the screams of horror and agony. "Tammy—"

"Yeah, I know." She slammed on the brakes. The back wheel slid sideways, but she kept the dirt bike under her. She turned back to look at the carnage.

Elliot shoved the shotgun into his sling and dug around inside the handbag. They were going to need the grenades. And a lot of luck. A *lot*.

"Yo, Stone! Come and get us, you redneck fuck."

"He-he's going to hear that?"

"He's still in my head." Tammy turned her attention back to the dark path that led down to the creek. She gave the bike a little gas.

Elliot pulled one of the grenades from the pink handbag. "Couldn't we have used one of the camo bags?"

Tammy revved the bike in response.

They shot across the last stretch of the driveway and onto the private lane, then they were on the main path down to the creek. It was dark and slick, and branches occasionally whipped out of nowhere to swat them.

Elliot cradled the grenade in his bad arm and risked a look over his shoulder. The Wendigo was behind them, and it was gaining. "It's coming fast."

Tammy gave the bike some more gas, and the rear end wobbled and nearly bogged down as they hit a deep puddle. Elliot clutched at Tammy and the lighter and the jar, for a moment unconcerned about the Wendigo. The bike stabilized and picked up speed, and Elliot released his grip on Tammy. He leaned over the jar until his head was on Tammy's back, shielding the lighter from the rain, then he struck the lighter.

Tammy smiled at the feel of his head against her. It was pleasant, comforting.

Elliot's first strike with the lighter didn't even spark. He debated tossing it right then and digging for some matches. He tried again.

A flame. Sputtering, but a flame.

He lit the fuse and tossed the jar onto the trail behind them. The Wendigo was silhouetted against the police car lights. It leapt past the bomb, and a second later an explosion flared. Something whizzed past Elliot's ear at the same time that something bounced off the dirt bike's frame.

Shrapnel. It's working. Somewhat.

He grabbed another jar. He tried to position it on the seat between him and Tammy so he could shield it again, but the motorbike began bouncing up and down on roots, and the slick glass slid from his hands. He heard it shatter behind him. "Shit."

"Yeah, great, El," Tammy shouted. "I'm fucking driving us blind in the storm of the century and I'm keeping us upright, and you can't keep a grip on a jar?"

Elliot grabbed the shotgun as it slid from the sling. He managed to secure it, then looked behind him. The Wendigo was closer.

Elliot pulled the third jar from the bag. He held it with a death-grip and got the fuse lit on the first strike. The fuse burned down as he tried to calculate the range to the Wendigo. When he was sure the fuse couldn't safely burn much lower, he heaved the jar. It detonated close behind the Wendigo.

The Wendigo lost its footing, as if its limbs had given out. It tumbled and bounced and rebounded off a thick oak trunk, howling furiously with each impact.

"Yes!" Elliot pumped his arm slightly and nearly fell off the dirt bike.

"You hit him?"

"He went down." Elliot began digging for the final jar. "Maybe gave us another minute."

Tammy slowed the bike. "Too much washed out, too many puddles. We're going to have to switch to a trail. That means slower and bumpier."

Elliot pulled his hand out of the bag and gripped Tammy tighter. "Okay. I'll just have to gut it out."

She turned the bike onto one of the trails that they had worn into the property over the last several years. "What do we have left?"

"One bomb. One silver shell."

Almost immediately, they heard something crashing through the undergrowth toward them. Tammy pushed the Kawasaki hard. Every bit of common sense in Elliot was screaming at him to tell her to slow down. Every bit of his blind animal will to live wanted to tell her to go faster.

Ruts, dips, rocks, roots: The trail swiped at them, tried to knock them down. They hit railroad tracks at far too great a speed, and Elliot knew they would be thrown to their deaths.

"Hang on, El. Just hang on."

"Just keep us upright!" His shoulder was no longer a thick, dull ache; it was a fiery bundle of agony. It felt almost as bad as when Simirita had separated it. He wished for just a moment of strength, just enough to be of some use.

The crashing was parallel to them. The trees were thinning. They were close to the creek, approaching the sandbar. Elliot fished out the last bomb and lit the fuse.

The Wendigo was near. Elliot swore he could see it.

It sprang out of the darkness, a swipe of jagged nails tearing into the back of the bike and raking Elliot's right thigh near the hip. The blow toppled the bike. Tammy cursed and did her best to control the crash, throwing a foot out and instantly regretting it; her leg didn't snap, but excruciating pain shot up it. Elliot went down hard, losing the shotgun and the bomb he'd just lit.

The bomb tumbled into the undergrowth several yards behind them and detonated.

Shrapnel whistled through the air, pelting Elliot and Tammy. They yelped in pain.

Elliot was sure his shoulder was dislocated again now. He plucked a small nail from his left forearm and looked around, hoping to get his bearings, but it was almost impossible in the near-complete darkness. He could barely make out the shotgun's outline a few yards away. Tammy was farther away, a dark shadow slowly getting to her feet. She staggered, possibly dazed, possibly wounded. After a second, she hissed and began hopping.

"Tammy, you okay?"

"My ankle hurts pretty bad, but I don't think it's broke. What about you?"

"Just the stupid shoulder, and he got a good cut on my thigh." He looked around. They'd lost the Wendigo during the wreck. "I think we lost him."

"We can't lose him, El. He's in my head."

Elliot dug through the handbag, pulling out a couple glow sticks. He bent one and shook it, tossing it near Tammy, then he bent and shook the other. Before he could toss it, the Wendigo stepped out of the underbrush. It was hunched, and it moved with a definite limp. Strips of flesh and muscle hung from its legs. Bloody snot streamed down its mangled face.

It straightened, sucked in a breath, and then laughed.

Tammy locked eyes with it. She spoke with the same calm, steady voice she'd used to lure it after them. "You have got to be the dumbest fuck in the world."

The Wendigo stopped laughing and took a clumsy step forward, tilting its head curiously. "Gonna…Gonna—"

"Yeah, yeah, yeah. G-g-gonna blah blah blah. Have you listened to yourself, Stone? Have you? Have you *looked* at yourself?"

The Wendigo laughed again, but it was an uncertain sound.

"Wasn't this all about killing some *subhumans*? Huh? Isn't that what they promised you? A chance to go after a whole bunch of people who really pissed you off because they weren't *white*? Because they were *different*? Well, look at you!"

The Wendigo looked down at its hands and arms.

"Yeah, that's right. Give it a good look. Fuckin' Neanderthal. You should see your face. Shit. You were a Creepasaurus Rex before with your beady little eyes and *I hate the world* tatts. Now? You're a fucking museum exhibit, about to be pounced on by a saber-toothed tiger."

The Wendigo rubbed at the holes in its chest.

"Is that what they promised you, Stone? You stink like ass. Like corpse ass."

For once, Elliot approved of pissing off the Wendigo. It was distracted and confused. She was reaching Glen Stone, or what tiny last bit remained of him.

Elliot began crawling for the shotgun. With only one good arm, it seemed a mile away, unreachable, but it was their best hope. His wounded leg was numb. It didn't seem to be bleeding much, and it didn't feel like it was going to fall off, so he kept pushing forward. He could hear the creek gurgling nearby. It was turbid, swollen from the rain. The little cairn was a black mound near the churning dark water's edge.

Tammy signaled for Elliot to speed it up. He tried.

"Did you negotiate the deal yourself, Stone, or did they trick you? You know the thing they put inside you? It's a Native American demon thing. You didn't even get a white man's demon. How sucky is that?"

The Wendigo snarled again, then it stepped forward and roared.

"Okay, fuck, Elliot. Today?" Tammy backed toward the creek.

Elliot could almost touch the shotgun. Stretched out, his fingers scraped the edge of the stock. The Wendigo turned to consider Elliot for a second, then it was on him. It snatched him up by the neck and drew him in to its ruined face, which stretched into a hideous, leering grin. Flesh tore and fell away until nearly the entire section of jaw—muscle, puffy gums, jagged teeth—was all that showed; it didn't notice. It breathed slowly, spraying Elliot with snot, blood, and foam. Simirita's stench was a freshly picked rose by comparison.

Tammy's heels edged into the rushing creek water.

The Wendigo tried to speak, but it couldn't manage anything more than a bestial grunt. It brandished Elliot as if to make its point.

"What?" Tammy took another step back. Frigid water rushed around her injured ankle.

"G-g-got...yer...*b-boy.*"

The Wendigo laughed its horrible, inhuman laugh, and Tammy realized she'd run out of options. She drew the *takoba* and pointed the tip at the Wendigo.

"He's not my b-boy, *douchebag.*" She took a practice swing; it was awkward and her ankle nearly gave out. She was hopelessly out of practice. "Okay, fuck face, put him down. No more killing people I—" *C'mon Tammy, you can say this.* "No more killing people I love. Let's get this over with, just me and you."

As casually as someone might toss aside a bunched-up wad of paper, the Wendigo tossed Elliot, then it crouched for a charge. Elliot landed twenty feet away without so much as a whimper.

Tammy's stomach knotted up. No more running, no more taunting, no more hoping for a lucky break. It was just her and the *djinn*, the Wendigo, the cannibal spirit.

The Wendigo charged, and Tammy could do nothing but brace.

Chapter Twenty-Nine

I ce-cold churning water tugged at Tammy's legs, trying to pull her off-balance and take her under. Putrescent winds that may as well have been Arctic-born drove freezing ice and sleet into her face, bringing tears to her eyes. It felt like a midwinter night, not one from early summer. She didn't have to look skyward to know the howling winds were twisting the thick, black clouds that had hung over Harrison Mansion for the last few days. Neither starlight nor moonlight reached her where she stood, shin-deep in rain-swollen Mill Creek. The only light was the blue-green fluorescence of a glow stick.

That was enough to reveal the Wendigo.

Twisted, deformed, lurching, the thing was the final shell of Glen Stone, a pathetic neo-Nazi. The Wendigo spirit had consumed Stone. It had taken innocent lives. It had taken Elliot and Tammy's family. It had defiled Harrison Mansion, their home.

And now it had them where it wanted them.

The water slowed the Wendigo as it lunged forward, but it stretched out to take advantage of its long arms. Tammy fell back and swung the *takoba*, her grandfather's holy sword. She put everything she could into the swing and lost her footing as a result. Out of sheer luck, the blade caught the Wendigo's left hand, slashing through the fingers at an angle that took off the tip of the pinky and most of the forefinger.

The Wendigo howled and recoiled, pulling the bloody ruin of a hand to its mouth. "Muh…muh fingers."

Tammy kicked along the slick, muddy creek bottom, trying to get some more distance while bracing with her right hand to regain her footing. "You think I was just gonna give up without a fight, you moron?"

Flashes of the dream she'd had in the hotel room hit her. She'd broken Stone's fingers, then she'd bitten them off when he'd stuck them in her mouth.

Prescience? A message? Daysi's drugs?

The Wendigo furiously slapped the water with its good hand. "K-k-keel…keel you!"

Tammy finally got to her feet. She was waist deep now, and the current was a terrible force that made it impossible to truly set her feet against the shifting ground. It felt like dozens of slimy hands were tugging at her, trying to drown her. She braced as well as she could, legs wide apart, one slightly forward, one back. Once again, she pointed the *takoba* at the Wendigo. The only strokes she could make now were overhead and somewhat parallel to the water's surface.

"You can't do shit all the way back there, Nazi bitch. Your masters told you to take me alive, so you better get your caveman ass in gear."

She took an ugly swing, once again nearly losing her footing. This time, she exaggerated her struggle, though, making it look like she almost lost her grip on the sword. Her teeth were chattering, her muscles were starting to cramp, and her ankle hurt like a mother, but she still had one good swing in her if he hurried.

The Wendigo surged forward, much slower now than it had been before.

"How's it feel being a total fucking failure, Stone? Huh? Is this what you expected when you signed on? Cannibal? Neanderthal? *Subhuman?*"

The Wendigo growled and leaned forward, once again extending its arms. Tammy could sense the attack coming and nearly swung down. It would've been enough to take the huge paw of a right hand off at the wrist, but the Wendigo drew back and Tammy checked her swing. It stepped back and considered her, black eyes blinking slowly, skeletal head tilted.

Wonderful. I finally get the chance to use Stone's dumb ass against it, and it gets all animal crafty on me. Fuck.

"Look at that, Stone. Now you can't even do what you want to do. Little A-rab bitch making fun of your ugly ass, and you just gotta sit there and take it. Damn. I hope none of your Nazi buddies hear about this. If they don't kick you out of their club for being so ugly, they'll definitely kick you out for being such a pussy." She jabbed at him with the *takoba*. "Your masters have a backup plan? Huh? Maybe you could give me an address to ship your corpse to when I'm done with it. Can you remember an address?"

The Wendigo shifted again, as if it were about to lunge at her, then it shook its malformed shoulders. For a second, rage flashed across the ruined, inhuman face, and its good hand clenched, then the rage was gone.

In that short moment, she could feel it: Stone had lost. Whatever was left of him was now just a prisoner in what remained of his own body.

An animal intelligence looked from the Wendigo's black eyes when it stared at her. Animal intelligence, and something ancient and inhumanly malevolent. It watched her, smiling when her shivering became too great to hide. It circled her slowly, putting its back to the current and forcing her to shift. She tried to set her injured ankle down, and it gave out. Tiny, slick hands grabbed her foot and pulled her off-balance, and the Wendigo surged forward, leaning in and reaching for the *takoba* with its ruined hand.

Tammy swung desperately and buried the blade in the Wendigo's collarbone. The strike was too weak to do any real damage, but the blade stuck.

The Wendigo growled and lightly swatted her left wrist. Tammy felt a jolt of agony, and then her hand went limp and she saw that her arm had deformed, as if a whole new joint had been created just behind the wrist. She blinked and gasped, and for a moment she thought she would black out.

The next she knew, the Wendigo was lifting her with its good hand by the windbreaker, holding her above its head.

He's going to toss me like he tossed Elliot. Throw me onto the sandbar like a seagull dropping a crab onto rocks to break its shell.

A form separated from the sandbar. It was a squat shadow washed in the blue-green of the glow stick, and it held something long and dark.

The Wendigo sensed her thoughts and turned to see what she had seen, but she could feel its recognition of what was just a shadow to her: *the other human, the weapon that hurts.*

Elliot! He has the shotgun!

She could feel its thoughts. It was going to put her in front so that Elliot couldn't shoot.

For once, Elliot didn't hesitate.

The shotgun roared, and hot pain ran up the length of Tammy's shattered forearm. She realized in a distracted way that she wasn't actually numb. She also realized the Wendigo had taken the worst of the blast, the right side of its face a gloriously mangled clump of ground-up meat and bone. Its good eye was frozen open in shock.

Lightning streaked across the black sky. The Wendigo arched its back and shuddered and released its grip on her. She fell toward the water.

More importantly, she fell toward the *takoba* still protruding from the Wendigo's collarbone.

She grabbed the hilt with her good hand as she fell and hooked her left arm over the top of that hand, throwing her entire weight down on the blade. It drove in deeper and cut through the collarbone, then it slid down between the Wendigo's ribs and sternum, and slid halfway down the chest before coming to a stop.

The Wendigo shuddered again, then it collapsed into the water, its good hand grabbing Tammy and dragging her with it.

Elliot dropped the shotgun with a curse. He thought he might have hit Tammy with the shot, but it didn't look bad. But the Wendigo had dragged her below the surface. She was a pretty good swimmer—much better than she was at running—but she'd said the crash had hurt her leg.

"Tammy!"

He tried to lever himself up on the cairn, but his bad leg wouldn't hold any weight. It had popped when he'd landed, as if whatever had been holding it together had finally given out. It still felt like someone had shoved a burning torch into the open wound.

He'd almost blacked out when that had happened; he wished he had.

Except Tammy needed him. He cursed and leaned against the cairn. Something rumbled within its depths. It wasn't an audible sound, but a sensation he could feel inside him: *manitous.*

There were *spirits* here! In the creek, along the banks of the creek, in the stones and mud, just as there had been on Tanegashima. They weren't mountain *kami*, but they didn't need to be. The Wendigo was wounded.

Elliot set the shotgun down and pulled himself up onto his knees, and bowed, facing the cairn and the creek.

"Spirits of this place, hear my prayers." His voice cracked, and his throat ached. There was no time for whimpering. "My ancestors respected you, revered you, offered prayers and supplications to you. This thing that pollutes you with its filthy presence, this thing that corrupts and destroys all that it touches, it slaughtered my ancestors, *your* worshippers. Now this thing moves again among man, taking and destroying and corrupting. As my ancestors before me, I come to you humbly. This thing of ice and hunger and destruction, it moves through you with impunity, wrapped in flesh that is not its own, hiding its true form. I beg that you help me see through its lies and wash this place clean. See this man whose body it has stolen on to his final resting place and banish this abomination from the world of man."

Along the shore, the waters seemed to churn even more than before. Elliot thought he saw a head pop out of the trees. In the darkness, the face looked long and narrow, with hair down to its neck. He couldn't see a nose in the profile. It disappeared, and he heard splashing. He grabbed the glow stick and crawled forward as quickly as he could. Clumps of sticks floated along the surface here and there, but they moved quicker than the current, and they disappeared beneath the surface.

Mannegishi? River spirits? Here?

He shifted the glow stick to his left hand and wiggled through the mud on his side until he was half-submerged in the creek water, then he twisted so that the left side of his body was above the water. He gripped the handbag with his left hand, keeping its top above the water. The current grabbed him and pulled him along, taking him out from shore into deeper water. It felt like long, watery fingers clutching him.

He panicked for a moment. He was an exceptional swimmer, arguably the best at his high school, but his right leg and left shoulder were useless. There was no way he could hope to survive the creek's raging current.

Then he thought of Tammy, and he realized he had to try. She deserved something better than the life she'd lived. She deserved something better than drowning in the hands of a Wendigo.

He closed his eyes and reached out to the spirits for their aid.

"*Mannegishi* brothers, spirits of the water, guide me to this creature! Guide me to the brave one who fought this abomination!"

The current moved him along. Churned-up mud left the water so brown and thick that the glow stick didn't penetrate much deeper than a few inches below the surface. It revealed nothing.

Elliot pushed himself. For Tammy. For those who had passed.

Tammy could feel the last of the Wendigo's strength leaving it. It wasn't struggling at all now. Its good hand had grabbed her as it sank, but there was no power to the grip. Still, the water was so cold, and the current so strong, she couldn't break free of it, and she wouldn't, not until she *knew* it was dead. Why try to swim for land if she didn't know with absolute certainty that she'd killed it? She'd seen enough movies to know how *that* story ended.

She needed to get it to shore. She needed to cut its fucking heart out. Then she needed to light that heart up like the Fourth of July.

There was a subtle shift in the current—no, not the current, but the direction she and the Wendigo were moving. Something tugged her jeans, pulling her up, up. Slippery fingers—at first she thought they might be snakes—skated across her chest and arms.

Her head broke the surface, and she gulped in cold, clean air.

She squeezed her good hand to be sure it was still wrapped around the *takoba* hilt. It was there, as was the Wendigo.

The Wendigo jerked.

Tammy looked into the water. Little humanoid things were tearing at the Wendigo's corpse, peeling away chunks of dead, white flesh and muscle. It looked like the water itself was also tearing at the corpse.

"Leave the heart, you little creeps!"

Elliot heard Tammy's voice ahead. He tried to swim, but he was completely at the mercy of the water spirits. "Tammy!"

"There's something attacking the Wendigo corpse!"

"Water spirits! *Mannegishi!*"

"Whatee whatee?" Tammy twisted around to look back at Elliot. He was coasting along like her, letting the whatee whatees do all the work.

"They're like...I don't know, like *djinn*? Spirits that live in and around water."

"Well, they're getting all kinds of groping in right now. Is that the ammo pouch?"

Elliot looked at the pink handbag and shook his head. *Only Tammy.* "Yeah."

Tammy groaned as she and the Wendigo came to an abrupt stop against the bank of the creek. Even after being in the freezing water, her broken arm ached. She looked upstream. Elliot was accelerating toward her. He was lit by one of the glow sticks. She crawled forward, her good hand still gripping the hilt.

Elliot shot up onto the muddy bank as she rolled onto her butt. He laughed, but it seemed as much a manic, surprised sound as jubilation. "You killed it!"

He held the glow stick up high, revealing the ruin the whatee whatees had wrought. Nothing remained of the body except bones, ligaments, and some other connective tissues.

And a black, glowing heart pinned on the *takoba's* tip.

"That's the Wendigo?" Tammy felt like grabbing the thing and stomping on it.

"All that's left of it, I guess."

With his good arm, Elliot dragged himself higher up onto the muddy ground, then he tossed the handbag and glow stick a little farther away from the creek. He turned around and gripped the skeleton by its ribcage and pulled it the rest of the way out of the water. It was smaller than he'd imagined, not much larger than Stone would have been. Serious breaks and deformities were visible everywhere.

Elliot wiggled the *takoba* by the hilt. "You stabbed him in the heart?"

"Sort of." Tammy crawled over to the handbag and grabbed it by the strings. She began the painful process of dragging it back to the skeleton. "Can you pull the *takoba* out for me?"

Elliot pulled the sword out, careful not to touch the heart or let it roll back into the creek. The black globe settled to the mud and throbbed malevolently. It gave off a rotten stench and a cold he could feel through the wind and rain.

Tammy hunched over the handbag to protect it from the rain, then she stuck her good hand inside and carefully dug around. "So here's the plan. I soak the inside of the bag with lighter fluid, you poke that piece of shit heart and put it into the bag, we drag the bag to that big rock up there, we hide on the opposite side of the rock, and we light the bag up. Kaboom. The End."

"How much gunpowder did you have in there?"

"A couple powder horns, about fifty shotgun shells, some fireworks, and a shitload of magnesium shavings. And the propane tank. I opened that up already. I'm emptying the powder horns now."

Red and blue police lights reflected off the dark clouds a good distance out. Throaty engines and siren wails echoed over the wind. There would be police combing the area soon, looking for Stone, looking for them.

"El?"

"Yeah, yeah. Let's do this."

He flipped the heart out of the skeleton and stabbed it with the *takoba*, then slid over to the bag. Tammy leaned the opening sideways to protect the interior from the rain. The black glow seemed to match the rhythm of his own heartbeat. He shivered at that, then he stuck the heart into the bag. Tammy emptied the lighter fluid all over and around the heart, then they both dragged the bag over to the large rock Tammy had spotted.

"Let's assume this melts the heart—"

Tammy snorted. "It will. I can feel this thing in my head still. It's fucking pissed and, I don't know, but I think *scared* is fair to say. If you weren't around, I'd crap into the bag before lighting it up. It knows that, so I think you've got a Wendigo friend for life. On the other hand, if Mr. Wendigo and

I meet up again, it's fair to say it won't be interested in taking me captive. Isn't that right?"

The sirens drew closer.

"So this finishes the Wendigo off. And Stone's dead. What do we say happened? We don't have an official deal, and if we did, it'd be for Stone captured alive."

"Fuck the deal, El. You know as well as I do, they never cared about me or you. They wanted Stone. They wanted the case closed and a bunch of good publicity for taking down a world-class fucktard neo-Nazi. It was never about getting my record wiped clean, not even for me."

Headlights were resolving into distinct beams. The police were close.

"So what do we tell them, Tammy?"

"The truth?" She held up a box of stormproof matches with her good hand.

Elliot chuckled and took one of the matches out. He struck it against the box, leaned around the rock, and tossed it into the handbag, then he ducked behind the rock and covered his head with his right arm. There was a quiet whoosh as the lighter fluid and propane caught, and a moment later, a deafening explosion. Secondary explosions sounded for several long seconds after, and pellets ricocheted and whistled past, some loudly plopping into the creek. Pieces of dirt and grass and handbag rained down around them, and little fires flared for a while before the rain snuffed them out.

Snuffed out, like Stone. And the Wendigo. Tammy could feel it. They were both gone.

Brakes squealed and tires squeaked. Doors opened, and radio chatter filled the suddenly calm and warm air. Someone shouted that they could see the kids, and the jangle of belts and other gear grew closer.

Elliot took Tammy's good hand in his and laughed long and hard.

They had faced the storm and come out alive.

Chapter Thirty

Riding in the elevator was like being in a mobile cage for Elliot, a stainless-steel and wood-paneled cage meant to hold the infirm and the dying. Even after they were freed, the scents lingered: disinfectants, salves, blood, death. Some things would never truly be free of their prisons.

The chime sounded: his floor. His last trip to see Tammy.

The door opened onto the lobby, opposite a nurse's station. He leaned heavily on his crutch and wished there were some way for his injured shoulder to heal quicker. Each pain-filled step forced a wince and a deep intake of the chemical-laden air. His hip was stiff and tender from the stitches holding the muscle together. The infection that had developed was well under control, but even in the hospital's air-conditioned corridors, he felt feverish.

A clattering rose from the nurse's station. Elliot spotted the source when he got close enough to the station to see over the walls: A young orderly was shuffling supplies around on a cart. Up close, Elliot could hear the muted ring of a telephone and the vibrations of personal devices—phones and pagers. Several orderlies were gathered nearby, their voices a subdued murmur; they went silent once they saw him.

Elliot frowned at the recognition. *Oh, there* he *goes. Yeah.* That *guy. Nice.*

A heavyset white woman with thinning blonde hair and far too much makeup sat at the nurse station. She set the phone receiver back in its cradle and waved at Elliot as her face broke into a warm, pleasant smile.

Elliot couldn't help smiling and waving back, even though he felt terrible.

"Can I—?" He jerked his head at the door to Tammy's room.

"You can go in, but she's got a visitor." Her smile faded and her brow folded as she looked at the two state troopers stationed outside Tammy's door. "They just can't leave her alone, I guess."

"Apparently not. Thanks, Donna." Elliot did his best to pick up the pace.

The state troopers flanking the door to Tammy's room looked up from their molded plastic chairs at the squeak-shuffle of Elliot's approach. Harden and Goerhardt; they'd pulled morning duty the last two days. Both were big, beefy, and pale-haired, exactly the sort who worried Elliot.

Harden stood, his eyes neutral.

"Is it okay to go in?" Elliot's voice was soft, calm, non-confrontational.

Harden held up a hand. "Detective Morales is in there with her." Harden opened the door and leaned in. "Detective Morales? Mr. Saganash is here."

Harden swung the door wide.

Elliot looked around Tammy's room. It was pretty similar to the one he'd just checked out of—two heavy, mechanical beds, one unoccupied; curtains on tracks in the ceiling; a nightstand beside the bed; a rolling food tray.

Tammy's head was elevated. Like him, she had a few butterfly sutures over small shrapnel wounds. Her eyes were locked on to a young man Elliot guessed might be anywhere from twenty-five to thirty-five. The man held a pocket notebook in one hand, a pen in the other. He was fit, maybe a patrolman recently promoted to detective. He definitely hadn't softened from long hours of desk work and fast food.

"Mr. Saganash." Morales pointed his pen at Tammy. "I was hoping to catch you before your discharge and have a word with you."

"Don't say anything to him, El." Tammy's eyes narrowed even more, and her chin jutted out angrily. "He's trying to pin a charge on you. He thinks you shot me."

Elliot shifted his weight slightly on his crutch. *I did shoot you.*

Morales's face hardened. "Your friend here is …" His mouth shut quickly, as if he might be fighting instinct. "She's a real little *luchadora*."

"You're with the sheriff's department?" Elliot motioned for Morales's credentials.

"Yes." Morales calmly pulled out his badge and showed it to Elliot.

Elliot made a point of looking at it hard before finally saying, "Thank you, Detective." He felt bad giving someone who probably shared some experiences with him a hard time, but he didn't care for Morales's behavior. "I'm happy to speak with you, of course. I'm sure my counsel could arrange a time for an interview. Do you have their number?"

"All right." Morales looked back at Tammy, his face screwed up in frustration. He loudly clicked his pen and pocketed it after a couple tries. He turned back to Elliot and gave a lingering, insincere smile. "I'll be in touch."

The room was silent until the door closed, then Tammy relaxed.

Elliot moved closer to her bed. "I—"

The right corner of Tammy's mouth rose. "You should have told him to eat a big, steaming pile of shit."

"And get slapped with obstruction charges? Tammy, you can't keep treating people in authority like that." *Regardless of whether or not they might deserve it.* "Look. Please, *please* control yourself during all this legal stuff. Every snide remark you make is just digging yourself into a deeper hole."

"These assholes don't have a clue what we went through." Tammy tried to cross her arms, but the cast on her left arm was too huge to move easily. She sighed and her chin dropped to her chest.

"And as much as we'd like to tell them what happened, they can't know what we went through. Not ever. You start talking to a court-appointed shrink about Wendigos, and you get a padded room and all sorts of neat medicine." He reached for her hand, then stopped himself. "Anyway, I'm not even sure …"

Tammy turned on him, her face again scrunched up in anger. "You're not even sure what? Say it! Maybe we need a padded room? That's what you were going to say, right?"

Elliot looked away, his head sinking lower. "Yeah." His voice had dropped to a whisper.

Tammy let it go. It would be easy to pick at him, to attack everything he was doing that pissed her off, to drive him away; she didn't want to. She wanted to see him again when the legal stuff was over.

"Are…are you going to visit me, El?" Her voice was as soft as his now. She wanted to hold his hand, maybe to hear him say everything would be okay and she wouldn't be alone again. Ever.

"As often as I can." He picked at the paper hospital ID bracelet around his wrist. "It's a long drive from Winnipeg, though."

Tammy's eyes rolled up in her head and her eyelids fluttered as if she had just heard the absolute dumbest thing ever said in human history. "Ever heard of airplanes? Big metal tubes flying through the sky from place to place at amazing speeds?"

Elliot laughed. He'd had enough of airplanes for a while, but she was right. "How's the arm?"

"The plate's a little annoying. Or maybe it's the cast. The swelling's way down." She shifted, and her gown opened enough to reveal ugly black and blue bruises on her chest. "The x-ray's over in the yellow folder there."

He waved away the offer. "I saw what it looked like on the outside. That's enough."

They looked at each other for a moment, neither able to say what they were thinking.

It was Tammy who finally spoke. "Thank you. For coming for me." Her voice was soft again, as if that were an admission of weakness. "I couldn't have done it alone."

Elliot finally worked up the nerve to take her hand in his.

She studied his face closely, saw his jaw clenching over and over, the rapid eye blinks. *He's just as scared as I am.* "El?" When he finally looked at her, *really* looked at her, she asked in a trembling voice, "Who sent Stone?"

"What?" Elliot tried not to react to the question, but his good hand was adjusting his glasses before he could stop himself. *How can I answer that? I have no idea.*

"Don't even try it. You know what I mean." She leaned forward and searched his eyes for some hint of what was going on in his head. "You heard what they said in the dream. There were people working against them. Lots of people. And

Stone wasn't smart enough to do everything he did, not by himself, and not with that Wendigo in him. Someone tricked him into taking that thing into him. I can't picture him letting a Native American do it, so who?"

Elliot thought back to the message on Simirita's phone: *Have you consumed him yet?* It was possible she was controlling Stone, but since she was serving—*allied with*—someone herself, it seemed unlikely. He wondered who was behind it all and if they would ever figure what was going on.

"Stone would have killed me if he'd had a choice. I mean, he never seemed to come at me like he could have, not until the very end. He killed everyone else like …" She fell back on the pillow.

Elliot squeezed her hand. *Simirita wanted Mangas's pouch, Stone wanted Tammy. Two different employers using ancients, or just two different people who played with our heads, and we're getting caught up in our own paranoid delusions? The pouch is probably worth a small fortune to some collector somewhere, but Simirita wanted the mystical foci, too. What are they worth? Stone didn't even touch anything in the mansion other than Tammy's focus. It doesn't add up.* He adjusted his glasses angrily.

"It's over, Tammy. We survived it."

Tammy heard the words, and she saw the all-too-familiar skeptical look Elliot had always fallen back on when he encountered something during a training session that he couldn't immediately explain. She looked away. *I need you, El. You're the only one who can figure this all out.*

"El." She said it low and soft rather than angrily. It was easy not to be angry, because the whole thing made her more sad than angry. She looked at him again, straining to replace the sadness with sincerity. "You can run from this all you want, but it's not going away." She sighed, feeling the emotion in her voice.

"I'm not running."

"Ignoring it isn't going to work. You *know* that."

The door opened and Harden stepped into the room. Donna entered, pushing a wheelchair and flashing Harden a cool smile. She scooted the chair forward, positively beaming at Tammy. "You all ready for discharge?" Her voice was cheerful and warm.

Tammy tried not to react to Donna's charms; it was impossible. Donna had made Tammy a special project, apparently attaching to her in some strange compensation for not having kids. Or at least that's what Tammy told herself. She swung her feet out of the bed, careful not to bump the inflatable cast protecting her sprained ankle.

Donna helped Tammy into the wheelchair. "You've just got to look at it as the start of a new life."

"Yeah." Tammy's lips quivered and her head slumped against her chest. She sniffled and wiped tears from her cheek with her good hand.

Donna's smile cracked and she shot an angry glare at Harden. She set a plastic bag with Tammy's belongings on her lap and wheeled her out of the room. Just outside the room, a large, bored-looking male orderly waited with another wheelchair.

Donna looked back at Elliot. "Your ride's here."

Elliot groaned quietly and settled into the waiting wheelchair.

They filed into the elevator, followed by Harden and Goerhardt.

When the doors closed, Elliot took Tammy's hand again and leaned closer to her. "You gonna be all right?"

"Yeah." She seemed to be bringing the sniffles under control. "It's only six months, right? Anyone can do that."

Elliot looked at the elevator doors. "It's just rehab and counseling. We're still negotiating to get it down to three. There's apparently a lot of maneuvering to look good for the next election cycle, but this story will be old news in no time. They'll budge."

The elevator doors opened onto the main lobby. Just beyond the revolving door and emergency double doors outside, the day seemed bright and hopeful. In the lobby, more state troopers waited; Sergeant Traxler stood among them. He looked from Elliot to Tammy before finally approaching.

Donna came to a stop and straightened, then she stiffly backed away. "This is as far as I go. You officers treat this young lady properly. She's been through more than someone her age deserves."

"You doing okay, kid?" Traxler's voice was heavy and slow, as if he'd gone too long without a good night of sleep. He gently patted Tammy's shoulder, then handed her something as Harden took over for Donna.

Tammy looked at what Traxler had given her. It was a business card. She held it up like a talisman against evil. "Thanks."

Traxler wiped an eye and looked away, shaking his head. After a moment, he looked to the orderly who was pushing Elliot. "I'll take this from here."

Elliot shifted uncertainly.

Traxler looked down. "If that's all right?"

"Yeah, sure."

Tammy anxiously waved at Elliot before Harden pushed her through the double doors and into the bright sunshine. They stopped at an unmarked SUV, and Harden helped her in. A moment later, the SUV sped away, and Tammy was gone.

Elliot's heart sank at the thought she was going somewhere he couldn't protect her. *We all have a price to pay, but it just feels like hers is unjust.*

Traxler stood silently for a moment. When Elliot looked up, Traxler dug a cigarette out of his pocket and stuck it in the corner of his mouth, then he pulled a lighter out of his pants pocket. Donna walked past, giving a stern look. "No smoking in the hospital."

"Shit." Traxler stuffed the cigarette back in his coat pocket. "All right, I say we get the hell out of here." He glanced down at Elliot.

"I've had enough of this place."

Traxler pushed the wheelchair across the parking lot to a plain black sedan. As Elliot struggled to get into the car, Traxler waved a security guard over and transferred the wheelchair to him. A moment later, Traxler slid into the driver's seat.

"Jesus," Traxler said softly. He dug into his nose distractedly for a moment, stopping suddenly and looking at Elliot with a sheepish smile. "Sorry. Paul—Henriksen—got on me about that. He was like my ex, only not as pretty." He put the car in gear and quickly backed out of the parking spot.

At the exit, he shoved the cigarette back into his mouth and lit it, then he pulled a long drag. His eyes closed as if he were embracing a woman he hadn't held for years. A second later he exhaled through his nose and mouth.

Elliot stifled a cough.

"Shit. Sorry." Traxler cracked the windows. "Where you headed?"

Elliot watched the traffic go by. "I need to rent a car."

Traxler tapped the steering wheel with his thumbs. "You up for a bite first?"

"Is this an interview?" Elliot fidgeted with his glasses. *Because I'm not up for an interview. Not ever again, I don't think.*

Traxler made a sound that might have been a laugh. "Can't get any further off the record."

Elliot knew what this was about, and it was horrible. It blurred the boundaries of reality. He hated the way his faith—in science, in logic, in rational thinking—had been shattered, but he and Tammy hadn't been the only ones that had seen…*things.*

"So, you want to talk?" The engine idled, and Traxler relaxed as if he could wait an eternity for an answer.

"I don't have any answers to your questions." *There are no answers.*

"Okay. What about this? We have two Native Americans, two Berbers, an Indian, an Iranian, a Peruvian, a Filipina, and a lady from Japan. All living in one old mansion." He leaned in close to Elliot, his breath rank from coffee and cigarettes. "What were they doing? Can you answer that?"

"Studying comparative religion, I guess." Elliot looked out the rear window, worried they might be blocking other cars. They were alone.

Traxler was in full interrogation mode, still in Elliot's personal space. "Mysticism? Magic? Anything like that?"

Elliot wondered if there was even an answer to be given.

Traxler held the cigarette close to his lips. "Maybe they possessed Stone? Hmm? Controlled him? And he broke free? I saw that in a movie once."

"What?" The question annoyed Elliot, as much for how close it was to the truth as for how wrong it was. *The truth. How can I even think that?*

"Sure. Crazy things happen in real life, crazier than the movies. This one time, I was chasing a kid through an apartment complex, and he jumped out a fifth-floor window. Hit the ground and kept running like nothing had happened."

"No. Nothing like that. They—we're not …" Elliot shook his head emphatically. "They were the victims, not Stone."

Traxler leaned back. He pulled into traffic and drove for a few minutes before finally pulling into an IHOP. He pointed toward the restaurant as he angled for a parking spot. "This okay?"

"Sure." Elliot hobbled out of the car on his own, pounding the crutch into the ground in frustration at letting Traxler get to him.

Traxler never offered to assist; he stood by and opened doors. They said nothing until they'd been seated and their waitress, a very young looking woman with blond hair and brown roots, came by and filled their coffee cups.

Traxler sipped his coffee and whispered, "Sweet ambrosia of the gods."

Elliot stared into his cup indifferently, his thoughts focused on Tammy.

"Look." Traxler scooted closer to Elliot. "We pulled enough crazy shit from Daysi Pizanga's room to make a legitimate drug bust. The DEA was all over what we sent them. Were they concocting some big psychotropic or something?"

Elliot understood that Traxler was trying to make sense of a world he had thought he had a solid grasp on until now. They both were. But that was a world before Glen Stone and Simirita and Wendigos and *rakshasi* and *kami* and *mannegishi*. That was a world that made sense.

"I've seen the footage from Trooper Murkofsky's cruiser. I've seen the footage from that night at the mansion. It makes the forensics from the mansion make a lot more sense. We both saw what happened." Traxler hesitated, hand circling distractedly. "To Paul. To three highly trained officers."

"Yeah."

Traxler pulled back from Elliot. "Yeah. *Yeah.* The only word that fits that is *superhuman.* Hell, if I'd seen that shit, I'd have done what Tammy did. She was right to flee the scene when Stone killed Murkofsky. And she was right when she told the SWAT team to empty their magazines into Stone. Fuck that. Into it. *It.*" Traxler rubbed his forehead.

It. Elliot balked at the word. It annoyed him. He just wanted to pound the facts until they fit reality, but they didn't in this case, and that made him mad in a way he couldn't understand. *Things need to make sense. I spent years refuting and arguing what they taught me. Years.*

The waitress returned. She didn't even bother to look up from her ticket pad. "What can I get you guys?"

Traxler looked to Elliot. "You buying?"

Elliot rolled his eyes. "Yeah."

"Steak, medium, eggs sunny side, toast, short stack of buttermilk, and an OJ."

"You?" The waitress looked at Elliot. "Hey, do I know you?"

"I get that all the time." Elliot winced at the cliché. The whole moment felt cliché. "Can I get a turkey club?"

"Sure." Surliness had replaced apathy.

Traxler waited until the waitress was out of earshot before leaning in close again. "You want another big juicy bit of crazy?"

No. No, I don't. I want the world to settle back into the confines of my comfort zone. I want it to follow the established rules of mass, velocity, and thermodynamics. I don't want to see what is plainly impossible.

"That skeleton? Stone's. Sort of." Traxler rapidly thumped the table with his finger. "DNA matches, but nothing else does. Dimensions were all wrong, teeth were all wrong. Hell, even the head was all wrong. So, how's that happen? How's Stone grow nearly a foot taller? How's his shoulder width go out nearly half again as much? And a skinny girl like Tammy kills his ass with a sword? Unless every damned fish for 200 miles took a bite out of his corpse, where the hell did all his skin and muscle go? And his guts? You think we got piranha up in that creek?" Traxler snorted angrily.

Elliot blinked hard. He took a sip of the coffee and let the bitterness wash over his tongue. He needed his mind in the moment, in reality.

"You ever seen a caveman?" Traxler's finger was now jabbing the air. "That's what he reminded me of. I looked up pictures online, trying to figure this out. That's what Glen Stone looked like to me. He looked like a fucking caveman. A goddamn giant caveman."

"You're sure it was Stone?"

"Four DNA tests. Three failed from degraded samples. The fourth was positive."

Elliot took another sip. He was tired of crappy coffee. He was tired of the questioning and conjecture and the general impossibility. Of everything. "Why are you telling me all this?"

"They're not closing the case." Traxler threw himself back against the padded seat. "FBI's taking it. Stone's activities stretched to Illinois and all throughout the South. DEA wants a piece of it, too."

Elliot took another sip of the coffee, finally dumping in a sugar. He stirred, tried it again, dumped in another.

"You sure you don't know something?" Traxler tried again. "I'd hate to see the DEA swooping down on you."

"You have no idea how bad I wish I could explain all this." Elliot looked around the restaurant. All around them, people ate and enjoyed a normal life. *Oblivious. Or maybe just sane.*

"Well, I've already put in a word for Tammy, and I'll testify when I can." Traxler pulled out his car keys and had them halfway to his ear before he caught himself. He set them on the table. "She did what she had to do."

"I appreciate that, and I'm sure she will too, even if she doesn't know how to express it."

Traxler slapped the table and chuckled. "Are you kidding me? She's a bundle of joy compared to Sharyl." He dug out a wallet and flipped through a couple of baby pictures that had him smiling. He stopped at a picture of a pretty teenage girl in a somewhat revealing cheerleader outfit. Her hair was straightened, and she wore a lot of makeup. She could have been a model. He flipped the wallet closed. "Fifteen going on twenty-one. Teenage daughters are the number one cause of suicides in America. Did you know that?"

"No." It sounded outlandish.

"It's not documented, but it's the goddamn truth."

The food arrived, and Traxler dug in like he was trading calories for sleep. Elliot took a few bites of his sandwich, mostly just to address the hunger he hadn't realized he was feeling.

He touched the table lightly, felt its solidity. He could describe with some accuracy what made it real. He understood it. He could give a basic overview of how organisms worked, what powered them. Dismissing Simirita was easy.

Jet lag, change in diet, drugs. He might have even been able to say the same of Stone, but too many had seen him and what he'd done. The police dash cams captured him on video at the mansion. It had real, undeniable results.

Elliot looked up from his musings. The parking lot was wet from a recent rain. Everything looked so real, and so normal.

And yet everything felt so wrong.

THE END

ACKNOWLEDGEMENTS

Thank you for reading *The Journey Home*. I hope you found it entertaining. Elliot and Tammy's story continues in *Rock of Salvation*.

If you enjoyed the start of the series, stick around. Please consider posting a review and letting friends know about the book. Reviews and word of mouth can have so much influence on potential readers.

For updates on new releases and news on other series, please visit my website and sign up for my mailing list at:

http://www.p-r-adams.com

ABOUT THE AUTHOR

I was born and raised in Tampa, Florida. I joined the Air Force, and my career took me from coast to coast before depositing me in the St. Louis, Missouri area for several years. After a tour in Korea and a short return to the St. Louis area, I retired and moved to the greater Denver, Colorado metropolitan area.

I write speculative fiction, mostly science fiction and fantasy. My favorite writers over the years have been Robert E. Howard, Philip K. Dick, Roger Zelazny, and Michael Crichton.

Social Media:
Twitter: @pradams_author
Facebook: PRAdamsAuthor
Web: http://www.p-r-adams.com
Email: Pradams_author@comcast.net

Made in the USA
Charleston, SC
17 February 2017